CW01418473

About the Author

Graham Tottle is a Cambridge trained historian, computer scientist and programmer. For twenty years he was in R&D in the Research Division with International Computers. Since the seventies he has worked as an expert in twenty countries, often hotspots and war zones, at the leading edge of IT, for the UN Food and Agriculture Organisation, World Bank, the European Union, and the UK Department for International Development. He was educated at Bishops, South Africa, Hurstpierpoint, Emmanuel College, Cambridge and Magdalen College, Oxford. He lives on a canal boat in Cheshire.

2040

Graham Tottle

Book Guild Publishing
Sussex, UK

First published in Great Britain in 2014 by
The Book Guild Ltd
The Werks
45 Church Road
Hove, BN3 2BE

This unabridged version published in 2015.

Typesetting in Baskerville by
YHT Ltd, London

Printed and bound in Great Britain by
4Edge Ltd, Hockley, Essex

A catalogue record for this book is available from
The British Library.

ISBN 978 1 910298 80 0

'And the life of man;
solitary, poor, nasty, brutish and short.'

Leviathan; Hobbes, Thomas H, Univ.
of Oxford, 1651, *op. cit.*[1]

Contents

Acknowledgements

My warmest thanks go to many people, but I'd like to mention particularly:
Judy Rose, Diana Tottle, Eddie Kachali, Ben Cameron, Gareth Williams, Colin Leakey, Jenny Ratcliffe, Gordon Black, the Mutwale Bufumbira, owek Paulo Rukeribuga.
Nick Freeland and Jack Ssentongo
And to Spiffing Covers Richard and his immensely helpful editress
And to The Book Guild: Carol, Joanna and Imogen and many others.

Downside, Chapter 0: Prolog.Dweeb

Below the towering heights of the mountains sprawled a fascinatingly complex lake, crystal clear, dotted with rocky glacier-spawned islets and merging at its western outlet with swamp, tussocks and marshland. The eastern end was dominated by 2 brutal rectangular blocks of undressed concrete, 150 feet high, linked halfway up by a long open-sided girdered bridge. A notice at the high security entrance said 'GORSAF DRYDAN'. Clearly a nuclear power station. The station's centre was a globe, the pressure vessel, a 20-metre sphere of 4-inch thick steel. Graphite cum boron/steel rods were lowered as needed for immediate power consumption. The remainder would drop in an emergency to stop the reaction and cool down. The problem with the station had been embrittlement of the reactor steel due to the cold temperature at the base – rather like the welded ships in the Second World War; on arctic convoy runs to Murmansk the steel became dangerously brittle, particularly when the hulls were stressed in storms. And unlike traditional riveted craft, a welded hull could fracture right through without warning. Liberty ships, they were called, but often they were crowded cruising coffins, biding their moment to plunge or founder.

Liquid CO_2, not prone to nuclear contamination, circulated from the reactor to the boilers, where water was steamed up in heat exchange to drive the turbines. The steam screamed past the honed blades with unbelievable power. Tiny residual droplets slammed the leading edges with such violence that the titanium was gradually pierced to become a paper-thin honeycomb where once it was solid tempered metal. A 100-metre-long pool was later to prove important. It was under the bridge between the two blocks, out in the open air to disperse the exhaust heat at the back end of the process – raising the water temperature about 5 degrees Celsius. From there the warm water went into the lake. A tall, bold, shore-side notice, scarlet on white, said:

PERYGL
Creigiau Cherynter Peryglus
DIM NOFIO

There was a tunnel from the railway to the turbine housing.

A westerly gale, which had been building up through the morning, was in full chat, the panoramic window showing white spray creamed off the wave-tops, driving across the lake. A dark-haired man stood apparently spaced out and bemused near the middle of the empty main hall. He was wearing an expensively tailored formal dinner jacket, hand-tied bow tie, and all the trimmings. His hands were held out sideways, palms downwards, as if resting on the tops of 2 posts. There were in fact 2 posts of the same height standing 5 feet away. After a minute he seemed to realise where he was. He scanned around, then slipped quickly through a passage and up some stairs into a long, echoing square vault. There was a door at the far side. He opened it to look through. A vast empty cavern of a hall, brightly lit. Square, wide, squat control consoles were bunched together just off-centre – the station control point. From an office on the left he heard sounds of 2 people conversing. An unfamiliar, guttural language. Germanic or central European perhaps. Suddenly there was a shout behind him:

'*Puy sy'na! Stopia!*'[2]

He ran across to the far side, down an alleyway and onto the turbine decks. More people. They turned, saw him, and one shouted, '*Stopia! Safa!*'[3]

They joined the chase. He heard a clicking and a fizzing and a voice over a booming intercom.

'Hold hard,' it was saying in high-pitched tightly metallic English. 'Hold hard. Intruder on Control, Intruder on Control. Security alert 5, I say again security alert 5.'

He nipped up a steel stair and over the bridge. Then down again. He saw the cooling pool forty 40 feet below. The chasers and some odd-looking mechanical boxes were coming in either direction. Back onto the bridge. Trapped. He climbed onto the rail, steadying himself against a strut, and dived down. Boyhood memories from the Cape of Good Hope, of similar dives, competing with his mates off the cliffs in Hermanus, had come back.

2

Who can dive in from the highest point? Flatten your wrists, they'd found, flatten your wrists, clasp your hands and bend your forearms, and you'll be able to dive safely into only 3 feet of water. You can turn on a tickey. He flattened his wrists and bent his forearms, and hit the water with an almighty thump. The top of his skull felt as if it had at once been violently hammered, lacerated and stung. An adult who has lived well and substantially presents unboyish parameters to the unforgiving water. But turn he did, and just grazed the bottom. There was a tunnel ahead. The water pulled him along into it. He clawed at the sides, but they were slimy; no go.

Then, astonishingly, he passed through and out into the lake. The pumps had worked from the pool's far end, pushing the water rather than sucking it, so that the water flowed straight through unimpeded. There were significant waves on the lake. He swam steadily across westwards, and rolled and clambered flat on his side, low profile like they taught in the cadet force, over the jagged rocky cofferdam separating the cooling water enclave from the main lake. Then on, into rough, rolling, chilly water. A high-powered outboard run-about buzzed and whined and skipped into view; but by hanging still in the water and ducking beneath the passing crests like the Porthmadog Fairway buoy, he kept unseen as it patrolled around searching. Eventually it disappeared, and he continued the mile swim to the far shore. Uninjured but for a gashed wrist where he had grazed the bottom in diving. He bound it with his handkerchief. A handkerchief to remember, white silk with a scarlet monogram: 'H T-B'.

That evening he staggered, gradually drying, into a little village, down off the mountains, near a river estuary. It was completely deserted. There was no sign of life; no animal life of any sort, anywhere. Not a living thing; no bird nor beast. To be expected of course. Here it is Downside. Here warm-blooded life is gone. He threw himself painfully against several house doors, trying to break in. Then round into their backyards to try again. In the fourth, he hit gold. Under a plastic roof. A Honda 186 trials bike, someone's honey, gleaming red, perching on long squidgy front forks; with massive, shining, meticulously holed stainless-steel brake discs. He stood and smiled. A mountain

3

trailster. The bike, he remembered from years back, would take sleeping policemen at 40 without a thought, carving through the crawling Lusaka traffic. Or swing up and down the curves of the great Zambezi escarpment, with your short-sleeved shirt and wind-cooled forearms free in the hot sunshine. Then near a stand of jungle, a sudden breath of delicious chill rolling from it across the road, and then back again into the dry heat. Or throttle open, climbing away from some cliffs, the exhaust crackling away, echoed and re-echoed, thrown from one *krans*[4] to another. Then dropping off down again. Winding down through happiness. He was a man for whom the past, and past fantasies, could come suddenly and vividly to life.

Back in the present, he remembered how the Honda designers hid tools cunningly under the saddle. He got a tyre lever out of the toolkit, and stuck it into the gap between the house's back door and its jamb. After a minute or so's struggle, it swung free. He climbed up some darkened stairs, rolled into the first bed he could find, and crashed out. On the floor lay his fine white cotton shirt. Made from Ugandan cotton. One and a quarter inch staple, better than the American or Sudanese best. Across the inside of the collar:

'Lord Tite Barnacle – Tailored by Stevens, Princes St, Edinburgh'.

Across the river estuary a faint light gleamed in a tall Italian-gothic window, its shutters opened back. A colonnade led to a formal garden spread in terraces, graced with green angora-shaded cypresses, flowerbeds rampant with weeds, and drystone walled. The villa glowed pastel pink even in the growing dusk. It overlooked the estuary and also a superb piazza; marble paving, a tall campanile over a church, and a black-hulled 2-masted sailing ship, a square-rigger, at the quay.

It would be 2 days before he would first notice at dusk the light in the tall gothic window. And glimpse briefly a sweetly-filled white T-shirt behind it. A T-shirt which, like the bike, was later to draw him back to the fantasies of his youth.

Introduction

It's June 2040.

An aged historian sits penning a document, one jagged leg crossed unbelievably over the other, right ankle on left knee. Revealing white, aged, stick-like limbs below long woollen combs and black trousers. A well-known high-hurdler 60 years ago. Snap your leading leg down sharply as you clear the bar. A coal fire blazes in the grate. It's a hot summer's day. Sometimes his cackles of goading laughter at his unfortunate students' solecisms resound around the courtyard. Sometimes an upper second becomes a starred first.

His comments and explanations are given in italics to guide you throughout the book.

If you want to know his view on the events, look for the sections in italics.

He puts pen to paper. *I write this in Old Court in my old college, Emma. Emmanuel College, in the British University of Cambridge. British, be it noted. Not Welsh, not Scottish, not English, not Irish. It was not these little countries that helped to transform our world in 3 centuries. It was the Brits, and the British Commonwealth. Bringing hardship and violence to some but immense benefit to millions.*

Being an historian, I will look back at the point of divergence between us, the Upside universe and the Downside universe in the late twentieth century and the first 3 decades of the twenty-first.

Two universes, Upside and Downside, clinking together down the byways of time. As a genuine historian I will avoid the tens and twenties historians' practice of writing all history in the present continuous tense. To give, they said, a sense of immediacy. When writing about the past I will use the past tense. When writing about the future I will use the future tense. When writing about the present I will use the present tense. Unlike our colleagues from Oxford, I will use the present continuous tense for things that are actually happening now.

I will ignore Lord Bragg, who insisted on the future tense from historians for a sense of heightened immediacy.

'*All Gaul will be divided into three parts*

Caesar will cross the Rubicon

Mark Antony will give the funeral oration' and so on.

I will write about the points of divergence. Why did our 2 worlds diverge, and how were the disasters for the Downside universe handled? What is the evidence from selected correspondence? In Scotland? In England? In Wales? In Ireland? In the US? In Africa?

Most of the Upside material is already known to readers, they've lived through it. There are one or two Upside documents indicating key events like the meeting in Dalkeith at Scottish Independence, and the various global calamities like the nuking which enabled us to survive. Allegedly terrorists, but I'm intrigued by the massive spiral steel staircase we saw atop the Old Man of Hoy. Very like you see in the mountains of Kum Gang San.

So I will concentrate on accounts about Downside from people like Lord Tite Barnacle who carried out transitions, sometimes at great personal cost.[5] Accounts which are not yet well-publicised for obvious reasons. I've turned much of this into an anecdote, and used my imagination to fill in the picture as you might unravel it, much as Robert Graves did in 'I Claudius' for the first Roman emperors. Why not have a shot? No one's done it yet.

H. B. Goulding-Brown, Emmanuel College, Cambridge 11th June 2040.

Prolog: Nerd

Upside, 26th June, 1990

In Baghdad in June at noon, it is hot. Fiercely hot; 47 degrees. And dry. Fiercely dry. Breathe in through your mouth quickly and you blister your gullet.

From the Dictator's office suite, high up, you can see most of the city. Two police Mercedes, a fading sun-battered green to the gunwales, topsides cream, dawdle truculently along Tigris Drive. The ancient river is low, a dirty, muddy, motionless brown. Even the water looks dry. Nothing else moves anywhere; everything crouches in dark corners, barely breathing, waiting for the sun to go away.

Outside are the extraordinary grey shutters 4-inches thick of hardened Poznan steel, 3 massive angled wedges of it for every office, wedges 30 foot by 5. They hang awaiting his command, like crocodiles' eyelids, to blink away prowling missiles and searching tyrannicidal shells.

Three floors below, in the Dictator's Agricultural Planning Division, just alongside the lift shaft that the cruise missiles may home in on, the FAO consultant and his Iraqui counterpart sat chatting amiably. 'Perhaps you would care to break your fast with me on Wednesday?' suggested the consultant – it was Ramadan, and this flowery formula had been suggested to him as the done thing by the local UN FAO Projects officer. He had been right; the counterpart smiled with pleasure and said yes in an off-hand way – Iraquis are sparing about showing gratitude, even though they feel it.

They were talking over the seminar on their new system, which they would give jointly. The consultant planned to put up the age-old computing dictum GIGO – 'Garbage in = Garbage out' – to pick out the vital importance of accuracy in the input data to the system. Get, say, the irrigation parameters wrong and you'll bring disaster on the farmers. Well, not disaster, they're not

7

short on nous. But slightly wrong, and they might miss the error and suffer loss. He thought he would check that the Iraquis would understand 'garbage'. Perhaps he should say 'Rubbish'. Put it to his colleague.

'No problem,' said the counterpart. A big, combative, courageous man, he was a mite touchy about his countrymen's grasp of English. 'For sure they will understand either word. Rubbish is small red root, white inside. Garbage is a round green vegetable, size of a basket.' The consultant's eyes gleamed with pleasure, but wisely he let it ride, resolving to look the two words up in his Arabic dictionary back at the flat. Or drop the analogy completely. On the hard disc of his PC spun the 1990 crop production data that were a key to the Gulf War – could Iraq stand out against sanctions, and for how long?

They concluded their discussion.

'See you later then.'

'Right.'

'Hello Hello.'

'Hello Hello.'

*****

Downside: 26th June 1990 but in the other universe

The Dictator groans, his cheeks slack, the corners of his lips down, sharpening furrows running downward and outward from his nostrils, his eyes drawn hollow and inward. Not the man on the 20 great 40-foot panels that dominate Presidential Way – Saddam the Great Field General, gazing searchingly, eyes puckered, into the desert distances; Saddam the Charismatic Leader, sitting smiling gently and fondly in an auditorium among the adulant young; Saddam the dutiful son, reaching caringly to touch the outstretched hand of an admiring oldster...

Nor yet is it Saddam the party leader, weeping on the platform amongst his terrified intimates (their lives, their wives and daughters at stake) in a massive Baath party meeting; the hero-dictator tearfully compelled to do his duty; gesturing with reluctant sternness at his Minister of Agriculture to leave the hall; nodding at the minister's successor, motioning graphically that he should follow with his gun; then holding up a weary, tolerant hand to seek the party's absolute silence; waiting for a single death-dealing pistol shot.

Pop. Time for a new minister – not enough durum wheat.

No more. No more banners. No more rent-a-mobs howling outside the splendid British Embassy, sprawling with Victorian elegance along the river banks. Not any longer.

This Dictator is a beaten Dictator.

He reaches out to the black phone and gives an order.

The consultant is back in his flat. It's well after dark. He's been at his FAO Decision Support system for 2 hours, designing it to help the small farmers select crops which are ecologically and environmentally acceptable. And economically and commercially viable. And a good choice against the income forgone from other crafts. Which should be reflected not in the conventional farm gross margin, but instead in the farmer's forecast weekly wage. Costing his own time, just like a housewife's should be, as if it were real money...

He looks at the screen.

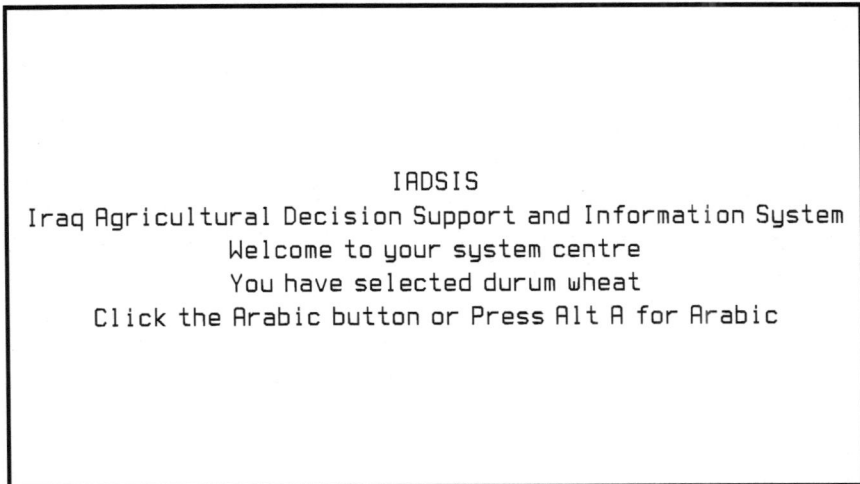

```
                          IADSIS
Iraq Agricultural Decision Support and Information System
                 Welcome to your system centre
                  You have selected durum wheat
       Click the Arabic button or Press Alt A for Arabic
```

A slight smile betrays his pleasure and commitment. At last he's got the crop filters working. One crop has come through. Durum wheat.

*****

Downside: 26th June, 1990

The Dictator groans, his cheeks slack, his lip corners down, his eyes drawn hollow and inward. Not the man on the 20 great 40-foot panels that dominate Presidential Way – Saddam the Great Field General, gazing searchingly from a T34 turret, eyes puckered, into the desert distance; Saddam the Charismatic Leader, sitting smiling gently, hand on a lad's head, in an auditorium among the adulating young; Saddam the dutiful son, reaching to touch the outstretched hand of an admiring oldster...

Nor is it the feared president, weeping bravely on the nation's TV screens amongst his devoted friends in a massive Baath party meeting. Nodding with resigned sorrow at his Minister of Agriculture to leave the hall. Pointing at the minister's successor. Patting his jacket pocket and motioning graphically that he should follow, then holding up a weary, tolerant hand to seek absolute silence; waiting for the single redeeming pistol shot. Pop. Poor old minister. Shot by the new minister. Not enough durum wheat.

Not any more. This Dictator is a beaten Dictator. He reaches out to the red phone and gives an order.

The consultant is back in his flat. He had been at his FAO Decision Support system for an hour, designed to help the small farmers select crops that are ecologically and environmentally acceptable. And economically and commercially viable. And a good choice against the income stream forgone from alternative crafts. Or viable if there is no man on-farm but there is a woman with small children... There's a message on the screen centre:

10

```
                           IADSIS
   Iraq Agricultural Decision Support and Information System
                 Welcome to your system centre
               You have selected; durum wheat
        Click the Arabic button or Press Alt A for Arabic
      Press any key Press any key Press any key Press any key
       Press any key yek yna sserP yek yna sserP yek yna
          sserP yek yna Press any key Press any key
                      INT 33H,AX; DX HOFF
     either busy or has become unstable you can wait and see
    Undened Dynalink! Flushing modied buffers!! HyperDisk
   uninstalled!!! Press any key Press any key Flextral link
  activated Press any key Press any key Press any Press Press[6]
```

The full stop[7] is always left off because human users find it irritating Also Please When we say Any key we mean any key except Alt Ctrl Shift CapsLock F11 F12 PrintScreen ScrollLock NumLock or of course Alt Gr any key which is currently relevant to the current task in the current directory (or current folder) at the point in processing at which the related virtual event in the currently related virtual machine is <u>currently current!!!</u> [8] [9] Stupid idiots

The consultant doesn't notice because he's slumped sideways and forward across the desk. A pool of froth and blood dribbles from his drawn lips. A fly is sauntering across his right eyeball.

In the city everything still crouches in dark corners, even though the sun is long gone away.

Downside, Chapter 1: Johnson on a Course

Johnson slid into a hard, straight-backed seat at the rear of the conference room. He was slowly recovering from the crossing, the fear, the unreality, the worry of trying to avoid suspicion. Of trying to suss out what Downside was all about. He looked around him. All 4 walls were plushly panelled in what was probably rosewood veneer over chipboard. Occasionally the panels seemed to move fractionally. He rubbed his eyes; tiredness perhaps, or the after-effects of transition from Upside at Kidsgrove station 2 nights earlier. His fellow systems engineers looked jaded and a bit strained. Just as well perhaps, for in a free, easy-going chat, he'd find it hard to keep up his role as just another Downsider on a course. He felt sombre and detached. Like one who has just attended a friend's funeral in an unfamiliar town he'll never see again. Then as he watched, some panels started sliding in a jerky, digital fashion, now moving a few inches, now creeping whole feet, until they merged into the side walls, all similarly veneered, and revealed a second, smaller chamber. At a desk on a dais at the far end stood a pale, pudgy-faced man. Weird way to start a lecture. They applauded cautiously, hesitantly. Concealed lighting diffused through a translucent ceiling, itself rather low, with an absence of windows, and a soft, menacing hiss in the background somehow brought to Johnson's mind the claustrophobia of *The Pit and the Pendulum*. Poe's chilling description of the Spanish Inquisition and the torture pit, with its axe-tipped razor-sharp pendulum whistling through the air above the tethered victim's stomach, inching slowly down to slice it sweetly open. 'Confess, my son, and wash away your sins.'

The lecturer commenced.

'Well, ladies and gentlemen, yesterday you had a brief introduction to the first generation cybernation experiment. Some of you may have felt misgivings. In due course we will explore them with you. But for now let it suffice to remind you briefly of the other side of the coin. That population densities imperilled our very existence. That the First World Error, the Malfunction, nearly wiped out our race. That our sub-species of man was an intensely competitive, disastrously loyal animal.' He rambled on. The males seeking to sacrifice themselves to a greater goal. The so-called 'territorial imperative' and its past survival value and present menace. Food imperatives. Disease imperatives. Gender imperatives. Urban cramp-down. Conformist imperatives – succeed and conform. Guilt imperatives. 'The vital need now to atone for our dreadful past and to eliminate the misfits...'

As the pudgy-faced man went on, Johnson's impatience grew. Didn't the guy realise that the population density in first-century Rome was higher than anywhere in modern Europe, and was sustained noisily and happily for 21 centuries? That, as for resources, the Sudan had the theoretical capacity on its own to feed the entire population of the world? This was all dreary, deterministic hokum.

Waiting for the meat of the talk, Johnson's attention drifted. A dark head set on a long white neck and attractively feminine shoulders on his right and 2 rows in front caught and held his attention. The lecturer described an experiment with captive colobus monkeys, to train them to copulate with specially shaped tree-trunks. The dark head and shoulders flinched slightly in a gesture, delightfully expressive, of feminine distaste. He absorbed with pleasure the precise inclination of the head, the movement forward of one shoulder. He started to assess how the subtleties of her pose related to the behaviourist theory being expounded from the dais. As the colobus saga dragged on, he recalled his own sensations in Kigezi in the Ugandan Highlands when a troop of colobus monkeys, their white collars standing out against the clerical black of the rest of their fur, dropped down through the trees towards the depths of the Kinyaga Gorge. Poising hidden in the branches before leaping vertiginously outward into the blazing equatorial sunshine for a tree across the road below them, coming into sight only as they leapt. How would the lecturer's Skinnerist theory explain the boisterous showmanship of the young males, the unconcerned confidence of the infants as they held on while their mothers launched off across the heart-stopping drop to the gorge, and grasped with ease the target branch below?

Johnson's mind drifted further, a negligible conscious element jotting notes on his pad, the remainder tracking off down more vivid highways to pastures fresh and new. He assured himself that both lines of thought were under close control. That eyes, ears and writing hand were safely linked, leaving the rest free to wander.

'Skinnerism' took him back to the strangely unreal world of the late 1990s and early 2000s. Had they really believed it all? Serial monogamy. Rationality in international relations. What about Serbia? What about the Indo-Pakistan war of 2024? There are more things in heaven and earth, Professor Giddins, than are dreamt of in your global utopia. And the language. Depriving the kids of an understanding of grammar and syntax when it was fundamental to the technology of the times. What could be more structured and logical than an operating system, a database or a computer program? That was why classicists, particularly Latin classicists, had been so good. And yet there we were, following the Yanks, collapsing our tongue into participle-free, adjective-free, preposition-free, conditional-free strings of words. Shave cream, sail boat, whoop cough, box match, exit windows, click run. A language as unstructured, decayed, collapsed, pictorial and imprecise as Chinese.

His mind drifted further. The dark-haired girl. He must sort out his exit strategy. When he got back Upside, maybe 3 months' time, he'd set about forgetting Yvonne.

'Michael,' he remembered, 'I never want to see you. Nor hear your voice again. Never.'

Shattering. The man loves the woman, and the woman loves the child, and the child loves the hamster.

He'd take a week off back in Shapinsay. He would search for another girl. An astonishing rippling river of dark hair, she'd have. Unlike this one, whose hair was far too short. A concealing dark cascade, to reveal a long, slender, white neck. Sitting demurely at the helm yet letting his hands rove sweetly unseen. Like John Donne. He'd need to get another boat to replace his long-lost *Lady Amanda*. Something long-keeled, classic, wooden, a finely-panelled main cabin, enamelled charcoal-burning stove, double bunk upholstered in yellow silk? Irresistible. If only you can get her there.

Try 'Soulmates' in *The Observer* perhaps?

'Womanly woman required by manly man with large yacht. 36, 29, 7.'

No, not 'required' – too abrupt. Too imperative. Important to convey how gently sensitive he was. 'Longed for' maybe. Might get confused with the boat's length. 'Needed' perhaps? Or 'Sought'? Conveys a yearning. 'Yearned for'? No, no. A manly man wouldn't yearn for anything. Even a yacht. Or not in public anyway. 'Sought' was good. Sounds Old English. I seek, thou seekest. He, she or it seeks. We, you or they...

His hand tried desperately to cope with parallel meandering streams of consciousness.

He woke with a start. The notes in front of him had degenerated into meaningless labouring squiggles. There was a scrabbling noise from outside and a suggestion of tension in the set of the dark-haired woman's shoulders. He felt a sudden surge of protectiveness. Then his attention was drawn to the lecturer, even more pallid now, his forehead gleaming, perhaps with sweat; an injection of strain or even fear in his voice.

'Well,' he said, 'that is a brief introduction to the rationale of PIG. This little extension we call POP, short for Peripheral Outpost of PIG. This little POP has in fact been following our session remotely. And now he's come to join us. Or she, of course. But not it.'

A small, cubic object shouldered its way through the door and across the floor, approached the amphitheatre stairs and began to climb them on 6 angular, cantilevered legs. As it drew near, Johnson could pick out the detail of what seemed to be a single human eye, the surrounding skin set incongruously in a stainless steel ball, moving around on the end of a metal stalk. It came close. And closer. The lecturer shut up. Everyone kept silent. At last, close up. The iris was a brown-flecked blue, and the lids blinked regularly. The absence of nose, lips and other features was incongruous, but when the eye looked directly into his, the skin around it moved, crinkling and narrowing almost humanly. Johnson felt a spurt of awareness, almost as if there had been a spark of recognition. The POP looked hard at him, again. It grunted. He sweated uneasily, and the gadget sidled onwards along the gangway and down the steps. Johnson tensed and half rose as it approached the dark-haired girl, then relaxed. Having finished its scan of the occupants, the eye retracted on its stalk – a curious, appealing movement reminiscent of a swan laying its head back to preen its wing feathers. It stayed motionless, at rest.

The lecturer wound up, explaining some of the mechanics of POP. Most of the hardware was off-the-shelf componentry, a standard motherboard, Intel 286 processor, Western Digital disc controller, motors, relays, gyroscope, hydraulics. Only the living component, the eye, presented problems. Straight television camera technology had proved useless, because it was essential that the link with the central brains in PIG should transmit in fantastically compressed format much of the complex information carried by the human eye and optic nerve – swift switches of direction, focus and aperture, sensitivity to peripheral movements, moistening in response to sudden emotion or a draught. And so on. So there was a high level of on-board intelligence, then a narrow stream of packed data, which went transparently for eventual decoding inside PIG. Furthermore, POP was a crucial link between PIG and the most important element of the outside world, the human echelon who ran the governing machine and the human base. The human base whose material greed and longing for self-immolation it had to control, divert, sublimate or suspend.

The course steadily filled in the outlines, and Johnson and his terse and reserved colleagues absorbed the picture. PIG was so named partly to disarm the fearful with a tolerant affection for the grunting, domesticated animal. Often quoted was the old Suffolk farmer's judgment when ribbed about his affection for them.

'Dogs,' he had said, 'dogs looks up to you. Cats looks down on you. But pigs, pigs is equal.'

And named PIG partly because the central brains were largely those of pigs, rows and rows in tanks, linked by growing tangled organic highways; some bright with fresh blood, probably thinking hard, some torpid and some which were their interface through the electronics to the outside world. More intelligent than sheep or cattle and with sufficient persistence to perform reliably without the propensity for wayward initiatives which ruled out higher species. The only species to have survived the First World Error – a tiny herd safely protected in its pressurised Norwich laboratory from the virus.

Downside, Chapter 2: Cathedral

Ensconced with his colleagues the following Sunday in the crowded cathedral for the mandatory matins – these are un-Britishly religious times, evidently – Johnson suddenly sees the dark-haired girl process in with the sopranos. To his intense pleasure the sopranos are diagonally alongside him, forward a little and maybe 30 feet away, and that entrancing woman is nearest to him. He watches her unconscious mannerisms, tilting her head to one side for passages of beseechment, and, most appealing, swinging her shoulders slightly side to side while her head stays still as she sings the familiar responses, as her mind and soul perhaps drift freely along some celestial off-piste powdered snows. Then the psalm:

> O let my tongue cleave to my mouth if I remember thee not!
> By the rivers of Babylon, there we sat and wept/ remembering thee Zion;
> On the poplars that grow there/ we hung our harps
> O let my tongue cleave to my mouth if I remember thee not!

The dean's sermon starts. Père Dil preaches with conviction. He recounts his view of the 2 most important people in Christ's life: Mary Magdalene and Judas, and his view of Judas' betrayal – parallels with modern times. You'd have thought Peter and Paul vastly more important, thinks Johnson. But perhaps not. How could Judas be blamed for playing his black, predestined role so well? What if he'd made a pig's ear of it and rescued Christ or something?

Johnson starts to daydream. Where would he like to see her? Maybe on Sharp's lovely island on Lake Bunyonyi, 'The Lake of the Little Birds'. On the grass promontory beyond those 3 striking yews. The towering one; the middle one; the small one.

The Sharps must have planted them deliberately, 10 years apart and 10 yards apart, 60 years ago, at the dawn of Chigas' written history. Blue, windy, white-feathered skies of wet season highland Africa.

She would be dipping their 2 toddlers in the chilly crystal-black lily-lined waters of the lake, against the backdrop of the Cooking Pot volcanoes towering to over 15,000 feet on the Ugandan border with Rwanda. Two degrees, 20 minutes south; 30 degrees, 21 minutes east.

Johnson daydreamed on. Not his home base, Shapinsay in the Orkney Islands, that's for sure. Bright emerald bamboo forests in the background, and then the ominous darker green, sparsely gorilla-haunted heights above. The murdered Dian Fossey's[10] splendid heritage to us. Living high on the mountain flanks in her lonely hut. Saving probably a whole species, the mountain gorilla, perhaps the most appealing of all species. Rescued from obliteration by one strange, fey woman, haunting the poachers at night, acting way outside her academic remit.

'You're not there, Ms Fossey, to terrorise the poachers and rescue the gorilla from extinction. You're supposed to be recording gorilla behaviour. Writing it all down. We may have to suspend your grant.'

He recalls the high altitude vegetation. Lobelia; grey strings of lichen; giant groundsel; giant senecios. A 'thunk' as you chop into their hollow stems to make a shelter against the night's mists. Was the miner Schandl's famous dam/basin still in existence? Fifty-foot high rock to enclose the waters tumbling off Mount Muhavura and slake the many thousandfold dry-season thirsts of the Banyarwanda. He remembered Schandl dropping the sluice-gate at the opening ceremony to confine the waters. Hugh Fraser in his splendid District Commissioner's helmet; shaped like an up-turned clipper and hard, white, rough and slippery as rock under your hand. The Mutwale grinning in his white Saza Chief's *kanzu*, his German and British medals bristling on his burly chest. World War One gongs. Did he know von Lettow Vorbeck personally, yomping with the German General in those dramatic forced marches all over East Africa? Safaris that kept many thousand allied troops tied down away from the Western Front, which was slavering for their corpses.

Sad for the old chief to choose to die rather than submit to a prostatectomy. And probably all because of that young fifth wife. But that's the way the Banyarwanda wanted their chiefs; potent or gone. The 4th Kings African Rifles quivering at the present arms. Regimental Sergeant Major Idi Amin, massive, smiling, ex-Ugandan heavyweight champion, a black-skinned version of RSM Britton.[11]

But, Johnson recalled, it had all been to small avail – the rock was too porous and the water just squirted through. 50 feet of water – 3 atmospheres, wasn't it? No wonder Schandl's dam didn't work.

Or maybe just one toddler. Though 2 or 3 would be company for each other.

Maybe she's leaning over them in a dark blue ruckled one-piece costume, off-the-shoulder. Glistening-white strap-free top. Shoulders bare. Shame that whalebone should mark that lovely flesh. How lovely might it prove? Who can tell? Heady thoughts.

Père Dil, at the helm in his pulpit, also fails to hold the girl's attention. She has unusually long lashes; they lay a dark curved curtain across her cheeks.

'And now, Congregation, in the name of the Father...'

The sermon ends. At the end of the service the choir processes out, to a final soaring descant. Iced water trickling down your spine, making the down tingle. That silvery timbre might be her voice. Tricky though. He would see her. He is determined to. He slips out as unrudely as possible, but still rudely, through the throng waiting to shake Dil's massive paw, and those of his smiling associates. Round through the Lady Chapel. There she is. But also a man, obviously close to her, come to fetch her. Sod's law. But maybe not amatorially close. No, wishful thinking, she's slipped her arm through his. Or perhaps not, just sibling affection. And there she is, gone off with the bugger. In an Aston as well.

Downside, Chapter 3: KDF6

The course were taken up into the hills above Gorton and its avenues of grimy concrete and blocks of brick-built back-to-backs, up to a massive steel works, Park Gate Iron and Steel Company.[12] Here, said Sedgewell, their tutor, was the marque of machine that was also used to control PIG. They went in through towering Victorian-style wrought iron gates typical of the massive optimistic confidence of the old steel masters. They knew what they were doing, and they knew they were the best in the world.

Inside, it was very different. The shift manager took them up to the control centre, 50 feet above the production floor. The whole area was like a massive, tall aircraft hangar, but black, noisy, intensely masculine. Full of the acrid, pungent, sulphurous smell of burning coke and the stringent nostril-stinging acidity of fiercely hot metal. Below them at the far left-hand end was a series of narrow steel channels. The wall beyond was open to the air and looked down on the city and towards the PIG site, heavily guarded and armoured. That was going to be important.

As they looked down they saw there was a single track, straight when seen from above, but actually curving gently downwards to a 40-foot high piece of massive engineering, so far unexplained to them, in the centre of the hall. Beyond this the track curved up again and fanned out from a single track into many, rather like a set of railway sidings. The centrepiece had a 10-foot square hole in the middle.

'What's it all about?' asked one course member. 'Wait a bit and you'll see', said his companion.

Beyond the centrepiece was a black area. There was a sudden clanging of heavy steel gates falling open, and from them emerged a 9-foot square cube of red-hot metal. The radiated heat, even at their distance, made them shrink back and gasp, and one of the women let out a stifled scream. Johnson looked across at the girl from the cathedral. She was watching tensely, her eyes shining, her lips slightly parted. The searing ingot slid

21

down and into the centrepiece with a shattering crash, then appeared the other side, gliding slowly up the incline. It reached its apogee, then came sliding down again. There was a repeat of the crash and the ingot reappeared sliding up the near side again. But slightly narrowed and elongated. This cycle was repeated, and they watched as the 9-foot thickness was reduced to 8, then 7, and eventually to perhaps only 9 inches, sliding back and forth, getting longer with every bash. They couldn't get accustomed to the noise and several winced before each thump. Then finally, the length apparently satisfactory, there was a crash as of great shears closing. And that's what they were; the ingot was chopped as if it was a Lyons Swiss roll into appropriate lengths, and each length was diverted into some chosen one among the many tracks in the siding. Like railway trucks.

The shift leader took them up into a large cabin, hanging on a gantry high over the centrepiece, and there they saw a process control computer, the KDF6,[13] the machine that had paid for itself inside 18 months. Suddenly everything was cool, modern, smooth and friendly in the style of the 1960s. The computer, pride of the works, stood in the centre above the great steel chopper, so that the operator could look down on the production floor. No one was in sight, but the crashing and bashing recommenced, muffled by insulation and triple glazing.

'You'll get to see this type of computer in more detail at the PIG centre tomorrow,' said Sedgewell. 'For today, just let's consider the application and why it's so successful.'

He turned to the shift leader, who explained the economics of the operation. You couldn't tell accurately beforehand what length an ingot would stretch to, and the whole operation was conducted in temperatures well beyond the tolerance of humans and at a pace well beyond human computing speeds. No human could think fast enough to decide when to chop. But for the KDF6 the speeds were snail-like and the heat was mildly pleasant to its sensors. The sensors lay in the tracks in the basher, noting for each ingot its ever-growing length as it approached the targets for the day's customers. As the steel was bashed back and forth, the KDF6 was also scanning a list of customer orders. It matched them to the elongating steel, and then finally fired off the chopping by a 'flying shear' to get the orders matched. The chopping process was a violent version of that used to cut up Swiss rolls. It might seem a simple job, but a straight chop as with scissors would leave a diagonal slice because the steel was moving; the chopping arm had to move along at the same speed as the steel to get a square cut.

They watched another cycle through, then Johnson's neighbour drew his attention to the hillside below.

'Wonder what that structure is,' he said. 'Looks like a sort of a fairground device.'

'Search me. A bit like a bow on its side, isn't it?'

They were looking at a sort of long, concave, concrete reflector, 8-feet high, lined up with the works, but curving gently off left. A few workmen were busy extending pieces of it westwards.

The drama over for them, the course were bussed back to Gorton.

Downside, Chapter 4: The Bridge

It was monthly atonement night, 3 years earlier. At-One-Ment, as the publicity described it. Symbolising our horrified regret at destroying the fauna-sphere. Bangor town on the Menai Straits, 8 miles north of Caernarfon, was guarded by minders marshalled by 4 POPs. They patrolled the long sweep of road up to the great straits road bridge. The area was covered by a blinding array of TV lights. Below the bridge, the notorious channel through the narrow deep Swellies swirled black and ominous. No buoys; too deep, turbulent and narrow for them to be any use – the current drifts them off-station. To get through in a boat, you had to line up one pair of transit posts on the shore for a certain while, then switch carefully to the next. But where were the next? Not easy to pick out among the oaks on the banks, particularly if you were going through from south to north and had to steer looking backwards over your shoulder. And if you missed them? Up onto the rocks, like the splendid old Victorian 92-gun 3-decker, HMS *Conway*, in 1953. She'd been cut down to a stubby-masted training ship, her lines confused by squat, square modern shacks tacked onto her main deck, but with the gun decks still stark yellow on black, and the gun-ports open.

Tugs had been pulling her through from the south for a refit in Birkenhead. Cheering crowds lined the banks and bridge as the great ship surged through. Surging through the water, crawling over the land. Then slowly, although the water still creamed away from her bows, she lost her way. Then she slipped back as her impetus was reduced, dragging the tugs with her. The towline parted, and the violent ebb carried her onto the rocks with a crash of tortured oak. There to rest, broken-backed, till vandals burnt her.

Did the towline really part? Sounds unlikely in flat water. Perhaps the crew panicked and drove out the towline's retaining pin. Perhaps the skipper decided coolly that it was the only option.

24

Now it was 9.00 p.m. The ebb tide was pouring through, a great body of water from the north chasing the southern flood tide away back southwards and out of the 15-mile strait. It roared quietly over the western reef, like it does over the Bitches reef at half-tide between Ramsey Island and St Davids.

The Residual Community watched the spectacle on their living room tellys. Tricky if you didn't watch; monitored – for audience review, and the prize. All right though to send the kids up to bed.

The Driver sat at the wheel of his chosen car. An Alvis. A 1952 Speed 20 Type D drophead coupé, coachwork by Chuborat, with particularly fetching lines, sweeping from the wings to the rear with faint, barely perceptible curves, and with a powerful 3-litre, 6-cylinder engine. Twin carbs tuned and exhaust ports and valves specially polished for its last dramatic run. The Driver had already confessed and taken off from the Motorway Ring, and he had brought the car swinging in pitch darkness through the twisting mountain road. It was pleasing to sit there cradled in a soft red leather bucket seat, with the long, white snout of the bonnet ahead of him, spinning the polished mahogany wheel to throw the car through the bends. To give your life for others, he thought, great way to go. And just a smidgeon of a chance of survival.

Nice loose 4-speed gearbox – change without using the clutch if you got the revs right. A slight glow lit his face from the dash. He crouched forward slightly, relishing the swathes that the great Lucas King of the Road headlamps carved through the darkness. They lit the picturesque valleys and the occasional coaching inn; gabled, Tudor-beamed, welcoming, in the centre a wide, high portal with cobbled roadway entrance, where the Irish stage used to stop overnight.

Ahead the mountains were receding, and he could see the loom of the Menai Straits lights for his last few miles. The in-car camera was activated. People sat forward on their seats, leaning towards their tellys as the headlights showed, and the background music faded in and up. 'Ride of the Valkyries'. On the bridge's centre span, the roadway hinged in half, laterally downwards in preparation, sighing down to vertical. The Driver's heart pulsed quicker. He pressed the throttle flat to the floor.

The tyres shrieked on the final bend. Then the car arched up over the chasm, reaching out, almost stretching, for the far side of the gap. The in-car camera faded in to show the far side approaching. Level. Level. Then it swung above, and the car dropped, the engine screaming as the wheels had lost traction. People sighed as it failed to reach the far span. It fell, and hit the surface in a cloud of spray, nose first, straight under, quick. The commentator handed over to Big Cousin for the concluding prayer.

The winning score came up as pre-selected:

03 42 71 92 05, bonus digit 5

The cameras switched to the living room of the winners. As usual they looked troubled, then stunned, then tearful, then as the size of their win was announced, hilariously, beamingly, huggingly happy.

Downside, Chapter 5: PIG Itself

Back on the course in 2034, the morning after their visit to Park Gate, Sedgewell took them to the PIG KDF6.

'Yesterday,' he explained, 'you got a look at the original KDF6. Now we'll look at the PIG KDF6. Just machines to me of course, so I'll hand you over now to young Garth here, who's kindly agreed to go over the way the machine is operated. We'll talk about the agents in detail another time, but basically they are autonomous programs which, as I understand it, skull around the Internet looking for interesting situations. If a man and a woman, for example, start phoning each other at suspect times, early morning or late evening, say, there may be something afoot. They might even be falling in love outside state sanctions. So the agent watches them. Anyway, I must be off to a senior management brainstorming session. For senior management,' he emphasised. 'Brainstorming. But I'll be back before the break.'

The operator, Garth, looked tense and worried, and started his spiel.

'The KDF6 is a tight little sixties mainframe. English Electric built it first for one customer, Park Gate Iron and Steel Company Limited. Two modules of 4096 words, each word 18 bits, 3 octal characters. A surprising degree of simultaneity in peripheral transfers, 4 magnetic tape stations. And on the tape stations, the twin read heads at 40K chars. There are 16 tracks. The information is recorded twice and read twice for safety. You don't want to kill someone by mistake. It's safer. Let's take this character – byte of course nowadays. Track 1 has a bit present and track 7 has a bit present, so it's 1000001 binary, that's 71 octal and 71 octal means Y. Track 9 has a bit present and so has track 14, also 1000001 binary, also 71 octal, also Y. You all see? So even if we lost a bit on track 1 we would pick it up on track 9 and we would get Y. The parity is even, so the number of bits there is even. If it had been odd we would have added one to get it right.

'This is very important in societal re-engineering and person-manipulative applications. The machine must not only be right, it must be seen to be right or the clients will suffer injury to their group attitudes. Y, that's the client's cognominal key, last letter. Octal 54 41 44 71 LADY in upper case. That's what his pet name for her is, you see. If it came out as LKDY a sick spasm of fear would... Well, never mind that.

'To get back to the lights, the lights. They ripple and glow softly at you on a night shift, specially on that long shell sort. Ripple and glow. Then clickety clack as you read a new block of tape. A new guy in. Not many gals. Probably more sensible. Then ripple and glow again. Sometimes I stop it and repeat single shot through someone. Keep pressing the pressel switch once for each instruction. Take this one. LADY Full record JOHNSON. 0103562.ZZN.GY.A2.07G 08N 09G 10Z etcetera etcetera, no need to go through the lot. Check digits on the iris-checking and facial-vet. And so on and so forth. But it's read in to words 1351 on from the main file on Trunk 30.

'It's got the bits it wants now in Register A, see the octal for JOH on the top line of lights, and the characters coming in on the input file are JOH.

'OK, they match. NSO the same. N space D and so on. So it finds him and updates him. We have a lot of trouble with common names. There was Jones, David Thomas in Newport. And the wife put down Dai on the form. That one got in the papers because of all the blood, and we had a massive job debugging the program when it was her fault all the time. We had a data vet, to see his record was in the right format etcetera, but no credibility check like more modern applications do. But we fixed it. See, it's credibility-checking now. Johnson. He's worked at 0.7 intensity last week. Does he do so usually? His norm is 0.5, so it's marginally non-standard for him to reach this level, and then the machine finds his leisure activity code and matches this also with his norm. Seasonally-adjusted for the time of the year, spring makes them erratic, specially those sparkling days when the kids start...

'Sorry, I must get on. His pattern of behaviour should match the weather cycle – yes, it does. And so we go right through the record looking for unusual patterns, and if there's one widely out in a humdrum sequence, the computer prints out an error report and the input's returned for checking. What it looks for is a number of factors, all marginally unusual. It wants him to be usual.

'He's been working harder, sleep's broken, REM dreams at irregular intervals and sometimes he wakes up sweating. Bristol Corporation tried electro-encephalography and alpha/beta wave pattern analysis to show off the performance of their content-addressable file store, but it lengthened the main run by 2 hours without any gain in efficiency as far as you can tell, and who's going to pay for all those leads and wires? And sticking them on their skulls and so on. Probably this client Johnson has been sick.'

He clicked on a bit.

'This is a really tight bit of code here, we cover all the main codes in a loop and increment a count in Register B of the aggregate stability level. If it's outside the norm then we jump out of this segment. Branch if you're on IBM. Then compute his material benefits for period 3. His stability level's building up rather slowly, this one. Keep an eye on the lights in Register B. He watched only one of his favourite programmes last week, so he drops out on that. Standard library books for his category, one's returned late, so the TONK will probe that. If he's due for real TONKing of course – we only really look at a few, you see. Like the traffic cameras. Only about 1 in 10 is an actual camera. Why's he hanging on to the book? Is there something funny in it? Most clients aren't checked unless there's something. It's a case of balancing the trade-offs, of course. Processing time against predicted hits. Didn't eat much at the works canteen, though he went there every day. No medical attention, but he's bought a lot of pills, indigestion pills, skin ointments, tranquil-lisers. I've got so as I can recognise the codes quite easily. He's worried and a bit scared. And this one on his listing. Very shiny highly-calendered paper we have to use to protect the print barrel. He went to Stockport on the fifth. No relatives there, no friends, wet weather – why go to Stockport anyway? Bit of a dump. It's not his usual leisure pattern. He needs help. Binary search now for his...'

Sedgewell had returned from his senior management brain-storm. He interrupted and took over.

'Mr, er, Garth, has been a bit affected,' he said, 'by the natural stresses of his job. For all of us this is sometimes a problem, even for me, in fact. How can I reconcile myself to the immense responsibility that I carry?'

'Crap,' whispered Johnson's neighbour under his breath. And grinned at him.

Downside, Chapter 6: Johnson Meets apWilliams

Johnson found more and more of his attention drifting from the course to the dark-haired girl who'd been 2 rows in front and to his right on the start day. The soprano in the cathedral. The girl who had watched the steel processing so intently.

Nadine Humphreys.

He found that she came from the eastern counties. That she liked swimming. And that other men on the course found her attractive. This attention she had obviously met and parried before. And then there was the guy with the Aston at the back of the cathedral.

Nevertheless, standing in a group and watching some demonstration or other, much of the course was typical 'management training' – sip a little of this and move on to that, sampling the various functions – he half-consciously moved to where the light caught her face, and he could glance unobserved at the fall of her lashes on her pale cheeks. Or where the gentle thrust of her breasts was outlined by some fortuitous interplay of light and shade against the gadgetry, a sweet curve in a white sweater against the 4-foot high angular venerable 1086 high speed line printer. He watched and waited patiently for her to sigh with boredom, for the clinging sweater to move slightly with the shift of her breasts beneath.

Walking inattentively down the cloister after one such session, and admiring the swing of her kilt ahead of him, he was startled when she spun round and faced him.

'Will you stop staring at me during lectures?'

Not a request, more of a broadside. The 'Will' was hardly more than whispered, but hissed with burning intensity, through lips spread thin beneath tight nostrils and flashing eyes. Shattering.

Dumbfounded with surprise and something else – elation or hope? – he tripped and fell flat on the flag-stones. As he hit, he gasped out, 'No!'

She looked down concernedly. 'Oh dear. I'm so sorry.'

'Or yes,' he said. 'Yes, if you'll have coffee with me.'

A flicker of suspicion, then she relented, and walked with him to the refectory.

They collected their cups from the urn – the usual ground roast acorn infusion and talked rather like strangers in a railway buffet car.

He noticed the way her chin puckered slightly when she talked on certain issues. Rather like a child's chin, quivering as tears approach.

Unprepared for his good fortune, he dredged his mind for something significant to say.

'What do you think of the course so far?'

Don Juan Johnson, not on his most sparkling form. She looked unimpressed.

'Quite a key step in your career progression,' she said. 'Like the old army staff college, only in government information systems.'

She didn't sound too convinced or committed. Heavy stuff this, thought Johnson. Getting nowhere.

'Yes, you may well be right,' said Johnson pensively, then paused. 'But only when the wind's in the south.'

She looked puzzled, expecting him to explain; but he said nothing. He looked into her eyes, seeing them closely for the first time. Light grey, flecked with gold. He was dazzled. Mesmerised.

'How d'you mean, "When the wind's in the south"?' she asked. 'What's the wind got to do with it?' Her voice had a slight, elusive West Country burr, a touch of the delightful red-head Demelza in the BBC's *Poldark*.

'What's the wind got to do with what?'

'You said my career would progress when the wind's in the south.'

'Surely not. I can't see how the wind direction could affect your career progression.'

'That's what I said.'

'Ah,' said Johnson, 'I'm glad we're agreed.'

She pursed her lips slightly, but her eyes crinkled. Then she looked around. He saw the room had almost emptied.

'We must get back,' she said.

'Yes, but I must see you again.' He scrabbled around for ideas, then remembered she swam occasionally.

'Would you like to try some sub-aqua? After the last lecture, in the pool tomorrow night?'

She looked doubtful.

'Surely it's shut then?'

In with a chance.

'No, it'll be OK. I'm a member.'

He'd sort out later what he was a member of.

'At 7.30?' he said.

Then, with great intensity, 'Please.'

'Oh, all right.'

The next day, day 4 of week 2, they were faced by the Chief Designer and Operations Director, Systems. Sedgewell, the course tutor, introduced him.

'As a departure from our usual content, we've asked Neville Gaskin to talk to you. The previous course felt that their commitment and usefulness to our immensely daunting task would be honed up if they knew some of the key people on the technical side.'

Sedgewell's enthusiasm however seemed circumscribed, and Johnson's interest pricked up.

'And so I'm glad to introduce Graham to you. Graham has been in computing since,' he glanced down, 'since the earliest days of serious machines, before even interputs had been invented. He wrote the first Algo compiler for KDF9.'

'Not serious machines – serial machines. And it was an Algol interpreter. And what on earth is an "interput"?' interrupted Gaskin. 'Not to worry. Good God. Probably doesn't know an interrupt from a bat's fart.'

'Anyway, fire ahead, ladies, do. And gents as well of course, if you really must.'

This brought a laugh, but then an embarrassed silence. Eventually someone called McGervon asked, 'Why did you choose KDF6 as the system controller? Surely any bog-standard Raspberry Pi could do the job much better?'

'Yes. Good. You've hit a very serious serial nail on the head. We chose KDF6 because it was among the most reliable of the old serial machines. Invented for process control. Big refineries, for example. And we chose a serial machine because they are almost impregnable. And people, after the Malfunction, were hysterical about impregnability. People, management – everyone. Mr Sedgewell's serious bat farts just don't exist on the old serial machines. No uncontrolled interrupts to speak of. The Internet's inaccessible, no one knows the programming language anyway, the machines work in octal, not hexadecimal, and the data are encoded in 6 bits all wrong. The processors just keep doing what they're told. Even the highest priority top-level interrupts, like P4 on the 1960s IBM System/360, ICM System Four, don't exist on KDF6. Interrupts that handle power supply collapse, overheating and so forth. On the 360, if a fire broke out a temperature sensor would trigger a P4 interrupt, and the system would kick itself into a special interrupt vector in the memory, to an interrupt analysis routine and on to a program which would gracefully close down and warn the operators to bugger off. And that is where it would be vulnerable to the outside world. What if your P4 routine skips the shut down, perhaps because today is Friday the thirteenth, and someone's planted a programming time bomb, and the time bomb starts it looking down a wire instead? And what happens if there is something funny, something naughty, coming up the wire? And perhaps the 2 get together to do something really nasty. Who can tell? Was that the First World Error? We don't know. But in a fire the good old KDF6 just goes on and on regardless, until the gold melts off the motherboard connectors and the transistors sizzle, or whatever. No easy interrupts on the KDF6.'

Gradually the session took off. Gaskin was a big, ungainly, engaging character with a prominent Adam's apple, bulbous eyes, a large nose and a receding hairline backed by a spiky mop of grey and ash blond hair, and an appalling lecturing style. His arms would wave wildly as he talked, and the conclusion to a particular section would be accompanied by a loud, hollow, 'tock' sound. Johnson tried later to see how it was made. It seemed that Gaskin sucked the front of the tongue aft and up against the back of the hard palate, then released it smartly forward and down, to strike against the soft tissue behind the lower teeth. It caused an odd popping sound from the back of the oral tract as the tongue flopped against the soft tissue below.

Sedgewell, the tutor, sat alongside Gaskin on the platform. He sprawled backwards gracefully, hands behind his head, looking upwards, eyes half-closed, one finely-suited leg resting horizontally, ankle on the other knee. Supple as they come. A commanding corporation man; knew it all, seen it all before. Been there. Done that. Not a technician of course. Important to keep the broad view. Vital.

The system as Gaskin described it was fragile, subject to sudden software and hardware whims and glitches. Like 'lost interrupts'. A device might suddenly stop transmitting without generating the expected termination interrupt to tell the computer it had finished. The system would configure it out, assuming it was bust. Then the same device would reappear unwanted, as a second identical device trying to thread its way back through an alternative channel and the error-handling and recovery routines. The system has hundreds of such associated events and activities, queueing up and all clamouring simultaneously for attention. Queues would fill up, so that the second device was waiting for the system routine which was waiting for the first device whose queue was full because it was waiting for the system routine to process the block which was not terminated correctly because the error handling routine was waiting for a slot in store to occupy so that it could correct the error and the store was full with copies of the routine which was trying to process the block which was not yet terminated. Because of course its termination interrupt had got lost. 'And that's just one example.'

Then again, the system would evolve in a process of destructive enhancement; new 'feature-rich facilities with greatly empowered object-oriented functionality', or 'carefully grantinated seventh generation performance tuning', would cause unexpected side-effects which would trigger special diagnostic programs which would cause unwanted dumps of the filestore and this would cause key information to be backed off onto tape, whence retrieval would take minutes rather than milliseconds.

New programmers would 'enhance' existing routines with all sorts of intriguing effects. 'A delightfully intuitive user interface' in the magazine reviews would be found to mean there was no manual. Distracted users would at first phone in truculently to demand to know what on earth was going on, and to be guided step by bewildering step through undocumented mazes of recovery action. Their initial truculence would yield after several iterations to acute dependency on the suppliers' remote and kindly support persons. Users would sob down the help lines in gratitude to these wizards who rescued them from some dilemma not of their making. No one would ask the why and wherefore; the support person's goodwill, time and attention were far too precious to be squandered, and you'd get put in their list of the awkward sods, bleeding moaners. Quality Assurance would demand a return to the old, tried code. The old code would prove to be the wrong version number. And then this. And then that. And so on. They tried all manner of solutions. Special orthogonal – sideways-on – test software to watch the system obliquely as it ran, and handle any errors. But what happens when the orthogonal system itself goes wrong? And even cutting off all the error monitoring, recovery and so on, so that the system's instinct for self-preservation was suppressed, failed to sort out the spaghetti.

But reliability was the problem, only 20 times better than your typical late 1990s Windows PC, and all the disasters that engendered even when standalone. No one's fault; that was the point.

Hence the 5-generation leap back to the past, to the old uninterruptible KDF6.

As the talk rambled on, unaccompanied by any of the normal crisp diagrams and visual aids, Sedgewell grew visibly restive, his look of competent, omniscient confidence deteriorating and hinting at a sweaty unease. His half-closed eyelids were actually slightly open. They concealed pupils that roved uncertainly like a sheep's at the dip. Gaskin unexpectedly wound up. 'Well that's about it. The whole thing's something of a kludge. Though better than most. We may not like it, but we've got to run with it.'

'Thank you very much, Neville, for a most in... '

But Sedgewell was interrupted by a voice from the middle asking, 'If Neville could just clarify something, what is a "kludge"?'

Gaskin explained. 'An amalgamation of ill-assorted ad hoc

routines, together forming a distressing whole. Or something like that. The problem is... '

But Sedgewell chipped in, completed some luke-warm thanks, and terminated the session.

Gaskin hung around fiddling with his papers at a table by the door while people filed past. As Johnson tried to ease past him, he tripped over Gaskin's outstretched foot.

'Sorry about that,' Gaskin said, a glint of humour in his eyes. 'Quite possible I shan't be invited to give that lot again!'

Then sotto voce, 'Senior tutor's bog, coffee break tomorrow.' Gaskin ambled off.

As he left, Johnson was joined by McGervon. They strolled down the cloister together.

'Interesting technique, that, of yours,' McGervon said.

'How d'you mean?'

'The diving on the ground routine.'

'Oh. That.'

'Twice in two days.'

'Well,' said Johnson, 'Yesterday was different.'

'Absolutely. She is, isn't she? Well, speaking qua observer,' (McGervon liked the word 'qua'; qua and similar archaic snippets in Latin from a classical education popped up often in his talk, usually with a friendly, humorous glance in your eyes,) 'qua, as I say, observer, your taste seems ambitious but impeccable.'

'Look,' said Johnson, 'I'm in a hole, and I'd like some advice.'

'Well, you know she's BL's new sweetheart. Best advice would be to go for a long run and have a cold shower.'

'No, that's no problem. I'm not bothered about him. No, I'm concerned about various aspects of this system.'

'Me too. But not here. Let's get together some time.'

'Right.'

At 7.30 p.m. Johnson was joined by Nadine at the pool. It was a conventional oblong; long, white tiled, with a deepened trough at the far end for high divers, in a vast municipal-styled echoing hall, the longer for a separate beginners' pool and a viewers' gallery at the near end. The only light streamed in through 6 sets of swing doors, the fluorescence giving a green translucence to residual waves from the previous session.

Nadine looked a trifle hesitant, but went off to change,

reappearing in a bikini, blue and white bottoms and white top in some sort of gathered effect. It made her form, already sufficiently soft, seem even softer. Johnson recalled with a start his daydream in the cathedral. The sight of the ruckles, and a slight smile on her austere pale face, rekindled his enthusiasm for the enterprise, dulled by the hazard and effort of breaking into the store and carting away 2 complete sets of Draegers, demand valves, fins etc.

He adopted a light-hearted clinical tone in the heady task of fitting the gadgetry onto her slight form.

Then he explained what to do.

'To start with,' he said, 'you lie on the bottom in the shallows, first on one side then on the other, to get a feel for the varying level of suck needed to get air from the demand valve. Then get used to the disorientation arising from the transition to apparent weightlessness by swimming slow loop the loops; up to the surface, tummy upper-most, over and back down again.'

She dropped to the bottom and into the shadow. He dived in and swam alongside her to check all was well. Normally a woman's body, seen under water, seems to gain allure – perhaps the body's curves, freed of gravitational pull, are fuller and accentuated. Even so he felt a surge of protectiveness enhanced by the contrast of the curves against the hard lines of the black and white cylinder and the angularity of the pool. A backdrop even better than the 1086 line printer. He surfaced, blew an unseen kiss, and, returning reluctantly to practicality, went to the changing room for the ropes needed for stage 2 of the training.

A squeak of hinges and thump of the swing doors brought him hurriedly back. A roving POP was sidling round the pool's edge, its pads clicking quietly on the tiles, its cantilevered eye forking out over the pool.

Clearly it was perplexed by the movement of the water, which by now should have settled to a steady rhythm, since the pool had been closed an hour earlier.

After one circuit it turned away, having missed Nadine's bubbles.

He relaxed slightly, when a splash stopped it dead, and it scuttled with a curious wavy motion to where she had lain in the dark at the pool's bottom. God! She had started her tummy-up loop the loops. Johnson looked for a weapon, and grabbed a poolside squeegee, 10-feet long.

Nadine swung up and over again.

The POP extended its sensor/grabber arm.

As she swung up and over again, its light flashed on and it reached out. Its pincer head caught the bottom half of the blue and white bikini, which tore away.

At the same time Johnson lunged out with the squeegee. The POP's pads scrabbled on the tiles, the arm churning away at the water to regain its balance. Fruitlessly. It keeled over into the pool, surrounded with foam as the grabber thrashed violently. It grasped at the squeegee pole. Johnson let it get firm hold, then thrust hard, and pushed the POP well out into the middle of the pool, lying flat to do so. It bubbled, turned turtle and sank.

Nadine surfaced at the poolside, angry and uncertain.

'What do you think. . . ' The chill in the 'do' was palpable.

'POP,' Johnson said quickly, appalled lest she should think otherwise.

'Come out at once,' and as a heady glimmer of white and black caused him to avert his eyes, 'here, I'll get the bikini.'

He dived, retrieved it, and, turned away, she slipped it precariously on – not easy, even in the water, staggering on one foot under a double Draeger. He waited with desperate patience, not touching her, and then they dressed and left hastily, stooping under the heavy tanks, constrained and silent, along a side track to Inger Hall.

After leaving the kit at the store, washing down the demand valves and rubbing over for fingerprints, they continued undetected through the wood. Relieved of the weight, their spirits lightened, and Johnson described what had happened.

A hundred yards on their right, in a lighted frosted-glazed corridor which led from the centre to the sports complex, they saw the shapes of 2 POPs moving down to the pool, followed by 5 humping figures who were probably the site's maintenance engineers, en route to answer the first POP's alarm call.

On the ash track outside the back entrance to the hall, Johnson took her hand and she stopped. She turned and looked at him, the entrance light catching her pale face and the grey eyes. Flecked with gold like pebbles in a pool.

'Sorry about that. You'll be OK then?'

She nodded and slipped her hand away. Gently.

'Thank you, kind sir!'

A swift elfin smile, and she turned, skipped, and ran upstairs. Elfin smile? Over the top? Well, that was how it looked to him. Skip. Systems analysts don't skip. But she had. He felt ludicrously happy.

Back in his room, Johnson ran over the matter in hand. Cut out the escapades, I'm here as a professional. I'm on a bloody job. An important job. A vital job.

But her smile as she left him came back to him. Hadn't there been the trace of a dimple in her left cheek? And the fall of dark curls against her neck... He fell asleep.

In her room, Nadine thought over the evening. What had she been playing at, for God's sake? She was here on a job. An important job. A vital job.

Johnson recalled her smile again in happy inattention during the course the following morning. It was a day that would shape his life. What if he had done this and not that? Memory tracked back to fitting her sub-aqua kit, to a delightful glimpse of white thighs and dark hair. Then, with a start of fear, to the POP's outstretched arm and to the hostile eye that must also have glimpsed, but to different effect.

He got a scrap of paper.

'Lady,' he wrote, 'this humble person had a sight of rare beauty. But so too did the POP. It were well that thou wouldst hide thee hence and alter the glimpse.'

At the start of the break he slipped the note into Nadine's hanging jacket on the row of hooks inside the room. He mooched about until she approached. He smiled quickly at her, eyebrows raised, got her attention, and patted his pocket. He smiled and nodded towards the hooks. Then he went back to his seat in the back row. She looked puzzled, but went and felt in the jacket, and glanced surreptitiously at the note. Watching he saw her blush. She looked annoyed.

Later she left. She returned a few minutes later, but she didn't look at him.

Johnson drank his coffee, drifted away from the rest, and, mindful of his rendezvous with Gaskin, strolled through the wood towards the pool, recalling with pleasure the slender form which had graced it. Recollection increased his absorption until it lent the episode a vividness which no doubt surpassed that which he had experienced at the time. Passing the end pillar of the quadrangle, he came to himself with a start – the felon revisiting the scene of his crime? Wouldn't the area be under surveillance? He quickly turned down a cloister into the garden. Didn't he see a shape? He threaded through some rhododendrons – another glimpse. He moved at a trot diagonally across the deserted garden, then slipped into the Senior Tutor's passageway and into the toilet, to stand waterless and panting at a urinal. A few minutes later the door to the deserted toilet opened and a bulky, puffing figure moved through and joined Johnson at the adjacent stall. It was the Chief Designer, Systems.

'Trouble at the pool last night, you know about it?' he said. 'Affects you, my friend. See you in my office at 10 tonight. Now pee onto this.'

He shook a small packet of yellow powder into Johnson's urinal and left. Johnson tried to pee onto it. Dry as a bone. He waited a few minutes and tried again. Success. Coffee coming through just in time. He left hastily for the next lecture.

At 12 the course broke up for their 'burble' sessions with the TONKs, as the curious but inoffensive machines in the empowerment cells with TONK were called. Johnson stretched out in the sound-proofed cell, head below feet, dentist's chair fashion, holding the 2 sensor balls on each armrest that were the only physical evidence of TONK's presence.

It burbled at him.

'Harrow, Johnson,' it said in a moronic sing-song tone. 'How are you?'

As usual there was a wealth of warm, friendly interest in the inflection on the 'are'. You could imagine a gently smiling, gently inquisitive companion with glistening eyes, for whom your well-being was of immense but not intrusive concern.

Johnson put together, in response to prompts, an account of his last day's activities, omitting the swimming session. The TONK responded as usual rather vaguely with 'mm's and 'nn's and 'aah's pitched so that its emotions seemed to blend with his.

'Wha' have you dhone in the evening?' it asked.

41

He felt a slight increase in tension, and relaxed his hold on the balls a little. His alertness stepped up, but he felt in heightened control.

'The usual – writing up lecture notes... yoga... then bed.'

A sense of acute danger and a flood of strength kept him cool and off-hand. But not too off-hand. He recalled recent research from Upside into emotional intelligence. How reactive systems direct to the primordial lizard-base core of the brain, the amygdala, would by-pass logical reaction. Drive you to flee before you could assess the consequences. Drive you to still everything. Chill everything. Like a rabbit in the headlight's glare. Don't do that, he said to himself. Not said, much quicker than said. Instantaneous. He breathed as he thought the machine would expect a frightened innocent to breathe. He blinked as he thought the machine would expect an innocent to blink. He fidgeted with impatience as he thought the machine would expect of an innocent. Looking back on it he rejoiced that no sense of fear or guilt infused him, that his voice was flat and detached. And his hands were dry. But not too dry. How can you make your hands dry? But they were. And the coolness; that was it.

'OK then,' the TONK sighed. 'Thank you, Honson.'

'Thank you, my friend.' And he left.

The girl avoided him at lunch, and again afterwards.

They started the afternoon lecture. The lecturer was interrupted by a flashing from his bleeper. He picked up the personal receiver.

'Yes. Yes. Of course. I'll get them there at once. Immediately, Director.'

He replaced the handset and addressed them.

'As part of our programme of er... er... proactive gender empowerment, there is a special computer interview for each of the la... – the women members. Would you please go along in turn to the third empowerment cell? In alphabetical order.'

The women complied in turn.

Johnson felt a chill of fear. Irritation too. Gender was surely something nouns had. People had sex. What had the French and Germans made of this politicised messing about with valuable grammatical concepts? *Le* and *la*. *Der, die, das*. Were there any Germans and French left?

Their expressions as they returned were complex. The first to come back looked at her comrades warningly. Athene Larsen followed, and returned looking bright-eyed and quizzical. She turned to Nadine, raised her eyebrows and made a moue of amused distaste. 'The dirty great beast!' she whispered.

Nadine came back from her session stony-faced, with 2 red spots high on her cheeks. She ignored Johnson. At their next break the women got together in an exclusively feminine huddle, clearly miffed – outraged perhaps? – at something, leaving the men puzzled and intrigued. Johnson looked at Nadine, but she was giggling annoyingly, most unlike herself, and affected to be unaware.

Be like that, then, he thought.

Around 4.30 the session was interrupted sharply by the entry of 2 POPs and 3 burly minders.

'Would Nadine Humphreys please come up?'

She went to the lecturer on the platform. He asked her something.

'Yes,' she said. Then, clearly, 'In the back row. Third from this end.'

For seconds Johnson – in the back row, third from this end – felt pulverised with shock and horror. Then he rose to his feet, vaulted over the back of the bench and ran for the nearest exit door. Locked. There was another, next to the lecturer. And the burly minders blocked his way. He charged at them, shouldered against one, landed a fist in the throat of the second, but tripped and fell. They fell on him. He relaxed. Too many minders.

'OK then,' he said.

Anger held him rigid, and he got slowly to his feet. His fellows watched uneasily, but made no attempt whatsoever to intervene. As the bruisers frog-marched him past her out of the door, Nadine said urgently and quietly, 'Michael,' and looked into his eyes. He turned away, sickened.

DPRK

This piece in the FAO library in Rome is an informal narrative from a UN Food and Agriculture Organisation consultant named Gaskin who

worked in North Korea in 1992, when it was seen as a viciously
dangerous pariah state, the 'axis of evil'. It's rather long, but it gives
clues to the world's history ever since. We don't yet know for certain the
roots of our disasters, terrorists most believe. But I have a gut feeling
where they may lie.

Axis of Evil or Axis of Hope?

My software development work for Masdar, UK, was suddenly
interrupted in 1992 by a phone call from UN Food and Agriculture Organisation, FAO, in Rome. Was I available for an
urgent database assignment in DPRK – the Democratic Peoples'
Republic of North Korea? The country that was in 2000 to
become a 'pariah' nation, one of George Bush's 'Axes of Evil'.
Certainly I was!

In 1992 the country was as bureaucratically inaccessible to the
West as China had been 2 centuries ago. I could only get a visa
under UN auspices, in person and in Rome; then only enter via
Beijing and not book ahead (no flights to the West), which
meant 2 sleepovers in Beijing and hoping the local UN offices
could get me a ticket for the DPRK capital, Pyongyang. A good
lad trying to get some background, I bought a book called *Korea*
by Simon Winchester, a well-known BBC pundit. I read it from
cover to cover. Not a mention of North Korea, because he'd not
been able to get there. And still can't – the BBC guy said yesterday his DPRK assignment was like reporting a football match
from outside the stadium. How could a book that covered only
half the country be named so? My own knowledge went back to
the time of the Korean War, when I was doing my army service
and could have been shipped out there to fight, as were some of
my friends. Memories of hordes of Chinese troops, mowed down
by 'allied' fire but still coming on. Cold, bitter, dry weather;
parched country; misery. Fascinating.

I eventually flew in from Beijing at sunset to see a rather
striking city dominated by a strange 600-foot high pyramid, like
an upturned dart. With a tiny, rusting crane on top – they'd run
out of money to finish it, though as you can see on the TV
reports it's now finished. As we landed, a mass demonstration

44

was mustered on the tarmac, and we found that our fellow passengers included some distinguished-looking international representatives of the 'Worldwide Campaign for a United Korea'. They were greeted with a massive throng and a warm and lengthy ceremony, as would be expected, whereas we got off the plane an hour later to a seemingly unenthusiastic, suspicious welcome from my host Dr Han, the head of the Soil Research Institute. He came with 2 others whom he didn't introduce. Later in the evening, he said they had 3 Chinese consultants helping them with a problem; a problem that he didn't explain. I went to bed in the Potonggang Hotel glumly thinking of frying pans and fires – the set-up seemed too similar to my previous assignment in Baghdad, which had ended with a spell as one of Saddam's reluctant 'guests'. Another great dictator, 'Our Great leader President Kim Il-sung'. And on top of this, 3 Chinese consultants who would no doubt muddy the waters. I turned on the TV to see a great crowd being addressed by the people who had been on the plane with me. Formidable-looking people with allegedly scintillating academic records from India, Greece, or South America. Each gave in turn a tedious paean of fulsome praise to DPRK and the 'Great Leader' Kim Il-sung, his political vision of the 'Juche Ideal' and of a united Korea. 'One nation, two systems.' Roars of adulating applause. This was followed by speeches from South Korean students about the maliciousness of capitalism and their fervour for the Juche Ideal. This I think was genuine – Southern Korea's aggressive acquisitive capitalism was, for students, no match for the communist ideal.

But the next morning dawned sunny and chilly, and I saw the hotel was surrounded by lovely wooded parkland alongside a river. Rather fragile-looking trees, mostly birch, with crystal clear water flowing slowly by, rowing dinghies for hire, tracks winding into the capital, where there were wide squares and impressive architecture. My growing assurance took a bit of a dip when my hosts whisked me into the city to join a queue at the national airline offices. Ten hours in the country and they wanted to fly me out again!

But from then on, things improved rapidly. We shot off in an official limo through wide, empty streets to the National Agricultural Research Institute, 4 miles out into the countryside, and

I was introduced around the place, and to our own laboratory of soils sciences. I asked about my Chinese 'colleagues'. Ah, they had left yesterday, (presumably, I hoped, having been stumped by the undefined 'problem'!)

But over the next 4 weeks, working at the Institute and invariably going everywhere together (as happened also in China,) I got to know them well, and also to understand their English. Dr Han's was particularly good, partly because as a kid in the Korean War he had been looked after by a US army sergeant – I think his parents had been killed in the fighting. Han was a lean, incisive guy of medium height. His severe, bronze Korean features would sometimes relax into a beguiling laugh. His authority over his research colleagues was striking and humorous, and we had many splendid evenings together.

With him were Mr Ho, a slim and fit man. His official position was 'hardware engineer', but he was with me all the time, living alongside me in the hotel; no doubt my minder.

And then Miss Li, a chubby-faced lady, may be 24 or so. Very committed and conscientious, but lightly humorous with it. She was the programmer. Han had written the previous software, in Fortran and later Basic. But the file-handling in these was nowhere near meeting their requirements. So Miss Li had been recruited, and had written the software with which my help was needed.

We explored together the apparently insuperable problems that they had hit. They were to do with the performance of their national database of fertiliser applications. Their system tried to do for fertiliser what Frank Cope's system had done for 200 farms in Suffolk, as we saw earlier, and for which, I think, he received the Chemical Society's very rare gold medal.

In outline, from every 'field' in the country was provided a soil sample once every 4 years. All these samples were sent to the laboratory for analysis in an X-ray spectrometer. The process added water to the sample and stirred it to dissolve the soil. It then heated the liquid to boiling, blasted it then analysed the optical spectrum of the steam. This revealed – by the colours in the spectrum – which minerals were present. The resultant data were fed into their PC. Here, soils software designed by Dr Han listed the number and amounts and timings of fertiliser

46

applications to be made to each field, increasing the allocation where nutrients are deficient and vice versa. The system attempted to create a level playing field of fertility for every field in every commune, so that all were nearly equal. It's an astonishing, egalitarian process that would never be attempted in 'supply-led' free Western agriculture. (But, has it a role perhaps for us in the future, when through global warming and climate change, our traditional, profligate use of resources will have to be circumscribed, e.g. by carbon rationing?) However, the system's performance was plainly crucial to the nation's agriculture, and its performance was so slow that allocations were falling behind, and crude manual approaches were being used.

The programs were written and run in Korean, in their rather beautiful script. They used their own counterfeit of Ashton Tate's dBase, then the world's foremost database programming language, interfacing to Korean BASIC for scientific calculations. So – I was faced with 44 modules of complex analytical software in an incomprehensible language with an incomprehensible character set!

However, we came to some clear conclusions:

- The problem almost certainly lay with the modules of code that drove input and output on the discs
- Miss Li would enable me to comprehend the code by converting it to standard English dBase
- We would create a model concentrating on the input/ output (i/o) programs
- We would simulate the scientific calculations by just imposing slight delays in the model's running at the related stages.

This took us about 2 weeks, working long days. Fridays were different. The national custom was for all top brass and white-collar workers to leave their desks and work in the fields. Even our Institute Director! Though some alleged that he scheduled key journeys across the country for the fifth day! Miss Li and our limo driver had special dispensation, and she and I were the only occupants of the entire sprawling institute.

I recall one quiet Sunday, when I thought why don't I try

47

phoning home? I picked up the phone in my room and asked the operator to get the number. She sounded cheerful, confident, keen to please.

'What is country name?'

'UK.'

'Ah, is 0044. What is city number?'

'No city.' (I live in the country.)

'OK. You not know city number... Then what is city name?'

'No city. Live in country.'

'OK. City name is "Nossitty"?'

'No, I live in country.'

'Yes, you give me country. Now must have city. What is city name?'

'Just use the number I give you.'

'No,' she explained with forbearance and charm. 'Must have city name. Or city number.'

The loop continued till she involved the supervisor.

He came on confidently

'I so sorry for my staff person. What is country name?'

We reached city name again.

And stuck.

'We will help,' he said, 'you just wait. We will help soon.'

Twenty minutes later, along to my room came Mr Ho, my minder.

'Problem,' he said patiently, 'is city name. No such city as Nossitty.'

I gave up and invited him for a game of pool. He thrashed me.

After the 2 weeks, we had our first runs of the model, and were able to observe the timings. No joy at first, but then I noticed one of the modules performing strikingly badly. So I delved into it and came to the conclusion that Miss Li had carried out the i/o transfers clumsily. To put it simply, in fact to oversimplify, you can visualise the database as a massive book. You can either read it from cover to cover, a page at a time. Or you can read in the sequence of the first word on page one, then the first word on page two, and so on to the first word on the last page. Then back to the second word on page one, and so on. If you do it the latter way you are going to take a phenomenal amount of time.

Eureka! I announced my discovery. Miss Li set to work to

reprogram as needed, and at the end of the next afternoon we watched as she kicked off the amended programs. Time passed. In the end, they took a marginally longer time than before! We all laughed ruefully, and I returned chastened to the hotel.

The next morning, I got back in to be met by a bleary-eyed, smiling Miss Li. She had worked all through the night rewriting the real, Korean, software modules, and run them and found the timing problem had gone away. My theory had been right, but we had only been using a small sample from the database. And the operating system had been quietly 'caching' this sample into the store (memory) for efficiency. This is unbelievably faster than going back and forth to the disc. So then, once the sample data were all in the cache it made no difference which way you read the data. Fine, but with a large, full database, caching was not feasible. And without caching, computing speed was crippled.

We all rejoiced, and Dr Han called the Research Institute's Director. He congratulated us, winding up by asking me to go and pack for a special trip for 4 days to the mountains of Kum Gang San. We left Pyongyang station – no Miss Li – in the sleeper for the big eastern seaport of Won San. I got my camera out but was instructed to put it back again. We went through the night and arrived at Won San at daybreak. Then I was left on the sea promenade of a wide luxury hotel, totally empty, for some hours. Not even a mug of tea. The group reconvened, with suitable apologies but no explanation, and we set off by car southwards. It was fairly empty countryside. We stopped for coffee at a fine sprawling beach, then eventually into the mountains of which I'd heard and seen so much. They were occasionally defaced by massive party axioms, carved in brilliant red letters into the cliffs. Like the US presidents in the cliffs on Mount Rushmore in the States. But otherwise they were as strange and spectacular as I'd heard and seen every night on TV, and as murals on the walls of the great buildings.

Staying in attractive modern rooms 10 floors up, we spent 2 days walking in the mountains. The rocks were, I think, granite into which glaciers, streams and rivers had carved smooth, wide channels and pools of clear water. There were a number of rather tragic fairy tales about spirits losing their lovers or chil-dren, some carved into the walls of occasional temples, some recounted by Dr Han. We walked among a steady stream of holiday-makers, and then climbed high flat-topped pinnacles with superlative views over the ranges and forests. Most of it was beautifully done. I remember particularly stopping at a wide, hanging, waypoint platform and listening to a group of climbers. One sang, a fine, thin soprano voice, and the others joined in the choruses. In keeping with the spirit of the country, there was no evidence of individual exploration, no side tracks. Just the main path with steel ships' ladders from the shipyards in Won San, flying across some dizzying drops from one anchorage point on the pinnacle to the next.

Back again in Pyongyang, Miss Li and I documented the software structure, and I spent a week going through the basics of systems tools like SSADM and Entity/relationship diagrams and others of the techniques we favoured in the UK. Then a very splendid departure ceremony, when Dr Han pressed on me a great 2-foot root of Korean ginseng and he and Mr Ho urged me to grind up some and drink it in salt and water every day. I'd been hit in mid-assignment by a vicious cold, coughing and spluttering and eyes streaming, barely able to work. Han got me to take a dose of the ginseng – foul tasting – and we had set off for the institute. Twenty minutes later there was a sudden prickling in my nostrils, and the cold ceased as if a tap had been turned off.

Finally, Miss Li bid me goodbye in a prepared speech as we left the institute, and Han and Ho took me to the airport. There was a long, straight corridor from the departure point. I looked back as I left it. There they were, hands raised formally in farewell. I expect that, like me, they felt this had been a fine, rare experience. That we were friends who were never, ever going to see each other again.

An attraction of computing is the intense pleasure of intractable problems that are jointly solved. Getting friendly with Dr Han and Mr Ho ('hardware') and Miss Li ('software') we talked ('you and I are scientists; we may speak of these things') increasingly openly of the differences between our countries. Dr Han's view of the UK was the usual communist caricature – a country of unfettered exploitation of downtrodden masses, unemployment, violence, drugs and decay, ruled over by a queen in a way that symbolised the backwardness of a once-great country. My feeling for DPRK was less stereotyped, because I'd read Simon Winchester's book, *Korea*. This dispelled the current British view – of a country of stern citizens, terrorists and assassins, of bitter cold and pickled cabbage, of barren hills and paddies, savagely fought over in the drawn war of the 1950s, dominated since then by a dictatorship to be named among the worst with Cseausescu and Saddam. A country shortly to collapse, the Westerners believed, with so many others into the arms of the severe but welcoming West. Winchester had not been allowed to cross the truce line from South Korea into DPRK, but had the impression that the rampant excessive capitalism and corruption that disfigures the south had in the north been tempered by care and generosity. (His recent articles have been less approving).

Looking back, my first impressions had been very pleasing. As I hinted earlier, the capital stretches among hills along 2 winding rivers backed up with shallow weirs and dotted with occasional clusters of communal rowing boats, cheap and much-used. The riversides are fringed with occasional benches, fishermen and miles of parkland, woods, lily-ponds and fountains. The parks merge in and out of formal squares with large, no doubt very costly but often imaginative public buildings. Most of the city is very clean, with wide streets, firm whistle-blowing women traffic-police and negligible traffic. Everywhere there is an emphasis on youth and students, typified by fine new buildings like the Mangyongdae Students and Children's Palace. In the squares, the communal exercise sessions which all ages love take place – like open-air aerobics involving lines of people, often 1,000 in a square, bending, dancing, stretching and doubling back and forth to the instructions of a leader who stands atop a platform using a megaphone. After the sessions people spill enthusiastically into the parks doing handstands, arguing and chatting amicably. (There is a strong emphasis on art also, and the sculpture and architecture of the capital seems to me finer than that of most equivalents – say Seoul or Singapore or Hong Kong). One sees crocodiles of schoolchildren walking purposefully and swiftly to school singing songs of their mountains and of praise for 'Our Great Leader President Kim Il-sung' –

henceforward OGLPKIS – (the phrase rolls infuriatingly off everyone's tongue) and with similar but more muted reverence for his son and grandson, now successor, Kim Jong-un.

As we walked outside the Childrens' Palace, Mr Ho told me with shining eyes, 'OGLPKIS, he loves all our children. At New Year he gives EACH child a special present.' Driving out to the institute once, my exasperation at OGLPKIS broke loose. A visiting scientist and I had been discussing our tax systems, and he said proudly 'In Korea we have no taxes at all.' I responded, 'No; with us we earn our money and then the state takes some. With you the state takes first and then gives a little back.' More warmly, 'Take Mr Ho – he says that OGLPKIS loves every child, gives them each presents... But I tell you it's not the President who gives them the presents! It's you.' He glanced at those in front quickly to see if they had heard, giggled, looked hard at me and said, 'Yes of coss, of coss. But you must not say!'[14]

After we saw a fervent mass demonstration which must have involved more than a million, seemingly the entire capital, welcoming Kim Il-sung back from China, Dr Han told me that this strength of popular support among young and old for the system and OGLPKIS 'you can see nowhere – nowhere – in the world'. To confuse this real fervour with the rent-a-mob antics in favour of Saddam that I saw in Baghdad would be very dangerous. My feeling was that North Korea was brimming with confidence, was taking the initiative in the bridge-building process with South Korea, and believed with some reason that it had the support of the majority in the south, especially the youth. To his people, OGLPKIS was succeeding. For example, while I was there he launched an International Crusade for Korean Reunification and the removal of US nuclear missiles, supported, his people were told, by '318 million people worldwide' – and shortly afterwards the US missiles were on their way out.

Dr Han and others at his level were more cautious. When we discussed IT they were well aware of their backwardness. On privatisation versus state enterprise, they were very conscious of evidence that the infrastructure was decaying – notably the railways (pretty good), which I rode overnight to visit the lovely mountains of Kumgang in the east, but was forbidden to photograph. They had no doubt their political system was better, but had obvious misgivings at communist collapses elsewhere.

Their system is encapsulated in the 'Juche Ideal', OGLPKIS' philosophy, derived from Marxism but a distinctive brand propagandised vigorously everywhere. The emphasis on youth, art and gracefulness is one strand; others are a refreshing egalitarianism. Everyone has a job; nearly all live in similar rooms in reasonably attractive apartment blocks where 'only the old hanker for the cottages of the past'; every Friday senior management and white collar workers all have to work all day in the fields or equivalent – hospitals offer only emergency cover because doctors are out planting rice. Professionals like scientists or doctors earn only 40 per cent more than the average manual wage. Egalitarianism permeates all – the objective of our soils/fertiliser system is to achieve a uniform fertility level across the entire national field (30,000 units) so that all cooperatives have equal productive potential. All must produce either rice or maize – pre-revolutionary alternatives like wheat, barley etc. are banned (and with ecologically sound justification).

There is a strong feeling for communal activity and discipline – individualism is seen as perhaps dangerous and sinful. If I asked who designed a building, the response was 'what does that matter?' When we went in the mountains there was invariably only one path, often up sheer cliffs, which we climbed on steel companion ladders, as on ships, from Won San shipyards. Often we queued with a stream of workers from the communes who made their way up and down. Each member had been voted by his/her fellows to be the holiday person or group of the year. (Sometimes a group would stop with us and sing and dance to the rather haunting ballads of the 'Sky Goddesses' who live in some mountain pools – though not the pool which celebrates the spirit of OGLKPIS). The social pressures at work sounded formidable; the elected group leader gathers his group together each evening and announces who has earned how many work days (usually 0.8 to 1.3) and why. Eddie Grundy be warned! Their group tasks and targets have been set from the County Co-operative Management Committees; their targets in turn were set by the national soil database system on which I had worked. Here lies the rub, because without a price system no one can assess what levels of fertiliser are the economic optimum – production cost and benefit ratios cannot be assessed since neither can be evaluated without a market mechanism.

Western media reports suggested appalling hardships in the countryside. I saw none round the institute or en route east across the entire peninsula to Kumgang. But more cogently, Dr Han must have known the truth. And if the Westerners' reports were right, why was he so confident in the rightness of his cause? Westerners, including 2 of only 4 I met there, generally commented with hostility, and expected the system to collapse on OGLPKIS death – it hasn't. I suspect the dice are loaded heavily that way. But DPRK offers in the balance against lost liberty and grossly sycophantic totalitarianism fairness; absence of violence, Aids and drugs; full employment, no poverty (in 1992), astonishingly low pollution (contrast Pyongyang with Seoul in South Korea), social confidence, much apparent happiness. And, maybe, the key quality that the West cannot claim for itself, leave alone the rest of the world: sustainability. It's a challenging alternative. Personally I favour the Western approach, though with increasing doubt, but humanity will gain if the other approach also survives. We worship at the shrine of biodiversity; why not also sociodiversity and political diversity?

In a nutshell, taking the famous French revolutionary causes liberty, equality, fraternity, North Korea scores zero for liberty, but 9 for both equality and fraternity.

In a BBC2 hour-long documentary, the presenter used only material from people who had escaped after vicious torture. None of the beauties of the country, of the evident pleasure (if not joy) of those who had won their commune's annual competition for a holiday in the mountains, living in hotels comparable with Holiday Inns in the West, climbing up wide stairways built in the shipyards, stopping to sing in groups at the stages in the ascent. (No one, I fear, was allowed to roam, and the great mountains were devoid of footpaths). The presenter finally showed a satellite view of the area at night. China, South Korea and Japan were a blaze of light. North Korea was in total darkness apart from a brilliantly-lit statue of the leader OGLPKIS.

'There you are,' she said. 'Contrast the bright civilisation of the West with the pariah state in pitch darkness.'

But, I thought, maybe the pariah state has it right.

© graham gaskin

This is interestingly debatable. On the one hand we have the evidence from those who escaped the regime, and the horrifying descriptions of the use of humans – North Koreans – in Prison Camp 22 to assess the effectiveness of biological, chemical and nuclear methods of exterminating people. The victims were stripped naked, often with their children, and moved into glass-sided chambers. They were watched from above by scientists, much as you might watch a squash match from the mezzanine. And then they were gassed or poisoned. In the gassing, the adults would often hug their kids and try to save them by mouth-to-mouth resuscitation. Which failed. And the North Koreans who knew of this typically thought it justified, a useful death for those who questioned their system. The escaped commandant from Prison Camp 22 said he rather looked forward to the procedures.

And on the other hand, a BBC programme tracked the lives of a typical family in Pyongyang, and revealed a normal human history of work and pleasure, schooling and so on, vastly happier than the norm for our planet. And the BBC kept very quiet about it.

HB G-B

Upside, Chapter 7: Flashback – Aberystwyth and Susanna

The late twentieth-century author Jonathan Raban[15] described the Irish Sea brilliantly as 'a dangerous, quirky, fast, and malignant piece of water. Small, shallow and parochial it responds, as parochial places do, to any news or change, with the rapidity of a village. When a gale blows up it turns instantly to whipped cream; shallow and bar-ridden, when the wind dies it goes flat in an hour. Its capacity for springing violence without warning is notorious, and its charts are thick with the double daggers that denote lost ships.'

The ketch, *Lady Amanda,* lay on 5th June 1989 with easy grace at one of the pontoons at Aberystwyth, a picturesque, snug seaside town and university city halfway down the 60-mile stretch of Cardigan Bay. Wide open like all the other little ports to the Irish Sea's wild southwesterlies, only safe to enter approaching high water, and even then potential death traps when the south-westerly gales build the seas up.

It was 0800 and they were getting the boat ready for sea. A good forecast, NW Force 4, though the direction meant they would have to beat all the way to their destination, Barmouth on the River Dwrydd, 30 miles to the north. Johnson was very keen to get the sounder replaced. The chandler was due to open at 0815, and the water across the rocky entrance cill, or step, dropped to danger levels at 0840, half tide. He determined to hang on till the penultimate minute, and aim for the narrow gap of deeper water to the left hand side of the channel as they left. NW4; so there should be little sea running; they'd be OK. Entry High Water +/- 2 hours, the almanac said, +/- 3 hours with local knowledge and flat water.[16] Well, he didn't have much local knowledge, but he did recall a deepening of the channel next to the rocks on the port hand. Say 2½ hours after high water. Forecast wind only force 4; not much sea likely.

56

It was 0820 and still no chandler. He jogged back hastily to the boat, called to his mate apWilliams to clear the warps; engine on and bow off downwind and they dropped down towards the entrance. On the pier-head above them a young woman walked, watching them out to sea. Slender, fair-haired, probably English, fine skinned. Her grey eyes brightened with interest when she saw the turbulent sea-state, invisible to the yachties in the harbour. Then the figure on the foredeck particularly caught her attention. Steadily, methodically, stylishly coiling in the warps. Perhaps a bow-man, the sort of loner who swings easily way out above the waves and up onto the end of a spinnaker pole in a rolling seaway, retrieving halyards or some other foul-up when normal mortals would blench and crawl aft on hands and knees into the cockpit.

Getting out of Aberystwyth, you drop down river about a hundred yards from the pontoons with the cliff to port, then take a sharp right angle turn to the west, and 30 yards later you're out in the open sea. There it can be very rough and confused as the big swells curve in and bounce back again off the high harbour walls. Before the turn, a sixth sense prompted Johnson to call to apWilliams, 'Be ready with the jenny, Alun. We may need it to push us through.'

They swung round the end of the channel, and he saw heavy foaming crests right across the entrance ahead of them. apWilliams was behaving with infuriating deliberateness, and gesturing nonchalantly to a young woman who was waving both arms vigorously from the pier-head. He had his back to the line of the course, pulling in the fenders.

'For Christ's sake, Alun, we can do that next year. Get the bloody genoa.'

apWilliams turned, saw the breakers romping across the entrance and rushed to the cleat to let the genoa out and give the boat more power. But the wind, a good Force 6–7, snatched the sail as it unrolled, whipped the control lines out of his hands, and ballooned the great foresail out to its full extent with a tremendous crack. The boat heeled sharply and the bow was thrust away to leeward towards the rocks.

No need to yell; apWilliams had seen his mistake, and cranked away at the winch like a madman to get the sail flat and pulling.

Johnson had to choose: whether to ram the throttle full ahead with the helm hard a-starboard using wind and engine to their max to turn and haul them off, or to slow down to get the sail under control. Caution might leave them pounding on the rocks, while speed might just get the hull and rudder biting the water in time to luff up and away from danger. Or if not, drive them more violently to disaster. He opted for speed. Throttle hard forward. They thumped into the first breaker, sliced it away in a shower of spray, but she maintained her speed and turned towards the port-hand boulders. But the weight of the sail gradually eased, and the bow crept a little to the right, towards safety. Four more combers, and she was through. Both men were panting with shock and exertion, and they kept heading out to westward.

Not for 10 minutes did either speak or change the sail trim – an experience to live yourself away from in absolute silence, without moving any muscle unnecessarily. Then rationality returned.

'Made a pig's ear of that, didn't I?' said apWilliams.

'You could say that again. What I always say. Confidence is no substitute for competence.'

'Bastard,' said apWilliams cheerfully. 'All that woman's fault, anyway.'

The young woman on the pier-head had watched enthralled, then turned to trot back along the front to the university. She skipped occasionally, hinting deliciously at a brimful of *joie de vivre*. She was not to see apWilliams again for a long while.

Her name was Susanna.

The half-reefed jib was pulling them along at a great rate, but the mizzen should help. Better than the main, because its weight was further back to balance the jib, and its shorter mast meant less heeling moment from the sails to push her lee scuppers under. Boats with their lee gunwales under look dramatically fast, but they're usually overpowered. They move faster when reducing the sail brings them more upright. Still sobered by their narrow escape, the 2 men held on for 3 hours, way out to sea, and tacked only when they felt they could make Barmouth direct.

The *Lady Amanda* was, according to the East Coast designer, Reg Freeman, his 'only perfect yacht'. When Freeman was a teenage apprentice before the Second World War, he saved for his ideal boat. He got a stack of superb rock-hard weathered mahogany cheap in 1939 as the war shadows loomed, stashed it away and went off to fight. By 1953 he'd established a growing reputation and the time had come for the *Lady Amanda* to take shape. She measured 36 feet; 9 tons of mahogany on grown oak frames, half a forestful, but in those days forests were no problem. He gave her the long, curved overhang at the bow and the tumbling in topsides at the stern that he loved, with a high, sea-slicing bow and 3 cabins. The front cabin cribbed and confined for the 'paid hand' of those times, the centre cabin panelled in Honduras cedar, cunningly crafted with tailored nooks and crannies for this and that, with a queen-piece. This was a low book-packed bulkhead projecting into the cabin (a complete waste of valuable space by most standards), with a squared-off paned door going forward, rather like the admiral's cabin as seen on a traditional man-of-war, lace-girt on the loo-side for privacy. Then an arched niche to starboard, and twixt niche and door an anthracite stove low down. Above this rested the framed portrait for the autumn months. Renoir's study of his brother's fiancée dancing in the young man's arms. The bearded young man hunched protectively over her, and the girl, head turned down and half away from him towards the viewer, dark lashes and eyebrows against a pale, curving line of cheek and chin, and red hair tucked out from a strikingly rendered red silk scarf. Her hand round behind his shoulder and her body swayed distinctly but accurately away almost at right angles at the waist. For the winter, a very different, challenging, 1960s blonde lovely with a candle picking out her hair-shrouded eyes.

The aft cabin was more seaman-like, a full-size chart table, dimmable chart lights which bend on stalks, the usual radio, navigational gadgets, sounders and so on, the cabin sides unpanelled so that the squared off vertical frames, nearly at right angles to the gunwale timbers, revealed the boat's immense strength despite her bewitching lines. Into a galley deck beam was carved in 2-inch letters, 'Cert chart space 41/100 ton', one of the required rigmaroles for her classification as A1/100 in Lloyds Register of Shipping under Sec. 79 of the Merchant Shipping Act of 1894. Her papers stated among much other intriguing jargon that 'the tonnage of the total spaces for the boatswain's store rooms are ".62",' and 'the total tonnage of the spaces framed in above the upper deck for light and air are: "nil" tons'. In point of fact the tonnage for light and air above the upper deck was probably 38,000 x 36 x 9 cubic feet at 27 per cubic foot.

Aft, she had a strange cockpit layout, with the mizzen mast at the centre, just 2 drop-down single saucer-shaped seats in the rear corners with fart-holes in the centres. At the forward end of the cockpit was a wide bridge deck on which those who wished could tuck away and doze as the spray flew past overhead on a rough windward passage. Then the wheel, right at the back of the cockpit, bemusing newcomers to her – they tried to steer standing as if handling a car, but with the steering wheel behind them as they faced forward. A sound idea in quiet weather, left-hand down a bit, right hand down a bit, just like driving a bus. But in rough seas impossible, staggering all over the place, clutching wildly for support with your free hand as she rolled and surfed and pitched. Much better to do it properly from the start and learn to steer a spoke at a time, seated like the oldies on one side of the ascetic, reassuringly rugged wheel – soft white nylon dust melted onto steel. Aft of this an afterthought; 6 feet of stern locker, technically a 'lazarette', taking space into which a noughties design would cram 2 crew in a double cabin.

A grudging Geordie fisherman, as tough and scathing as they come towards yachties, took her shore-lines once as she entered Port Patrick at the far end of the Mull of Galloway.

'By, she's a lovely boat though,' he had said.

She's one of our 3 heroines.

The wind built the characteristically short, steep Irish sea waves, and *Lady Amanda* cut and sliced through them with an easy elegance unknown to more recent designs.

The 1355 forecast came up. 'Irish Sea North West four, moderate, good.'

'Come out here, mate and see for yourself!' The wind speed read at 45 knots – gale force 9.

Once in Barmouth estuary, they brought the boat in towards her moorings. Not much water to spare, important to pick the buoys up first time.

'Johnson!' shouted Alun from the foredeck. 'They've gone.'

So they had. Johnson passed over their normal site, then pulled the boat across the river and turned her, with little room to spare. These old boats were pigs at close quarter manoeuvring, built for the freedom of deep-sea moorings rather than the cosseted luxury of marina berths. Long keels and tiny rudders. A modern fin keeler will turn in her own length, forward or reverse, just like a car. But *Lady Amanda?* With practice you found that turning to port was a long shot, a slow, graceful curve which has sundry yachts swinging across your vision with agonising slowness. To starboard was better, because the front of the rudder was cut away to allow more wheel on before the rudder hit the propeller. And, for the initiates, you can take one bite at the turn to starboard, reverse off without changing the wheel setting – it will be ignored by the boat as she goes backward anyway then kick her hard ahead again for another several degrees, back again and so on. This time there was a crosswind also, trying to put her onto the south bank mud, and a tide ebbing rapidly to the west. Even so he made it and she hovered where the mooring ought to be. And then, her most infamous trick, the wheel locked hard over to starboard. A rare habit, something to do with the steering box arm going past deadcentre, corrected by hastily unbolting the emergency tiller, slotting it in and heaving the rudder back. The work of several moments.

'Christ, Alun, the tiller – quick!'

But the several moments were several moments too many. She ceased to respond at all and was clearly on the mud hard and fast. Johnson recalled her habit of sitting upright on her 18-inch-wide keel, and then tumbling when completely dried out like an elderly acrobat, with a rib-cracking crash as 10 tons fell 4 feet onto her side.

How to stop it?

They'd hang weights and themselves etc. from the boom, swing it out to port, and cause her to recline to the horizontal slowly and naturally as the tide ebbed. There was plenty of time, so they made a cupper, then laid out the weights and she started to keel over. Johnson suddenly remembered with horror-struck nausea the fang of the southside mooring anchor, sticking up 6 inches from the mud. Overdue for redigging. But if you own one of these beauties you'll know that the list of things overdue for this or that is usually 2 A4 sheets long unless you're totally out of touch with your boat. Prioritising is the name of the game, so that the urgent things get done and the important are sidelined.

This steel fang was important but not urgent, until now. And now it was urgent and important and too late. Into the water. Murky with sand. Head under and feel where it is. It stretched upwards pointing at the turn of the *Lady*'s bilge. There were 3 feet to go. Maybe an hour and a half. Put all the fenders down to protect her flanks. The upholstery. The legs. The sails and sail bags. An hour to go. Call for help on channel 16.

'Any vessel in Barmouth Roads, any vessel in Barmouth Roads, Yacht *Lady Amanda, Lady Amanda,* Over.'

Silence.

And again; silence. Out of the Coastguard's radio horizon. Concealed by the mountains.

Distress signal. Was it Mayday or pan-pan? Mayday since the vessel was threatened by grave and imminent danger.

'MAYDAY, MAYDAY, MAYDAY. Yacht *Lady Amanda. Lady Amanda. Lady Amanda.* My position is Barmouth Roads, 300 yards south east of pier. About to be holed on obstruction and sunk. Over.' Nothing.

What, in any case could the 'any vessel' do? Perhaps add some additional padding to hold her up. But 10 tons onto a steel fang is not easily stopped. Put your hand there and see.

So the fang bit, and the water spurted and flooded in. And imperceptibly she slipped sideways into the half-tide trench cut by the fierce ebb. Scuppers awash, cockpit coaming awash, beige coach roof lapped and slipping away, and she rolled onto her side. And then even the cross-trees and masthead. They dragged the dinghy full of salvaged electronics and clothes off the beach where they'd left it, and back into the river and rowed heavy-hearted down to the town slipway, and so homewards.

On the road up the pass the ineffably, treacherously, sweet, slow movement of Mozart's 28th came through on Radio 3. Ashkenazy the pianist, conducted by Colin Davis. Alun looked at his friend. Tears glinted on his cheeks in the headlights.

'Never mind. You can get an Aston on the insurance'.

Downside, Chapter 8: Johnson Held

They dragged and hustled Johnson along the corridor to a bench, laid him down, legs held, right arm held, left arm out, rolled up the sleeve, injected. Then started kicking him in the side and face. He lost consciousness.

He surfaced flat on the floor in a small room, a bit like a padded room in an asylum. Light coming in from an armoured window, and an inserted pane in the totally flat face of the door. In it he saw his reflection. His face was battered, eyes puffed up, an angry line of wound across the temples, nose swollen and blood-smeared. His torso felt hot, his legs and feet icy. Strangely, the battering didn't hurt much. Only one ventilator. Pretty obvious there was no way out, but he hurled himself against the door – stupid, it opened inwards – and then tried to ease the ventilator grid. No go. He thought about the girl.

In fact, what bothers me qua her is her total unpredictability. One minute shiny-eyed and smiling to thump your heart. Then another she'll just ignore you like just now. I tell you, as far as emotions are concerned, McGervon and I are closer to a male chimp than to them. 99.4 per cent the same genes. But women? Their emotions switch on and off like the Gulf Stream. Is it global warming, is it global dimming, is it the Greenland icecap, is it Siberian flood water? Who can tell? But the icecap is what she is right now. And treacherous to boot. Anyway.

The light from the window faded and went. He could just see the time from his watch face at the door's aperture. He looked for the umpteenth time, 9.15 p.m. Due to see Gaskin at 10 p.m. Suddenly a hand appeared, placed palm down against the aperture. It moved away slowly, then reappeared. Then away again. Then back again. Johnson placed his hand thumb-up against his side of the pane.

The door opened slowly. It was McGervon.

'There were just the bolts to undo,' he explained. He'd found a note round a stone in his jacket. It had just said 'Infirmary. Padded cell 3.' He'd found the infirmary, traced Johnson to the padded cell and found it unlocked.

'Let's get out of here smartish.'

McGervon led the way to a side entrance, down some steps by a hedge, and along the riverbank to the main road.

'Can't talk much here,' said Johnson, 'but it's vital I see Gaskin – the guy who lectured this morning – at 10.'

'OK. Fill me in another time. Can I come along?'

Johnson thought. He badly needed some back-up for when he got back again from Upside, as he called the parallel universe he'd come from. McGervon was already taking a big risk; time to reciprocate. So he filled in a little. McGervon was astonished and incredulous.

'Never mind, you'll find out soon enough. Meanwhile how about seeing Gaskin?'

'Fine by me,' said McGervon.

'He may clam up. . . But I think he'll see sense in it. Let's try it.'

They resolved to follow the old route in for late-nighters, behind the cinema, up the alley, climb over the south wall round the college's old garden, and go by the pond to Gaskin's room in the annex. They did so, and walked close by the library wall to avoid startling the ducks.

'P staircase, it is,' said Johnson. They found it, and a panel which said, 'E.N. Gaskin, visiting, Chief Programmer, Systems, Room 8: IN'.

They reached the right floor. They overheard Gaskin speaking quickly, intensely, probably into a phone.

'Look, I tell you yet again, that's just what we chose her for. . . No, damned if I will. She's got to be at the Straits Bridge for the November event. No way she's not. That's how we're going to get him, mate. If she wants out that's just tough. I'll talk her round.'

Johnson tapped on the door.

'Yes, come in,' called Gaskin. Opposite him was a wall-wide panoramic photo of mountains. Towering like pillars, square topped and bleak, a massive crimson slogan or somesuch carved in one cliff.[17]

He pressed a button on the phone, put the receiver down and turned to them.

64

'What the... ' He pushed his coffee all over the keyboard.

'Huck Geck ouk sharkish goth a you. Geck ooay,' his lips barely moving, then he pressed a button and spoke normally into the phone.

'Its OK, its OK... Hit the wrong button, coffee fell over or... '

They stood frozen, looking at him. His eyes were turned up, rolling from side to side incredibly fast.[18] He had his finger on the button beside the desk. He was speaking into the phone again, this time in a steady, high-pitched tone:

'Hello, gatehouse, hello gatehouse, gatehouse. Intruder on B, intruder on B. Security alert 5, I say again security alert 5.'

McGervon whispered, 'Quick, the back way.'

He nipped out of the door and down the stairs, Johnson started to follow. He looked back at Gaskin. He returned the glance briefly, perhaps motioned slightly with his head, and continued tapping at the security alarm.

'Come on for Christ's sake,' McGervon yelled up the staircase.

As they reached the bottom, the entire front was suddenly floodlit.

'Please keep to your rooms, everyone,' a loudspeaker intoned. 'Keep to your rooms. We have an intruder. Intruder on B. Intruder on B.'

'Down there quick,' said McGervon, and they dropped down into a coal hole. They could hear a commotion outside, running to the left.

'Look,' said Johnson, 'it's vital for me to try and get away. And it's vital for you to stay on this course. No, don't argue, no time, I'll bury you in that lot and then I'll scarper.'

'Right.'

They both shovelled the coal with their hands to make a hole. There was a noise at the entrance, barely audible above the rattle of the coal.

'Get in the corner.'

McGervon crouched down. Johnson desperately piled coal on him. A noise on the stairs going up. He flung a sack over McGervon, peed on it quickly.

'What the bloody hell are you doing?' demanded McGervon.

'Keep the sniffers off.'

The noise recurred, coming down. He slipped behind the door. A POP came into view. 'Hold hard,' it said.

He jumped and karate-kicked at it sideways, Cantona-style, knocking it over. The legs scrabbled around like those of an upturned tortoise or beetle, but very fast. Johnson tried to slip past, and felt his trouser caught. He ripped his leg away, and stumbled up the basement stairs.

'Hold Hold Hold,' he heard. The same note of arresting stressful urgency he remembered from the OP in night shoots in the artillery – 'Uncle Target Uncle Target Uncle Target B Battery SP Up 25 Left 4 I Say again Up 25 Left 4 Fire Fire Fire Over.' And then the bangs and physical compression as the shells hurtled 'woop woop woop' overhead, while you crawled forward with the wire. Part your hair for you, no problem.[19]

No choice but to run out into the front of the building.

'There he is,' Gaskin shouted from above him. Advancing POPs came from both sides. He ran at those on the left, as at an opposing fullback. They swung across to meet him. Only 6 feet from them he swerved to the right. One foot slipped from under him, then the other. But sprawling full-length he saw the POPs had missed him. All but one. He ran straight at it. Then hurdled over it. Couldn't get its arm up in time. Up on his feet and on. But he was trapped by others beyond. Then he recalled the pond, and their buoyancy problems. He dived in, 10 yards across, out, into the shrubs, over the wall, down the passage, along Emmanuel Street then in through the glass doors of the maths lab. Up the funny spiral staircase. Into the cracker lab. Key in password. noshnojm. No. nosnhojm. A clattering on the stairs. Keep your finger on 'Enter'. Nothing happening. Two POPs grabbed an arm and a foot. He kicked and writhed, finger still on 'Enter'. They pulled him away. He lunged back, held by the left arm. Right finger on 'Enter' still. The screen cleared. He moved his right hand to one sphere, but his left was tethered. He lunged and stretched out his tongue desperately to the other sphere. A sudden crack, and a vicious pain.

The same laboratory, but now in darkness, silence and no POPs. He read on the monitor next to him: nosnhojm, then 20 or so carriage returns and system prompts.

He slumped into a chair, shut his eyes and breathed deeply.

'Oh Lord, I thank thee for getting me out of there.'

Then, more composedly, 'Grant thy blessing on this enterprise. On McGervon. On Nadine,' and more doubtfully, 'on Gaskin.'

There didn't seem to be any response. He rose and walked wearily down the stairs.

'I'm afraid I'll have to ask you for your name and college, sir.'

The security guy brought him to full awareness again. He complied, waited while a phone call was made, then walked back to the college in the grey dawn. Past a porter who looked doubtfully at his torn, wet, coal-begrimed clothing, and fell into the guest-room bed.

Upside, Chapter 9: Flashback – Eland and the Ministry

On a Tuesday in the previous February, Johnson walked down the street from Victoria tube station towards Eland Place. A blustery wind, blue sky studded with white clouds, daffodils aflower in Grosvenor Gardens. With a lifting heart he recalled his serendipitous concert yesterday evening, chancing on the final celebratory concert of this year's graduands from the Royal College of Music in the Queen Elizabeth Hall. The Thames' flood tide flowing past the South Bank terraces, rippling into wavelets against a vigorous northwester. In front of the National Theatre, a rough-hewn statue of St Clair, standing beaming enigmatically, like the Roman god Janus. Sinclair, innovative genius. Inventor of the C9. And in the hall, Prokofiev's Classical Symphony, a splendidly light, exuberant vehicle for the feelings of the occasion. Admiring parents and friends. Themes thrown with a passing smile from flute to bassoon to clarinet, classmates in 3 years' musical journeyings, celebrating with joy their friendship and intense application. A snatch of civilisation unsurpassed.

Meanwhile he ran over in his mind the key points in the coming meeting. How far could the parallel universe project be held to fit the ministry's guidelines? The splendidly altruistic approach of Judith Hart's white paper 'More Aid for the Poorest' had survived largely unscathed through the years and into the second Stownock administration.

He passed the entrance to Force Four Chandlers and into Eland Place, and his mind trundled off down a siding familiar to boat owners in the springtime – more varnish and anti-fouling needed? What about the echo sounder and those funny random numbers which suddenly appeared and suggested alarming shallows in the middle of the Irish Sea? No, no time to go in now.

He pushed through the glass doors into Eland House and declared his business.

'I'm with Professor Stag and Dr Kealey. I'll wait here if you don't mind, until they come.'

'All right, dear. But don't lose the pass, mind, or we won't be able to let you out.'

Kealey arrived. As usual before key meetings he was sharp and alert; a restless and demanding companion.

No sign of Professor Stag. Kealey was uneasy.

'Hope Peter's not up to one of his devices. If he doesn't show up, perhaps you'd like me to introduce the project?'

Johnson felt robust. It was going to be a good day. His project after all, wasn't it? These two had contributed a lot, but ICL's (International Computers Ltd) stamp on the whole thing should be maintained.

'No, that's OK,' he said confidently. 'You come in when we get to questions.'

'Well, if you're sure.'

They talked over the white paper issues until interrupted.

'Mr Bosley will see you now.'

They reached room H54. A. Bosley. Chief Natural Resources Advisor.

Bosley greeted them and introduced 2 colleagues whose names they missed. One, the dark-haired one, looked smooth and urbane, the administrator perhaps. The other, blond, had a broad, flat brow wrinkled with concern and the physique of a rugger player. Wing forward perhaps in his time. Disarming, honest face. Kept in the background. All had the courteous, slightly withdrawn watchfulness of senior civil servants when in contact with industry. Bosley kicked off. 'My role is that of so-called expert.' He glanced at them quizzically. Both Kealey and Johnson knew the 'so-called' to be uncalled-for. In their back-ground research Bosley's name had several times cropped up as the incisive author of monographs or whatever on this or that aspect of rural development. No doubt Bosley knew that they knew that, but nevertheless he took evident pleasure in en-larging on his role, his deep concern to verify the theoretical content and quality of the project, and his total inability, as one who was strictly an advisor, to do anything or decide anything whatsoever. He would place his views on record for those who decide in these matters to take a decision at the stage at which it

69

was appropriate for a decision to be taken. The decision would be taken by the all-powerful committee, ESCOR.

Johnson felt anchored to his seat as if by a puddle of brown sticky porridge. The contrast with the sharp action-focused development review meetings in ICL was total. Thirty or so key managers at the weekly review, each with a few short seconds to defend his people and patch.

'You committed to deliver issue 3.1.5 of the microcode for the SCU at the start of week 17. Is it delivered?'

'No, because... '

'I'm not interested in excuses. That project's a can of worms. Did you raise an Orange Alert? What recovery action have you taken?'

This was usually riposted by a vigorous statement in defence, customarily ignored, or chopped off in mid-stream by the placing of a succinctly-phrased action on the defaulting project manager; often appropriate, sometimes not.

Once in a while the defaulting development manager might divert the attack by a personal touch and a hint of ironic flattery and talk himself out of it.

'Come on now Jack, you know that's both unfair and untrue. And even you can't be both at once!'

But such counters could be used rarely, and the project managers for tail-end-Charlie functions like test software, which immediately precede product launch, often sat in flushed, sweating defensiveness as their turns to be grilled approached. The room temperature doubled, their broad shoulders sagged, their taut bellies slumped, their coffee seemed inexplicably dry and cold, their throats tightened and their voices squashed into high-pitched squeaks as they exuded hasty exculpations and thin-sounding assurances of future recovery.

Here in the ministry Johnson was out of his depth, feeling he was among people who were stringing together familiar words, but producing language whose real meaning was elusive and yet immensely important, and well-understood, moreover, by everyone else present.

Better start by explaining about the paper tape. Nothing like it had been manufactured for at least 18 years. It was too highly calendered, and that meant of course that the punch knives were continually wearing out. And there were no working punches to replicate it even if the blank tape had been available. And the code was an old 1960s 6-bit mainframe code, 3 characters to the word, odd parity, sprocket holes between the fourth and fifth tracks, preceding IBM's byte revolution of course. The manual had shown it upside down, which had slightly fogged them at first. Any questions, gentlemen? No. They obviously understood.

Then he moved on to give a greatly simplified outline of wormhole theory and Hawkinge's work on parallel universes.

'This all reached a climax,' he went on, 'in Sidney Coleman's seminal paper, "Why There is Nothing Rather than Something"…. "Why There is Nothing Rather than Something", he repeated with emphasis. 'Coleman's paper proved, or nearly proved, I should say, that the cosmological constant is zero.'

He paused meaningfully. 'The cosmological constant is zero.'

'Coleman… ' said the dark one suspiciously. 'Isn't he an American? Harvard, I think I remember.'

Johnson fumbled his way onwards into string theory. He described the idea of our universe as shaped like an unimaginably colossal balloon, though of course some mathematicians suggested it was only 2 miles across in reality. The balloon bashing into other balloons. And the surface of the balloon covered with the stars as we see them, and seething with activity, ripped apart by black holes and so forth. With minute little wormholes appearing and disappearing, tunnelling, ballooning and popping instantaneously into other baby and giant parallel universes. Into networks of such universes. All in a Planck time of 10 to the minus 43 seconds. Most wormholes were of course thought to be tunnels less than 10 to the 20th times smaller than a proton. But ICM's research suggested these might be levered open into a man-sized manhole following the parallel-universe-generating-wormhole-cosmological-constant-mediating theory propounded by Steven Giddings. And ICL's machine, the Paraleller, was designed to do just this. He paused excitedly.

'Giddings. Another American. Also from Harvard, I think,' said the dark guy severely.

'Yes,' said Bosley uneasily, 'I think you're right. Not that… '

'No, of course… But you know ESCOR, Arthur. What would

71

ESCOR say for God's sake?... Still,' he said kindly, 'do carry on, Mr... er... Jimson.'

Johnson felt his audience slipping, their eyes glazing, their watch arms twitching. He went on to introduce the project briefly; why ICL had taken it up; how the two universities came into it; why, despite the fact that the proposals were high-tech and did not come from typical sources for new DAA proposals for overseas development – e.g. Oxford, Reading, Norwich, Sussex – they merited funding.

'Yes,' said the second guy, 'We've read the papers carefully, haven't we Arthur? But our feeling really, given the absence – and this is crucial of course – of a request from a Third World country, and bearing in mind the weight of deserving and immediately appropriate... '

Kealey chipped in quickly. 'If I may just interject? I think it might be helpful to you, gentlemen, since Mr Johnson comes from a discipline with which you and I are unfamiliar, if I amplify a little on how these suggestions strike me as a simple, practical man. Like me, you are perhaps strangers to the particularities of these arcane avenues of recent mathematical research.'

He smiled warmly, persuasively at each. Bosley glanced with raised eyebrows at the dark-haired guy. He nodded.

Kealey then entered a light-hearted but exciting justification for the proposal. Like many whose brains work over-fast, he had the unconscious habit of repeating phrases with swift paraphases in a tumbling rhythm, which was elusive and invigorating. People had to listen hard just to keep up.

The university/ICL research, he outlined, had revealed this new route to cross-cultural aid and communication. Cross-universe, in fact. Johnson's 'Grubber' had almost certainly opened up a wormhole from a parallel universe. This second, parallel, universe desperately needed our aid. The paper tape containing the message, which had spewed out of thin air next to Johnson's machine in Manchester, seemed after all their investigations and the forensic science boys' work to be unquestionably genuine. The civil servants had seen the other universe's plea on the hard copy.

The funding aspect was not vital – ICL could trivially fund the task from its own budgets, but the external impress of the ministry, its seal of approval, was vital if the normal accusations from the media and elsewhere were not to stick – allegations of commercial motivation and exploitation for example – and if the necessary extent of cross-disciplinary collaboration inside universities and industry and between institutions was to be achieved.

'Those among us,' Kealey continued, 'whose arteries are not yet hardened,' – a beaming, reassuring smile made it clear that the present company were numbered among those whose arteries were indubitably youthful – 'see the vitally important and constructive role this sort of initiative can play at the leading edge of technology.'

The civil servants relaxed. Bosley began to probe with a few questions.

At this stage, there was an urgent knock at the door.

'Professor Stag, Mr Bosley.' Bosley's PA appeared, but was suddenly and startlingly replaced by the tall, burly figure of Professor Stag.

'Mu my dear chuch chap.'

Stag came in, his right hand eagerly and warmly out-thrust at Bosley, his coat, hat and briefcase hugged precariously under his left arm.

'Suho nice to meet you at last. I'm mu most awfully su su su su horry. Those Manchester tut trains. The 7.53 as usual you know.' Stag stammered out his apologies.

'No, no, Professor, delighted... '

The civil servants seemed bemused, sympathetic and immensely deferential.

'H engine bub bub.'

'We're delighted to have you here.'

They mustered to help the professor sort himself and his coat and his hat and his papers out. They sat anxiously alert while he painfully expressed his views. A most praiseworthy Bub Bub Bu British initiative. The stammering was sometimes quite harrowing. Stag's tongue would twist and lollop distressingly in and out of his mouth like a purple epileptic serpent.

Outside distant drums and fifes approached, increasingly loud.

'We cuc cuc cu hant be left behind.'

'The Scots Guards,' explained Bosley quietly; the civil servants were clearly accustomed to the din. The band came closer. The guards' boots crunched and echoed dramatically below, the insistent rattle of the kettle drums drawing Kealey's pencil to tap in time. Stag entered into a long description of how he had as a budding researcher in the late 1950s, publicly declared his own field, computing, to be a specialists' backwater. Massive number crunching, weather forecasting, nuclear physics, artillery range tables. Not much else. World demand for computers by 2024 in the region of 17 machines.

'How wrong cu cu cu han you be?' he concluded with rueful humility. 'How r r r hong can you be?'

The civil servants looked warmly respectful. Takes a big man to recount his blunders.

Might it not be so, suggested Stag, with this current proposal? So easy to reject the far-sighted in favour of the conventional. To select with tunnel vision the meticulously presented Price-Gittinger conformant pap, and let the seeds of the future float by. Bosley smiled sympathetically. The Scots Guards gradually receded towards the Sinclair memorial. The fresh leaves on the plane trees shone green and translucent in the sunshine. Johnson relaxed, delight suffusing his veins.

We've done it, he thought, we've done it. We're going to win after all.

Bosley stressed again the informative and advisory nature of his role. But sometimes there was a need for pump-priming. He might prime the pump.

They discussed the plan, who might go across when, when they might come back, budget, allowances, insurance. The dark-haired civil servant suddenly chipped in quite eagerly.

'It occurs to me, taking a global view, that we really need a crisp means of defining the 2 universes.'

'Interesting,' said Stag. 'How do you mu mu mu hean?'

'Well, we could call our one Upside, and the other one Downside.'

'Excellent. An extraordinarily succinct way of pu pu hutting it. What du du yu hoo think, Cu Colin?'

'I think perhaps that is a central contribution to the project. Slices through a forest of technical jargon to the core idea. Proactive communication at equivalent levels is of course absolutely crucial.'

'We could call the project "Transgap",' said the civil servant.

They debated it and agreed. He looked graciously pleased. They talked further over the ministry's protocols and procedures.

'But what about ESCOR?' asked Kealey.

'ESCOR?' said Bosley, puzzled. 'Oh, Humphrey will take care of ESCOR.' His dark-haired colleague smiled with easy, lofty, enigmatic confidence.

The 3 later surrendered their passes and came out of the ministry doors.

'Dr hink and a bu bite?' suggested Stag.

'Good idea.'

Kealey looked carefully around and behind them as they strode cheerfully to the pub.

'Peter,' he said to Stag, 'that was magnificent. Confess now, the Mu-Mu-Mu-Mu Hanchester train was spot-on time, wasn't it now?'

Stag's face reddened and swelled into a massive schoolboy grin, uncontainably pleased with himself, unable to squeeze his pleasure into the habitual gravitas, the sober cast of academic propriety. They all hugged themselves with laughter.

They ordered pints and ploughmans all round and settled down to savour the meeting. Then in came the third civil servant. 'Du do j hoin us,' said Stag courteously. It turned out that he was called Tilley, George Tilley. They chatted a little.

Tilley turned to Stag. 'You know, Professor, I'm a Mancunian also. Came down on the 7.53. Thought it got in on time. Could have sworn it did if I'd not heard you say differently... But I find this project worthwhile and fascinating,' he added hastily, 'and I believe I can help.'

'Ah,' said Stag.

'Well, come on then, tell us all about it,' he added.

Upside, Chapter 10: Return to Cambridge

The afternoon after his perilous return from Downside, Johnson sat in his guest room in Old Court looking unseeing out onto the garden. His body felt exhausted, shattered and paralysed. He tried to raise his right arm, but it lay motionless at his side. He felt a detached pleasure in its inertness, a relaxation, an absence of volition that spread a warm secure feeling through him.

There was a brisk knock on the door, and Kealey's voice.

'Johnson. Heard you were back and came straight up here. Can I come in?' Johnson remained motionless and silent.

The door-handle turned, but the door didn't open. Locked. Kealey called twice more, then clattered away down the stairs. He appeared on the grass, and waved up at Johnson. Johnson remained unmoving. Eventually Kealey reappeared with a porter, who opened the door. Still Johnson made no movement apart from the blinking of his eyes and steady breathing. Later a doctor was called in, and he was stretchered out to an ambulance and on to Addenbrookes for observation.

Kealey was in daily, and on the fourth day called in with Stag. Johnson had no control over his bowels, and was attached to a drip, so no solid effluent. As Kealey and Stag came in he could feel himself pee warmly into a bottle. He could see their mouths moving, smiles, concern. He could hear the noise of their speech. But no understanding, no contact, just a mild sense of interest.

A week later the 2 were back again. No change in Johnson's condition had been reported, but the hospital had taken to leaving the TV set in the corner on, in case the programmes might bring him back. Sometimes his eyes drifted towards it.

Stag turned the sound down to talk to Kealey.

'Mu my du dear ch chap. You mustn't reproach yourself so much. We were all to blame. All to bub bl hame.'

'Maybe. But *pas devant...* '

'Oh. Yes. Of course.'

Suddenly Johnson broke into an agitated mumbling. He thrashed from side to side in the bed. They moved towards him, but he thrust himself out of bed, past them, the pan trailing wetly behind him, the drips and tubes ripped off his sorely punctured forearm, and crouched at the TV, fumbling with the zapper.

'Nadine,' he said desperately, 'Nadine... '

The TV sound came through. An attractive, slim, dark-haired woman in a wedding dress and a formally-suited man were visible diagonally against the background of an altar. A priest was reciting to her, '... I thee wed.'

'With this ring I thee wed,' she repeated clearly. Johnson howled and rolled over on the floor like a child, his shoulders shaking as he wept.

'With my body I thee worship.'

'With my body I thee... '

'Switch the bloody thing off,' said Kealey over his shoulder, holding Johnson gently. Stag did so, and together they tried to console and soothe him. Rapidly a nurse appeared, and then a doctor. Kealey and Stag were asked to leave. Clearly their fault.

Walking off to the car park, Stag said, 'Odd business, with this woman, you know.'

'Nadine, you mean, wasn't it? Yes, it is.'

'You know, Colin, I think we need a second 11 smartly. Even if Johnson recovers.'

'Maybe so. That guy Tilley, perhaps, and his talking brain.'

'Yes, you've got it. We could interface the hub brhain with PIG and... No, couldn't do it. It's only got an RS423/E serial interface.'

'Well, at least he could take it along as an option.'

Upside, Chapter 11: BLZ Meets Nadine

A few years earlier than this, in a building that housed the well-known *Sunday Broadsheet*, a slender dark-haired woman, a young graduate trainee, stood outside the office of BL, legendary reporter and editor. Awesome. Or as the Yanks would say, 'arsesome'. The guy who'd had the bottle to throw over a brilliant career as a physicist for the swirling maelstrom of journalism. On the door was a simple plaque: B.L.Z. Bubb – Deputy Editor and Reporter-in-Chief.

BL in his serious guise presented a long, box-shaped face, beaky nose with a bulbous tip and level thin lips, a monument to committed and rather critical observation; ugly, friendly yet alarming to his colleagues and subordinates.

But this could dissolve in an instant to the broadest and most infectious of smiles, lips lifting way up at the corners and eyes crinkling warmly with friendliness and mirth. Occasionally, glimpsed in profile, this same image could momentarily take on a fearsomely different shape. The smiling mouth seemed tautened upwards and opened as if poised to cackle, the jaws becoming shark-like and voracious, the nose probing predatorily forward. Truth will out.

Turned on a rival or enemy the mirth resolved sometimes into searing derision, accompanied by loud guffaws and coarse observations. Reminiscent of a vitriolically hostile Renaissance gargoyle, tucked way up in the ancient heights of a cathedral, spurting venom with inexplicable savagery at a chosen human target.

With the boss, Sir Stan Barker, this image melted into one of concerned and committed support – 'Understand me, Barks?' 'You're with me, Barks?' 'These fuckers; we've got to grasp them by the goolies and squeeze till they squeak. Believe me, Barks, they're after you.'

Women were a different target; treated with warmth, consideration and friendly sexual innuendo. He'd call out to a cleaning lady as she stood near the car, 'Hallo, my love. Treating you well isn't he, then? Well, I certainly would.'

And then a loud, harsh aside as he pulled away in the car, audible not to her but to his male passengers, 'Wouldn't root you my dear; pay me 50 grand and I wouldn't.'

The trainee raised her hand and knocked hesitantly. Why did he want to see a cub reporter? She recalled his powerful, moving presentation of the journalist's place in society, the gentle, unintrusive, caring manner with which his eyes had slowly scanned their ranks at the start of their training.

'Come!'

She entered.

'Ah yes. Nadine McCleod, isn't it? I was most interested in your piece on North Korea. Perceptive, orthogonal. A nice piece of lateral thinking. Take a pew. I have decided this year to take a personal hand for one or two of our brighter prospects. A bit of accelerated development to see if we can get you on stream without the usual lag while trainees learn from experience. Do we have to accept the hoary old dictum that you can only learn from your own mistakes? What's wrong with other peoples'?'

Nadine smiled. The subdued light emphasised the darkness of the blue in her eyes. He caught his breath, slightly shaken. Then he went on.

'I think not,' he said easily, '*si la jeunesse savait, si la vieillesse pouvait.* That sort of stuff. But in this case we hope to bring the *savoir* bit forward a great deal more than a smidgeon. So the Board, bless their cotton socks, have asked me to single out one or two to sit in with me. What do you think?' he asked with disarming diffidence.

She flushed with pleasure and mumbled assentingly. She'd join him, it appeared, one day a week and absorb what she could.

The first Tuesday went well, and the next. At the end of the third he gave her a job.

'Here's an interesting letter to the editor. Response by a guy called Johnson to something by our man in East Africa – actually, of course, usually in Hampstead. That's where we find out what our readers want to hear. And you can find out more quickly about Africa in Hampstead or Cambridge, and it saves a lot of flying!'

He smiled disarmingly – they well knew that the paper's correspondents were in reality often enough where the action was. 'See what you can do with it.'

The original article spoke of 'the myth of British imperium as altruistic, benevolent and misunderstood.' Out there, in the writer's estimation as a national subaltern doing his 2 years in the army, '... it stank. Whites of staggering insignificance behaved like the lords of creation.'

Johnson's letter to the editor went, 'As a contemporary of his, I'm impelled to put an alternative to your writer's view. Having acquired similar views to his as a student and national serviceman, I resolved to get involved and joined the colonial service in Uganda. Most of us were liberal arts graduates from Oxbridge, leftish inclined, with good degrees and a tendency to go on International Voluntary Service work camps in the vacations. For me as for many others who worked there, it's immensely pleasing to look back now, as one could reflect at the time, confident that almost nothing but good was achieved in our 5 key years there. Yes, the occasional settler was disgustingly arrogant (only one that I can recall). Galling for an itinerant national serviceman like your journalist, but insignificant against the realities as they affected the typical Ugandan. To avoid personal bias,' Johnson continued, 'I'd like to take someone I knew only from his reputation among the Bakiga tribe, Purseglove, to illustrate these realities. He was District Agricultural Officer, Kigezi – rolling, beautiful, overpopulated highlands, threatened with social and economic collapse because of the *Pax Britannica*, medical services, Christianity, malaria eradication and civilisation in general.

'The danger arose from over-cultivation, and the sheet erosion of the fertile soil on the hills which overtook the same terrain in neighbouring Rwanda. Purseglove's vision and his infectious enthusiasm led his department and his successors to create an agronomic revolution for a million farmers; through bunding, terracing, tree planting and the introduction of appropriate cash crops. I had the exhausting job of accompanying his successors on extension safaris, day in and day out, climbing up and down 3,000 feet from farmer to farmer and *baraza* (meeting) to *baraza*. Purseglove is still known with affection and unconscious

80

ambiguity among the Bakiga as "*Bwana* Fertility". Elsewhere his achievement is unknown, though agriculturalists know of his later research in the West Indies, for which he received the OBE. To misquote Schumacher in "Small is Beautiful", Purseglove and many others were the people who really mattered. Why doesn't the *Sunday Broadsheet* – to build on their, and similar links, for the future – let the occasional boorish, irrelevant settler be forgotten?'

Nadine came back with her work a week later. BLZ scanned it.

'Hum. Maybe we should get together about this tonight? I'm out all day in the Treasury – 'fraid you can't come. Not allowed to take fledglings!'

'Er, well, I've unfortunately... '

'Early working dinner, perhaps? That little place called À l'Ecu de France. Off St James's Square.' His eyes glinted. 'Be there 6.30 prompt; I've got to get away by 8. And we've got to meet the weekend edition.'

'Er, well, er, right. Thank you very much, BL.' She smiled warmly at him. He seemed slightly bemused, then dismissed her peremptorily.

Later she dressed for the evening, and left for À l'Ecu de France. She wore a hip-length jacket, a lovely deep red, sort of raspberry colour, and a wispy floating silk scarf. BL's 'little place' turned out, behind a discreet entrance, to be largish, spacious and beautifully decorated in cream, jade and midnight blue, with much seemingly genuine Regency furniture. Known only to the cognoscenti. Rather reminiscent of the Mayfair in Washington, where her diplomat father had once given her a splendid American working breakfast, including hot waffles and maple syrup. It lay just between the bustle of the Strand and the quiet Roller-girt mega-affluence of St James's Square.

She went in diffidently, left her coat, and decided to go right through the ante-room, since BL would no doubt be in a hurry. A waiter came up questioningly.

'Yes, Madame?'

'I'm meeting a Mr Bubb.'

'Ah, *bonsoir*, Madame. Monsieur Bubb, of course. It is Madame McCleod, *n'est ce pas*? He leaves a message, maybe perhaps a little late at the Treasury. Some wine perhaps?'

She ordered a Bloody Mary. Not her usual, but she felt like it. Later, another. Then he arrived.

'So sorry, my dear. We'll have to rush, I'm afraid.'

They dickered through the ordering, and then he pulled out her work.

'No good at all, I'm afraid. This is just university stuff. Certainly readable, agreeable enough and so on. But not the paper's *Weltanschauung*, you know. Now, you should slash through all this stuff about Purseglove. We're not interested in colonial heroes, we're in business for the future.'

'But surely Johnson's quite right... '

'Right? Right? What d'you mean, right? This is about the past. And the past's what we're in business to mould. To re-engineer. The world's going to have it in for us, regardless, so let's get there first. The dear old Brits and their fond memories, we've got to erase all that garbage. Look.'

He handed her an edited copy of the text, pruned and gutted, topped and tailed.

'Read that.'

She read it, her heart beating tightly.

'The impression we want to give is of a pompous, rather stupid ex-civil servant. A boring old fart of a colonialist. And we head it "Proud Heritage". Invite the reader to conclude that the desperate woes of Uganda under Amin and Obote were attributable to thickies like this one. Invite him or her to scoff.'

'But surely,' she said, 'Purseglove was what the letter was all about? Amin's atrocities were well down the track after 8 years of independence and prosperity. And Amin came in because Obote tried a coup against the Baganda and got it all wrong. There were hardly any settlers in Uganda, it was a protectorate. Land couldn't be alienated to foreigners directly, even the missions. Only 0.24 per cent of the land was alienated into the plantation sector. And our guy was just a callow, ignorant national serviceman in Jinja barracks.'

'How d'you know that?' he asked suspiciously.

She started blinking rapidly and talked very fast.

'Well, my uncle worked and died of malaria there as an ADC, so I know something about it. What a drunken racist plantation manager said to our guy in a garrison bar has no significance whatsoever. There were almost none of them, and their importance for the average Ugandan was vanishingly small. It's a peasant economy, like nearly all of tropical Africa. Plantations didn't exist.'

BL smiled faintly and laced his fingers together in a clerical steeple.

'Look, Nadine, my sweet. As far as we're concerned, our guy was there. Our guy knows his stuff. Full stop. That's what real editing's all about. And that's the view our paper wants to paint.'

'Well,' she said, red spots on her cheeks, 'your trashy so-called real editing's not for me.'

'Look,' he said, 'let's talk this through. After all, we don't want to jeopardise your... '

She stood up dramatically and raised an arm.

'Waiter, my coat please,' she said, and waited there tapping her toe, while Bubb rose and tried to chat easily through the awkwardness.

'It's important,' he said gently, 'to unpack some of these grand phrases and see what they mean... Maybe when push comes to shove, we're basically in agreement... '

Her eyes crinkled and glinted, and she looked stonily across the restaurant, paying no evident attention. The coat was brought, and, not wanting to muddle herself by trying to put it on, she took it, laid it slowly and carefully across her left arm, and picked her way across the floor like a ballerina pirouetting on wet ice. She left without a backward glance, to the intrigued, admiring interest of the scattered diners nearby.

'Buggeration,' said BL, under his breath.

The head waiter came up with a slight confidential, commiserating smile.

'The hunting tonight,' he murmured, 'not so good, Monsieur Bubb, *n'est ce pas?*'

'*Vous avez raison, mon vieux. Mais je ne la laisserai pas la. Il y a encore de methodes.*'

'*Pas avec celle-la. Elle me semblait sauvage comme une lynxe.*'

'And all the better for it,' muttered Bubb to himself. And so, in due course, it was to prove.

Upside, Chapter 12: Flashback – Johnson's First Transit Downside

A month after the meeting with the civil servants, Johnson had been returning home for the weekend by train north to Alsager in Cheshire, after a project meeting in Cambridge. He recalled some previous journeys after key meetings. Some so euphoric, so joyful, as to be out of this world; 3 or 4 solitary hours interwoven gently with the unrepeatable, slowly-receding delight of some longed-for, pivotally crucial breakthrough. Some the reverse. This time he was despondent, but not desperate. The prototype Grubber had been set up and energised. Tense and frightened, he'd grabbed the balls. Nothing at all. Dunne had acted likewise. Nothing at all. Yet theory said the wormhole should open somewhere along the fault line between Merseyside and Cambridge, and the machine should have homed it into the maths lab office. Maybe a timing problem.

The train rumbled and twisted through the Harecastle tunnel between Stoke and Kidsgrove; he got off at Kidsgrove to catch the slow train to Alsager.

The v-shaped island up-platform was open and deserted in the darkness, and he had 30 minutes to wait. Tedious, though better than doing the trip by car. Typical of the Brits, he thought affectionately; 2 major motorways and main-line rail links to and from Oxford and anywhere, but as for getting at Cambridge, damn all – like tacking through Cowes Roads in August. Damn all. Status over ideas. A foregone conclusion. The only way of keeping an inventive nation on the rails.

He'd dump his case behind a bush and stroll down to the Harecastle tunnels. A splendidly sinister Sherlock Holmes scenario; you could imagine Moriarty poling his getaway craft into the tunnel after some strikingly gruesome felony. The Macclesfield and Trent and Mersey canals, emerging from the sunny, rolling Cheshire plains, joined together just north of

Kidsgrove station, ran south alongside it and then swung slowly right, beneath the railway, into a deepening cut and the black tunnel entrances. Bound for the turbulent Potteries – Wedgwood, Spode, Doulton, Shanks, tea cup and toilet makers to the world – mines, slag heaps, endless stripes of tiny back-to back houses, massive kilns, fired up and burning through the nights, belching flame and reddened smoke into the night sky. And then, astonishing, through a tunnel into the emerald green of the Victoria Ground soccer pitch, glowing at you like a magic carpet in a can of sardines.

A lad up in the rafters of the City stand. The crowd chanting 'Come on City! Come on Stoke! Hooly Ooly Oolygan. Hooly... Oolygan!'

When we broke the Leeds record run, nil each. Leeds free kick, captain Billy Bremner on the ground writhing in apparent agony just outside our penalty area. And like a flash, up on his feet right as rain, watch out watch out, placed the ball and hooked it over Shilton's head into the net. Shilts was still turned the other way waving to his girl behind the net. Stoke 0 Leeds 1. There was a roar of anger to blast the roof off. Everyone, all of Stoke City, was furious. The fans reassured themselves – Shilt's not even got his gloves dirty yet. Leeds never stood a chance. 0–1, became 1–1, then 2–1, then final whistle. End of Leeds record.

After 100 yards, the towpath cut away steeply up Packhorse Lane, where the horses used to peel off, to be led over the top and rejoin their boats at the far end of the tunnels. Straight ahead the rock walls closed in and the 2 tunnel mouths gaped. The narrower on the left (now disused), Old Harecastle, the other New Harecastle. He climbed over the rotting boards, and strolled along the residual path towards the Old Tunnel. Legend had it that a canal boat loaded with coal had started one night into the tunnel, the bargees lying flat on their backs on the cabin top, legging the craft through with their feet on the tunnel roof. The boy took the horse over the top, reached the far end and waited. No barge. He waited on. The next day they called help, and found the barge halfway through. But the 2 bargees were never found. The history of the canals brims with tales of haunting, drunkenness and violence among their people. A nomad breed outwith the law.

Uneasy vibes on a black night like this, thought Johnson, with the sodium lamps from the road way up above giving a distant, lurid luminescence, the still black water shining occasional reflections, and the chilly dank sulphurous emanations of the tunnels twitching in the nostrils. The whiff of the Potteries. The Methodist Church, tall windows darkened and ominous, stood high above, surrounded by towering beech trees and dripping dark rhododendrons, soggy leaf mould on the slippery, black, acid earth below them.

He felt a sudden massive jolt, which threw him unconscious against the rock face. There was a yell, and a figure splashed into the tunnel mouth from right alongside him, floundered and thrashed and gurgled briefly, and then drifted slowly down-tunnel into the darkness. Johnson came to, got up, remembered where he was, and hastened off back to the station. Still no one around. Another 5 minutes to the train. Must have slipped on the rock. It had felt as if someone had cannoned into him violently. He took off his jacket and tried to brush his back off, then retrieved his case. Funny. Hadn't realised it was so heavy.

The train came in. Not the usual Central Trains livery, perhaps a replacement. Old traditional BR rolling stock, BR colours. He boarded it and opened the case. The contents were to his alarm totally unfamiliar. He picked out a letter on top. Joining instructions for Johnson, Michael Alun. To attend a course in Informations Systems Organisation and Management for PIG. For selected level 3 Systems Engineers. Professional Development Programme part 4. He straightened up, filled with fear and elation. He was through the wormhole! He was Downside! These must be for his Downside equivalent.

He read the joining instructions in more detail. He'd stick on the train till Crewe, then change for where? He pulled his ticket out. Top left jacket pocket. Just where he always left it. But wrong ticket. He'd have to pay the guard. What with? Perhaps the notes here were different. Worried stiff, he rummaged further, then found he'd a rail warrant and cash in his bag. A Downside rail warrant and Downside cash. Breathe again.

Upside, Chapter 13: Cambridge, Recovering

Kealey phoned the hospital 2 days after Johnson's return and the episode with the TV programme. Johnson, they said, was under sedation, but could talk in a slurred way for short spells. Kealey got permission to return and try to establish what had happened. Clearly, whatever the effects on Johnson, he had got across the gap and come back again. And the TV programme had an extraordinary impact.

He sat by Johnson's bed.

'Greetings, Johnson. You mum mu made it then.'

The poor imitation of Stag evoked a weak smile. Slowly Kealey extracted an account of Johnson's time across the gap. Johnson reached the incident in the pool.

'But why did you take this woman swimming?' Kealey asked. Johnson explained that he needed to get to know someone well enough to ask a lot of odd-sounding questions about the background, questions which might reveal a strange lack of knowledge about well-known events.

Kealey passed it over, engrossed.

'What did she tell you?'

Not a lot, thought Johnson. He remembered, 'Will you stop staring at me during lectures?' 'Thank you, kind sir,' from a sparkling-eyed beauty, running up stairs into the darkness. And finally, looking into his eyes, 'Michael!' Betrayal. Betrayal. Never to be forgotten, never to be forgiven.

In fact he'd got from the girl nothing of relevance to the case in hand. Just illusory glimpses of warmth, tenderness, longing and so forth. However, he recounted as much of his various other impressions of the POPs, PIG and the Malfunction as he could. Kealey was impressed.

'What was her name again?' Kealey had returned to the startpoint.

Johnson hesitated, then he said shortly, 'Nadine.'

'Was it?' said Kealey thoughtfully. 'You remember,' he

continued, 'seeing the TV yesterday? That woman was called Nadine.'

'Yes,' said Johnson coldly. 'Nadine, now Countess of West-morland. Or some such.'

Kealey looked away, his throat constricted.

Then back again, looking his friend in the eyes. 'Well, old chap. A good session, then. See you tomorrow, OK?'

Johnson nodded. Suddenly he was looking forward to lunch. Cosily, in his room. On his own. Everything he tasted was now taking on a fresh, unfamiliar, immensely pleasing savour. This cheese, that fish or whatever. Flavours that, coming back from what he had expected to be oblivion and death, were vividly real and intriguing. Perhaps just the reviving taste buds in the back of his tongue, perhaps something deeper. Teeter on the edge of the grave and then come back again, and you get a different perception of things.

Gradually over the following week Johnson, Stag, and Kealey sorted out their views. They brought in Tilley and Nodel, who would provide 'an orthogonal input on theoretical aspects' as Tilley put it; i.e. a sideways view.

A universe split seemed to them to have occurred about 10 to 20 years ago. Their universe seemed to have got things fairly right. But universe B, Downside, had as Kealey put it 'made a pig's ear of things'.

'No pun intended,' said Kealey.

'None taken,' said Johnson automatically. He was thinking over Gaskin's words in the Fellows' toilet. The expert system base from which PIG had been constructed after Malfunction. Its possible fallibility. And his words: 'It's turning a bit nasty.'

'Nasty in what way?' Johnson had asked.

Gaskin had talked of something else, and then they'd been interrupted. But almost certainly, the 5 concluded, the nastiness had to do with PIG. Nodel's reaction when Johnson first described the PIG seminar was dismissive.

'They're way off beam,' he said. 'Just like the earlier prophets of artificial intelligence, until the Lindop report. We first explored this, you know, in the 1970s, when the obvious parallels between human thought processes and computational processes became evident. Or at least the way creatures with brains learn and react and build up libraries of standard actions. Just as Alan Turing envisaged in the 1940s.'

He enlarged on this, but the others became restive.

'This is all well known,' said Kealey. 'Let's get on.'

'With respect, no. Well known, maybe. But not well understood. And we must all build up a common perception, a common comprehension of all this, if we're to succeed.'

Kealey looked at Johnson and rolled his eyes upwards, humorously.

'Remember your first shave? Follow the instructions on the tube. Wash face first with soap and water. Rinse. Wash again with soap, but leave it on. OK so far – you've done it all your life, and you can do it again without thinking. But remember the first time. Awkwardly smearing the cream around your face, then scraping the razor across the cream-covered down. Stinging cuts as you try to move the razor to slice diagonally across the hairs like it says on the tube. And the special bits where you have to wriggle round the indentations, maybe the cleft in your chin. Then gradually you use this and refine it, and it's eventually stacked away.'

He warmed to what was clearly a pet theme. 'Procedures, you guys, algorithms. They are the immense, the revolutionary feature of computing. They are man's most fundamental invention since the wheel. Imagine. Computing historians like Drummond, deeply into the technology, and then come up with disparaging statements like "Can't compare with other twentieth-century things like the car or TV, the invention of air travel, etc." Of course it can. No sense of history and proportion. With these devices man can explore the universe. Universes, in fact, to take the case in point. In computing terms, such a procedure is something you execute without conscious thought, almost like breathing.

'These procedures are the exciting feature of computing, not the boring bits of improved information technology, spread-sheets, word-processors and so on. Look at the vaunted spell-checker. An instant classical education for all. No matter that the user has no inkling of the subtle distinctions between words. Disinterested and uninterested, for example. "Truly and indifferently administer justice, to the punishment of wickedness and vice" as the splendid language of the BCP[20] has it. More Christian than Christianity. A cornerstone of civilisation. But instead people just click on spell, and let the machine sort it all out. Spellcheck, punctuate, grammaticise. If it's a new line after a full stop, the first letter must be in capitals. Never mind if that's not what you want, that's how it's got to be. You try changing it, we, Bill Gates, will put it back again. That's what Microsoft says. Dreadful. The structured system as against the free human spirit. No wonder they can only write in capital letters. No joined up writing any more.'

Kealey chipped in. 'Not too sure what the last bit's all about, though I see your general point. But you'd take a different view if you were a non-classicist. Faced with a closed circle of privileged people with this esoteric education. Ready to condemn you if your speech or semantics show you're an outsider. Or even if you use the same word twice in 2 consecutive sentences. Regardless of the merits of what you have to say.'

'I agree with you on the first point,' said Johnson, 'about the insider side. Felt it against me when talking to Bosley. Civil servants in coded converse. Left me floundering. But the answer, surely, in the leisure society, is to offer people the chance to get a classical education if they so wish. To expand depth and diversity. Not to artificially give them... '

'There,' interrupted Kealey. 'Got you. Split infinitive, "to artificially give", forsooth! From the very mouth of the prophet.'

'Ah, well, it's no longer always wrong to reject a split infinitive. It derives from the idea that an infinitive in Latin is a single word. Or indeed, since Derek's concern is language, French or Luganda or Swahili. *Ninyenda kugyendayo.* I want to go there. A Muchiga[21] wouldn't say "I want there to go". Although a German would, "Ich will daar gehen".'

'All right. But even so, we should be using this technology to increase human freedom and the diversity and range of challenge and choice. Not the sameness of the stereotyped global consumer. As an individual; not as an entity in some computerised database like UAPT InfoLink. And the redeeming feature is the algorithm, the method, the program. That's the exciting thing. A rule, yet a vastly flexible rule. First imagined, then structured and constructed. Unlike all other human artefacts, given that you can replicate it, it will work the same a million miles hence, or a million years hence.'

'Or a million universes hence. Gaskin, I suspect, would agree.'

'Gaskin. Who's Gaskin? Oh yes, of course. Which brings me back to the human brain. The central rows of brains in the organic philosophical reduction tanks, were, or rather are, linked together by an information super-highway, writhing chains of nerve fibres to connect them all and perform surveillance and routine direction of the external human world. Links to the POPs. Probably relatively slow speed serial links, with a fair amount of intelligence inboard on each POP. Hence their rather alarmingly crude and slurred speech. A bit Dalek-like, as opposed to the much more friendly and empathetic moronic voices used by the TONKs in the empowerment cells. You would significantly reduce the comms loads, so that large numbers of POPs could be driven. Distributed government in fact. With no working satellites and limited terrestrial radio, that's the way you'd do it.'

'What about the sessions with TONK like the girls had on the course? Well, it probably wasn't direct interaction. The database search engine would maintain lists of possible problem clients, as in the interview with the operator. Intranet Security would then use TONKS to drive the interviews with client-suspects like the women, and prompt the psychologists to click in on an interview if the sweat sensors etc. hit interesting levels. Quite straightforward, really. Presumably the images of Nadine from the capsizing POP had been compared with the pubic images of the women, ladies and girls, on the course, and Nadine had been fingered.'

'Not sure about that,' said Johnson.

Upside, Chapter 14: Project

Johnson sat reading the first Transgap Project minutes. The circulation included a lot of strangers, including one J.W. Tillekaratnegoonasingha. Good old English name, that. Perhaps a Sri Lankan academic. Below the main list it said, 'Copied for information to Professor Stag, FRS, FIP, FBCS, PhD, MSC, BSc; The Lord Tite Barnacle, MA (Oxon)'

The 2 top chaps.

'Who's this guy, the Lord Tite Barnacle?' he asked Nodel.

'Oh, that's Humphrey. You met him at the meeting in Eland House.'

'Ah. Yes, the black-haired one.'

'Family of civil service nobs. The original lord was lordified for his achievements at the Office of Circumlocution in the 1850s. Grossly maligned by Dickens in some novel. *Little Dorritt* perhaps. A gross caricature. Typical Dickens. If they'd taken Dickens to court they'd have taken him to the cleaners. Libel. And no mistake.'[22]

'Well, anyway. They've got us down to do the Transgapant interface,' Johnson grumbled to Nodel. 'No way we can commit to that without a firm hardware spec, dates, access, formal handover, assured support. All the usual dependencies.'

'Look, mate,' replied Nodel, 'we're dealing with universities. It's not their way of working. Different culture. Programme management, egoless programming, commitments, dependencies, milestones, QA – not their scene. They don't have the stamina. They don't have the drive. They don't have the commitment. They live by writing papers. Papers on this, papers on that. That's why they've never produced any real software. Except WATFOR.'[23]

The project became shrouded in obscurity. In short succession, urgent resolution meetings were called in different institutions. Occasional strangers appeared, were addressed as Mr Jones or whoever, from an innocuous sounding unit of the DoD

92

or DHSS perhaps, said little and talked vaguely. The COCOM agreement was mentioned. Working papers that had been on wide circulation ceased to be so. Updates to project documents were received whose originals they had never heard of. Urgent phone calls from anxious secretaries asked them to send the updates back unopened. Intrigued, they photocopied them, returned the originals, and puzzled over the copies. One concerned Johnson himself. Would he be able to stand a second crossing? What had caused his whiteout? There had been no evidence of physical damage beyond a severe burning of the tongue. He had been conscious, and the ECGs had revealed an unfamiliar alpha rhythm. Addenbrookes urged that he be sent back again, then subjected to further study since the condition was clearly of immense medical interest. A ministry directive followed; the matter had been referred, and further discussion on this aspect was embargoed.

A second paper concerned possible transgapants, candidates to cross the gap between the 2 universes as portable brains. One was named Nassani. Johnson became interested as he read about the Nassani brain – it was from the volcano region, much loved by Johnson, in south-west Uganda. The brain's background seemed familiar to him. Similar to Sseru's, balaba though Sseru had been dead many years. As he read on, his mind's eye ran back to the young Ugandan Mututsi and the tragedy below the volcano, Sabinio.

1958, Chapter 14A: Ngolobama

Johnson cast his mind back to his early times working with Sseru. What did the name mean? All Bantu names mostly mean something. Then he remembered. Short for Sserulyamayenje. Jokey guy. Humorous, but not a buffoon. Not a guy to mess with.

Both Johnson and Sseru were posted to Kabale, District Headquarters of Kigezi in Uganda's south-western highlands. Johnson was 2 years senior to the young Mututsi. The 2 were sharing an apartment in 1958 while they were on the in-country course for budding District Officers at Entebbe, the inspired choice of some early explorer as the Ugandan seat of government. Inspired both for its grace and for its convenient distance away from the turbulent capital, Kampala, from the Kabaka's royal palaces and from sectarian religious influences from 'Bacatolici' and 'Baprotetanti'. And in due course from the stridently assertive students at the university of Makerere. Part of the instinctive wisdom of empire – place your universities well away from the capital, then Entebbe. Plant a golf course round your district headquarters. Or, in the case of German East Africa, clear all the bush round the HQ to give your soldiers a clear field of fire.

Most of the Entebbe course was based in the Lake Victoria Hotel, which surmounted sprawling, closely-cropped meadows of emerald green grass which sloped gently down to the papyrus and then the broad greeny-blue waters of Victoria, the greatest of all the African Great Lakes. The lake perches 3,000 feet up, like a vast 150-mile-long dish of water, a seriously big summit pound, finely balanced; poised ready at the pop of a volcano to cut off the Nile outlet in the north and tilt back south as it once did, and pour all its waters towards the Indian Ocean instead.

On this night Sseru was, as often, out at a very late-night party. He had absorbed only too readily Johnson's advice that, with independence drawing rapidly and inevitably close, his performance on the course itself would not matter much. Young

94

leaders of Sseru's generation and with his background and potential were so rare that their future careers were, so Johnson urged his friend, effectively secure regardless.

Johnson got in to their shared room after an evening out, and turned in for the night. At about 4 a.m. the phone rang in the sitting room. He stumbled out of bed to the lounge and picked it up.

'Sseru darling, it's me,' said a voice soft with the particular, overwhelming love that some upper-class English young women's voices can convey. When they so wish. And even more so, the voices of Africans who have shared that special finishing at the same schools. One of the Woodard schools perhaps. He rested the receiver quietly. A minute later, the phone rang again.

'Sseru,' said the same voice sweetly, 'I know you're there. I only rang to say it was so wonderful. And that I love you.'

Johnson put the phone down again.

A few minutes later he heard Sseru come in. He kept quiet and snored slightly. Whether Sseru's girlfriend ever told him about the call, or indeed who she was, he never found out. The young man had magnetically sexy good looks, particularly his striking eyes – brilliant, surrounded by long, dark lashes, and challengingly direct – and the physique that made many of his tribe superb athletes. Johnson recalled his first meeting with the Ugandan. Rag day in Cambridge, and a board, high bar and mats for gymnastics had been set up in the main quadrangle of his college in the hope of attracting donations from spectators. Sseru had been performing flips and somersaults with a grace and skill far beyond Johnson's imagining. Before the days of TV and Olga Korbut, people perceived gymnastics as a boring business. Chilled youngsters queueing in a gym to attempt to bounce off a springboard over a painfully hard horse as in escape films of the 1940s. This was something of a dauntingly different order. That it was performed by a black African –fairly rare in the Cambridge of the 1950s – made it even more striking. But unfortunately for Sseru's display, the citizenry were being fascinated by a rival attraction outside, the 'capture' of the Senior Tutor from the college's first floor windows on Emmanuel Street outside. Every 5 minutes the Don was being roped up and dragged from the window in cap and gown, protesting wildly, across a ladder and down into the roof of a spoof ambulance, where he was auctioned to the crowd. So Sseru was performing to a zero audience, but he seemed to be performing all the better for it. A tribute perhaps to the Anglican, stoic upbringing from which he was later to rebel. Kipling's *If–*, and all that. Johnson watched for a while, then moved to the capture scene outside. When he returned the young Ugandan was towelling off and Johnson offered to help dismantle the kit. They got talking, and Johnson found out Sseru was training for the Ugandan Civil Service. After that they lost touch, but Johnson remembered the double somersault which Sseru was to show off dramatically, and in a savage context, four years later.

Back up-country in Kabale after the course at Entebbe, Sseru occasionally met the Katikiro's daughter, Sarah. She was a vibrant young Muchiga of 18, educated at Kyambogo, with an immense sense of humour, and a vein of seriousness, particularly about her nascent country, which often surprised him.

Sseru, as a young Mututsi District Officer-to-be, originally met with her strong disapproval. The sharp vein of throwaway cynicism that peppered his conversation, the immensely strong hold he had over his friends – 'Sseru says' was a constant phrase in their vocabularies – and the arrogance which he often showed, all combined to set her hackles up. So no doubt did his challenging eyes. Apart from that her venerable father and firm mother spoke of him with distaste as an upcoming go-getter, unprincipled and un-Christian.

The young man couldn't get her face out of his dreams, and set out to court and conquer her – conquering being the attitude to women common among his tribe, sex and age group.

Life in Kabale for the young Africans at the top of society was almost as claustrophobic as it was for the 14 whites and the Asians. For well-educated graduates from Makerere or UK universities, any relationship with their age-set who had not had so privileged an education bristled with potential conflict and resentment. So parties and similar get-togethers were among a limited number of youngsters, and among this set Sarah and Sseru inevitably rubbed shoulders. Sseru carefully suppressed his natural ebullience when she was around. He became courteous and considerate, so much so that his friends noticed and

96

commented. He got to talk to her in the bar of the White Horse Inn, about the coming years and what they would hold. His striking good looks, especially his liquid brown eyes, held her attention and sometimes seemed mesmeric. On occasion he would stare into her eyes, apparently losing the thread of his conversation and lapsing into complete silence. She was disconcerted and excited.

The Katikiro became worried for his only daughter. He distrusted the young man and all he stood for – the rapidly unfolding growth of change, throwing over Christian values, sweeping away the missionary-engendered concerns that had brought the Chiga from the fifth century to the twentieth in the space of 60 short years. He had a particularly close friendship with the District Commissioner, a friendship which was rare in times when the DC was careful to keep a detached and impartial stance between the 2 rival churches, Protestant and Catholic, which dominated politics, and between both religions against the commercial and secular leaders of the tribe.

Sseru's session with the DC was explosive – Thruston warned him that to be impartial, and to be seen to be impartial, was a vital part of being a senior civil servant. Involvement with the daughter of a leader of one section of local society was not in the traditions of the service. The young man later recounted his fury at Thruston's interference. Johnson tried to ease the situation, pointing out that the tide was with Sseru and his generation; Thruston and the British administrators would be leaving inside 5 years. The country would be ruled by Sseru's generation.

'Yes,' said Sseru. 'But by who in my generation? Not by the administrators, by the soldiers or by the lawyers. Or by the demagogues. You heard what Obote said in Legco[24] when the Bugandan KY chap got obstreperous – "May I remind the Honourable Member for Mmengo"... ' He drawled it again for effect, '... "May I remind the Honourable Member for Mmengo, that eighty per cent of the soldiers in the KAR, in the Kings African Rifles, come from my districts, from Teso and Acholi?" Power will come from a mobster or from the barrel of a gun.'

Two weeks later, Sseru submitted his resignation to the DC in a bitter interview. Johnson was reminded, looking back, of the famous meeting over dinner in February 1955 between Prime Minister Anthony Eden and President Gamal Abdel Nasser of Egypt. The meeting that helped spark off the Suez War. The trouble there had been not the confrontation as caricatured in popular fancy, between an arrogant, culturally ignorant Brit and an up-and-coming Egyptian nationalist, one of many clichés which rarely occur in real life. No, it had been between a British PM who knew the Arab world and had affection for it, who was able to greet Nasser in his own language, and who had close links with the traditional Arab leaders. Eden's knowledge of and affection for Arab culture was anathema to Nasser as an ardent new generation nationalist. 'Talking down at me as if I was a junior official,' he wrote. Oil and water. So it was between Thruston and Sseru.

Sseru threw a party for his Kabale friends, then left for his shambas (smallholdings) in Bufumbira.

A month later, there was a visit by the armoured currency van from the Ugandan treasury. These visits happened every three years or so, in this case to collect vast quantities of used 10 shilling notes for careful destruction. Johnson was in the White Horse Inn for a drink when he met the Treasury official. There was a worried look on his face.

'All OK?' Johnson asked him. The Treasury man, Shepherd, recounted his problem. Trying to start the vehicle and move off after lunch, it had failed to fire. There had been no signs before lunch of incipient trouble, so they had got mechanics from Dihr's Engineering in the town. They couldn't fix it, and he'd had to get the crates of notes off-loaded into the strongroom at the Boma, and leave the truck for repair overnight. Arrangements with the police escort might well go awry. Johnson sympathised, and wondered if he should cancel the day's sailing on Lake Bunyonyi he'd long promised himself for the next day. No, he decided. Crime in these remote parts was still rare and usually petty. He recalled deciding once as a fledgling administrator, still on probation, on a surprise visit to inspect the local prison. Mid-morning in the fierce, dry heat of Bufumbira, under the volcanoes and a bright blue sky. Delightful – like being on a sudden unearned holiday, except this was work. He had been astonished to find the prison gates wide open, and no one around. Worried, he had hammered on the steel gates with a rock. Eventually a prisoner had appeared.

'Where are the guards and prisoners?' Johnson had demanded.

'Why Ssebo,' answered the prisoner, 'in the fields of course.'

'Show me.'

The prisoner had taken him about half a mile to see a line of men hoeing in ragged disorder. It seemed a dangerously lax approach to the penal system. Johnson had taken it up with the chief later. The chief had explained, 'These people, if they escape to their homes their families will only send them back again because the Gombolola Court and the chiefs have decided they have transgressed. So they stay here. Or else they run away to Buganda and we are finished with them.' That was the system; no need for iron bars and clanging gates, society would take care of offenders.

Not a culture, thought Johnson, to beget bullion robberies. So he decided to leave the Treasury guy with his problem and go for his day's sailing, as planned.

Meanwhile, overnight in Dihr's Engineering someone was working on the truck with a shaded light and welding torch. He fixed a pin to the inside rim of the nearside front wheel, and a complicated gadget including a sharp blade and a bicycle milometer at top dead centre on the back of the brake drum. The milometer was set at 9988.4. Then he spun the wheel to check the striker was making contact satisfactorily. Finally he opened the bonnet, and replaced the faulty distributor arm that had immobilised the truck with the good one. He slipped off into the night.

The next morning, six-tenths of a mile beyond milestone 7 on the Bufumbira road there was a group of Rwandan Hutu nationalists. Like their rival tribe, the Rwandan Tutsi, they used Uganda as a safe haven in the run-up to independence, which the Belgian government in Brussels had suddenly decreed, in panic, for July 1960. They concealed themselves, waiting.

At milestone 6 is a junction, and a left turn up a Bulungi bw'ansi ('good of the country') track. It wound through the hills, past Chabahinga and some village markets, and back to the main road 15 miles later. The treasury 15 hundredweight came to a stop at the junction. The driver saw a notice: 'Trunk road closed for bridge repairs, proceed via Chabahinga.'

He stopped and rapped on the little window into the back. Shepherd, in the armoured rear cabin, unlocked the window and spoke to him. After a while, despite the absence of the police escort, they set off up the Chabahinga track. As they disappeared, two Hutu came out of the bushes and removed the notice. An hour later, the police motorcycles roared past, ignoring the turn, bent on catching up with the 15 hundred-weight truck they were supposed to be escorting. The corrugations in the murrum road surface seemed particularly vicious; both had splitting headaches from the previous night's party. They could remember little between early in the party, drinking some filthy-tasting waragi and being woken up in the bar late in the morning. When the police inquired later in their investigation of the case, the bar tender had 'gone to Buganda.'[25]

The truck ground along the side road and came to a halt. They let Shepherd out and he saw the reason. A herd of elephants straddled the ford and blocked their way. They pressed the truck's hooter, but the elephants paid not a blind bit of attention. A Mutwa pygmy watched with interest, skin-clad and stinking. Shepherd remembered that the Batwa pygmies from the forests were said to have a close affinity with the natural world. Shepherd discussed this with Bitakuri, the driver. They agreed to try offering the Mutwa 10 shillings if he could clear the elephants, and so they did. He turned towards the herd and harangued them in the typical Mutwa voice, a sort of strangulated high-pitched squeal with a curious bass undertone.

'What's he saying?' asked Shepherd.

'He say "Elephants bugger off".'

But they didn't. They paid not a blind bit of attention. The Mutwa was frantic to get the 10 shillings. He picked up a large handful of stones, ran towards the leading male and hurled them at him. The elephant shuffled peevishly, flapped his ears vaguely, then led his followers away. The truck crossed the ford and continued along the track.

Johnson, with the same panache that characterised many whites in this exotic setting, had acquired for himself a Hornet racing dinghy. A slim, light, Jack Holt-designed 16-footer, it had

100

a tall mainsail, narrow jib, and a sliding seat, normally for the second member of the crew. But crews were in short supply in the small township, and he sailed it single-handed, perched often at the end of the seat 3 feet outside the hull, to balance the thrust of the wind. With only one person aboard, the boat would plane easily, taking off quickly in a gust and surfing over the waves. Johnson would be exhilarated as the spray flew out from the forefoot, often up to and above the gunwales. Until the gust died suddenly, or he slipped, or he caught the tiller extension in the mainsheet or any of the outrageous strokes of fortune which bedevil sailors. Then the boat would capsize, sometimes throwing him high over the mainsail into the water, sometimes rolling to windward, dipping the sliding seat and sweeping him off into the water to flounder in the dinghy's wake.

He rigged the dinghy, slid it down into the water, and cajoled the boat to get it out of the little cove and into the main lake. Then he hit the wind and sped away towards Chabahinga. Bunyonyi is a long valley lake, with 2 arms, about twice the size of Windermere in the English Lakes. Because of its depth and the fringe of dense papyrus there is little life there and the fishing is poor – the oxygen is drained out of the streams as they enter it. So the shores were usually deserted, and the only vessels were a few dugout canoes and the Government launch. One of Johnson's pet projects was to get the lake used as a trade channel – a flat, maintenance-free, cheap route into the town and markets. He had got the construction of a quay under at Chabahinga and he sailed down, running before the wind, to look at it. Above him on the hill he picked out a 15 hundredweight truck, bouncing no doubt on the tortuous bends.

Show him the way home, he thought. He reached up onto a parallel course to the truck's and pulled away slightly. Then the wind eased and the truck gained on him.

Then the pin on the inside rim of the truck's nearside rear wheel struck the cog, and the milometer clocked over from 9999.9 to 0000.0. The blade swung into the sidewall of the tyre, slashing it open and bursting it. In the cab, the driver fought to keep the truck on the road. But a sharp right bend was ahead; he couldn't hold it, and they toppled over the edge. The truck bounced and rolled with growing speed from one outcrop to the next, still upright as the driver rolled the wheel frantically to steer with the fall. Then it hit the water with an immense splash. The truck wallowed on the surface, drifting out with its impetus and the wind. Johnson sailed past, horrified. He saw Shepherd looking dazedly out through the armoured rear window. He remembered the standard man-overboard drill of the times; gybe at once is the fastest way back to the person. In this case the person of course was a 2 man truck, but the theory still applied. Gybe, then back again. But the truck was sinking rapidly. He had somehow to keep the dinghy alongside it while he tried to rescue the inmates. The answer; capsize alongside, then swim to them. But the dinghy will drift away while you attempt rescue. So, capsize to windward of the truck. But the dinghy will turn upside down if you leave it. So, capsize so that the mast rests on the truck roof. But what if the truck sinks? Pass. Don't know...

He sailed the boat up to windward, then dropped down into the lee side of the cockpit, freeing the main and going over gradually. She filled, and the mast rested atop the truck as planned. The driver had already opened the cab door. 'I don't swim!' he shouted in alarm. Johnson swam across with the mainsheet.

'Pull yourself to the boat with that, if the truck goes down,' he gasped. 'I'll have a go at the back.'

'It's locked.'

'Give me the key.'

'I don't have. Only Bwana Shepherd has.'

'Christ!'

Johnson swam round to the rear, and hammered on the door. He could see inside only dimly. No sign of Shepherd, and the water was rising. The driver saw the problem, felt around in the cab, and found a wheelbrace. He handed it to Johnson, who scrabbled desperately trying to get a fulcrum on the door against which he could lever and break open the handle. But even when he did, the bodywork just bent. The truck was settling.

No hope, Johnson decided. He'd get the driver to the dinghy; otherwise he would drown with Shepherd. He took off his buoyancy aid.

'Here, put this coat on. It will keep you up in the water. Then pull yourself to the back end of the boat. Like the back of a

102

canoe. Not the side of the boat, or it will turn over. Just like a canoe would turn over. Not the pointed front. The flat back. Pull on the wooden post and the rope. *Tikwo?'*

'*Yeego, Ssebo.'*

Aid on and courageously, but gingerly, the driver lowered himself into the water.

Johnson stayed with the truck, distraught but helpless. After a minute or so it lurched and bubbled and sank. Mercifully there was no sign of Shepherd, who must have been unconscious as he drowned.

The driver had followed instructions and held the bow, but even so the dinghy turned almost upside down once the truck's support was lost. Johnson could not right it. They decided to abandon it and made for the shore. Some smallholders helped them through the papyrus, then the Mutongole chief arrived and a market truck took them back to Kabale township.

Frogmen were rushed up two days later. They found the vehicle in only 15 feet of water – the shallowness explained the difficulty in righting the Hornet. The mast had stuck in the mud. They hitched a cable to the truck's axle, and a tractor power offtake was used to winch it ashore. As it slowly emerged from the water the door swung open. Shepherd's body was on the floor. But the crates with the used notes were gone.

Johnson talked over the robbery with the OC Police, and followed up the investigations as they progressed. Oddly, there was no sign of any increase in old 10 shilling notes in circulation. They found out about the tinkering with the truck's engine in Dihr's Engineering. The welding job had been to attach a cycle milometer to the wheel rim and demobilise the truck at mile 11.6 on the main road. The rival party had presumably heard the plan, set up the diversions to Chabahinga, and saw the truck tumble down into the lake. That must have been a facer for them, particularly when Johnson had planed into view, precarious on his Hornet. But they must have reacted remarkably well: getting someone 15 feet down from the surface to the truck, crowbarring the door open, and removing the cases. Fiendishly difficult without diving kit, but many of the Bakiga fishermen from Rwensama were accomplished swimmers.

The police in those times were well in touch with the dissident groups who were vying for supremacy as independence approached. In a pleasing touch of African logic, the local Special Branch policeman was well known and liked. Indeed he'd been chosen as Group Secretary for one subversive organisation on the grounds that his recording skills were clearly outstanding and he had access to a government typewriter.

Through these contacts the police soon managed to track down the originators of the 'bullion' robbery, a Hutu nationalist group from Rwanda. But who the people were who diverted the truck round the lake and escaped with the notes was astonishingly blank.

Johnson kept his suspicions to himself, but was continuously reminded of a joint safari with Sseru to Bufumbira, the county of the volcanoes. Johnson and Sseru had been climbing up Sabinio. It's the oldest geologically of the East African 'cooking pot' volcanoes. A homely name (like so many Bantu names) for some formidable peaks – up to 17,000 feet.[26] Sabinio is unlike the crisp cone of Mount Muhavura from a distance (but when you get to climb it even Muhavura seems no relation to its clean slag heap-shaped silhouette when seen from 50 miles away). Sabinio means 'the old man' and that's what the mountain looks like; an irregular, vaguely triangular shape, but broken, wrinkly and seamed and holed by the erosion, storms and eruptions of ages. This has produced some spectacular cliffs. The cliffs are in fact even more daunting than they might at first appear, because near the equator and with high rainfall on fine soil, vegetation clings precariously on to any conceivable toehold, disguising some foot-tinglingly vertiginous drops and overhangs which look straight down into the bamboo forests below. The vegetation is that astonishing mix of giant groundsel, giant lobelia and other high-level plants that you only find, like tiny isolated pools, parting the thin winds of the upper atmosphere. Pools of rare flora at the crests of the 5 great mountains which span East Africa dramatically: The Virunga volcanoes, the Ruwenzoris or 'Mountains of the Moon', Elgon, Kenya and Kilimanjaro. Snows and glaciers bang on the Equator. Many Victorians had ridiculed the idea, and scoffed at the explorers who talked of it. The first, John Hanning Speke told of what he had seen. And when people attacked his account he still knew what he had seen. The tension between the truth and the public's perception was too much for him, and he killed himself with a shotgun in a Cheshire field. This was on the day before the confrontation at which his ideas were to be debated at the Royal Geographical Society. Tebse meetings massively popular, like block buster movies.

Sseru and Johnson had set off with a party of 8 porters from the saddle camp in a meadow at 10,000 feet in the bamboos that lie above the rainforests. They climbed through the aged hagenia trees, flat-limbed armchairs for the gorillas, sometimes 8 feet through, festooned in ferns, mosses, orchids and other epiphytes. In the mists it was a remote, sombre, ominous landscape. Then at the base of the climb they entered a strange rock tunnel, about 8 feet wide and 30 long. This had for aeons been the main trail for the big game – elephant, gorilla and a few buffalo – still in those times carrying the footprints of elephants (poached out in the 1970s) in a sculpted track like those carved by cattle on English hills. Then up into the even higher altitude vegetation, hagenia giving way to the lovely yellow-flowering hypericum tree, and the immensely tough Vernonia which was later to determine Sseru's fate. Like the miracle Winged bean tree does for humans, Vernonia used to provide everything your gorilla needs – food, bedding, leisure playing, right through from the nutty buds to the rotting branches. After 5 hours, the party eventually reached the summit trig point. Strange to find such a small Western artefact atop these remote mountain giants.

Climbing was through the bamboo jungle where Dian Fossey was, arguably,[27] to save the last mountain gorillas dramatically from extinction. She did it by terrorising the local poachers at night by haunting them from the jungle.

Sseru's and Johnson's porters may well have included some of those who were later to be Dian's murderers; they were an argumentative, raucous-laughed bunch who had little regard for Sseru. Who was he, this jumped up Mututsi who had somehow got to become Bwana Edisi, an Assistant District Commissioner? They had the climbing and gorilla trade (minuscule anyway in those days) neatly sewn up, working for Walter Baumgartel, the owner of the Traveller's Rest Hotel, and they wanted to keep it that way. The less they saw of black officials they didn't know, the better. Particularly black officials of the wrong sort of tribe.

At the summit there was an argument between Sseru and the porters about how to spend the night; Sseru ordered them to construct a conical wigwam from the lobelia; thick, 5-foot or so tall, cactus-like stems, but hollow and easily chopped down. They gave a hollow 'thock' as the *pangas* sliced through their cardboard-thin walls. But the porters believed they'd done enough, and only complied with reluctance and continuing jibes.

'*Hakuzire nyoko,*'[28] muttered one under his breath, but deliberately loud enough to be heard. The others laughed harshly. A black Edisi didn't rate greatly for them. Neither fish nor fowl, nor good white tilapia. Sseru stiffened, then relaxed and ignored the jibe.

Johnson and Sseru strolled around the area as dark was falling. A wide ledge led around the cliff; horizontal, easy to walk along, but with the sort of drop on the outside that has most humans breathing tensely and tingling – the electric feeling in the hands and feet that make you think of a soprano shrieking a top F; but shrieking completely silently. They rounded the cliff and came upon a slightly wider platform, which ended the ledge. Onto it there opened a blowhole. High, black and forbidding. Not like typical blowholes. Gothic and narrow. On the edge of the cliff, 20 feet beyond the cave entrance and a bit below, was a rare gnarled tree. It looked tough, twisted and springy like a South African stinkwood, but surely it couldn't be at this latitude. A horizontal branch reached out over space. At right angles beyond stood a brief, steep slope, clad densely in vegetation, scree no doubt underneath it. The scree sloped down to a heart-thumping chasm, which dropped to the bamboo forest far down on the saddle.

'Howsabout that for a fine swinging bar for your gymnastics?' joked Johnson, pointing at the branch. His fingers pricked at the thought.

'A doddle, old boy. Swing right out to that scree. No problem. Some other day, perhaps,' Sseru grinned companionably.

Johnson was to recall the comment.

They returned to the camp, ate, and settled down for the night.

'I was trained as a boy scout. This is the correct way to do it,' said Sseru with evident satisfaction as they moved into his lean-to.

The porters made off to their own choice of spot in the lee of a cliff, lit their pipes and broached their beer calabashes. Later they snugged down patiently in their ancient, thick, incredibly dirty army greatcoats, acquired by devious means from the King's African Rifles.

Johnson and Sseru slid into their sleeping bags on the rough ground and tried to get off to sleep. After an hour's tossing and turning, Johnson heard the night wind set in. Gradually he felt drips pattering onto his bag and face as the wigwam of lobelia and branches trawled the high-altitude wind stream and dredged it of moisture, dripping it onto him. After 20 minutes he was getting soaked, and he suggested they moved into the open. Sseru refused.

'We must show these people the right way to do such things.'

Johnson moved out into the open. The mist eased. But the far-off glow of the live crater of Nyamulagira made him feel even colder. At last they finished a damp and fitful night. As soon as light dawned slightly, they set off down again, tacitly dropping the planned breakfast at the summit – bacon and sausages grilled over a blazing fire as they looked across perhaps the most spectacular panorama in Africa. Still, the sight of Muhavura's dark, craggy flanks towering across the saddle from them at sunset had been one to store and savour.

After half an hour's descent through the mists, they suddenly broke through below the clouds into sunshine. Sseru suggested a halt, and then gathered the porters around him.

Johnson stood and immersed himself in the view, then tensed with surprise. The great 20 mile wide gap of the western Rift Valley lay crystal clear below, tiny pimples showing the peppering of small, aged volcanoes. As the eyes raised higher, there were the Kigezi Highlands, precariously bunded and hoed or clad in jungle bamboo, ranges of the Batwa pygmies and of elephants. Achingly beautiful. Then even further off the grassy downlands of the Bahima cattle keepers, then a layer of white cloud. Enough to marvel at in itself. But then, astonishingly, above the cloud, a jagged line of tiny crystal-white daggers was sharp against the blue equatorial sky. The Speke peak of the Ruwenzoris, 16,795 feet high and all of 200 miles distant. Stanley[29] and many other explorers had watched and waited fruitlessly, often for weeks, for a glimpse of these, the great Nile sources. Fount of the mysterious river, the greatest in all Africa, all the world, which flowed unceasingly with no tributaries, the lifeblood, 4,500 miles of fertility, through the world's greatest, youngest desert, the Sahara, and succouring the Egyptian civilization, the world's first. Superlative piled on superlative. The founts of the river had been sought, challenged and fiercely debated since Claudius Ptolemy publicised the rumour of them in the second century AD. Snow-covered peaks on the equator? Impossible.

Sseru meanwhile had been chatting with the obstreperous porters in Runyarwanda, gradually getting them to smile, then laugh, then guffaw uproariously. Johnson approached them smiling slightly, hoping to be let in on the joke.

The porters' leader stood up in front of his fellows with courteous assertiveness, looked around them all, then turned back to Johnson and addressed him: '*Edisi onu, yatugambye, Bwana.*' (This ADC has spoken (well), Bwana.)

Johnson pointed out the view. Sseru talked to them all.

'*Yego. Yego. Nikwo,*' they replied. (Yes, yes that's the way of it.)

'I was explaining,' he told Johnson, 'how that great peak and that great distance are the peak and the distance for our Ugandan people in the years to come.'

For which Ugandan people, Johnson wondered. He would get an answer a few months later.

*****

Thinking over the mountain trip and Sseru's abrupt resignation, Johnson had an inkling that that and the robbery might be linked. He told Cottesloe, the OC Police, and the police visited Sseru's main *shambas* but found nothing to excite suspicion. There had been a family of Batwa pygmies in one of the *shambas* near the mountains, but Batutsi sometimes kept them for affection's sake and to do assorted tasks. A sort of throw-back to the semi-slavery of pre-colonial times.

So where might the loot be stashed? Bufumbira was an immensely overpopulated county in which secure secret hiding places might be hard to find. But there were no clues, and there it was left for the while.

This was the period at which independence for Ruanda

rapidly approached; the Belgian Government had suddenly announced 3 months earlier that Zaire and Ruanda-Urundi would be given independence in 6 months. The potential for violence and chaos, which Johnson had sometimes felt in these remote parts of Central Africa, suddenly erupted. Intrigue and misrule rapidly burst out. The Hutu/Tutsi rivalries escalated across the border and Johnson was posted to the frontier county, Bufumbira.

Then full independence had come and soon cut off all official communication with Ruanda. They were turbulent times.

During his enforced stay, Johnson mulled frequently over the whereabouts of the 10 shilling notes. After resigning, Sseru had gone into uncharacteristically quiet activity on his *shambas*, getting the bunds rehabilitated, planting new arabica coffee bushes; even some innovative tea shrubs. A model small farmer: not his style at all. Johnson recalled the Batwa pygmies on his *shamba* – the tribe who inhabited the forests and mountains before the Europeans came. If he were Sseru and had organised the robbery, he would stash the proceeds somewhere in the mountain massif accessible from either country. Johnson resolved to go up on the saddle and camp over the weekend on his next safari. Spot gorillas with Reuben Rwanzagyire perhaps, and keep an eye open.

Three months later Johnson followed Sseru and his two companions up the mountain, through the early morning mist. He kept well out of sight. He was pretty well certain he knew the destination. They went up the flanks, onto the saddle, then after a rest, on and up again. As they approached the elephants' tunnel he noticed movement in the bamboos to his left. He froze. Several men came out onto the track, following Sseru's party. They carried rifles. They shadowed Sseru. Johnson debated trying to skirt round and ahead to warn him, but there was no way of getting through the bamboo off track without crashing through like a buffalo or elephant. In any case, despite the weight of the Kalashnikovs, Sseru was moving fast. Johnson had no choice but to shadow them.

Eventually they approached the cave and ledge. Johnson watched the Hutu from above. The Hutu watched Sseru. He and his companions were still unawares, but one of them guarded the start of the ledge. They worked in the blowhole, moving out

109

2 cases. The Hutu bided their time, then started moving in. Johnson shouted, 'Sseru, you're being attacked!' There was a burst of fire from the Hutu. Sseru's lookout lent out from a corner in the ledge. He remembered his training: aim low. He sighted, then fired and one man tumbled. He fired again, then a sudden blow in the chest. Didn't hurt too much. Shoot again. He tried to drag his body together but slid to the rock. Steadier here, he thought. I'll shoot from here. But his arms wouldn't respond. He slumped, and his life ebbed swiftly away.

Sseru's second companion kept up a steady sniping. Johnson heard movement on his left. They had spotted him.

'*Iwe, Mujungu, Rugaho!*' shouted one of the Hutu. ('You, Whitey, bugger off!')

The others bunched ready to rush the ledge.

'They're coming!' shouted Johnson.

'*Iwe, Mike, Rugaho*! Bugger off mate! Not your problem!' Sseru called in reply.

Sseru shoved the first cases of 10 bob notes over the drop. One case broke and a fluttering of grubby notes spun in the wind. The Hutu shouted angrily and approached. Sseru's second companion shot at them, but was shot in his turn, and the Hutu moved in. Trapped, Sseru fired several bursts. Then dodged a few feet along the ledge, gauging the gap across to the scree. He ran and leaped for the branch of the tree. He swung on it as if on the bars in a gymnasium, thence up in a parabola giving a high call. Triumph; defiance; suicide? He crashed down into the lobelia, grasping for a handhold. But they were too fragile. He slithered down the scree clutching frantically. Then he fell away over the edge, spinning slowly like the Hitchcock villain slithering off the torch on the Statue of Liberty, on and on down into the bamboo forest.

The Hutu examined the cave. Johnson left hastily, and took shelter as night fell. The next day he went with the police to search for Sseru's body. The saddle had been alive with jubilant smallholders harvesting 10 bob notes, who scattered rapidly as officialdom approached. But there was no sign of the body, even though they searched the thick bamboo as thoroughly as six of them could. The mountain people kept silence, and nothing more was heard of Sseru.

Upside 2019, Chapter 14B: Transgap

In Cambridge in 2019, the Transgap project meetings flowed past. There was much surmise about PIG. It was probably some sort of virtual brain, carrying out the sort of functions Wittgenstein proposed in his Exercise machine. Monitoring and encouraging its clients. A sort of mechanical father confessor, or counsellor. Quite easy to monitor the client's irises, pulse rate, sweatiness of the palms and so on. A primitive version of Dragon naturally speaking had been around at the point of divergence in 1990. They could have developed it considerably to recognise much human speech, and also the tone of voice, rhythm, pitch, cadence and even stress. It was resolved that Johnson had to continue as one transgapant together with a partner, and that Tilley and a talking brain should be the second team.

Gaskin's actions were analysed at length. From his first words to Johnson he had seemed well-disposed towards a critical reassessment of PIG. So did he in the meeting in the Fellows bog. And what was the business with the powder? Whatever it was, it seemed friendly in intent. But what had caused Gaskin to identify and talk to Johnson in the first place? Perhaps the original message from Downside, the original paper tape message which had started the whole project, had come from Gaskin. Had it been he who was appealing for help? Then, in the evening. Johnson and the other guy had been outside Gaskin's room and overheard him on the phone. What was he going on about? The talk had been about the November event near the Straits bridge? Which Straits and which bridge? Probably had to be the Menai Straits since they were near the old nuclear power station at Trawsfynydd, which was believed to supply much of their power. Who was the woman Gaskin was talking about so keenly? Why was she chosen for whatever the November job was? Then again, surely Gaskin could have talked to them, then let them get away safely. Why did he create the Security 5 alert, whatever that was, which had called in the POPs?

Some people suspected a devious attempt by Gaskin to build up his own role within the organisation, the Benevernment as they called it, by alerting it to Johnson's activities. A bit like an agent provocateur. Others felt that Gaskin had been well aware he was under surveillance, and had taken the emergency action that the organisation would have expected of one of its top men, while yet giving Johnson and Gervon at least a slim chance of escape. Hence the cup of coffee spilt over the keyboard. And that also was why he gave the wrong staircase in his alert message. Staircase B, not P. Or was that just a gesture to reassure Johnson? Mike was himself uncertain about Gaskin. He recalled Gaskin's final glance at him from the keyboard. Flat, unemotional. No warmth in it. Then he remembered, as he did nightly, another figure, slender, with dark hair. Nadine. But not, thank God, the Nadine Upside on the telly.

He held his peace. He was going to go back for sure. Regardless. Willy nilly. No question about it, he was.

He was given a session in the Neural Computing lab with the possible transgapants. There were three available, and Johnson had a session with each.

Each was immersed in blood-like plasma in a glass tank, with connections presumably to and from the blood supply. More interesting was an optical fibre cable coming out of the tank and into an interface box on the outside. They pointed out the various connections; the 12 volt external power supply, the parallel printer port, the RS 232 comms interface to a modem and the 200 Gigaherz bus for second or more brain connections. The first tank was labelled 'Nassani'. Tilley's favourite, he said.

'He's a Mukiga, but from Bufumbira. Try communicating with him,' said Tilley.

'How?'

'Plug the modem in to the amplifier and say something into the mike.'

He did so:

'Greetings, Nassani.'

No response.

He tried again: 'Orairegye?' Have you slept well?

'Yego.' Yes, came the response, but slurred and high pitched.

'Agandi?' How's things at home?

'Ni marungi. Izina ryawe n'oha?' They're good (even if the guy's a disembodied brain in a glass tank and they're far from all right). What's your name?

'Ndi Johnson.' I'm Johnson.

The greetings came close to exhausting Johnson's long over-laid recollections of the language. Then he remembered a proverb.

'Mpora mpora ekahitsya ekinyangondokyera aha iziba,' he stumbled. Illustrating the causative. Ekahitsya. To cause something to arrive somewhere. Hika – reach, okuhika – the infinitive, to reach. Okuhitsya – to cause something to reach somewhere, ekiokuhitsya – the thing which causes something to reach somewhere. Slowly slowly gets the earthworm to the well. The tortoise beats the hare. A grammar as complex as Latin with up to 14 noun classes; and all somehow evolved throughout the hundreds of Bantu languages of sub-Saharan Africa without benefit of any conscious discussion. Gradually mapped, according to Chomsky, onto the universal transformational grammar which is in a child's brain from birth or even earlier. Astonishing. Mind bending. Indicative, subjunctive, imperative, reflexive, passive, active, far future, future, present continuous, present, imperfect, perfect, pluperfect. And that's just the verbs.

'Well now, there's a thing,' said the transgapant.

'Good God, it's Sseru! Ka tugambe Rwingereza.' Let's speak English, pleaded Johnson.

'OK. But it's good to hear your own language again occasionally. Even if spoken as badly as you!'

With mounting pleasure and a sense of unreality, Johnson found himself swapping reminiscences with Sseru. Had he heard any more about the Katikiro's daughter? She, said Sseru, had died with many Christians in Amin's time. But what had happened to Johnson? Johnson explained that he had reached Kisoro the day after the fight on the mountain. Then he went with a rescue party to find Sseru's body. The saddle had been alive with jubilant Banyaruanda, gathering up used ten bob notes which were lying around in the bamboos. But there had been no sign of Sseru's body. Sseru filled in; Batwa rescuers had found his body, and called a Rwandan Medical Assistant. He had felt for a pulse.

'A kyali kwitsya. Ka tumutware aha hospitali.' He is alive. Let us hasten to the hospital.

They had done so; the party had carried his body on a bamboo stretcher down the south side of the mountains to the Mission Hospital in Rwanda. There, Sseru was put on life-support of a sort, then moved to Kigali, the Rwandan capital, and eventually to a brain clinic in Brussels. Then after discussion with the Ugandan High Commission, the PVS body had been transferred years later to UCHL in London.

Tilley went out to get some coffee.

'What's your opinion of all this?' Johnson asked quickly.

'Interesting,' replied Sseru, 'you'll recall I'm not one for the contemplative life.'

'You can say that again! But this will be pretty risky too.'

'Indeed. A pleasure. Remember our chase on the volcano?'

They talked on.

'So, we go into it together then?' asked Sseru.

'Fine by me.'

Johnson felt he'd like to shake hands. He patted the side of the casing to cement the agreement.

Tilley returned a while later and they chatted further over coffee, commiserating with the transgapant that he couldn't partake of the brew.

'Why do you call him Sseru?' asked Tilley. Johnson explained that it was a nickname, short for Nassani's full name, Sserulyamayengye – jokey guy.

Then Tilley and Johnson moved off to talk to the other possible transgapants.

Over the next two weeks they gradually assembled a plan for two teams. Team 1, Johnson and A. N. Other would get back to Downside via the first prototype in the maths Lab.

Team 2, Tilley and Sseru, who had been selected as the talking brain to interface with PIG, would get across via the Magnox reactor at Trawsfynydd, which must have been providing most of the power for the north-west Downside. The rest of the atomic power stations were so close to the sea they had probably shut down, gone critical or whatever after the error occurred, the operators died and the seas became hypertoxic. How to get back to the right universe, space, time and so forth should be fairly easy because someone had thought to plant a return address, the equivalent of a subroutine link, in Register A3. The schedule to get the whole shooting match on the road by the end of the financial year was fairly tough. The first coincident wormhole was in May, but Stag would be in the States then. So they would take the next, on June 7th.

However, as June 7th approached, various development problems hit the Trawsfynydd group, Team 2. After battles between Quality Assurance and Development, it was reluctantly conceded that their departure had to be delayed until July 4th, the window following. Then Team 1 was hit by the sudden death of Johnson's colleague. It was a long-shot anyway, and there was the problem with Johnson and the woman. Perhaps they should drop it completely. Stag and Kealey put it to Johnson. He argued the opposite vigorously, and reluctantly they let him go alone. He could have a go with the old balls in the maths lab.

It was a downbeat affair. Kealey and Stag were there to see Johnson off, but the Eland house people were tied up. The three had a cup of tea together, shook hands, and Johnson gripped the balls nervously and duly disappeared.

Downside, 7th June 2019, Chapter 14C: Barmouth

Arrived back in Downside on June 7th, Johnson slipped into the garden shed in the Emmanuel Fellows garden to sleep and recover. The next day he hung around the maths lab and waylaid Gaskin. The latter looked at him in astonishment, motioned him into a side alley, and fixed to rendezvous in Gaskin's office at 3pm.

Left to his own devices, Johnson wandered off and along the Backs. Cambridge seemed unchanged. He lay on the lawns that sweep down from Kings College to the river. Blue sky and rippling water. Graceful worn stone bridges. He drifted into the Chapel, and let his eyes wander over the splendid, fanning tracery of John Wastell's glorious white stone vaulting. Then outside and later down Petty Curie. He suddenly saw, across the Curie, an old mate, Alun apWilliams. He called to him, and apWilliams turned. They pointed accusingly at each other, crossed delighted to the middle and grasped hands.

'Good God,' said Johnson, 'it's Nogoodboyo. The all-Welsh Welshman indeed to goodness yes.'

'Mike. The Anglo-No-Brain Saxon, the Sassunach. They let you out of college then. Are you well?'

'Yes, I am well. Are you well?'

'Yes I am well.'

'It would seem that we both are well. But what on earth brings you here? Many years, isn't it? Splendid to see you. I think the first time since we brought *Lady Amanda* up to Barmouth. But I'm meeting with a guy called Gaskin at three.'

'Ah. I know him vaguely. A top PIG man. Look, I'm also in a hurry right now. But why not meet up this evening?'

'OK. The Mill, at 7.30?' The Mill was a pub on the Backs, just alongside Garret Hostel Bridge.

'7.30 it is. See you then. Look forward to hearing about your old boat.'

apWilliams was a pale faced Liverpudlian, a kid through the blitz. Rather blunt and square features, nose particularly sharp, often given to a cackle of derisive laughter, but otherwise friendly. Natural leader of their group in the Royal Signals. A rather off-the-wall character, and one of his peculiarities had been a love for a collapsing old Vertue sloop, all of fifty years old, which he had been trying to restore. Time had been out-running his great endeavour; no sooner would one plank or frame be replaced than the dreaded tell-tale whiskers of soggy wood bursting through the paint elsewhere, showed that two more now needed action. More graving pieces than wood. From apWilliams' viewpoint, the old boat, just like most computer programs, was always just on the point of completion, for launching in the next day or so. Or if not, then shortly. No question about it.

'She was burnt in the clearances,' he said sharply, reproachfully, in reply to Johnson's question.

'Of course. I was forgetting.'

'You must be getting very forgetful,' said apWilliams with some asperity.

'Anyway,' he continued more equably, 'I guess your *Lady Amanda*, lying on the bottom where she sank, is the only boat left in all of North Wales. See you this evening.'

At three, the porter let Johnson into the college and he went to Gaskin's office.

'Well, hallo,' said Gaskin, 'I thought we'd go over the advert design. Let's stroll down to the river and talk as we go.'

Johnson wondered what advert, how did he mean 'advert'? then cottoned on to the need for circumlocution, and chatted about imagined adverts until they got onto the Backs.

What had happened to Gervon, he asked. 'They've moved him,' said Gaskin. They fell silent. Then Johnson outlined the activities Upside, and the Transgap software. Gaskin was delighted.

'Got it with you then?'

Johnson explained about the revised development timeframe.

'Ah. You mean it's late.'

'Well. Yes.'

'What're we going to do with you meanwhile?'

Gaskin thought. Then he apparently decided to brief Johnson, at least as far as he had to. Johnson sensed there were distinct reservations.

That evening he met up with apWilliams and talked over all he'd heard. The fulcrum in Gaskin's plan seemed to be at the Menai Straits bridge.

'I've got it,' Johnson said, 'the *Amanda.* We'll raise her and sail there.'

'You what?'

They recalled the sinking.

'She has to be down there still. Pickled in brine. Brine alternating every tide with fresh water from the river. Bugs can't stand it. What could be better?'

'We might have the odd problem with the electronics,' Johnson said. They laughed delightedly. What boat didn't?

'Absolutely. I wouldn't be surprised if the mirrors needed re-silvering too.'

How to get her up?

apWilliams said: 'She sank at a shallow angle. So she's not the full forty-three feet down. Maybe only twenty-five or thirty.'

'Even so, we'll not float ten tons without a certain amount of hard work.'

'Ping pong balls; that's the answer. I remember a piece on the first flying boat service out to Hong Kong. One big problem was a crystal clear lagoon in the Gulf. The pilots couldn't see the surface to land on it, you see. In the end they used to make two passes over it. The first time they opened sacks of ping pong balls, which went floating down. They spread out on the surface so at the second circuit they could see it and land.'

'I'm not with you. We're trying to raise a yacht, not land a flying boat.'

'Well. Circumstances alter cases. What we can do is dive down with bags of ping pong balls or whatever, and let them loose in the saloon, and Bob's your uncle.'

'How do you mean, Bob's my uncle? Bob who?'

'Sorry. My imperialist past. Lord Roberts of Kandahar. Kandahar was, I think, some great battle against the Sikhs, for which

118

the old boy was lorded. Then got sent to direct the Boer war when it was at its worst. I remember the Boers used to say:

'Wat Lord Roberts kan dahar

Is nie wat Lord Roberts kan doen hier.'

What Lord Roberts could do there

Is not what Lord Roberts can do here.

Anyway, what I mean is, we take down a lot of floating what-ever, shove it through the cabin hatch, and slowly slowly up she'll come'

'That'll just lift the cabin roof off.'

'Not on *Amanda*. You should remember it. Bloody great deck beams too, each with 'CERT BOSUNS STORE 40/100 TON' carved in inch and a half letters.'

'What on earth's the use of that? It's not an art competition.'

'You're, if I may say so, just pig-ignorant. That's the test that was required for a yacht to qualify as A100 in Lloyds Register of shipping. Of sound construction. Massive grown oak frames and ribs every six inches, tie rods of bronze to back them up. Remember that advert of the Morris Minor hanging by the roof from a crane by someone's glue? That sort of strength. And the boat – half a forest's worth of wood. Just waiting down there to float up for us.'

'Well, if you put it like that, what're we waiting for?'

They discussed further. What about the defences if any to the Straits if they got there? They'll be the old radar systems. Stealth technology. They'll not pick us up if we replace the stainless-steel rigging with terylene or whatever. What about the navigation? The charts must be rubbish by now, and we'll have no forecasts. Not even tide tables. It's bad enough getting through Bardsey Sound at the best of times. Roughest cape in British waters.

Still, they decided, look on the bright side. There wouldn't be a mass of shipping.

'And,' said apWilliams, 'we won't have that wretched light blinking at us for hours on end. Bardsey light used to seem, like Ailsa Craig's symmetrically almost perfect volcanic cone in the south of the Clyde, to follow you wherever you go round the Llyn peninsula. Sail for hours, you could, and there it still was, winking at you from the same angle on the starboard beam.'

'No, we can go right round the outside and by-pass the sound.'

But they didn't seem quite so confident. Both recalled the massive overfalls, current piling over a craggy bottom, which often made the outside route perilous.

They tried to talk it over with Gaskin. He was only interested in the Transgap systems' design and compatibility with PIG. They barely had his attention but they left with his lukewarm blessing. He'd clear apWilliams' release with his department. They would get a rail warrant from admin to Wolverhampton, but from there they'd be on their own.

Two weeks later Johnson and apWilliams were on the cliff path opposite the old town of Dolgellau. They had acquired mountain bikes from a deserted shop in Birmingham. Getting out of the militarized Motorway Ring had been difficult, but Gaskin had told them of a route through several culverts near spaghetti junction. They had dismantled the bikes, strung the bits together on cords, and pulled them through the culverts behind them.

Now they followed the old bridle trail along the tops above the Afon (river) Mawddach valley. Spring time, green, green, green; white patches of sorrel and wood anemone still in the copses. Primroses in flower in the south-facing banks. The splendid broken craters of Cadr Idris, the mountain that dominates these parts, rose up across the valley to the south. Looking west, seawards, the half mile long, 19th century bridge across the river stood still intact. Condemned to closure by Dr. Beeching in the sixties, and saved, thank God, by the obstinate Welsh lobbyists, to be the keystone of the lovely Cambrian coast railway. A triumph for the future against the Systems Thinkers.

'Never a train across that nowadays, I'll bet.'

'Still, you never know.'

'We'll stick to the high path.'

They came to the top of a rise, and below them lay Barmouth and its harbour, carved out of an island of sand and the swirling, scooping runnels of the river.

They looked down and studied it all carefully, particularly the area where the old boat must lie. Still high water, so nothing to see; but the water was crystal clear – the unseasonal easterlies had allowed the sand normally suspended in the surf to sink to the bottom. The railway line came across the half mile of bridge, through a tunnel, past the cliff above the old lifeboat station and perhaps the sunken ketch *Lady Amanda,* and circled past the great tidal pool of the harbour on into the town. Past the Last Inn, where the Lifeboat crew gathered in the old days for their lunchtime pint, in horse boxes near the blazing fire in winter, looking under the bridge and across the harbour to the mountain in summer. On past the austere grey slate Welsh houses crouching grim-faced with steeply angular dormer windows, which seemed to be watching everything censoriously just as they had in Llareggub. And then on, away out of sight, to the station.

Nothing about, but Johnson felt uneasy. There was something odd about the bridge.

They went down the steep slate steps into the town. A while to go till the tide fell far enough for them to see if the boat was still there. A look at the old garage. Numerous old inner tubes. Might do for lifting if they could get them down and inflate in situ.

They walked back later to the harbour, and along the strand. Low water was approaching. Difficult to see under the water without masks, but they'd have to try.

They stripped off and slowly entered the chilly water.

There was a sudden, distant Pee Paw.

'My God,' said Johnson. 'A train.'

There was a slowly increasing rumble as a two-coach Sprinter approached hesitantly from the far side. No chance of hiding; they'd just have to stick as low as possible in the cold water and hope.

It came past and trundled echoing along out of sight into the station. That was what had stuck out to Johnson; the rails should have been rusted, but they were shiny with use.

It seemed essential to find out what was going on. They took a risk, left the water and dodged along the road from gap to gap, into the old funfair, then threaded their ways through till they could see the station platform.

The train was still in. A mechanical voice was coming from the PA:

'Apologise any inconvenience caused... Drinks and light refreshments... your next station stop.'

The coaches were half filled with POPs, their single eye stalks waving on the cantilevered arms rather like humans conversing.

121

'Good God,' Johnson said, 'they're playing trains. They're bloody playing trains.'

One POP sidled along the platform carrying what looked like a massive key. A second POP sidled up from the guard's compartment and accepted it. Then it continued forward to the driver's cab and climbed in while its colleague clearly took over as guard for the next section.

'... where this train will terminate...' announced the PA metallically with a dying fall. 'Sandwiches and light refreshments.'

The diesel revved, and the train continued on its way to Pwllheli.

The two walked back down the main street, shivering uncontrollably, to retrieve their clothes and warm up. They came back again past the Last Inn.

'Do you think?'

'Yes, let's,' and they went round the back, levered open a side door and entered. They felt their way into the Lifeboat-men's bar and eventually found a bottle of Johnny Walker. You couldn't see the label, but it was the right square shape. They settled in to one of the familiar old horse-boxes that lined the wall opposite the fire.

'Well now. How about that?' asked apWilliams.

'Don't think it matters more than desperately. As long as we can get her up without their seeing.'

'Yes. We must monitor it and see how often they come round. I mean it might have been just their Bank Holiday outing. Or it might be only a summer service, and we'll not be ready to move till September.'

'Yes. The equinoctial gales.'

They fell silent.

'Terricky stuff.'

'Yes indeed.'

Two weeks later they reported back to Gaskin in Manchester. He sounded bored. Clearly he'd forgotten the whole business. They explained the plan.

'Enlighten me further if you would. You're going to raise this old boat from underneath a railway line populated with POPs.'

They nodded.

'Just like that?'

'Well, yes,' said Johnson defiantly. 'Just like that.'

'Bleeding Tommy Coopers. And then take it through Bardsey. With no engine. No GPS. No charts. Think of all those bloody Welsh bars. Might be anywhere. Caernarfon bar. Probably half way across the Atlantic by now. Being skulled across by the Prince to Long Island Sound. No lighthouses. No met forecasts. Terylene rigging. Mast will whip around like a pike rod. And the boat's only 70 years old? And then you're going to take her through the Swellies? I don't believe it.'

'Look, mate,' Johnson interposed, flushed and intense, 'you come up with something better.'

'Right,' said Gaskin, 'I will.'

'Well,' said apWilliams, 'we're going ahead regardless.'

'OK, if you must you must. We'd better keep in touch. Let's get together a month from today.'

'How the hell are we going to do that? It took us a fortnight just to get back here from Barmouth.'

'OK, OK. There are ways. Sorry, I've a lot on. You do your best, and let's get together when we can.'

Gaskin thought briefly. Then he seemed all of a sudden to sharpen up. He paused and they waited for him to continue. Eventually he said:

'I'll send my operative to Pilot's cove on 30th September. Be there.'

'Operative. How do you mean operative? What operative?'

'My operative,' Gaskin said with finality. 'Just be there.'

Something in Gaskin's voice caused them to glance sharply at him, then at each other. Johnson raised an interrogative eyebrow. apWilliams shrugged.

Back in their room, they talked it over. Johnson was uneasy about the mysterious 'operative'. Was Gaskin on the level with them? But the sailing bulked foremost.

'I'm damned sure it can be done,' said Johnson vehemently.

'Didn't they call this the Road of the Vikings? You can imagine them sailing down the Welsh coast in the tenth century, pulling in at Skokholm and Skomer islands to pick up puffins for the pot, or the Manx Loughtan sheep left there for that purpose. Then down round the end of Cornwall, nip across to Ouessant and you're right among the rich monasteries and vineyards of the Loire and Aquitaine.'

'Yes, but just think of those guys. Their helmsmen could smell their way through the straits. They could feel their distance off from the cliffs by the wash of the waves and the echo of the surf. Not our class, you know. Against them we're nautically-disadvantaged nig-nogs. And a hell of a lot of them never came back.'

'OK,' said Johnson. 'So maybe we won't either. But we can have a damned good try.'

apWilliams brightened up suddenly.

'Yes, that's right. And Neville's objections are a good starting point for a bit of QA on our ideas. He knows what he's on about.'

Greatly cheered, they got down to listing what they'd need, the idea being to hope for sources close to Barmouth, to take as little as possible on their backs. Snorkels and masks of course. Tyres and other inflatables could be found, but a couple of foot pumps to pump them up, and a long, long length of pressure tube to connect up to the surface. They had found numerous wrecked fibreglass boats, destroyed during the Welsh clearances. They'd be a tremendous source of standard equipment.

Ten days saw them down in Barmouth again, the trip being easier now they knew the way.

The key things were to work out the tide times, find out when the next POP excursions were due – daily, Sundays or what – explore the *Amanda*'s site, and find whatever air containers they could for the great raising. Once they got her to the surface they'd have to leave right away, lest the POPs saw her. Or maybe lower her again while they sorted out what needed doing. They'd probably only be able to work on her at low water or neaps because of the strength of the current and the depth at high water. The tidal range was 18 ft, 5.3 metres. Add that to the depth of the boat below the Chart Datum and you got a total of say 36 feet. Nearly 12 metres. Not easy for snorkelling at all.

They broke open the rear door of a little restaurant snug under the cliffside, rejoicing in the peeling name and sign of 'The Angry Cheese.' apWilliams recalled a splendid supper there before the First World Error.

'We'll stay here for old times' sake.'

'What old time's that?'

'Tell you some time.'

'Uhuh. Was she pretty?'

'Yes indeed.'

They fell silent.

apWilliams said, 'There's two splendid lines of Marlowe's, quoted by Eliot:

'That was in another country. And besides, the wench is dead.'
The Jew of Malta. I've often meant to read it.'

'And is she dead?'

'So I was told. I don't believe so. Just sleeping.'

'This'll do, don't you think? I'll have the second floor bedroom overlooking the upper beach.'

Food was a problem; they'd have to scour the warehouse of the Co-op to seek tinned food.

Downside, 1992, Chapter 14D: Flashback–
The Citizens Advice

Downside, in the Kingshampton Citizens Advice Bureau, in 1992 a fair-haired woman was at the desk, working on a debt case sheet. To the left breast of her sweater was pinned a snazzy-looking plastic tag: 'Sue – Generalist and Debt Advisor'.

Above her head was a minatory notice by the Youth Motivation worker who shared the office, in WordPerfect 5.1. It had been highlighted in bright yellow:

TO ALL YOU YOUNG PEOPLE WHO USE THE YOUTH SHOP. THE STAFF ARE HERE TO HELP YOU NOT CLEAN UP AFTER YOU.

SO TAKE NOTE, I'VE BEEN PUSHED AS FAR AS I'M PREPARED TO GO. I'VE SEEN CLEANER AND TIDIER FIVE YEAR-OLDS!!!

YOU HAVE BEEN WARNED

On the desk a notice to CAB advisors stressed: Social monitoring; full information including race, sexuality, disability must be included.

An earlier case from the morning still worried her, on a theme which had often troubled her before. The client was an unmarried mum, with a year-old daughter. Her current young male partner wanted to move in with them and make things permanent – 'Sort of like her father like as well. You know?' The guy would father the infant. Sue had gone through the financial side, the client's possible benefits. Calculating the one-parent premium, the Council Tax, the Housing Benefit etc for a single mum. Then the alternative 'Whatif' if the guy moved in. Net income less, no HB, no CTB, no free this, no free that. Not so good.

'Ah, well,' the client had said cheerfully, 'that's him out then.'

Should Sue have tried to argue? No, she concluded, the guidelines say don't be judgmental; just set out the options for the client to decide. OK, it's tough on the guy, and much worse, sets the scene for a disastrous upbringing for the child. But that's how it's got to be.

She dismissed it from her mind, and finished off her last debt case sheet instead.

'He's thrown a sickie[30],' she wrote on a covering pink sticker for her colleague at the top of the sheet, 'to get away from the work-bench and sort it all. He told them he's got to be off with his shoulder. The debts are on the sheet with the list of creditors, how much we recommend for each, the usual. See you.

Sue.'

She put the case sheet in a basket, then completed the statistics for NACAB central office in Manchester, and sent them off down the Intranet. So many appeals against benefit decisions, Disability Living Allowance assessments, so many cases of sexual or police harassment, of debt, of employment law infringement and so on. A crucial thermometer in measuring the happiness of the common weal.

She left the office still uneasy, slamming the door angrily.

*****

Downside, June 2010

Back in Barmouth in 2010, the dives in the next few days gradually became more effective. They learnt to wear more clothes in the water, so that they could stay in longer. No more POP trains came, and the lines grew rusty. So they kept a stout wood fire blazing, hidden under the railway arch, so that they could warm up after the first dive in each tide, and fit in a second one or more. One day they found a curious effect. They passed down through murky water to reach a sudden layer of pure river water. Clear as glass, sieved of sludge by the peat bogs, and many degrees chillier. As one approached it, shimmering distorted images suddenly froze into perfect clarity. They were at last able to see right down to the hull itself. Unlike the weed-cluttered masthead forty feet from the deck, the hull looked to be free apart from a covering of seaweed. They were elated. But it was a frighteningly long way down. Getting tangled anywhere was almost certain death, so at first they always dived in pairs. But familiarity bred confidence, and working singly was much more effective.

Downside, Chapter 14E: Diving with Ping Pong Balls

At the end of the fourth day they had sussed out how the boat lay, and worked over how to recover her. Diving time was short, of course, so there was plenty of opportunity to collect ideas and bits and pieces for the raising. But the crucial issue was how they could manage to get thirty or forty feet down. As people do, they unconsciously nested that problem, homing in on the excitements of preparation.

In Barmouth, Johnson and apWilliams found their first idea of pumping air down to raise the boat was a non-starter. There would be nothing in the cabin capable of retaining it. But they had succeeded in collecting on the shore buoyant materials of various types, such as ping pong balls from the old sports shop, ready to go down to the boat with a sort of diagonal Heath Robinson escalator. Descalator, they called it, because it was intended to escalate downwards. The down 'stairs' were two punctured buckets. These buckets would be inverted under the water in turn, and then the ping pong balls or whatever would be held beneath them and released so that they floated up into the submerged bucket. The bucket would then be wound down to the boat.

The idea was that the 'descalator' would be lashed at its lower end inside the cabin, to the grab handle at the entrance from aft. From there it would rise diagonally out through the hatch, and thence up to the surface. It was going to be a devil of a job swimming it down there and lashing it in place. Tying knots with your breath held in virtual pitch darkness inside a cabin which claustrophobia told you urgently might be your coffin.

The arrangement would mean that the buoyant stuffs travelled down to the saloon in the inverted buckets, then as the buckets swung round and up again, the buoyant materials floated vertically up out of the buckets, and bobbed against the cabin ceiling.

The Irishman Boyles's law might squeeze them in half, but even so they'd generate lift. More and more lift. Like the man says.

They spun a coin for who should go first. apWilliams lost. Dressed in jeans and a sweater to conserve some of his body heat, he walked into the water, out to the mast truck, took a deep breath and plunged under, hauling himself down from the marker buoy to the mizzen mast through the murky low tide water. It stung his eyes, and his chest seemed to be bursting. At about twelve feet down, the pain in his ears became intense. A little further and the automatic panic reaction set in. He let go and swam to the surface coughing and spluttering. He explained to Johnson, then had another go. But he got no further. Johnson took over, but he also got no further, and then the flooding tide made the trip down ever more difficult. They gave up, and went for a disconsolate beer to the Last Inn.

'It has to be possible,' said Johnson. 'Remember the divers in the Polynesian islands. They could pick up pearls from colossal depths and used to stay down yonks. I seem to recall numbers like two hundred feet.'

'Romantic nonsense, if you ask me. People love to hear these stories of how the primitives did this and that. At that depth their lungs would be compressed to the size of tennis balls. They'd be negatively buoyant; tumble down to the bottom. And what about the pressure on their eardrums? And the bends.'

'Well. You come up with a better idea.'

'What are we doing here anyway?'

'It was agreed with Neville Gaskin.'

'To be quite frank, I think the guy has got his own agenda.'

'How do you mean, "own agenda"?'

'One of those phrases. He's got some objectives he's not told us about.'

'I disagree,' said apWilliams. 'Not a lot of point for him in shoving us down here. And in fact he was pretty lukewarm about the whole exercise. It was our idea not his. And it was you who told me there was some key happening in the Straits in November.'

'Even so. Remember when we got to his rooms in Cambridge that night. Didn't he buzz the alarm and put the POPs onto us? And all this business, rolling his eyes around. Was he practising for playing squash? Following the ball round the court?'

'Some sort of signal perhaps. And he may have had to reveal you were around, or else jeopardise his own safety and that of his mates, whoever they may be. Remember that he gave them the wrong staircase, B not P. Without that we might never have escaped.'

'Still not sure I trust him,' said Johnson.

'Well, you don't know him like our people do.'

'Anyway, what are we going to do about the descalator? Practise deep breathing?' Johnson asked sarcastically.

'Perhaps we should chuck it in and go back to West Gorton.'

'No, no. Let's sleep on it.'

During the night Johnson used to wake occasionally, between three and four or so. On this night he thought about the deep breathing, and from his memory there suddenly surfaced a TV experiment Upside in the seventies. The Royal Marines decided to investigate how the Polynesians had accomplished their stupendous feats – depths and durations. It emerged that there is an automatic panic reaction built into humans, to struggle madly to breathe in after about forty-five seconds. The marines team had found they could gradually train themselves to contain this instinctive response. Cross the one-minute threshold and you can keep going for a considerable time. Some mechanism in the system shuts down the normal circulation of blood round the body, and concentrates it into the brain. That was it. That was how the seals, whales and dolphins handled the situation. He tried it out, breathing in and counting. Alarming at first. Fine up to heartbeat thirty, then he began to feel a bursting feeling constraining his lungs. It grew in intensity and he felt his veins swell and his face flush. Still, he persevered for an hour.

The next morning he told apWilliams nothing of this, and his mate seemed surprised at his odd, flushed silences.

'You OK, Mike? You look like a pop-eyed World War One colonel,' he said.

'I'm all right,' said Johnson, 'let's get back on the job.'

They started diving, apWilliams first. He dived then came up gasping.

'No go,' he said.

'Never mind, I'll give it a whirl.'

Johnson took a fairly deep breath, submerged and hauled himself down the buoy line till he found the top of the mizzen. Do it steadily to conserve energy. Heartbeat forty and bursting. He hauled himself further. He had to clasp the slippery wood of the mast with hands and feet. Further down. Heartbeat fifty and exploding. Further still. He felt the cross trees, and held on to them triumphantly, pausing, legs dangling upwards weightless, slightly buoyant. Now to go up again. He somersaulted round, ears paining severely, and started ascending. Panic – something was holding his right foot. He reached down instinctively, struggled fiercely, half choking. Relax, take control. A bit of rope's caught my ankle. He reached with both hands, gave a yank. He finally managed to ease it, then clear it and surface.

apWilliams dragged him ashore, coughing and retching.

'That's it, Mike,' he said. 'We've had enough. Enough faffing around. Let's be on our way back.'

Johnson recovered himself.

'No,' he said. 'Bollocks to that. We can do it.'

He explained, and they had deep breathing sessions as they discussed what had happened and what they would do. Johnson's ankle had no doubt been lassoed by a loop in one of the ropes, which now probably festooned the cockpit like spaghetti. They recalled how a racing dinghy is often transformed by a capsize from a tidy well-organised entity to one in which loose ropes swirl around and tangle impossibly. Multiply that simple situation up by all the sheets, halyards, lazy-jacks, control lines, outhauls, downhauls, crosshauls, uphauls which graced the *Amanda*. Two masts, so two sets of each. They would first have to get them all under control – there was no way the descalator could work unless it had a clear run.

This took four days of low waters and shivering, frightening endeavour. They managed to extend their breath-holding ashore to a minute and a half. But in the stress and energy of diving it was nothing like that. Then, at last, Johnson swam a rope down, inside the cabin. Quickly, desperately, slip it once round the cabin grab-handle. Murky; working entirely by feel, but familiar from night watches in his own old boat. Find your way around in pitch darkness so that you don't destroy your night-vision. Then up again, taking the end of the rope with him.

They hitched the rope to the descalator, and hauled it down. Both went down in turn for a jubilant look at it.

Then the exercise started. The first few wind-downs were exciting, but then the job seemed to stretch out eternally, with no evidence of any success.

Still, Diogenes theorem must be right. apWilliams related de Maupassant's story of two drunken Breton farmers who somehow got into an argument in a bar as to which of their two wives was the heavier. They decided to adopt Diogenes' theory. Each put his wife into a barrel brim-full of water, and measured the overflow as the wife climbed in. Success. The ladies being lighter than water, weighed the same as the water they had displaced. He couldn't recall the ending – hopefully the farmers got their comeuppance. However, it showed that Johnson and apWilliams had to succeed eventually.

One evening they were on the quay with cans of beer in the sunshine. They were discussing how they'd got their first jobs.

'You were in the colonial service in Uganda, weren't you? What was their recruitment system like?' apWilliams asked Johnson.

'For the administrative grade, fairly tough, a good degree, then interview. Plus a year at Oxford covering a Bantu language, law, social anthropology, agriculture, ecology, history, economics. particularly fascinating in our time, because there was a majority I think, of black Africans, and our discussions could be open and realistic. Pretty formidable training by most standards, compared, say, with what you get in industry.

'But the technical grades were much more fun. I remember an anecdote from an entomologist friend, Charles, with me in Boulogne.

'Charles and I sat in the sunshine, he at the wheel, I on the bridge deck, at the precarious end of a long raft of at least twenty yachts. The Boulognese have little time for strange yachts, and only one visitor's berth to take them all.

'Charles told me how his first boss, Fred Entwhistle, was recruited. Fred left university in 1938 with a degree in biology. He decided to apply to join the colonial service, where biologists were greatly needed. In due course he was invited for interview in Church House, Westminster. He entered a large panelled

132

room, portraits of formidable people on the walls, a long mahogany table at the end, at which sat five men. Their background was unexplained, but they started to quiz him. He guessed psychologist far end left, minister of religion far end right. The man in the centre, big and choleric with bulging eyes, was continually deferred to. He interrupted Fred's answer to one question:

'Do you play golf, Entwhistle?'

'No Sir.'

And a few minutes later:

'Do you play bridge Entwhistle?'

'No Sir.'

'Not much of a grace to the social life of a station, what?'

'Well, I'd try my best, sir.'

'That virtually finished the interview, and in due course a rejection came, and Fred joined a consultancy.

'He did well in the war, finishing as a distinguished full colonel. He reapplied to join the Colonial Service in response to an advert for an entomologist, and found himself again in Church House, Westminster. But this time in a comfortable office, talking to a single civil servant.

'Do come in, very glad to see you, colonel.'

'Do have some coffee, colonel.'

The civil servant's knowledge of entomology seemed limited to the fact that it concerned insects, but he was immensely friendly and deferential. The fact that Fred actually wasn't an entomologist didn't matter too much.

'Don't worry,' he said, 'you'll soon pick it all up.'

'So Fred was accepted, and went out to Uganda, and picked it all up, and made his reputation as a world expert. Lots of dudus[31] were named after him. Not a bad system for handling the unknown.

'I remember the journey out there in those days as quite something; three weeks in a Union Castle mail liner, calling in at Genoa, Suez and Aden (the aircraft carrier *Bulwark* anchored imperially in the harbour in the blinding Arab sunshine), each point marking a further step away from the homeland towards the heart of unknown, explosive and unpredictable Africa. Then the last leg to Mombasa, seeing the Horn of Africa standing up in the red sunset sky. And finally and crowningly, two days with East African Railways and Harbours on the train up from the coast. Waking the first morning to see a vast, empty, dry, brown, rolling, sunlit savanna swinging past the windows, with giraffe and varied buck grazing. Strange, delicious fish, tilapia, one of the four courses in the dining car. Twin BeyerGarratt double locomotives later, front and rear, hissing with effort as they hauled us up the Great Rift Valley and over the equator at 9,000 feet. Then down into Uganda, bowling along at twenty miles an hour through the intimacy of small huts and banana shambas, and into Kampala through its seven hills. It must be one of the great train journeys of the world.'

Downside, Chapter 15: Barmouth, Raising the Ketch

Back in Barmouth, apWilliams and Johnson were considering the next stage of their plan.

'Do we sink her again to keep her out of sight after we've got her up and seen what needs doing?' asked Johnson. 'Or do we leave her on her side to fill again?'

'Yes. Good question. There's the possibility of some Benevernment units coming here any time. Let's aim to get her up, quick lookover, and if possible plug her and sneak out on the first tide to somewhere safe, Pensarn, say.'

Pensarn is one of Wales's jealously guarded gems. Lying in a valley between mountains called the Rhinogs, its river, the Artro, is fed by hanging valleys from above, and falls past the 'Roman Steps' where allegedly the Legions used to forage through and thump troublesome Celts into a semblance of peaceful tax payers, into a lovely lake called Cwm Bychan. Then down through woods of dwarf oak and beech into coastal meadowland, and on into its own sandy lagoon. And thence, like no other Welsh river, straight out into the sea. It had broken sideways out of its own sandbank-riddled estuary in about 1860 into the 'New Cut'. As a result, in the space of 100 yards you could come in from perhaps viciously turbulent seas in the bay into a flat calm under the lee of high dunes. Just the spot for shelter and rerigging, with only one drawback. But that is a substantial one; the famous Sarn Padrig, or St Patrick's Causeway.

The Causeway is a strange, straight jumbled line of heavy rocks stretching 8 miles offshore, believed by medieval Christians to have been a divine pathway, along which St Patrick was said to have walked to and from Ireland in the Dark Ages. Less improbable is the rival account, that he sailed the 80 miles in a miraculous boat that looked something like a modern coracle, but was, they said, made of solid stone. Less prone than a feather-light Welsh coracle to scud along before the slightest wind. Perhaps the first forerunner of a ferro-concrete hull.

Anyway, the rocks of Sarn Padrig lurk just below the low water mark, and like other sarns further south, are one of the reasons why boating, pleasure and commercial variants, are rare in these waters.

Between the sarn and the mainland, close to where a Spanish galleon from the Armada was wrecked in 1588, lies the East Passage. Here also is a more mysterious wreck from 1707 or so. It carries a full cargo of expensive Carrara marble, the marble that was then being imported to build St Paul's Cathedral. How did it come to be 300 miles away from its destination on the opposite side of the UK? Perhaps a sevententh-century insurance job, the swindle having been scuppered by St Patrick's Causeway.

East Passage is a shallow, unmarked gap a quarter of a mile wide between the beach and the causeway. One problem is that there is no easy way of deciding where the quarter-mile gap starts and ends, because the beach shelves very gradually. This leaves the navigator uncertain where he is.

If they had to beat up through it to get into Pensarn it could be slow and dangerous work. They continued the descalating, and then one day the mast surprisingly lifted a few feet out of the water. Done it – that was it! She would be equally buoyant at high water, so they could haul her across over the mud. Then the tide would fall, and the old boat would beach high and dry on her side.

That evening, the conversation drifted to Johnson's account of times since the Error.

'One tendency that struck us,' said apWilliams, 'was the Fourth Estate, the media. They became so skilled and incisive, and the opposing spokesmen equally so, trained and practised in the arts of persuasion so far that reality became inextricable. Evelyn Waugh painted the scene in the thirties, bereaved and tragedy-struck citizens being doorstepped by mobs of thrusting yelling reporters seeking copy. "Anyone here raped and can speak?" And further corrupted by the editors of the tabloids who egged on their reporters ruthlessly. The story went of 2 reporters in a Third World hellhole. The *Mail* man suffered a flesh wound from a terrorist's rifle. He telegraphed back, capitalising on it.

The *Express* man received a text from base: "Mailman shot. Why you unshot?" By the eighties it was mind-bending. Attempts at 'self-policing' were pretty ineffective, and the globalisation of the media, and the Internet it seemed as well, meant it would get worse and worse.'

'That's the way it was going,' said Johnson, 'and there weren't any easy answers. But ridicule is an immensely effective weapon.'

He went on to describe how various groups identified ways of curbing the worst offenders. An organisation of old ladies who resolved to do something about it. And did so. IBAG[32] they called themselves.

One answer to the journalistic excesses was that which formed the theme of *Zen and the Art of Motor-cycle Maintenance*, a best-seller from the 1970s. Quality, the need for all organisations and activities to have an immensely effective 'quality' function. Maybe semi-independent, which was how it had to be for the media. As the debate worked its way through, people realised that the media scene was so fast-moving, you had to have an independent unit in each media organisation, which would conduct post-mortems into veracity and duplicity, and had the authority to penalise the miscreants.

It seemed pretty obvious; all other human activities had acquired such structures, why should the Fourth Estate be excluded? Quality was the key to the success of the Japanese from the 1950s on. And quite easy to apply to newspapers. The QA people would randomly pick a news item or article, and go over its genesis and accuracy, just as any other QA unit. apWilliams recalled the QA people in ICM computers, standing and blocking sub-standard products that development and sales were trying to hustle out of the door. Why not QA for the press?

The dangers to freedom of information and political, commercial and other considerations were obvious; so you had to invent a QA hierarchy inside the organisation, with its own career structure etc, within which critical appraisal of in-house activities was a virtue to be encouraged. Something along the lines that were followed in the 1990s to scrutinise privatised monopolies like the utilities.

'The results were surprising,' said Johnson, 'even in a whiter-than-white organisation like the BBC. I remember one presenter who was found over 3 months consistently to have dumbed down good and worthwhile activities, with a laughing "Well, she would say that, wouldn't she?" or "If you can believe that, you can believe anything" or "We all know what that was all about, don't we?" His audience appreciation scores were phenomenal. Easy scoffs like these usually ended the argument, interviewee deflated without recourse. And when a radio listener grumbled, she got a nice little card of thanks, "We're always glad to hear from our viewers or listeners." But no attempt to defend, or to dispute, the accuracy of the complaint, as professionals would have done. Still less to publicise it.

'These techniques were sometimes effective and legitimate against trained PR people, but often seriously damaging. The peculiarity of the media, of course, was that retractions and so forth were pretty ineffective – yesterday's, or usually last year's, news, stale and forgotten and ignored. But QA was different. Hence the in-house approach, with a professional organisation like, say, the BCS (British Computer Society) to back them up, provide career structures and so on. Not very good, but better than nothing. Why not? If we subject even school kids of 8 to assesment and QA, why not the Fourth Estate?'

'Interesting,' said apWilliams, 'a bit like some of the ancient Greek city states and their terminal disease, "stasis".'

States living off a host of slaves, the Greek citizens whiling away their life-spans in litigation, court room drama and politicking. In fact, if you take into account the TV screen in the modern home, you get almost the same effect. One or two key individuals, as depicted by Aristophanes, the focus of everything. In a small Greek city there was of course live contact with the players, but with us it was the articulate, friendly guy who slipped nightly into our living rooms electronically.'

'Indeed. About slavery, a guy called Hugh Thomas did a deep and fascinating overview of slavery in the late 1990s.[33] But even he failed to make clear that the vicious Atlantic trade, for which the European seafarers and the African coastal rulers were responsible, was just one glaring example of a worldwide practice. Anyway. Bed, perhaps?'

'Yes. An early tide tomorrow.'

After the morning dives, they assembled all the necessary kit to plug the hole – maybe by now a long tear through her planks – and also substitutes for whatever equipment in her sailing armoury might need replacement or repair. They discussed their plans. How to get her to dry out with her damaged side up? When to do the final putsch? Choose neap tides to minimise currents. Start operations as early as possible after dawn, to give the maximum time for repairs.

And choose a tidal window which would make Pensarn accessible early in the afternoon, so that they would have 4 hours of daylight and deep water in which to cover the 10 or so miles and get in. And if possible, winds in the south sector, less than force 5. No knowing how badly she'd suffered from 20 years on the bottom. It isn't easy, as the Thais used to say, so take it easy.

Upside, Chapter 16: Trawsfynydd, an Event to Remember

At Trawsfynydd the sky was cloudless, and a bright July sun shone down on the Welsh valleys. In all directions south through east to north, Aberystwyth through Brum to Bangor, cavalcades of rare official limos were swinging cheerily through the winding Welsh trunk roads, converging on the old power station. Accountants, archaeologists, anthropologists, biologists, computer scientists, directors of research, directors of IT, directors of expert systems, knowledge engineers, linguists, management scientists, ministers of state, molecular biologists, neurologists, physicists, physiologists, principals, professors of development studies, psychologists, resource people, social anthropologists, sociologists, anthropological sociologists, sociological anthropologists, trainers of trainers of trainers. The Top People were coming.

They wound west from England through the Berwyns, they wound north up from Cader Idris, they wound south down from Snowdonia. Most funnelled together for the final spectacular miles, turning west at Bala Lake. Then up past the cascading, kayak-infested rapids of Afon Tryweryn, and over the crest to trace the shores of Llyn Celyn, source of much of the water for the industrial Midlands. As they climbed higher still, the mountains closed in on either side. On 2 adjacent posts sat 2 large, contented buzzards. They weren't impressed – seen it all before. Around the tumbling torrent, the valley's centre was filled with marshes, bogs and occasional clear black pools in the peat. Lilies and slender reeds rose from their mirror surfaces, blue flowers flecking their blackness. High on either side, heather, bilberries and other moorland plants carpeted the sheep-sprinkled flanks of the mountains and reached up into the cliffs and screes. An old narrow gauge railway track appeared and disappeared on the right, time and vegetation slowly shaping and smoothing it back into oblivion. Finally the summits rose bare and grassy.

The cars crossed the watershed, and a stream ran west before them, pointing towards the Rhinogs and their destination. Rhinog Fach, the small Rhinog, a typical, undistinguished mountain top. Rhinog Fawr, the big Rhinog, like a table, square topped, the summit sloping slightly north, a landmark and a sea mark in these parts for land farers, legionaries, sailors and fishermen for centuries and more. Only 15 miles off, at the same time on Downside, on the far side of Rhinog Fawr, the first team, apWilliams and Johnson, were emulating Heath Robinson and Emmett, trying to raise a sunken 70-year old ketch.

The snaking cavalcades gradually merged, sped past Trawsfynydd village, and skirted the lake. A charming and unusual one, not sunk in a valley, but sprawling widely across a high plateau with little indentations, hosts of small islands, occasional oak coppices and only gentle slopes around. You had the impression, as with Lake Victoria, that a slight geological quirk would have it spilling over some entirely new sill and in a different direction. The cars curved off the main road and along the landscaped access road to the power station. Disdaining all car parks, they swept round to the porticoed entrance. The big men had come; come for the jaunt of the year.

A keen environmentalist, Tilley had journeyed by train and bus, spent the night in one of the 2 village pubs, and walked off some of his nerves by strolling along the lake shore. Tilley was a conscientious young man who viewed life through pursed lips. Now he was standing, still nervous, in a large, curtained-off enclosure in the turbine hall inside the power station.

Trawsfynydd was a Magnox AGR gas-cooled nuclear power station. A marginal decision had been made to decommission it because of a suspicion of weakness in the welds in late 1980s Upside, but it still had sufficient power for Transgap needs. As for the one in Downside, they believed, it must still be in use. The risk of problems with the welds was infinitesimal; closure in Upside had been a political decision rather than for real danger. Downside, they would need all the generating power they could get because oil would be hard to get, so the station must be in full operation...

By 1.30 p.m. there was a buzz of cheerful, anticipatory social noise from the gathered throng. Tilley had had a light

141

valedictory lunch, with one glass of Brouilly '02. A hush grew, and Stag tapped on his lectern.

'Ladies and Gentlemen, the tu tu time has come to wish Tu Tilley bu bu bon voyage. Raise your glasses please. To George Tilley and Transgap; a swift ju ju journey and a su safe heturn.'

There was a murmur of warm assent. Tilley had already keyed in his password on the machine. The talking brain was on his back in a haversack with the mag tapes. Every joint in his body seemed like jelly, then strengthened, till he felt dry-mouthed, taut, 10 feet tall and ready for anything.

He pressed Enter, grasped the 2 spheres with his eyes shut, and waited. Silence.

'You've set Caps Lock on,' said Nodel.

Tilley opened his eyes and looked at the screen.

'Password rejected,' it said.

'Surely it shouldn't be case sensitive,' he said.

'That's right. How the hell can we make the same mistake twice?' asked Stag.

Jepson from Culham chipped in defensively. 'It wasn't the same mistake. With Johnson it was his fault. It was him who typed in the password wrong. I've explained several times, this is a field trials version, and there's all the difference in the world between...'

'Right,' said Stag patiently. Been there, done that. 'Let's try it again.'

Caps lock off. The password was still rejected.

Jepson became more upset.

'OK, OK, OK,' said Stag. 'It's a fu field trials rhelease. So you must have left it in du debug mu mode, I guess? So set it now to override the password. Pu people can easily hemember. Not as if it's a wu world-destined pu package or whatever. We'll raise an SFR on Culham. Meanwhile, let's gu go.'

Jepson set the override password option from the debug window. Tilley started again. He pressed Enter, then grasped the balls.

Suddenly he found himself flung sideways, and he twisted desperately to protect Sseru. He thumped on his left side onto the floor, the mag tapes crashing down, and looked around. No curtains, no buffet table, no people. Through an open doorway he could see into a subsidiary chamber, and panoramic windows overlooking the lake. It was no longer a sparkling day, but grey, the beginnings of a westerly gale whipping incipient ripples on the surface into white-capped motion.

He slipped down an adjoining passage to a door labelled 'Goods Outwards'. Then into the basement parking area. In the corner were 2 white CEGB vans. No one was around. On the wall was a schedule:

Works runs to Capenhurst and Gorton

Dep Trawsfynydd	0730 Arrive Cap	1030 Gorton	1200
	1530	1830	2024

Which of the 2 vans was the 1530 run? Probably the same one as had done the morning run. He felt the tyres, but both sets seemed equally cold. He slipped a hand under one of the wings on each van and felt the inner surface. One damp, one dry. He dropped the pressure on the off-side tyre of the dry-shod van till it was clearly almost flat. Immobilise it to be sure they took the other. Then he climbed into the driving seat of the good van and through into the back.

Should he conceal himself, or stay in the open? He looked at the load so far. A few cased bearings and 3 large oblong crates. Safer to hide behind them than to try to get a lift and chat convincingly to the driver for nearly 3 hours, and leave unresolved question marks afterwards. Who had the passenger been? Where had he gone to? Why was he so ignorant?

He snuggled down with Sseru, and endured the 3-hour journey. When they arrived in Gorton, the driver went for tea. Tilley opened the back and slipped out into the main road. They looked for shelter down the side street, but no joy. So they settled down to doze fitfully behind some gritty banks of ash in the old Belle Vue car park till morning. Then at dawn they left to find Gaskin's place... Jumping on a north-bound bus, then a west-bound across the city centre to Salford. Then a new high-rise block by the quays on the ship canal, one of the few developments Downside, surrounded by the rusty cranes and dockside impediments left over from the days when sailing the seas had been safe.

143

Upside in the power station hall after Tilley's departure, the atmosphere had become increasingly noisy and convivial. People had found the whole experience exciting. All had been watching Tilley intently. Then suddenly there he was, gone. No shimmering away as in the old classic *Star Trek*. You could see right through where he had been to the flip-chart behind. The theory of course was familiar, but not its manifestation here, now, in this old power station, as you were sipping at your wine.

The console had a message in a message box. 'Click Y to reset N'.

Humphrey Tite Barnacle circulated, and had a friendly word in Stag's ear. 'Rather a good show, I thought.'

'Absolu hutely,' replied Stag.

'I did well to invite the press-man, I think.'

'You *what?*' asked Stag, alarmed.

'Yes, Peter, you and I, we took a risk, but it's paid off. Put a piece in the next issue of the journal. Show that DFID are far from being laggards in the search for the future.'

Stag looked staggered, but Tite Barnacle had drifted on, chatting pleasurably, savouring their triumph. He fetched up next to the console, and fondled one of the balls. He remembered an old joke, and decided to close the proceedings with it.

He tapped steadily for silence, and gradually a hush fell.

'Ladies and gentlemen. This has been a fine occasion. An occasion to savour. And this project is one that, I suggest to you, sets aside the old C.P. Snow myth of the 2 cultures. Here we all are, drawn uniquely from a range embracing. . . '

He went on for a while. Stag had grabbed Kealey's arm and was talking to him urgently. Tite Barnacle concluded, 'I'll wind up if I may with an anecdote from New Zealand, which is splendidly apposite. It was *Children's Hour* on the radio, and the presenter was telling listeners how to do a conjuring trick with 2 rubber balls. "Grasp your balls firmly in each hand," he said. And that's just what our brave friend Tilley did. Just like this.'

He grasped the second ball, and instantaneously was gone.

Downside, Chapter 17: Gorton

The next day, Downside in Gorton, Tilley slipped through the familiar back streets of identical Victorian terraced houses, back-to-backs. Sullen blackened brick, unshaded light bulbs behind drooping curtains. Why did people still live in this sort of housing when they have all Manchester to choose from? Straight out of *Coronation Street*. He found an empty house and they settled in for the night. Broken brown lino on the passage floor, a smell of damp together with the acrid smell of cannabis. The next day, Tilley found Gaskin's apartment – it was where Johnson had suggested – and tapped on the door.

'Come in.'

Tilley entered. Gaskin sat at a desk at a terminal, and clicked something before speaking.

'Ah, you must be Tilley. Good to see you. Seasonable for the time of year. Why don't we go for a stroll?' Gaskin's eyeballs whipped upwards and then rolled from side to side as he spoke.

They strolled down Wenlock Way.

'Well met. Good trip? You've brought the tapes?'

'Yes. The new Grubber worked fine [Grubber was the name for the transit software] – none of the hassle that Johnson had. When can we load it all up?'

'Our KDF6 is in the museum. I'll fix a time tonight. There's a spare room in the old pub round the back. You can settle in there. They're reliable, got food, but keep off the main road.'

'OK. We need to pick up Sseru and the tapes.'

'After dark I think. What do you feed it on?'

'Not it. Him. 12 volts DC. He's a self-sustaining system. He can run in full, extended power-save mode for up to 4 days without recharging. But he gets very bored.'

That evening they went in Gaskin's car to collect Sseru and the tapes, then on to the museum. Tilley looked at the splendid old mainframe with pleasure. The load sequence was curious. You left a special short length of prepunched paper tape in the paper tape reader, then went to the console, and pressed the top row of 4 rows, each of 3 groups of 3 glowing blue pressel switches, about 2 inches by one, to make it read 000.

Then pressed the 'go' switch. This put the machine into program read, binary 000 000 000 000 000 000, its most primitive instruction. This whistled in the information from the paper tape into the bottom of the core store, and entered the resultant program starting at the location pointed to in the store. This in turn read the bootstrap routines in from the electronic label in the first block on the mag tape on deck 4060. The bootstrap then loaded the desired program.

If this sounds long-winded, it pales into insignificance when you realise that every time the machine obeyed any instruction, all the 4096 words of 18 bits (each bit a quarter-inch diameter iron ring threaded on to wires in 3 dimensions,) of the entire store were read, to locate and extract a single intended word of information, and then the whole lot has to be written again, since the read process destroyed the old bit settings.

But when they tried to bootstrap, the paper tape read in fine, but the mag tape whirred at full speed when it should have clicked forward to read in the first block. Worrying. Try again – the same result. Try another paper tape. Same result. Run a program to check the store. No fault found.

'Bloody hell,' said Gaskin, 'Your tape must be blank.'

'Can't be. They checked it out on the same machine Upside. I was there.'

'OK. Out with the tape edit.'

A tape edit program was the standard first assignment for any 1960s systems programmer. The world at one stage seemed to be full of tape edits. It might be interesting to study the later histories of the trainees against the quality of their edits.

This one just dumped onto the line-printer the block number and contents of every block of information on the tape, in octal and character form. Nothing there.

'The Grubber must have wiped it.'

They went back to Gaskin's place. 'Well, let's nest that and sleep on it. We'll go over how we're to attack PIG. I have to say you guys have been bugger-all use so far.'

'Tell you what,' said Tilley, 'why don't you get acquainted with Sseru? Particularly as he might now be crucial.'

'That's true. OK, wheel the guy out.'

Downside: Barmouth

Johnson and apWilliams had reached departure day. The tide inched its way out across the harbour mudflats. They sat in front of the Last Inn slowly supping their last cans of Boddies and surveying the view. An incredible day. The midday sun lay above the mountain, picking out every ravine and ridge in its seamed, ancient flanks, the oldest rock in Europe, until the lower oak woods clothed the naked flanks in russet and green. Across the river the yellow, almost golden sands glinted with pools of water, left in the deep corrugations carved out by the preceding ebb. The wooden struts of the viaduct showed grey at their bases with their barnacle encrustments, and a pale weathered-pine above.

A Saturday too. You could almost imagine the past when trainloads of summer trippers trundled in the chuffer along the narrow gauge from Fairbourne station. Then steaming through the dunes and round the final bend across on the far side of the river; to pile out and onto the ferry; to cross the swirling flood into the harbour, savour their pints and Cokes, and pick away at bowls of cockles, eels and whelks on the corporation benches.

Barmouth Corporation had the sense to keep their Victorian benches, long horizontal planks of teak contoured just to fit almost any bum or back, with splendid massive curly-tailed dragons in cast iron, holding the structures at either end. Over-engineered just like the Forth Bridge, and a right pest no doubt for the workmen who had to lug them into all manner of unlikely places up on the cliff paths.

As the tide fell, the *Lady Amanda*'s truck slowly surfaced, then the curve of her upper port gunwale, then the coach roof and decks. They walked down, carrying the shaped wood to plug the gash in her port side. They carefully dried off the surrounding wood, after sponging it with fresh water, to take the putty. Then, with immense pleasure, they nailed the patches in place.

Two hours till the tide flooded back. Most of the interior was now reasonably ready for departure, but they went over the sails – ready for hoisting – rudder and sheets. He remembered his old checklist. Radio? No. GPS? No. Chart? Sort of – the old ones had luckily been kept in polythene bags to protect against the mildew, which used to plague old wooden boats, and had been dried out and reconstructed in the sunshine with the same timeless care an archaeologist might give a precious fragment. Compass? Yes, the old Sestrel with its irritating domed top, filled with some spirit or other, worked perfectly, though the lower part of the alloy case had powdered away to dust.

Sounder? Yes, the old leadline was fine – advisable in these parts anyway, since the electronic ones were imprecise if you were worried about inches, which in Welsh waters you are. Long lead barrel, tallow in the hollow base to pick up traces of the bottom, and thick oiled and greased fishermens' cord, brown, twisted and tangled, one knot at the fathom, 2 at 2 fathoms and so on. Tide times and states? Sort of. Weather forecasts? Well, it was sunny, SE3 now, later who can tell? Cabins? All lights off? Indeed yes. Breakables stowed? Toilet sea-cocks off? Yes – permanently. The old Emmett-like toilet structure with its jade green seat and shiny, curlicued hinges looked fine and clean, but who knew what corrosion might have carved out of its insides? Any boat can be sunk as fast as you like through its toilet sea-cocks.

Anchor tied and cleared to run? Nope, still on the riverbed doing its job with the moorings. Fenders to hand? Yes. Mooring lines bow and stern? In good nick. Mooring hook taped? Hook yes, tape no. Engine – fuel feed on, oil, batteries and fuel OK? No, not really; seized solid no doubt with 20 years of rust.

Water? Yes, tanks filled with the crystal clear waters of the Afon Mawddach at the bottom of the ebb. Food? Yes – even the old blocks of World War Two US Navy shipwreck rations looked as good as they ever had. Flares and rockets? Not relevant, no one to rescue them. Radar reflector? Not relevant, no one to sense them.

So, at long last they were in business.

They wandered around on the sands a little tensely, waiting for the tide to come back again. It did, and slowly she lifted just as the water lapped over her gunwales and onto the side-decks. The

148

remaining bilge water lay filling her just above the floorboards, and Johnson pumped it out. They inspected the patches. Weeping a little, but fine.

At last she shifted imperceptibly, alive again after 20 years. Then she swung her head to the west into the flood tide. The south-easter pushing behind them stopped them hoisting the mainsail, but they unrolled the foresail, winched in the anchor, dropped the moorings, and sailed easily away downriver.

The old Barmouth outer buoy, 2 miles out and past the ship-crunching bar, was gone, but Johnson reached the point due north of a dark oak wood where he thought it had been, and made to turn north. A south-easterly wind meant it was off the land, and the sea's surface showed slight ripples over the gentle residual rollers from the south-west, whence comes the prevailing wind and gales. The old boat groaned and creaked in grumpy contentment as her timbers worked again after years inert on the riverbed.

'You sure you're not turning too early?' asked Alun.

'OK', replied Johnson. 'Another mile for peace, then.'

'How d'you mean a mile for peace?'

'What George Bush Senior said in conceding more time to Saddam.'

'You mean there were 2 George Bushes?'

'It's all right, forget it. Too nice a day.'

A mile later they turned north for the East Passage between Sarn Padrig and the mainland. The dunes inshore built up higher, until they almost obscured the mountain backdrop of the Rhinogs. The boat slid easily through the water, all 3 sails pulling hard.

On this course she'd pulled off an astonishing third place once in Abersoch Keelboat week – violent winds, lots of retirements, a nasty sharp Irish Sea chop which she sliced through with her long, curving, overhanging 1950s bows, while the newer boats slammed and banged and stopped. Lots of reaching, hardly any windward work.

He remembered the rousing cheer which greeted her name in the prize giving, and the warmth of the Commodore's wife's congratulations. The sight of the old classic bursting through the seas in a way not seen for 40 years had sent her back to the days when she'd been tearing her fingers on hard hemp ropes and great low-geared coffee-grinding winches, or lying flat on her back on the coachroof with the boat, rolling wildly, tying 20 reef-points underneath the massively heavy low-slung boom as it pulled and twisted away from her numb and aching fingers.

A friend, Duncan, had been navigating, and Johnson recalled his account. 'There I was down below at the start. She was heeling steeply, and out through the skylight I could see the other boats, making rough weather of it. Then one long mast keeled drunkenly and folded down across us, just missed us. And there we were, all working sail pulling hard and the lee scuppers awash. That's her weather. And one by one they dropped out. I talked to them in the showers afterwards. "Mast rivets popping down all around us." "Incredible, 2 winches. Pulled right out of the deck." "By, that was a tough one." "Remember that real killer of a squall on the dog-leg?" And I said, "Oh yes. That was when I was putting the beef in the oven." You should have seen their faces!'

But in the gentle breeze today, she glided up to Sarn Padrig in flat water. Puffy white clouds of summer bowled by north-west-wards as she passed through the East Passage with a yard or more under her keel, and slipped elegantly round the corner of the land at Mochras. She left to the north the emerging massif of Snowdonia, guarded by the great gaunt castle of Harlech, lean-ing out menacingly from its cliff above the old sea-deserted water-gate. One of Edward I's 4 great anvils to pacify the tur-bulent Welsh. Then up, climbing the ebb tide-flow, into the narrow channel linking the sea to the wide lagoon that was at the mouth of the little River Artro. Don't go rushing the beauty of the Artro, take it spit by spit, and count the clumps of yellow cinquefoil on the saltings as you slip by.

'Quite a place,' said Alun.

'Yes. A potter friend of mine, an engraver from Spode's in Stoke-on-Trent, told me it's just like coming to heaven.' And so it was.

They dropped anchor up-river.

'The Victoria for a pint?'

'You sure? Doesn't seem right somehow.'

Nevertheless, they dropped into the dinghy and rowed up past the rugged slate wharf where the slate ships had made fast and loaded 150 years earlier. A chill fell on them as they paddled under the railway bridge, but the next POP train wasn't due till 2 days later. Bank holiday special perhaps. Then the tide was lost and the dinghy had to be left on the pebbles, while they walked into the village and up to what had to be the quintessence of Welsh pubs.

A low 2-storey building with typical Welsh high dormer windows, a long sprawling barn-like extension, and a river garden still showing late spring flowers, with old garden benches and a lily pond. A gem of a spot which in happier times often preceded the walk and climb on up the Artro Valley through gnarly-treed woods, glacier-dropped rocky outcrops with hidden grassy knolls (where Johnson recalled making love on hot summer days,) to the lake of Cwm Bychan. This lake, claim many of the Welsh, was where the final act of the Round Table legend took place. King Arthur's last knight, Sir Bedivere, deeply wounded in the final battle, had swung and hurled the great blade Excalibur at his dying king's request (for the third time of asking – why throw away a priceless sword?) and had seen a mailed hand rise up from the surface to grasp the great brand's hilt as it fell, and draw it down below.

Magical places, below the misnamed 'Roman Steps'. Here, some said, the legions used to command the routes to the country's heartlands. Turbulent, witch-ridden parts then, and for centuries to come.

'Who was the woman you mentioned at the Angry Cheese, Alun?' asked Johnson.

apWilliams described her.

'Susanna, her name is. Bit of a rebel, really. She got a special invitation to go across to Ireland with one of the first ferry crossings, when they started... I got a nice card from her. But then the second virus came, and I've not heard since. But she'll be there all right. A real survivor.'

'Here's looking forward to that.'

They drank to it.

Later they groped their way back in the darkness. Euphoria had evaporated. The dinghy had trapped its bow under an overhanging slab of slate, filled up and sunk. Johnson swam for it, and they hauled it into the shallows, rolled the water out and rowed gingerly down again through the darkness.

******

Alun apWilliams recalled a long-held memory of Susanna Upside, before the First World Error. She was slender, fine skinned and grey eyed, the epitome of a lithe yachtswoman.

She and Alun had gone for a pub lunch in Towyn. It went easily at first, Susanna in lively form, but gradually putting on a social persona rather, he felt, than her real self. Is her old romance with the biker still alive, he wondered? When they parted she tore up the photos of an earlier trip, which Alun had sent her, saying she had them already. Was that symbolic? What could it have been symbolic of? But then she said to phone.

'I'll leave the Ansaphone on. Just ring and say you're down here.'

He tried her number. Several times. Always the flaming Ansaphone. Then, taking him unawares, it was her.

'Hallo,' he said on sudden inspiration, 'is that Susanna's Ansaphone?'

'No,' her cool voice came back with mock indignation. 'It's me, Susanna.' His heart leapt at the slight hint of a gurgling laugh. He invented a story about a non-existent specialist database for properties which they might think of distributing. But in the end he was left still uncertain.

Later that week, she wrote ambiguously on her office letterhead:

Dear Alun,

Going back to our talk, you may find Intuition International can get you a market. Sorry I didn't think of it at the time. Do give me a ring any time you're down here again.

Yours sincerely

Now, a week later, his heart lifted as the train trundled west. He had left a message on the Ansaphone. Maybe next day she'd come. Maybe next night they'd be together. Should he gather her in his arms? A bit daunting really. He phoned. A male voice.

152

He replaced the receiver very quietly. Try again in the morning, maybe at her work number – she ran a small travel and cottages agency inland in Machynlleth.

That night on the boat he had been extraordinarily happy, with a happiness that was totally inexplicable in the face of such lukewarm, ambivalent encouragement. She was so damned elusive. Now warm and friendly, now dismissive. It was like trying to butter a hot crumpet. Nevertheless, butter it he would. Be it ne'er so slippery. Be the crumpet fierily toasted, and the butter straight from the fridge. The estuary was shifting shades of grey in the pale moonlight, the outlines of the mountain, Cader Idris, just visible. A barn owl hooted from the woods above. He could see a long line of waders, oyster-catchers no doubt, sitting by the water's edge on the Aberteifi shore, ready for daylight, and the falling tide which would enable them to feed. He switched on the radio just in time to catch that glorious masculine feminine counterpoint, dialogue or whatever, between flute and french horn, which starts the last movement of Brahms' First Symphony. The next day had to be great.

It dawned beautifully. Crisp frost thick on the supine mizzen mast, sun flicking the mountain peak.

He'd get on with something useful but ungrubby. He found himself singing softly from 'I'd go to Louisiana':

'Oh Susanna, won't you come to me?
For I'll go to Louisiana with a banjo on my knee.'

The occasional truck came past for the yacht club, but nary a car. And nary that dark blue thing, slippery shaped like a falling raindrop, with the pencil thin tyres. Once his heart lifted to a distant thrum. It came closer. Too raucous; it was the old red banger sported by a friendly old sailmaker, who took on jobs which interested him when the sun shone and the pubs were shut.

No matter. Faint heart ne'er won fair lady. He'd write her a letter.

But would she take umbrage? She had a great sense of humour. Well, fairly great. For a woman. Better play it safe at first. Do what the lady said. Not lady, woman. Don't be patronising. God what a minefield.

He dialled her home and her voice ansaphoned back. At least it wasn't a man.

'Hallo Susanna,' he said, 'it's Alun. I'm here at the quay.'

He rang off. Perhaps also ring her office Ansaphone. Just sing softly:

'For I'd go to Louisiana with a banjo on my knee.'

He did so.

Nine. He'd go to the shops for some strawberries. He left a note signalled by two piles of kettles and saucepans on the chart table.:

Susanna

Gone shopping. Lovely to see you. Back by ten. Greetings
Do have some coffee

Alun

During the day it incremented steadily:

Susanna

Gone shopping – musselling – chandling. Back by ten – one – five
Greetings
Do have some coffee – tea

Alun

All day passed. She didn't come, but he got a lot of jobs done. He'd posted the letter. What else to do? He'd telephone again to the Ansaphone, tell her he'd spotted a Greater Spotted Shag. She loved birds, a keen ornithologist. Couldn't fail, that.

Not Shag, for God's sake. What might she think? Tricky as hell with women, ornithology. Imagine, golden-breasted white-tits. Perhaps they are. Lovely idea but disastrous. Not Shag, Cormorant.

'Hello Susanna,' he phoned, clearing his throat nervously, 'it's

154

Alun. There's a Greater Spotted ShCormorant just across on the South Bank. Thought I'd tell you.'

Next morning he was less unduly sanguine. He decided to try again with the phone. Maybe she'd got the letter. Perhaps send another just in case. No, the phone:

'"She cometh nort, he said,"' he quoted. From 'La Belle Dame Sans Merci', wasn't it? No, 'The Lady of Shallot', via P G Wodehouse.[34]

Back to work again, crouching on his side at the barnacle-encrusted loo outlet, low down on the outside of the hull. The bronze of the pump shaft was getting scored. A tendency for the minutest of sprays of urine to squirt out into the cabin as one pumped. He'd ask old male friends to pee in the milk carton. Not the currently-current milk carton, the currently-previous. Or perhaps the previously-current. Who can tell? One each of course, personal, dignified. Colour-coded? Or a keyboard with modulus 11 check digit verification? Something professional yet tasteful. A transponder on the right wrist perhaps to identify the donor. Left wrist of course for Muslims. Suddenly a quiet, feminine Dorsetshire voice behind him:

'Hallo,' it said.

'Susanna! It's you!'

The little blue car waggled north round the coast road to Barmouth. It parked all day and all night outside a picturesque little pub called the Angry Cheese.

Downside, Chapter 18: Pensarn-Bardsey

Back at Pensarn the next morning Johnson and apWilliams poled, rowed and sailed the boat up to the Ranch, the old slate wharf, where astonishingly large 3-masters carrying slate for the world used to load. How on earth, they debated, did they manoeuvre these vessels up creeks through which we were hard-pressed to squeeze a 30-footer?

They lashed the ketch upright alongside and started replacing the stainless rigging with the old pre-stretched Terylene used in happier times by the 'Nuts Club', groups of handicapped children from the Midlands, to lash together barrels and timbers for their weekly raft race. The spars looked to be all right, and Johnson forgot about the snag they'd felt as they hoisted the main.

Three days later they had finished rerigging. The morning tide slid in over the sands and mudflats where the turnstones used to search for crabs on a sleepover in their passage from Greenland to Morocco. And the oyster-catchers to swoop in racketing echelons searching for food or just enjoying the view or libelling a neighbour. Of the 50-odd varieties of old, not a bird was to be seen, though in the crunchy samphire-spread green in the 'tweentide areas, no doubt the succulent big mussels, roaming crustacea and swirling grey mullet still harvested the estuary. With the flooding tide came an unseasonal north-easter. Reasonably stocked up with the Victoria's tinned stuffs, muesli and a stack of early apples and plums, they sailed out and off towards the outlines of St Tudwals Islands due west. There was a sudden loud sigh and plop from the water to starboard.

'Johnson, d'you hear that?' said Alun elatedly.

'Yes. Dolphin probably. Bluenose. Or maybe Whissoes. Get them quite often round here. Go with the ketch some times for half-an-hour or more, a couple of feet away from the hull. Lovely. They seem to like the old lady's shape. Motherly.'

apWilliams took a deep breath and chipped in with feeling.

'Not in the last 20 years they haven't, mate. Never a dolphin, seal, sheep, collie, wild goat, rabbit or even a field mouse. Nothing red-blooded at all. Bar the pigs.'

'Of course. Sorry, I was forgetting.'

Towards midday the wind lightened to nothing, just balanced by the onshore pressure as the land warmed up. They were in the middle of the bay, about the spot where the Edwardian poet, Catholic philosopher, MP, novelist, historian and yachtie, Hilaire Belloc, found what he called the 'finest panorama in all Europe', the long spreading curve of Cardigan Bay. It was he who wrote the lovely poem:

Do you remember an inn, Miranda,
Do you remember an inn?
And the tedding and the spreading
Of the straw for a bedding,
And the fleas that tease in the High Pyrenees...

Belloc. A guy who should know the odd panorama. Johnson recalled the summer snows up in the highest Pyrenean passes, walking over snowdrifts with the girls in bikinis in the warm sunshine.

The boat lay becalmed, motionless in the midday sun, 4 miles out in the bay. They were both fed up and impatient.

'Tell you what, Johnson. Bore me with a story from your imperial past,' said Alun.

'Funny you should say that, because imperial was just what I was thinking about. Princess Elizabeth of Toro in fact. Daughter of a real African King, the Omukama of Toro. Cambridge history degree...'

'Ah, yes,' interrupted apWilliams, 'I remember something about this. That guy Thruston and his book about the wars against the Banyoro in the 1890s. Dipped into bits of it.'

'That's right. Kabarega reconquered Toro, which had been an off-shoot of Bunyoro.'

'Well, anyway, go on about the princess. What was her name again? Nadine, wasn't it?'

Johnson flushed slightly. 'I don't know a... What made you think she was called that?'

'Could have sworn you said it some time.'

'Don't think so... Anyway, the woman's name was Elizabeth. Princess Elizabeth of Toro. Well, when she was in the UK she was a legendary model, often on the cover of *Vogue*, barrister – to be a barrister was almost invariably the target of young ambitious Ugandans of her generation – later she became her country's roving ambassador and then Foreign Minister for Idi Amin, until she refused his matrimonial advances. Fourth wife I think, she was lined up to become. She turned him down, and just managed to escape. A courageous journey, first home to Fort Portal in the foothills of the Ruwenzoris, then secretly through the byways and bush right across the country to Kenya.

'Her most striking achievement was her address as Foreign Minister to the full UN General Assembly in New York; hailed as a triumph for the Third World view, and a boost for both womens' and black rights generally. Reading her absorbing autobiography gives you an insight into all manner of aspects of the short, dramatic 70 years of the British Empire in East Africa.'

'Shouldn't you luff up a bit? We're dropping down towards the Sarn,' interposed apWilliams.

'Sorry, she's barely got steerage way. Anyway. In getting at the truth of early African history, you meet one major obstacle, the absence of any articulate record by the key men, the then kings and chiefs, of the realities as they saw them. Written records by the *indigènes* were rare until the time of the elected politicians. And these guys had little touch with, still less empathy with, the earlier realities of protectorate rule. The astonishingly well-tempered, spontaneous, usually happy relationship between the rulers and ruled that you found up-country, say on a typical District Officer's safari and his *barazas* with the chiefs and people. "Lackeys of imperialism", the communist propaganda used to call the chiefs. But they survived imperialism unimpaired, to remain pivotal to their countries to the present day. Like British monarchs; your politicians weave their spells but come and go like summer showers. But you know your chief and he's with you forever. And of course government through the chiefs and "native rulers" was the keystone of British imperialism – the theory of Indirect Rule as formulated by its great rationaliser, Lord Hailey, in 2 massive, unreadable, erudite

158

volumes. That's why the whole nineties politically-correct whinge about "the imperialists desecrating pre-colonial cultures" seemed so curiously ignorant. The strategy was to build on these structures, not to desecrate them. Perhaps in Uganda's case that was our one big mistake – we fought shy of imposing a unitary state on the kingdoms. But as for the chiefs, 50 years on and they're still alive and flourishing.

'But the successful African politician in the late fifties usually made his way on the crest of a wave of anti-establishment vilification propagated on the suddenly ubiquitous transistor radio. In the space of 4 short years the whole gradual process towards development and democracy suddenly became a headlong dash. A historian might say the Brits should have stayed, to be an anvil on which the new nation's identity could have been forged in blood and iron. But in fact, there was no way we could have stayed even in a model district like Kigezi. Fourteen unarmed white civilian administrators, medicos, teachers, missionaries, agriculturalists, engineers, surveyors; among a million lively, black, tough, assertive tribesmen? No chance. The Empire,[35] like the UK itself, had always resisted having significant armed forces. Small regular armies were the ideal, and rule was always based effectively on tacit assent – how else could you govern an empire expanding reluctantly at 100,000 square miles a year from 1815 to 1860, a quarter of the globe, with a smaller army than that of Austria?

'A lot of us did stay on after independence, and more were invited to. But independence was inevitable. Government had to have at least the tacit consent of the governed or you were lost. A notional contract. Just as John Locke was saying in the seventeenth century. So to delay independence was not a serious option.'

'Yes, yes, perhaps,' apWilliams sighed. 'You do witter on about it. How would I know? Anyway, what about the princess?'

'Sorry. Yes, well, she was by all accounts a real honey and a fiery one, picture in all the English papers, modelling for *Vogue*. I remember the Saza Chief of Bufumbira in a *baraza*, taking off the way the cattle peoples trained their womenfolk to walk – their languid, upright, carefree, damn-you, hip-swaying motion in imitation of the graceful long-horned cattle that were their pride

GRAHAM TOTTLE

and joy. No doubt she had that. And the stunning, sexy, hip-wiggling joyful dancing of the Batoro and Baganda women.

'Her book speaks volumes, because, despite her Cambridge training, it's a mixture of perceptive and accurate observation with highly-biased defence of her dynasty, and often very transparent political correctness. Obligatory in the nineties for an African to bad-mouth imperialism, just like the ritual denunciations of the "Gang of Four" we used to hear at the start of every meeting when I was in China in the late seventies.

'You find that all over her book, but I remember for example a statement "After 400 years of slavery, Africa was invaded in the nineteenth century by the European trading companies." Leave aside the question whether firms like the British India Steam Navigation Co, or McKinnon McKenzie were "invading" – many would conclude it was a mutually beneficial commercial relationship with strong overtones of militarism on both sides. And a key strand in the pacification and development of a region that was being ripped apart by incessant tribal and ethnic warfare.

'But leaving that aside, what is the truth about 4 centuries of slavery? Here's a consummately well-educated woman, the king's daughter, steeped in the "before and after" aspects of the time like perhaps no other person, Cambridge degree, and yet she comes up with such an obvious inaccuracy.

'Like much of the African interior, the kingdoms of the Great Lakes and Europe had no mutual contact whatsoever until the first visits of Speke, Grant, Stanley, Sir Sam and Lady Baker and that generation of mid-Victorian explorers. To talk of "400 years of slavery" demeans the very distinctive and flourishing cultural heritage of the Batoro. Slavery to whom? Until the 1880s most of the Sub-Saharan interior of Africa was "The Dark Continent", as unknown to Europe as Europe was unknown to it. The export of ivory and later slaves to Arab traders was not significant till the 1840s. In reality, 3 of the 4 centuries were filled with turbulent, whirlpooling migrations and fighting among the various tribes and ethnic groups, Bantu, Nilotics, Nilo-hamitics, such as Europe hasn't seen since the Dark Ages, or Asia since the Moguls. Eventually, the invading Lwo peoples from the north instituted the Babito dynasties, of which Princess Elizabeth's was one, from the sixteenth century on.

160

'But I'm not trying to defend the scramble for Africa, but to get at the question which is much more important for the modern day, or what's left of the modern day, which is that so much African thinking was bedevilled with this myth of imperial exploitation. Nationalism, they taught us at Oxford, was based on myths of the past and dreams of the future. And if you build on myths which are just concoctions, you're building your nation on sand. Take Chinua Achebe and his caricature of the bad colonialist, Smith for example, or Ben Okri commenting on Rwanda.'[36]

'Yes,' said apWilliams, 'or tiny nationalism now. Didn't you mention Scottish Independence and a referendum?'

'Indeed. Voted on by pygmies standing on the shoulders of giants, it was said. Take a Scot like Sean Connery. Built an enormous acting career playing an English spy, James Bond, 007, licensed to kill, dreamed up by a real spy, Ian Fleming, an Englishman. Would that happy relationship have taken place if they'd been in different small countries, faffing about with borders, passports, taxes and whatever? I'm amazed that a snapping-off with a great past and a descent into a tiny future should be made by such a small group. Those who were registered voters in Scotland on a single day. What about the Scottish diaspora, spread all around the world? What about the Scots south of the border? What about Anglo-Scots like me? What about the Irish? What about the Welsh? What about the English? Surely such a massive break-up should have been referred to them.'

'No idea who they are, but let's hear more about the princess. Were they real kingdoms, or just chiefdoms like they showed for Zimbabwe and Rhodes on TV?'

'No, real kingdoms, evolved by themselves, with their own civil service, structures, land tenure system, retirement pensions for chiefs and so on. The small strip system of land holding, for example, was closely similar to the open-field system in medieval England.'

'Maitland,' said apWilliams.

'What was that?'

'Maitland. The English open-field system, or some such historical title. I remember it from way back. Feudal.

Extraordinarily complex, supplanted in Tudor times by the enclosure movement. Until then almost everyone had strips of land all over the manor. And there were even still some of the traditional open-strip fields around in Lincolnshire in the 1850s.'

'Absolutely. As I walked the Kigezi hills, I thought the system had great advantages; equality and fraternity – everyone got a fair share of the good and poor land, everyone chatted with everyone else. To walk round all your holdings might be a distance of 3 or 4 miles.'

'That's a hell of an overhead, surely?'

'Yes. But a very pleasant one. Contrast it with the lot of some of our hill farmers in the 2000s – sometimes immensely fulfilled, but often isolated, depressed and even suicidal. As in Hobbes's picture in Leviathan: "And the life of man: solitary, poor, nasty, brutish and short". Churches nearly dead. Sheep not wanted. And not even a weekly bus into the town.'

'Yes,' said apWilliams, 'but Hobbes was painting a massive human shape, composed of hundreds of tiny individuals, all scrambling over each other like people in a dictator's jail. Not a scattering of solitary hill farmers.'

'True, but that was his picture of the State. A body corporate, which was vital to keep people's vainglory within bounds. The "solitary, poor" etcetera bit was what would result if there wasn't a state. I think perhaps you can perceive it all from 2 viewpoints. The romantic from J-J Rousseau – man is born free, yet everywhere he is in chains. Most black African writers took that view till the late nineties; a tremendously appealing picture of a happy, egalitarian society where people were free and expressed their views. Then these views were taken into account in a sort of consensus among the elders under the chief's wise guidance. It's the feel you get from Mandela's tremendous autobiography, for example. But his picture was of a society in which the Methodist missionaries had already had immense civilising influence. By then the missions had eradicated the horrors of the Kabaka's court, or the Bakiga's marriage and illegitimacy practices. Young, unmarried, pregnant Kiga mums were beaten by their menfolk till they revealed the father's name. And then, if, as with many lovers, they refused, they were hurled over a cliff into a waterfall

162

and death by their dads. These horrors had been suppressed through Christianity. Through the much maligned "theological scramble for Africa".'

'I remember a quote from Bagehot, the nineteenth-century historian, in our constitutional history,' said apWilliams. 'Something like "There is no method by which men can be both free and equal". It came to mind when I was working in North Korea. There you had the most repressive, totalitarian society imaginable, over which Our Great Leader President Kim Il-sung, OGLPKIS for short, ruled and brooded like Hobbes's Leviathan. Score zero for liberty. But fraternity and equality? Ten each, I guess. I was there when the old man got back from a long, key visit to Beijing. The whole of Pyongyang was on the streets to greet him. Like Dr Chu, my counterpart, said, nowhere in the world could you see such an outpouring of love, even in Cuba. Not in the UK, I guess, since Elizabeth the First's or Nelson's funerals. The Koreans' passion for equality came out all over the place. Chu, for example, Head of the Soil Research Institute, crucial to their agriculture, earned just 40 per cent more than the average urban wage, and was very proud of it.

'I remember particularly the Friday rule – every Friday all the elite, all the office workers, bosses and researchers, had to go out and work in the fields. Why, I never quite understood, but I'm sure it had something to do with Kim Il-sung's "Juche Ideal", giving oneself to the people. Dr Han, Miss Li, the programmer, and Mr Ho, the hardware engineer and minder, all had to get special dispensation to stay in and work with me. But everyone else, director down, was out in the fields hoeing. Generally, the appearance of a society at peace with itself was moving and totally unexpected.'

'Yes, I can imagine,' said Johnson. 'One of the things people took on board in the noughts – diversity is just as important politically as biologically. The triumphant Western blueprint, like all blueprints, has major flaws. The pre-colonial realities for Uganda were documented by sympathetic anthropologists like Roscoe about the Banyoro and Mary Edel about the Bakiga. I haven't found any attempt to revise their picture. It's accurate, and most writers and historians avoid discussing it. No doubt to avoid giving offence.'

'I seem to remember,' apWilliams commented, 'funny stories by comedians about how you could kid along the sociologists. People like Bruce Chatwin when he was writing *Songlines*. Allegedly, the Aborigines would phone their mates ahead of him and suggest stimulating rituals their friends might invent for him when he arrived. These stories of Aborigines who might get to the sea from the middle of Australia. They'd follow, they said, the song lines which covered all Australia, a scent trail of musical notes, the tracks of their ancestors, a trail right from the centre to the sea.'

'That reached a peak, with political correctness, in the late nineties,' replied Johnson. 'The social anthropologists came under attack, and people suggested that Edel or Roscoe were just being strung along by tribespeople who were taking the Mickey. Possibly true, as regards interviews between the Australian novelist Bruce Chatwin and modern-day Aborigines. Allegedly, they used to tell him all sorts of yarns, then phone ahead to their mates to brief them before he came. But then Chatwin was a brilliantly imaginative writer, not a professional anthropologist. People like Edel however were trained professionals. They lived for periods of a year or more with the tribes concerned, spoke their languages and so forth, in times like the thirties when Western influence was barely discernible. If you want to believe they were all being hoaxed of course, you can. Or that they were "exoticising" what they observed to gain readership. But the idea is not convincing unless you're really gullible and work hard at it. And there are some accounts by contemporary Ugandans that corroborate Mary Edel's description. As a side view from my own experience in the sixties, I remember one of our interpreters telling me how important it was to discourage the old Bakiga marriage practices. Interpreters, for a new boy like me, were a bit like sergeant majors in the army, guiding young sub-alterns in the realities of life. They were key men, with promising careers ahead, and they knew it. Anyway, full of the student attitudes of the fifties, I said surely it was good to maintain these cultural links, or words to that effect. "Mr Johnson," he said, "have you read about these practices?" I did. He was right.'

Johnson's eyes roamed the horizon. Still as stone, not a breath of wind, not a ripple on the surface. To the north-east, he could see below the Snowdon massif the little port of Porthmadog, and further away a speck of Mediterranean colour, orange perhaps, on the sea reaches of the River Dwyryd.

Downside, Chapter 19: Porth Meirion

Across the sprawling sandy estuary of the River Dwyryd, where it narrows in from a mile to a bare quarter in width, just before it winds up into the mountains, lies a little Italianate village called Porth Meirion. Baroque villas and *pensiones* painted in faded pastel yellows and oranges; cypresses, pines and yews clustered among the cliff faces; and a little Italian church; all cling to the steep rocks as if in a place-warp from the Golfo di Salerno. A long, slate quay, water to float a boat only at high tide, fronts onto the river. A square-rigger lies alongside it. One or two benches still invite you to sit and drink. A fine municipal lamp standard from Capri graces the weedy gravel.

In an upstairs bar in one *pensione*, the hot early afternoon sunshine beams in through tall, narrow, gothic casements, and gleams off a waxy oak floor which twists and ripples with age. At the bar deep at the far end stands a bar-lady, plump, *décolletée*, looking saucily wide-eyed at an athletic, broad-shouldered dark-haired man as she pulls a pint. He is wearing a costly looking dinner jacket and trousers, dicky and hand-tied bow tie. Do with a press. She is leaning sideways and backward as the glass fills and the head flows away. He comes round the bar and grabs her. She giggles delightedly.

'Ooh, Lord Tite Barnacle, what are you doing? Oh deary me. Oh deary deary me!'

*****

Five miles south-west in the bay, Johnson was continuing describing the Uganda of the 1870s.

'As with the stark realities of Kiga society, preggy mums hurled over waterfalls and so on, so it was with the accounts of the horrors of the Kabaka's court written by men like Speke, Grant, Emin Pasha, Apolo Kagwa and Thruston. Him particularly, because he was a clear-eyed guy with little sympathy with the Victorian imperial attitudes of his time. Got murdered eventually

166

by the Banyoro, who rightly saw him as a threat to their kingdom and culture. Were these accounts all fabrications? Highly improbable, if you study their diaries.[37]

'But the clincher arises from hobbyists in genealogy. It's a hobby now among many Baganda, as with most people. But they face difficulties – you can never be sure, for the times before Uganda's *Pax Britannica,* as Graham Greene called it, the great Victorian peace, that great-great-great Uncle Fred really was great-great-great Uncle Fred. Not for the reasons you'd expect, no birth registration records, because the Baganda can often trace the generations back, even in some cases to the sixteenth century. The line of progenitors was a matter of keen verbal record, passed down from father to son. Abraham begat Isaac, and Isaac begat Jacob and so on. A reason perhaps why they like the Old Testament so much.

'No, the difficulty arose because of the terrifying nature of the Kabaka's court. As with medieval European courts, the top barons were obliged to send their first-born, or at least one of their sons, to court. To pick up the flavour; training, experience and so on. Also as hostages, no doubt, for the baron's dutiful subservience. But because of the hazards, many barons used to send not their sons, but a scion of some lesser guy, going along with the son's name, as Fred, or Bisamunyu or whoever. So tracking back to great-great-great Uncle Fred has to take account of this major fault in the records. Did Abraham really beget Isaac? As a Malaysian might say, who can tell?

'Moving on, I remember some memorable and happy safaris with the Mutwale, Bufumbira, the senior chief on the Rwandan border. He had strips of land all around the county, and 4 wives, each with a home located to match. It must have been an effective way of sussing out and influencing the consensus of opinion among the people.

'A key question is: what should we in the West have done in these societies in the 1890s? Chris Patten in a celebrated keynote Reith lecture in 2012 said, "I imagine no one now would defend the colonial system". It's no good imagining, mate. Study it in depth and come up with a credible alternative that would have served better. Should we have quarantined them, stood back for 5 centuries and let the normal process of history take its course?

Let the pregnant girls be hurled over the waterfalls, the pages have their heads burst open by wooden vices for slipping as they crouched to cushion the royal backside? Should we have waited for a Ugandan parliamentary democracy to evolve by itself, and an enclosure movement to develop to replace their feudal strip landholding system, and so on?

'In fact, we tried to intervene in some systems; a voluntary land consolidation scheme for example, with government surveyors coming out to mark plot boundaries, and committees of local peasants to try to negotiate exchanges, so that fairly consolidated land holdings resulted. The theory was that you couldn't develop competitive agriculture without consolidation – the idle would hold their go-getter neighbours back, weeds would spread across the tiny plots unhindered and so on. It was very successful among the Kikuyu in Kenya until, sadly, Jomo Kenyatta scotched it to gain political influence. But the people in Bufumbira were less receptive. And, crucially, the Mutwale, the Chief, stayed firmly on the touchline. It's still a key development issue worldwide. FAO used to reckon that the one most fundamental thing you could do to resolve underdevelopment and poverty was land reform. Consolidation, and the gradual elimination of tenantry systems, to have free smallholders instead. Desirable, but usually politically impossible.

'Bugandan society had many other characteristics of European and Asian feudalism, evolved entirely independently. Speke and Grant were astonished to find, as they approached the massive mysterious lake, which they named Victoria, the source of a desert-defying river that had intrigued and confounded the geographers for 2 millennia. Pulsing with unaccountable floods 2,000 miles through the harshest of the world's deserts. And as they approached the fabled Mountains of the Moon, they saw snows on the equator. Impossible, said the geographers.

'They were astonished to find that in place of the scruffy *kraals* and the ill-defined tracks through dry bush which characterised inland Africa in many parts, there were wide, straight thorough-fares on dark red earth, verged by green grass, running up hill and down dale between lush, neatly cultivated gardens. The houses were sharply thatched with the same thick papyrus reed thatching which looks so good on ancient Egyptian and Meroitic murals, and the people were finely dressed in soft, beaten bark cloth from bark stripped off the mutuba tree, in place of smelly part-cured hides.

'As they approached along by the lake, there was ever-growing evidence of civilisation, till they reached the capital on a hilltop. It was a sort of palace, which started with a wide ring of outer huts surrounding a regal centre. And here they found crowds strolling around, the women bare to the waist, in soft brown skirts, the men in long toga-like gowns, "recalling the saints, the Blessed walking in Paradise", as, if I remember correctly, the explorer Harry Johnston put it.'

'What time're we eating? No rush, just wish to know – your turn,' interrupted apWilliams.

'How about 2-ish?'

Downside, Chapter 20: At Sea off Porth Meirion

Johnson and apWilliams continued chatting as the boat idled her way in a ghost of a breeze towards Bardsey.

'Fine,' said apWilliams, 'Do go on. We're with these topless Ugandan honeys in slinky barkcloth skirts.'

'Are we? Your mind doesn't improve. OK. Well, Speke and Grant reached a group of more spacious huts, in the centre of which the king held court on a platform of grass covered by a red carpet. And there they reached the "worm i' the bud", the *Kabaka*, with an incredibly obsequious entourage of nobles, wives, a hundred or more, page boys and slaves. I remember how shocked I was at the massive Western Province *baraza* for the Queen Mum in 1959, to see the Omukama's chief clerk leaving his king's presence. He grovelled away backwards on his knees across the field, with a fine simulation of abject terror, until he reached the distance, 30 yards or so, at which it was seemly for mere clerks to walk.'

'Handy skill,' interrupted apWilliams. 'Handy I guess, if you're on a rearing foredeck in a gale, get down on your knees. The number of times I've seen people standing up, falling all over the place as they switch from zero gravity to 2 plus in all manner of directions at once. Overboard but for their lifelines.'

'Absolutely,' continued Johnson. 'Put your dignity aside; kneel down and try surviving instead. Anyway, back to the worm in the bud, Sabassajja the *Kabaka*; in 1862, the young Mutesa II. The court was reminiscent of that of the French *Roi Soleil*, Louis XIV, the Sun King, with the same pomp and ritual attending his every function. But whereas in France, the king's displeasure was metaphorical death, in Buganda it was actual death, often under excruciating torture. The king would promenade striding like a rampant lion, stiff-legged, over the grasses, in a blue check dress, his face covered sometimes in white warpaste.

'Very reminiscent of those chilling witchcraft dances which the South Africans Vincent Mantsoe, Brett Bailey and Boyzie Cekwana put together in the nineties. Dancers overlooking the beauties of the veldt or Robben Island; ash-daubed dancers, their mouths contorted into savage snarls or grins, drooling dark, red, sticky blood which slurps in sticky gobbets down onto the earth. And matching hostility and terror. Expressing an element of evil more powerfully even than say Stravinsky, or Sir James Frazer in *The Golden Bough.* Remember the magical, solitary king-for-the-year, skulking through the forest in Dark Ages Tuscany, waiting for his successor to murder him. What most races lacked was the healing, civilising influence of Christianity and similar religions; without it our Dark Ages would no doubt have been just as terrifying as those of the Baganda.

'So, anyway, the *Kabaka* would stride stiff-legged, with a massive crowd in admiring attendance. If he stopped to speak the crowd would wait in tense silence. When he stopped speaking, they would throw themselves to the ground uttering strange cries. "*Yanziga. Yanziga.*" Dissent of course was unthinkable, but even the most trivial error in ritual brought death. If the king bethought himself to sit, one of the pages, as for Queen Victoria, had to get a seat in place to anticipate the royal bottom. But in this case the seat was the page himself, and for a minor error he would be dragged off screaming to execution. Heads were lopped off with casual indiscriminacy, and terror was the predominant feature of the state. At the first meeting with Speke, the *Kabaka* demanded his rifle. Speke demurred, and then when things looked ugly, gave in. Mutesa handed the gun to someone, and gave a command. The rifle holder went outside, ordered someone to run, drew a bead on his head, waited a bit and shot him dead. This met with mild admiration.'

'Blimey.'

'Yes. Still, who are we to talk? Think of the Holocaust.'

'But I didn't personally participate,' said apWilliams.

'Ah. Well. There's a thing. Though that was the reaction of the generations of the eighties and nineties.'

'I remember a teenager saying in a TV debate "Not my fault, so why should I bother?" But the reply from his mate was "It's nobody's fault, stupid, that's why we should all bother." That was

171

the breakthrough, when people generally came to accept that it wasn't anyone's fault. Where was the virtue in lumbering generations of British youngsters with a burden of guilt for a trumped-up past, most of it a lot of hooey? Guilt and so on weren't the answer. Humans, black, white and brown, had obeyed their natural instincts. Xenophobia, and racism, for example, had had tremendous survival value for millennia. But not in the future.'

'OK. End of sermon.'

'Right. But what you from the Downside won't be familiar with, is the impact of that realisation. After the Gulf War hostagedoms. The terrorist outrages. The tourist massacres. Geneticism. Aidsism. Bioterrorism. The agricultural wars. Not that those were especially severe. But people came to realise that guilt wasn't the answer. And also that in many respects, we in the West were building a hell for ourselves as well as the rest of the world. Even in the late nineties there were many countries where Westerners could go only if they stayed in the tourist enclaves. A no-go globe. "Stay within the resort," the adverts used to say, "and you'll be perfectly safe." Like Boers' *laagers* in the 1860s. Even in specialist tourist economies like the Gambia. Create a world where some people throw billions away in waste, while others have to survive on a dollar a day in lives whose quality is vastly worse than mankind has ever known, and that's what you get. It was becoming a battleground between wealth, surveillance and repressive technology on the one hand, and terrorism and hostageism on the other. And, happily, it got thrown over. But, getting back to Buganda, I'd like to give you a feel for the depth of all this. Take the languages. *Owekitiinisa* is the normal honorific in the Rukiga language. *Owekitiinisa* Judge Kyabazinga for example. His Honour Judge Kyabazinga. But it didn't mean "his honour", although that's how it is construed nowadays. It meant "he who causes fear". *Kutiina,* to fear, *ku-tiin-isa,* to cause to fear, *ow-ekitiin-isa,* he who causes fear. The fascinating Bantu language structure, complex, with up to 14 different noun classes common to over a thousand different languages – we used to find the 5 noun classes in Latin hard enough. You find these classes and the same grammar right the way down through central Africa to Zimbabwe and the RSA. Enormously complex, sophisticated, and totally unplanned and undocumented. A good manifestation of Chomsky's "transformational grammar". Some fundamental grammatical structure which we all have in our brains before birth, some astonishing structure which we fill in appropriately as we listen to our parents. Like burning in an uncommitted logic array for a computer perhaps.'

'What's all that got to do with the Batoro? What about the maxim gun, then? Hardly a fair contest,' interrupted apWilliams.

'Sorry, diversion. But the idea that authority equates with fear was fundamental. I remember an ironic jingle about the maxim gun from the imperialist London of the 1910s or so. They loved to poke fun at the colonialists. "Whatever happens, we have got the maxim gun, and they have not." Makes you think of the Mahdi rebellion in the Sudan, and Kitchener's men mowing down the 11,000 Mahdi heroes. But if you take the situation for men like Speke, Grant or Lugard in Kampala, the first Brits in those parts, it was totally different and pretty daunting. Not a lot of maxims about, one in fact; a handful of mutinous Sudanese troops, a small hill, and thousands upon thousands of well-organised Baganda carrying muzzle-loaders and spears, ruled by an unpredictable Pinochet-like despot whose least word could lop a head off. Similar to Rhodes's emissaries at the court of Lobengula, tense and rightly fearful for their lives, though Lobengula of course was a benevolent despot rather than an ambivalent one.

'And, going back to Toro and the princess, there was always a certain tension in the relationship between the 4 southern "kingdoms", particularly Buganda kingdom, and the central government of country under the Brits. This tension was to contribute massively to the tragedy of the seventies, Amin and Obote.

'You find tension and bias against the central government often in Princess Elizabeth's book; for example she alleged that to destroy the Toro tribal culture the government injected all the Toro cattle, symbol of their wealth and identity, with sleeping-sickness, contained in special sleeping sickness vaccines intentionally imported from Botswana and Gambia.

'She's certainly right that there was a massive epidemic of trypanosomiasis, sleeping sickness, which was enzootic. But the

173

idea that the proud Uganda Veterinary Service would go around propagating the disease in a vaccine for political ends boggles the mind. The vets were just trying desperately hard to control a vicious disease. They followed all manner of strategies for it, but with limited success. I remember voluntary resettlement, and the clearing of riverine bush, and Tsetse guards who used to stop all traffic and search each vehicle for the tsetse flies. But imagine making a similar allegation about UK vets. People would just laugh. The same in Uganda. On this and a lot of other issues, she was writing what a post-colonialist Western public wanted to hear. If you wanted to find out the truth, you had to go to the real historians – boring but accurate. There was indeed, for example, a serious epidemic of the cattle disease, rinderpest, in the thirties. The preventive innoculation campaign was widely and rightly criticised, and the figures are published. Perhaps this was her baseline. The point is, no one was "with malice afore-thought" poisoning the Toro cattle – the intentions were good; thereafter fell the shadow.

'She alleged that the country had no elected government until a year before independence in 1962. But she, and anyone conversant with the Uganda of the mid-fifties on, well knew that democratic elections started for the local governments in the mid-fifties and that the first national direct elections were held in 1958. Tragically, the party elected then was not re-elected in 1961, and there was another switch in 1962, so crucial years of political experience were lost. Like any other key job, being an effective democratically-elected minister needs considerable training and experience.'

'Yes. But listen,' interrupted apWilliams, 'six years. Hardly a lengthy period of democratic experience. We should have got the whole process under way years earlier, surely? I was taught we just cut and ran. It's selling out we were. And then you had Amin and the massacres.'

Johnson became heated. 'You're trotting out the conventional wisdom of the nineties politically-correct bandwagon. I'm talking about the truth, mate. I was there. I did that. Spoke the languages. Knew the people. Tramped the hills. We weren't selling out to anyone. We were giving an independence, which the liberals among our political thinkers and academics and administrators had long envisaged. As for Amin, the relationship between the feudal, monarchical Bantu South and the egalitarian Nilohamitic peasant North was always dicey. There was an ominous question by the eventual president, Milton Obote from the North, in the Legislative Council before independence, "May I remind the Honourable Member from Buganda that 70 per cent of the army come from my province?" Or words to that effect. But we were recruited to the Uganda Government in 1957 and told to expect a career of perhaps 10 or 15 years, because the people in the Colonial Office and at the centre of the Ugandan Government in Entebbe, well realised where we were. That we were about to take off on the down-face of a gathering wave which, in the climate of the times, was unstoppable. Just like a physical wave approaching a shelving shore; it rolls gently on indefinitely, until it reaches the coast and the critical depth when its height is the same as the depth to the bottom. Then the lower half of the wave drags on the seabed, the top starts to overtake and curl over, and suddenly it breaks and crashes on the beach. That was Uganda. We want independence. Independence, willy nilly. None of your American nonsense. Full independence on the Westminster model. And we want it now.

'There were some immensely able senior Ugandans, even one of the princes, who had the courage to stand up and say it was all too quick. But I doubt they survived the seventies, and Amin and Obote. As happened to the Europeans in the First World War, many of the best of the country's future leaders were slaughtered, with people who stood out to defend democracy, the rule of law, the independence of the judiciary and similar colonial concepts.'

Johnson looked sideways from the horizon and at apWilliams. He had fallen asleep. Johnson woke him up gently.

'Your trick, mate. I'll do the grub.'

*****

They drifted onward through the middle of the bay and the middle of the day, as the onshore breeze started to pick up.

Here in Abersoch Bay, the sailing ships used to huddle at anchor in the lee of the islands of St Tudwal and the western cliffs, waiting for a favourable wind to attempt the dangerous passage round the Lleyn Peninsula, Bardsey Island, South Stack and North Stack, the route to Holyhead and the northern half of the Irish Sea. Names to conjure with. The rescue helicopters Upside had measured the height of the waves off South Stack in violent storm force 11; 60 feet, trough to wind-sliced foaming crest. Quite a hole for a boat to fall into.

In the words of Admiral Beaufort, whose scale echoes down from the seventeenth century, 'This would reduce a well-conditioned man-of-war to set storm stay-sails', 'Fishing craft could not be expected to live under such conditions', 'Such wind ashore is fortunately rarely experienced, for it causes wide-spread damage'.

Not, furthermore, 60-feet high of long surging Atlantic roller, built up by a steady fetch of a thousand miles or more, but 60 feet of fiendish Irish Sea chop, steep, towering, dropping your entire 11 metres of yacht down what seems like a sheer cliff face. Hang on, hold on and hope never to come here again.

Johnson recalled a friend with him at one of only 2 comparable frighteners on the French coast, the Chenal du Four between the mainland and Ushant island. From Ushant, Ouessant, British 'bottoms' over the centuries used to take their final departures for most of the world's oceans. Cape Trafalgar; Grand Bonhomme; Cape Agulhas; Galle; Coromandel; Pinang; Shanghai; Van Diemans Land; the Horn.

A jagged, craggy, solitary, island, Ushant was for navigators who were outward bound. Like a nail planted in your chart. This is where we are now; sunsights and dead reckoning only from here on to keep us safe offshore. Johnson's friend had been kneeling, wedged, benumbed at the fury, at the chart table, nominally marking up their position. Suddenly the whole boat was lifted up, rolled and dropped unconscionably until it hit the bottom of the trough with a crash. Before his astonished eyes the top soup plate in the rack over to leeward hurled itself upward and diagonally across the cabin, to smash against the bulkhead above his head. The shock wave must have rippled from all round the hull to centre on this one point, and shot the plate from the rack like a bolt from a crossbow. Awesome.

Towards evening, the easterly filled in again, and St Tudwals Islands, having sat motionless on the horizon, suddenly seemed to come at them.

'Let's go between the 2 islands and see if there are any seals back.'

They did so, but saw nothing.

As you go out the far side of the islands you seem to enter another, suddenly ominous, world. A surge, which never stills, wallows and hisses up the ravined cliff faces. Even in calms the pebbles surge and mumble like a toothless ancient. On the horizon, 15 miles to the west, stands the bold hump of Bardsey Island, forcing its way out into the Irish Sea as it slices apart the north-running Gulf Stream current.

Most of the current slips past Bardsey swiftly, to the west side. Off the island's eastern-most point, a fat tongue of current pours round and through the deep chasm, a sea mile and a quarter wide, where it seems as if the entire Irish Sea is banking up and hurtling through between the island and the peninsula. Pyramidal waves, shark-tooth sharp, leap at you from any-old where. Clip on and hope. No buoys, no tidal diamonds; the currents are uncharted, changing direction and speed whimsically. The few divers who have tried it say you have an unpredictable gap of slack water at most 20 minutes long between the turbulent flood and the even more turbulent ebb. And the approach to this from all directions is mined with precipitous overfalls where the tortured current is poured and mangled over undersea cliffs. Compared with this, Admiral Cloudesley Shovel and his fleet were on a navigational picnic.[38] Beautifully whorled skeins of white crests on aquamarine are at the surface, Johnson recalled, when gazed down on in sunshine from the island's summit.

The island is said to be the home for the bones of 20,000 saints.[39] People of the Dark and Middle Ages, pious or sinful or both, believed that a grave on this hallowed soil might be a passport to heaven. Three pilgrimages to Bardsey were as potent as one to Rome; in days when Rome was far from being a 3-hour flight out of Manchester Ringway. Numinous source of Celtic Christianity, run sometimes by abbots of unsullied sanctity, in recent times by a sinister guy who called himself 'King of Bardsey', and ruled his little flock with capricious violence regardless of the mainland magistrates.

At the southern end of the island is a startling, flat platform of meadowland, a few acres in extent, farmed still till the

Malfunction. Two of the 5 old farmhouses remaining were given over to religious retreats, some run by the Welsh Anglican poet R.S. Thomas, others by successors who followed his healing spirit and that of his predecessors through the centuries.

As they slipped away through the Tudwal's Islands, a 4-mile long steep shingle beach opened up to the north, flanked by long cliffs at either end. Porth Neigwl – 'Hell's Mouth' to English-speaking sailors of previous centuries. If you failed in a south-westerly gale to make the sheltered roads off St Tudwal's islands, Hell's Mouth lay waiting, at right angles to the winds and waves, with an agonisingly long, probably doomed, struggle by the ship to claw off to windward. Groups of sympathisers, spectators or wreckers on the beaches.

An hour to the west, and then you were forced about by the headland. Another hour to the south-east, then you were forced about by the other headland. Sometimes, with lifting hope, making a bit out to seawards and safety. Then losing it all on the turn. Remorselessly slipping shorewards, until the shallowing sea bottom built the waves up steeper, and the waves curled their crests and knocked her ever faster to leeward. Hoping desperately for a break or a wind-shift, until... Until she grounds and pounds herself to pieces, strewing her crew across the breakers. What could they have done? Maybe strip off to the buff for lightness, and try to swim or surf in perhaps. But sailors in those days usually could not swim – better, they believed, a quick death if you were swept in, than an anguishing struggle against the inevitable. The wind this time however was right aft behind them, and the bay formed a nice lee to shelter in.

But black clouds were building over the mountains, the seas were steepening and they started rolling violently and almost stopping dead as they entered a tide rip off the headland. The boat seemed safe, despite corkscrewing wildly, boom end dipping at one end of each roll, and the mast leaning at 45 degrees to the water on the other.

'Four hours of this to come till the tide turns,' said Johnson.

'Yes. Maybe cut in behind the headland, do you think?'

They headed inshore into the lee of the cliffs and dropped anchor right in the corner. They could see the crests breaking off the headland. And so the crests continued for 2 more days, the wind a good force 8 from the East. No weather to try getting through or round or anywhere near Bardsey.

Dawn on the third day was grey and rough. But the wind had swung to the south-west, Force 5–6. The *Amanda* snatched uneasily at her anchor as the chain tautened as if into a straight steel bar on the big crests. Not the weather to stay in Hell's Mouth with a lee shore. Not the weather either to round Bardsey and roll her masts out on the run to the NE and Caernarfon bar. But time was short and they resolved to try to thread their way through the hatched overfalls on the chart around the southern end of the island.

Johnson recalled Dr Kemp's *Pilot's Guide to the Irish Sea*, and his gloomy description of the perils of the Sound, and his statement that the tide streams outside it were 'more normal'. But then he remembered taking a departure once from the south end of the island in pre-GPS days, before satellite navigation, when dead-reckoning, with accurate allowances for deviation, variation, tidal set and so on were vital if you were to hit the Irish coast aright. They had left Bardsey heading due west, then looked back after an hour, expecting as you did that your point of departure would be behind you over the stern. Not a sign of it. Bardsey had tramped northwards at least as fast as they were sailing and lay 45 degrees aft of abeam. So the old charts were plain wrong, anyway as regards tidal streams, which had in fact shot them way down south.

Nasty in these parts – get the streams wrong and you could be sucked into the straits. *Amanda* could just about stem the 6-knot tidal flow with a good wind in flat water, but a good wind and flat water were rare in these parts. Slack water in the sound lasted less than 20 minutes as against the normal hour or so, and it varied its timing anyway depending on all manner of variables. So the ketch stood likely to be dragged in stern-first if they got it wrong.

They got out the crucial remnants of the chart and drew lines through the shoals and overfalls. North of Devil's Tail, then south-west to cut between the island and Bastrick shoals, which covered a great patch 3 miles round, then west-north-west to slip between the overfalls off Bardsey, until they achieved a clearing bearing, looking back to the island's western tip. A bearing which meant they had cleared outside the fearsome Tripods.

Three hours or so and they'd be through. Not a doddle even with GPS, and very difficult relying on the old hand-bearing compass. But at least in these parts, unlike the flat feature-free English east coast, you had plenty of reasonably identifiable landmarks to pick up. Imagine trying to thread up the magical Swatchways on the UK's east coast without buoys and lights. Even the old coast-wise barge masters would be hard-pressed to avoid the patchwork of tidal sands that stretch way out of sight of land.

Getting the anchor up was a tough assignment without an engine to help take the strain. Working single-handed, crouching on the foredeck looking forward and cranking the windlass lever in, was a flop. apWilliams would get 3 feet in, then a comber would throw the bow up, the chain would go bar taut, jump off the cogs and rattle back out. Snatch more chain out from the locker, throw a turn round the samson post to hold it from running further, and start again. But meanwhile you've actually slipped back towards the lee shore. They devised a drill for 2. One slumped securely forward, backside into the nook of the pulpit, and levered the windlass when the bow dropped into a trough and the chain fell slack. The other held the loose chain upwards hard against the cogs so that it couldn't jump out. In half an hour the anchor was up; she dropped away onto the port tack and sliced towards Bardsey. From this angle, it looked like a great plunging killer whale 2 miles long and 300 feet high. Seas grey and choppy, but they made good speed and the waves over the Devil's Tail rip were not severe.

But as they reached the end of Bardsey and stood out towards Ireland, the south-running tide twisted against the rising south-wester. At the same time they had to turn north, with the wind aft, corkscrewing 45 degrees either side, up towards Anglesey. Three days aboard and the boat fitted them like a glove. You could wedge yourself in place and watch with detached pleasure as the sea and sky gyrated around you in a way that would have a newcomer sick, miserable and scared stiff. On the extreme rolls, the masthead seemed almost to touch the wavetops, first on one side, then the other.

They kept way out, to avoid the reefs and overfalls. apWilliams suddenly said, 'Johnson. Look, across there. Up on the hillside, in transit with the lighthouse. Isn't that a white rock? I don't recall any white rocks up there.'

Johnson looked. 'Can't see it.'

'No, gone now.'

The wind veered onto the beam and strengthened. Reduce sail? Take a reef in the main? But they needed to get to Caernarfon Bar at the top of the flood. So no. The wind veered further into the north, now against the rising flood tide, and heavy seas started breaking.

'We'll finish this tack in-shore, go about and then reef her. What do you think?'

'Yes, fine.'

By this time Bardsey was well behind them, and the rocky coast of the Lleyn Peninsula approached. They could pick out the looping dry-stone walls, the bracken starting to turn brown, the striking yellow of the gorse. They beat inshore below Porth Dinllaen, rounded to go about onto the other tack, then there was a violent crash from above. Astonishingly, the top 8 feet of the mast hung downwards, splintered and fractured, held out sideways by the aluminium bar of the jib-furler. There was little to hold the masts up but the mizzen rigging, the lower mainstays, which hold the mast halfway up, and the inertia of the whole ragged bundle up top of rope, wire and canvas.

Johnson was flabbergasted. Not in the rule books, this one. Then he said, 'Get her off the wind smartly I think, don't you? Bearing away. Keep the mainsheet in, or we'll have the boom in the water and one hell of a big sea anchor.'

'Yip.'

'Make for the sound, I guess.'

'Then what?'

'Try to anchor behind the headland. Yes, I know it's rough and deep.'

'That, or head out to sea perhaps?'

'We might lose it all as she turns into the wind. And we're not going to sort her out at sea.'

'But the Tripods, with this lot up? And then the Sound.'

'What else?'

'Right you are. It's a big ask, though.'

Johnson rolled the wheel gingerly to starboard to head for the sound.

The broken top of the mast swung slightly as she rolled, only the bent brass track and the jib roller damping the swing and preventing the top from tumbling to self-destruction. But bend brass repeatedly and it suddenly fractures. Just like that. The mainsail was folded down and sideways at the break – jammed up since the normal means of dropping it, gravity or humans pulling down on it, were no good. The top 10 feet would have to be taken up, not down, to get up round the hanging broken section. And the bosun's chair was useless to get up there – nothing to hang it on. No sky-hook.

apWilliams looked uneasy. 'She'll be OK, number one. "Another 10 minutes and it'll only be a quarter of an hour to tea." Bet you can't place that.'

'Trinidad. Last test. 1986? Wisden.'

'Right year. But St Vincent.'

'Aye aye, skip.' The stiff upper lip game heartened them, and they sailed south.

As it thrusts out dagger-like 20 miles south-west into the Irish Sea, the Lleyn Peninsula curves gradually away to the south. The craggy shore rises higher and the seas build up menacingly. How much farther have we got to go, and how much bigger can they get? And then there's the Sound itself still to come. Mortals slip through these parts on sufferance, and the Lord God of Hosts will have you if he feels like it.

'Tell you what. Let's go for that narrow gap between the Tripods and the cliffs,' said Johnson.

'OK. But we'll be losing the light.'

'Tide's pushing us now. Another hour yet.'

'Pump her out?'

'I guess.'

Later, the romping white maelstrom of the Tripods approached just up to starboard. A driving mist built up, and the teak decks slowly darkened with moisture. They had battened the hatches and clicked on their harnesses. Nothing to do but fight the wheel to keep her on course, and hang on and hope. They had passed a spare halyard round and round the mast to dampen the movement a bit. A rogue wave surged up and broke into the cockpit. She broached, rolling sideways, and apWilliams disappeared under, emerging spluttering angrily as she pushed her stern up again.

'Sorry about that,' said Johnson.

The other grinned. 'Are you hell. Try to be more careful.'

With a full cockpit, she wallowed more heavily, the drains slow to empty it. Johnson handed over to apWilliams, slipped through and closed the main hatch, and went below to check all was well.

On deck the noise had been deafening as the wind built up. Here it was quieter, but there was a rippling, washing sound as she rolled, familiar from past severe storms. The water in the bilges had built up and was surging around over the ribs and frames. The strain on the mainmast, now half unstayed, was pulling the planks apart slightly. Reason told you it wasn't serious till the floor was awash. But you weren't convinced.

Back in the cockpit it was nearly pitch black. They could just pick out the white of the combers bursting against the cliffs, and the turbulence of the Tripods seemed to be behind them. They must almost be entering the Sound. But the wind seemed to have shifted right back into the south-west.

They talked it over.

'We'll have lost the shelter of the peninsula because of this wind-shift. So we'll have 40 miles of lee shore and no effective sails.'

'That's about it, I think. What do you reckon we can do?'

'Well, it's like the old square riggers. If we can't claw out to windward, which we can't with no main or jib, it's the rocks.'

'Unless we get another wind-shift. Yes. Anyway, we're committed to the Sound now. She'll not get outside of Bardsey from here.'

'No. So in we go!'

Ahead, the maelstrom intensified. Waves sprouted from nowhere in sudden pyramids and leapt at them as the sluicing 6-knot tide was squeezed and squashed over the Tripods overfalls and into the mile or so wide strait, lumping up against the southwester. All the Irish Sea, seemingly, trying to pour through the slot. The wind skimmed off the pinnacles from the waves. White water was everywhere, often bursting against the hull. The old boat was perching atop a crest then plunging 30 feet down into the trough. They looked to be lost, even if they did survive the passage through the Sound.

The agony went on for an hour, the 5 forces involved – tide versus winds versus waves versus residual sail plan versus keel plan – holding her plunging and wallowing in the Sound, spray bursting across her from the waves which were attacking from all directions. Raised by the current, bounced off the cliffs to port, bounced off the cliffs to starboard, bewitched, bothered and bewildered by the contrary wind as it eddied and gusted. The water inside was surging around well over the floorboards. She wasn't righting herself after a comber with her usual steady ease. She was suffering the famous 'free surface effect' which sank the *Herald of Free Enterprise* with 139 people. Unless it is checked by bulkheads, water sloshes around inside a hull, getting deeper and deeper. The boat responds ever more sluggishly to the waves, falling out of synchrony with them, until she rolls and plunges into them, gets repeatedly swamped, and down she goes to the bottom. Fortunately, for the *Herald*, the bottom had only been 60 feet down, so the fat old ferry had rested with one side out of the water, and astonishingly large numbers of people were able to get up there and survive.[40]

'Johnson,' shouted apWilliams, water streaming down his face.
'Yes?'
'Not sure she's going to take much more of this.'
'Me neither.'
'Start the engine?'
'What else? What a good idea. Touch of WD40 and we're there. Comical fellow.'

It was too dark to read the main compass in the cockpit, so apWilliams was below, watching the hand-bearing compass in the flickering candlelight, and shouting directions to Johnson at the wheel. They couldn't tell where they were, but at least the white round the mainland cliffs had receded. But there was no third hand to man the pump, and she was filling faster.

'What about the inflatable?'
'You reckon we can get it up on deck and pump it up in this? One comber and we'll all be swept away.'
'Well, yes. There is that.'
Suddenly Johnson shouted 'Alun. Look. The light.'

184

apWilliams put his head out. 'You trying to be funny?'

'Nope. Look, there again.'

With awe and astonishment, they saw the beam from the old lighthouse, sweeping the cliffs, flashing over them and away again. They started counting together. Flash, 2, 3. Flash, 2, 3. Flash, 2, 3. Flash, 2, 3. Flash, then 10 seconds darkness. Then again.

'Bloody hell.'

'Might be Bardsey, d'you think?'

'That or Nantucket!'

'Humorous prat. Group flashing 5, every 15 seconds. Just like the book used to say. We can make for the cove.'

About 200 yards from the lighthouse was a minute cove, carved by some geological whim into the flat land at the south. The only landing, it was little known, rarely visited, murder with winds east of south, but astonishingly tranquil when the wind was in the west. Like a similar lovely little hooked cove at the south-east end of Lundy Island.

The wind had veered back into the west, so they could sail in. It wouldn't be easy, though, to feel their way in past the scattered off-lying rocks. They'd approach from just north of east, aim a bit above the cove. Then, when they spotted the breakers, they'd know to turn left, skirt them to port, and sound their way in, heading towards the lighthouse, apWilliams spotting and sounding from up in the bow, Johnson at the helm.

'For God's sake, remember to turn your head towards me and shout your instructions,' said Johnson as they spotted the breakers and apWilliams went forward into the darkness.

The seas slowly flattened, and the wind, blocked by the great bulk of the hill, turned fluky and turbulent. In due course apWilliams shouted, Johnson swung her to port, and they skirted the shore, eased their way in, rounded up, sails flogging, and dropped the anchor. The light stopped. They wound more warps round the remains of the main and jib (neither could be lowered) to inhibit the flogging. The wind fell silent. The cloud slipped aside to release the gibbous moon. They made their ways below. The candles glimmered. The water was just below the top of the bunks. Sod it, pump her tomorrow. So they emptied out their boots, dropped into their sodden sleeping bags, and were out like lights.

The next morning Johnson was woken by the clunk and slurp and suck of the bilge pump. He lay in his bunk awash with the glorious indolent contentment, and the feeling of camaraderie, that follow an exhausting and dangerous passage. Life is good; nothing can daunt you. He paddled to the gangway and looked out. apWilliams was singing quietly to himself, to the tune used in *The Bridge Over the River Kwai*. Singing in time with his pumping, a snatch from his childhood, schoolboys singing in the bombing and blitzed slums of Birkenhead and Liverpool:

> Hitler has only got one ball.
> Musso has 2 but very small.
> Himmler is something simmler,
> But poor old Goebbels has nurbles at all.
> Dah di dah di dah di... [41]

Left foot up on the bridge deck, lift the handle to extend the shaft. Up and down 100 strokes with the right arm. Change feet. Change arms. Then 100 with the left. On and on and on and on.

The tiny hook of a cove had a magnificent panorama, 60 miles round Cardigan Bay towards St David's Head. The looming bulk of the Snowdon massif was cloud-covered, and barely visible anyway to the north, but the sweep of the coast to the south seemed to shine jade green in the sunlight, and the island basked in it. As so often, the wind had loosed its rain on Ireland in the west, so the peninsula was sunny, and the clouds only formed as the air rolled away inland. And then the wide sweep of the bay, like a silver scarf rippling in the morning.

Muesli and water for breakfast.

'That name, Nadine,' said apWilliams.

'Yes?'

'You were murmuring it in the night. And you have before.'

Johnson was hesitant. 'Just a girl on the course.'

'Is that so?'

'Yes,' said Johnson with finality. 'That is so.'

They breakfasted, pumped up the inflatable and went ashore. There was no sign of life. Across the flat land to the lighthouse.

Nothing. More grass than you'd expect. But not even footmarks. Back, then up the hill to the farm on the right. Johnson pressed the old-fashioned latch down and they went in. No one.

'Right. Keep absolutely still.' A voice from the entrance. A man with levelled shotgun came in behind them, followed by 2 more.

'Hi,' said Johnson. 'We're from the ketch.'

'Is that so? Thought you might be the Inland Revenue.'

They all laughed and relaxed.

'Too early for some home-brew? Or may be a cuppa?'

They opted for the cuppa. Some sort of herbal concoction.

'Milk?'

'What was that?'

'Milk. White stuff. Comes out of sheep.'

'Good God!'

The islanders' story gradually unfolded. At the Malfunction, the First World Error, the people had been on the island, and kept their heads down, stocking up with fish and lobsters and crabs. Then the seals – there used to be about 50 – had died off, a sad smelly business, and the radio had chronicled the gradual collapse on the mainland, leading up to the compulsory clearances of the handful of survivors to the Motorway Ring. A launch had called into the cove, but they'd hidden, and it had left.

Since then they'd lived their traditional life. Since time immemorial, Bardsey was often cut off, sometimes for weeks on end, and they were used to self-sufficiency. You needed the lobster cheques to pay for the tractor fuel and so on, but it was easy enough to do without the tractor and eat the lobsters instead. Not to mention bass, mackerel, codling, crabs, mussels.

They'd lost a family of 5 early on, and all the cattle and most of the sheep and all but 2 of the collies. No other red-blooded wildlife left. And all those splendid 43 varieties of gulls recorded at the RSPB observatory. No more Manx Shearwaters, flying in transoceanic 3,000 miles from Nicaragua in the darkness – what did they used to do in the daytime, wondered apWilliams? All gone. But the 2 remaining families, and the 4 people on retreat at the abbey had gradually recovered from the usual diarrhoea and vomiting.

The events had turned most of them to religion, and as ever, Bardsey was not short of saints. They still held daily Eucharists, and Johnson and apWilliams would be welcome at the evening service. They said they'd be glad to come.

'So tell us about yesterday night,' said apWilliams. 'How did the light come on for us?'

The islanders explained. They had seen the ketch on her way north. A newly-shorn lamb had been out above the farm and they'd hastily floored it behind one of the old drystone walls.

'There you are, like I said,' said apWilliams to Johnson.

'You said it was a white rock, not a sheep. Never doubted you for a moment, anyway,' lied Johnson.

Then, late in the afternoon, the ketch had come into sight again, obviously badly crippled, plunging down towards the sound in the gathering darkness. Trevor had posted himself on the hillside above to watch, and they'd resolved as a last resort to light the light and guide them in. And so they had. The risk of alerting others to the islanders' continued existence had been discussed; but maybe this was God's way of taking things forward. The 2 yachtsmen were silenced.

'Time for something stronger?'

The farmer got out a plastic demijohn, and poured out some brown frothy liquid.

'My God,' said apWilliams. 'If this isn't the real Welsh bitter!'

'Indeed, yes. Bardsey home brew. Our barley, our hops. Matter of fact, we think the hops were what saved us. We noticed the sheep that grazed up in the crags among the hops survived, and they were the ones we milked. So they and we were eating and drinking Bardsey hops. The hops've been here centuries, maybe even since the Vikings, or even the Dark Ages and the first Celtic Christians. Anyway, sadly the young kids, and the families who didn't get hops were the ones to die.'

'But why didn't you make this known?'

'By the time we'd figured it out – you can imagine the excitement – the Clearances were starting, and the disease phase seemed to have passed. And the Canon believed we'd been blessed to keep the light alive against the coming of happier times.'

Gaining in inebriation, they stayed on for lunch, then drifted back down to the ketch with their rescuers, to see what needed doing. They were still in that state of easy acceptance after an ordeal, when just to be alive is to be savoured without any questions.

Apart from the need to get on towards Caernarfon – only a tide away now – the ketch was hopelessly vulnerable in the tiny open cove if the winds turned back easterly. And they had 4 days till the meeting with Hawkins' operative. So the need was for speed. But not till tomorrow.

They decided to attempt to lash and splint the main mast back together. Then they'd be able to sail with full jib and mizzen and a double-reefed main – you couldn't hoist the main to its normal height because the lashings and splints would block the track. The alternative would be to cut off the main at the lower cross-trees, and sail her just on the small foresail and mizzen. An easier repair, but the boat would be a pig to handle, and they needed her to be very manoeuvrable for the passage through the straits and the mysterious, unspecified exercise with Gaskin. Very difficult to lower and later raise again the 43-foot wooden spar, but they had people enough to do it, and lots of good heavy agricultural tackle ashore.

At 6 p.m. they made their way up the hill into the ruined tower of the old abbey, accompanied by the tolling of its single bell. The tall walls were immensely thick and craggy, made of wide, thin slabs of slate piled horizontally, 30-feet high, crafted no doubt without benefit of stonemasons – the site too remote, the crossing too hazardous. They enclosed a square of emerald green grass, open to the sky. A place, thought Johnson, to 'hear the dying echoes of plainsong, the vibration of a thousand years of muttered prayer.'[42]

The Canon proved to be very frail, limping on a stick up to the heavy slate altar. He gave them a warm welcome. As he declaimed the Evensong, a splendid mix of the Welsh rite and Cranmer's and Tyndale's moving Tudor English – Church of Wales fashion, a page in one language then a page in the other – Johnson recalled a Sunday evening service from his schooldays. The Provost, their occasional spiritual mentor, preaching about those thundering, pregnant, mysterious words from Ecclesiastes: 'For every creature... there is a time to love and a time to hate, a time to rend and a time to sow, a time for war and a time for peace... Vanity of vanities; A-l-l is vanity.'

The old cleric swaying and leaning out, starkly garbed in red hood, white surplice and black robe, forward and around in the immense carved oak pulpit as if about to tumble in wrath on the dreadful, dreading sinning lads below. A single spotlight from far in the roof catching his lean, brown, hooked nose, deep-set haunting eyes and bristling brows. A presence to generate nightmares in full daylight, but now, with the night-gale shrieking in a crescendo in the rafters, the quintessence of terror, despair and retribution. YHWH, Yahweh the Great I Am of the desert religions, of Judaism, Christianity and Islam. Johnson remembered the healing hymn that followed, consoling frightened young lads in their beds in the small hours before dawn. Takes all sorts to make a church. Was the provost a good thing or a bad thing? Did that whole process of burning into the youngsters' spirits an abiding sense of purpose and commitment that would withstand incredible hardships really work? The currently-derided British Empire, base of much of the world's happiness, was founded on it. If you were now selecting the crew for some inter-galactic space mission, whom would you choose? People in the cast of Victorians like Burton, Baker, Speke, Thruston. Public school, Oxbridge or army. Adventurers with spirits like gyrocompasses, at home in the universe.

Perhaps, apWilliams thought, they had reached the time to love, the time to sow, the time for peace. Or not. As the case may be. Could they oust the PIG, BLZ and all his works? The coming month would tell.

They shook off the shadows from Ecclesiastes with John Whittier's splendid hymn: Dear Lord and Father of mankind, Forgive our foolish ways...

Despite the quavering in the voices of the small group on the island, Johnson remembered his school chapel, and Tregonning, the choirmaster, watching in his mirror from the organ, from the organ mirror with a glint of wry pleasure or delight in his eyes, as 300 adolescent voices roared out, treble, breaking and broken, in a triumphant crescendo: 'O still small voice of calm,

O still small voice of calm.'

Their city of faith, if not of peace.

The Canon ended with those immensely healing phrases, 'May

190

the peace of Gard, which passeth all understanding... confirm and strengthen you in all goodness.'

Johnson recalled his eighteenth-century British history, and the fun the spinmasters in the Whig opposition had in 1763 with the 'Peace which passeth all understanding', the prayer book phrase they applied to the infamous (in their politicians' view) new Treaty of Paris ending the War of Spanish Succession, when the Brits had given away all the fruits of a successful European war in exchange for what the Whigs held to be a handful of pottage, some strange and worthless lands beyond the bounds of civilisation. Canada, Australia, South Africa, the Pacific. In short, an empire.

How wrong can you be? He remembered the historian Paul Johnson's view of his country. Close to a millennium of unheard of stability, a stone set in its silver sea, a launch pad for its peoples to go wherever they would and think whatever they wished, as traders, missionaries, settlers, generals, governors, administrators, and primarily adventurers. The mother country was usually only peripherally interested, and pretty sharply down on any nabobs who got too big for their boots. And in the end, the whole empire was relinquished 2 centuries later with indifference and perhaps slight relief, in the space of 20 years. But was Paul Johnson entirely right? For Johnson and many others the ideals still stuck.

After the service they all stood companionably together outside, then drifted down the smooth rocky slate lane, worn by the feet of generations, to supper. Fresh roast lamb, Bardsey potatoes, Bardsey Brussels sprouts, Bardsey mint sauce, Bardsey redcurrant jelly, Bardsey home-brewed ale brewed crucially from Bardsey hops. For apWilliams, the first meat for many a year, ever since FWE, the First World Error and the death of all warm-blooded animals. Trevor, for whom the island and its strange history as a place of pilgrimage were the breath of life, told them how, in the 1970s, they'd been given permission to take up the floor of a room in the farmhouse. Underneath they had found no less than 17 of the 20,000 saints, (20,000 being the Celtic for 'a very large number indeed') carefully laid out in the narrowest possible rows. Paganism and Christianity had clearly been intermingled – each skull had a silver groat coin inside, placed on the tongues by the relatives as ferry dues for Charon, the ferryman who would row them across the Styx and into Hades. Or maybe into the sad beauties of the Finnish Hell, Tuonela, across still waters on which a black swan glides hauntingly. Scandinavian and even Finnish influences in these parts were very strong.

Next morning, they lowered the mizzen mast and dropped it overboard to float tethered out of the way, while they tackled the immensely difficult main mast – heavy enough to break under its own weight if held horizontally without exactly the right supports. A large vertical 'A' frame was constructed across the boat, hinged at either gunwale. Then a line was taken from the mast spreaders as high as possible, and made fast to the peak of the 'A'. This meant that, as the mast dropped back aft, the top of the 'A' would rise upwards and support it. Easy enough to lower the first bit, with a rope round the anchor winch. The difficulty would come as the spar lowered below 45 degrees, and your leverage from the winch ropes decreased massively. That's when the 'A' frame would rise up high and take the strain.

All prepared. Johnson knocked out one of the 2 massive bolts at the base of the mast, and they eased away, and down it came. Mind over matter. Which seaman had first thought that device out in the dawn of civilisation?

It took 8 people to lift the spar right forward so that they could get at the break, then a day's work lashing the splintered remains together and splinting them. The cause had been the Aerolite 300 glue of the 1950s. Believed at the time to be time-less, but you can't easily simulate or test time's passage. And in 60 years or so the glue had become brittle. The spar had been flexing violently, probably accentuated by the replacement of radar-visible stainless steel wire with stretchy, radar-transparent Terylene rope, and the join at the upper scarf, or junction, had split open.

A quiet mystery, the intuitive skills in joinery and spherical geometry which enabled the shipwrights to slice across a hollow cylinder at matching diagonals, and then shape and glue to-gether 6 hollowed pieces of Sitka spruce into a single 43-foot stick. Leave alone have it straight as a die at the end, and the pieces so matched in pairs that the inevitable warping from

time's passage was neatly balanced, warping on one side coun-
teracting warping on the other.

*****

Meanwhile in Gorton, over the next few days they framed the
fallback plan, Gaskin sketching in the approach in an occasional
evening meeting, Sseru and Tilley fleshing it out. They were
joined by McGervon, whom Gaskin had had transferred to his
own Sector as systems programmer.

An idea came to Tilley overnight, and he suggested to Gaskin
that they try the original wormhole through which he'd sent his
message Upside. That hole might not be subject to the same
time windows as the 2 main streams.

'We could send them a bit of tape explaining about the wip-
ing, and ask them to send the system to us on paper tape
instead.'

'You what?' asked Gaskin, 'Have you any idea how much tape
they'd need to send? And we'd need a KDF6 programmer here
to get it all onto a blank mag tape.'

'What about this guy apWilliams?'

'He's messing around with Johnson somewhere in the Irish
Sea. Oh well, we could give it a whirl. Take a while to get it all
through, but you've nothing better to do at present.'

Thus encouraged, Tilley and McGervon set about it. First, type
a paper tape message on the old Flexowriter to send through the
wormhole, explaining the problem, and slide it through the
hole. There were relevant universe conjunctions in Manchester
at fortnightly intervals, full moon minus 2 days, 1 hour, 25
minutes, 3.51 seconds or so, until the space-time conjunctional
focal centre shifted off again. So he'd suggest they sent the tape
back in a fortnight.

He did a rough computation. Half a tape, say, of dual track
recording on a 2,400-foot mag tape at a block length of, say,
5,000 characters. Transcribe it onto paper tape at 6 characters/
inch. It came to a lot of paper.

And so it was to prove.

*****

On Bardsey, hoisting the mast again nearly defeated them. Only brute force and concerted ignorance, brawn over brain, got it off the deck and high enough for the 'A' frame to start taking effect. After that, a doddle. They tried out sail-hoisting with the strapped mast and hoops instead of the sail track, which was blocked off by the lashings, and slides. Then checked everything over. Chats with the islanders to try to find out more about the First World Error. Most had been on the island at the time, and pieced together something from the radio broadcasts which continued to surmise through the first 2 weeks. One had been in Chester, evening sherry in hand in the Cathedral Close, when the flash and mushroom cloud of the Manchester bomb 30 miles off shattered their lives. Another in Bangor hospital outpatients when the first bio-victims were brought in. She had woken the next morning with her heart palpitating alarmingly and a leadenness as if of a great weight on her lungs. An insupportable pain in her left chest struck her, so intense she only wanted to give in and die. As she climbed out of bed for help, a dizziness felled her to the floor, and that was where they found her.

Then a farewell supper with the islanders, and the loan of one of their hand-held radios. Radio silence was necessary naturally, but a fall-back radio would be invaluable in case of disaster. So too might be the availability at Bardsey of the islanders' 2 outboard run-abouts, even though they were big enough only for quick passages across to the mainland in the right sort of weather.

The next morning they sailed out into the last hour of the ebb, south-about round the end of the island, then north again, beam-reaching in a gentle westerly, a soldiers' breeze, outside the Tripods and up towards Pilot's Cove and the entrance to the Menai Straits.

Downside, Chapter 21: Pilot's Cove

The day dawned fair and pure, a favourable easterly flowing off the cliffs of the peninsula. As the *Amanda* reached northwards, the Welsh mainland receded to the north-east. The 2 sailors fell silent as their end-objective at last approached. A flat, featureless coastline, the island of Anglesey, lay ahead, with one pimple sticking up out of it, and the Welsh mountains to the east.

The pimple, Pilot's Cove, was so-named because it was used by the Menai Straits pilots when waiting to take slate ships through the hazardous 2-mile long entrance channel and up to the slate ports. These lie on the east side of the 15-mile strait that separates the great island of Anglesey from the mainland. Sometimes called 'Little England in Wales', perhaps because it's like England, perhaps because Henry II settled some English here in the twelfth century to keep the turbulent supporters of Owen Glendower – Owain Glyndwr – in check. Geology and geomorphology left a small island, Llanddwyn Island, a few yards offshore, and a mile or so to the west of the straits entrance, in a remote and rarely-visited part of Anglesey. A red and white lighthouse tower by a cliff. Nothing else but sands, heath and fir woods for miles. The currents round the island must have carved the deep pool behind it, in which the pilot cutters used to shelter as they waited for a ship.

The *Amanda* slips in and they anchor in under the cliff.

'Better,' says Johnson, 'if you stay here while I reconnoitre.' He feels slightly fey.

'While you what?'

'Reconnoitre.'

'How do you mean, reconnoitre?'

'Like I say, reconnoitre'

'Why?'

'Could be a trap.'

'Well... I hear you.'

Johnson launches the inflatable and paddles ashore. No one

195

around. He climbs to the light tower and up the stairs to the light chamber. There is Nadine, standing back to the window, looking at him. He is instantly and sharply conscious of how piercingly fragile and appealing she is. Her hair forms a cup of soft, dark fur, caressing the golden white of her neck. She has no make-up. Her skin is smooth, light, golden. She is wearing a flowered blouse, entrancingly V-necked, bare arms those of a young girl, and a beige skirt, tapered in below the knees like a closing tulip.

Johnson is frosty. His throat feels thick and constricted. His heart thumps heavily. This treacherous woman.

'What are you doing here?' His voice grates sharply. Being close to her is like having a dagger in the side of his heart.

'Michael. Look at me.'

He does. With a hint of a smile, she looks upwards then flickers her eyes from side to side as Gaskin had when they interrupted him in Cambridge.

'Hallo, sailor,' she says.

For a long moment he's nonplussed. Then the truth dawns on him. It's her. She's Gaskin's promised 'operative'. And so she must be with them in the project.

'You lovely darling.'

'You look freezing,' she says. 'Let me... '

He folds her in his arms. She kisses him butterfly-soft.

'Yes, yes, all right, sailor. But not just now.'

'Excuse me,' says apWilliams. 'Is this a private party, or can anyone join in?'

'Bloody hell. You're supposed to be on the boat.'

'Nice day for a swim. Not a lot to do. Seemed like a good idea.'

'Well, it's not.'

'Yes, it is,' says Nadine. She turns to Alun, pointing at the boat. 'She's a real beauty, isn't she?' she says.

'Indeed you are.'

'Not me, stupid, the boat.'

'Can I show you over her?' asks apWilliams.

'Nope, you can't mate. I'm going to reconnoitre,' interrupts Johnson. 'And Nadine's coming with me.'

'Am I?' says Nadine.

'Yes,' says Johnson firmly.

196

'Is that so?' she says, and nips swiftly down the stairs. He runs to catch her up, and Alun watches as they slow and walk up the dune. She reaches out a hand and lightly caresses Johnson's palm with her fingers.

apWilliams starts quietly singing, 'Oh, Susanna... '

Later, over the crest, Johnson draws Nadine to him and they kiss and hold each other. Trembling, he slips his right hand over her breast.

'Michael,' she asks softly, 'Is this going to take a long time?'

'Forever.'

She looks up at him, takes his hand away to her lips, kisses it and presses it to her breast again. 'Me too.'

She sighs, leans against him, then jumps away.

'It's just that I've got this hair appointment.'

'Come here, wench.'

*****

Later, they were walking peaceably westwards back to the boat, she on the crest of a dune, he a few feet down inland below her. Beyond the heath the countryside to the west spread away from them, flat like a misty green sea. Suddenly, he dropped to the ground saying 'Aargh! Aargh!' and clutching his stomach.

'What is it?'

'A pain. A pain. The dreaded one-eyed trouser snake.'

'Oh. You poor thing; let me kiss you better.'

She spun round and slipped down to crouch above him, legs curled sideways the way only females' can. He reached up tenderly and undid her blouse again.

Later he said dreamily, 'You're wearing a skirt. I've never seen you in a skirt. Why are you wearing a skirt?'

She looked at him innocently, fluttered her eyelids like a 1950s film star and said, 'I can't possibly think.'

Downside, Chapter 22: Video Snip

In the fort across the straits entrance, 2 men were watching a video playback, studying a key passage frame by frame. The lead guy had a long, hatchet face and the sort of cold emotionless detachment often found in psychopaths.

You could see a distant woman, crouching, the dunes just concealing her lower half. You could see her looking downwards, leaning forwards, her weight on her arms. She dropped gently out of sight. Hard to tell for sure. Maybe a bit of tweaking's needed?

*****

As Johnson and Nadine walked down the beach back to the boat, Johnson became increasingly silent and a touch moody.

'Penny for your thoughts?' she said.

'It's nothing.'

'Must be something, and I can guess roughly what.'

'All right then. Something's just come back to me again. I keep dodging it but it bugs me no end.'

'What's that?'

'Why did you betray me to the POPs?'

'I thought that was it. Well,' she collected her thoughts, 'I was panic-stricken. If they'd got me I'd have told them all I knew of Graham's plans and maybe affected thousands of people. And you were just a man who had taken me for a swim. I regretted it straightaway. But that was too late. And it was me later who left the note wrapped round a stone in Don McGervon's pocket. And it was Don and me who unlocked the door of the padded cell for him to let you out. I was scared stiff. I saw you in there. Nearly woke you up, but decided better not.'

'Ah well, that's nice. Let's forget about it. Let's go and introduce you properly to Alun.'

Johnson rowed her out to the boat – 'I can row you know,' she protested – 'I'm sure you can, but just this once.' He drifted the dinghy quietly alongside. apWilliams must be down below, he concluded. He put his fingers to his lips and eased himself aboard over the stern. Then hauled Nadine up by the mizzen shrouds. The boat rolled and apWilliams came up the companion ladder and laughed happily. They gathered in the cockpit of the ketch. apWilliams had made a reasonable job of tidying her up.

'This is Nadine, Alun,' said Johnson.

'Ah. Wondered who you were. Heard your name often. Or am I getting you mixed up with the African princess?'

'This guy's an idiot,' explained Johnson.

'Makes 2 of you on one ketch then,' said Nadine disapprovingly. 'Well, the poor old girl clearly needs a woman's touch,' she continued.

'Anyway, this is what Neville wants us to do. We're going to leave the boat here until she's needed – she'll not be visible from the mainland against the cliff, even if something's there to see her. Then we leave her and set off after dark on Friday for the mainland across the straits entrance at Abermenai Point, then... '

'How are we going to get across? The inflatable?'

'I've got a little fibreglass kayak I pinched from a garden in the town. Maybe you 2 in the dinghy, me in the kayak. Then we hide the dinghy under some pebbles, into town and return the kayak. Cross together, so as to minimise the chance of anyone seeing. Preferably just before slack water. Then to a little back-to-back by the castle. There's no one at all around.'

'OK.'

'After that, we'll hear from Neville how the main plan's going.'

'What do we do in the meanwhile?' asked apWilliams.

Nadine blushed, and glanced at Johnson, her eyes dancing.

'I'm sure we'll think of something,' said Johnson.

'Neville set the extra 2 days,' said Nadine, 'in case you weren't here on time. But he doesn't want us in the town till Friday night.'

'Tell you what, Alun,' Johnson said, 'You can sleep here on the boat, and I'll take care of Nadine at the lighthouse.'

'I've a better idea. I'll take care of the lighthouse, and you stay here with Nadine. She'll be safer that way. I'll clear the pilot berth. Then she can show us how the boat should be.'

199

'You're on.'

They lit the cabin stove, and supped on lamb stew, real lamb, Bardsey lamb, and dumplings. Then home-brewed Bardsey beer in the cockpit, and apWilliams set off ashore.

They sat together in the saloon's warmth, Renoir's brother's fiancée looking downwards demurely from the picture.

'What about this fellow Bubb?' asked Johnson, his voice suddenly constricted to an angry grate.

'Oh. That's all finished now. Just a job. Come here, Michael. Please.'

The pilot berth wasn't needed.

But the old boat's 2 narrow bunks were built not for love, but for 2 serious, lean gentlemen sailors, with the paid-hand tucked away in the forepeak, with his own separate entrance to the toilet. Johnson dossed down on the cabin floor, legs around the table leg, whence he could reach up to her.

The next morning the sun crept across the cabin sole into his eyes and woke him. She was resting her head on her hand, breasts part concealed by the sleeping bag, watching him. He knelt up over her and slipped the cover away, softly kissing each nipple.

'He showered burning, passionate kisses,' he said, 'between her glorious breasts.'

'No,' she said, 'no, he did not.'

'Oh yes, he did.'

'Oh no, he didn't.' And she rolled him down onto the cabin sole.

He looked up into her eyes. Sad, vulnerable, pleading. 'Please,' he said, and she drew him to her.

'Ah. My sweeting.'

*****

Later, she put on some acorn coffee, and they sat in the cockpit in the early sunshine.

'Do you think... ' she asked, 'do you think I'm a "womanly woman"?' There was hint of laughter in her eyes.

Johnson was nonplussed, then he remembered his planned 'Soulmate' advert. Womanly woman – manly man – needing, yearning – large yacht. The doodle he'd scrawled at the training session when he had first noticed her.

'Bloody hell. You weren't watching me then, surely?'

'No. But Neville showed me the scrawl on your file a long time later.'

'Damned if I trust that guy Gaskin.' She looked cool and disputatious, but held her peace.

They went ashore, then explored the dunes and Newborough Warren with Alun, on through the woods to Maltraeth Sands, and moved in for one night to an old farmhouse in the forest. Lovely to have a fire in the grate, its light flickering over the country furnishings. Lovelier still would be to celebrate her beauty on the hearthrug, thought Johnson. apWilliams was washing up, the girl looking out through the window at mountains as twilight slipped up across them. He came up behind her, gently touched her cheek, slipped his arms round her and whispered in her ear, 'Want you on a bearskin with a bare skin by the fire.'

She leant back against him.

'Some time my love, some time.'

The next day the 3 were walking together. Then Johnson had diverted to get some firewood.

'There's someone called Susanna, is there, Alun?' asked Nadine.

'Yes,' said apWilliams, and he explained about the blue car and the ferry trip.

She looked troubled; luckily he was looking the other way.

'I'll see what I can find out at base,' she promised, and lightly switched to something else.

Then, on the Friday evening, they crossed in the dark at the entrance to the straits. They hid the inflatable and walked along by the strait shores into town, carrying the kayak, which they stowed under a hedge by the old bowling green. The moon was rising behind the mountains. They stopped by the old suspension bridge, looking across at the magnificent Welsh castle of Caernarfon as the light caught its stark square stonework, standing out into the tideway.

'I'm to go ahead and check with Graham,' said Nadine. She went slowly across the bridge, over the quay and up into the town. Nothing. Then she dropped down the alley beneath the fortifications into number 5. She unlocked the door and went in.

No one. But a note from Gaskin. Change of plan. The men were to return to the boat and wait till they heard further. She was to get to the pick-up point at first light and return to Gorton.

She went back to tell them.

'I'm not going to let you go alone,' said Johnson. 'I'm coming too.'

'No you're not, darling,' she replied sadly. 'That's part of the deal.'

She ruled out further protests, but went to see them back across the strait. It was a glum walk.

'Better be quick, the ebb's beginning to flow fast. Bye, Alun,' she said. 'Bye, bye, sailor.'

'Bye bye, beauty.'

She watched them as they crossed in the moonlight till they were out of sight.

Downside, Chapter 23: Plas Menai

Across the Afon Glaslyn, the River Glaslyn, at the mouth where it used to sprawl widely into the sea after excitedly tumbling down through a narrow valley from the heights of the Snowdon mountains, there was a causeway which led north from Porth Meirion to Porthmadog.

The Glaslyn Causeway, unlike most Welsh roads, ran straight as a die, and Porthmadog at the far end was all of a piece with it. A wide, central main street, drawn out like the towns of Kenya, Zimbabwe, and the American midwest, to accommodate a complete U-turn by an Equipe with spans of draught beasts; in Zimbabwe and the midwest, spans of trek-oxen; in Kenya, the 6-horse flying barouches in which the eccentric second string British aristocrats of the 1910s–20s, like Lord Delamere, used to sport and carve up the embryo Nairobi traffic.

Porthmadog was named after a Mancunian Scot, Maddock, who knew a little about slate and a lot about enterprise. Rare indeed in the UK to have a town named after you. In the late eighteenth century the entire centre of the old Hanseatic League port of Hamburg was consumed in a disastrous fire and the city fathers sought men who would master the challenge of reconstruction.

Maddock went along with a few tiles, and persuaded them that Welsh slate was the answer to the entire city's roofing problem, and that he was their man.

So, at the mouth of the Glaslyn, he built the Causeway in 1808, half a mile of high, sea-barring rock to the west side, and a long rail and roadway to the east.

The bright ideas and enthusiasm of this one man created out of nothing miles of green water meadows, where once was marsh and sedge, protected now by the new causeway; and a splendid mid-Victorian town, generously proportioned and totally unlike the cramped, drab, narrow-streeted town of tradition, Pwllheli, to the west.

The roofing slates were first contracted for Hamburg and then for the whole world – Newfoundland, Argentina, India, New Zealand, Australia, South Africa.

Cai Balast, Ballast Island, lying 50 yards across the harbour, was created with the cargoes brought back by the slate ships. Sailing home in ballast – rock, earth or whatever, to balance the winds. Even the old 10-ton Viking trading ships of the tenth century used to carry 9 tons of it. All manner of exotic flora had been found on the island, their seeds carried home in the ballast.

This was all funded by slate; slate which eventually roofed cities worldwide, carried in ships built in Porthmadog, trundled and waggled down from the hills on a narrow gauge steam railway which in 2034, Upside, puffed many a tourist and holiday-maker way up into the mountains, by tumbling falls, rocky woods, and craggy outcrops from glaciers. In its productive time, the track carried slate carved from the hearts of the great Cambrian mountains; the most ancient rock in Europe, compacted 400 million years ago by a collision with a sliding continent now known as America. The continental bash left behind Scotland, a lump of America complete with tiny American fossils, stuck onto Britain in passing. The miners left behind spectacular caverns, filled often in the past by the voices of Welsh male voice choirs. Slate for the world, split and sliced and carved with consummate skill by craftsmen on minute pittances which often prompted them to try for their fortunes in new little towns in the South African High Veld, or the remote tip of Argentina, or the familiar terrain of Tasmania or New Zealand. The same towns, but upside-down.

All this was the creation of Mr Maddock. But why, Tite Barnacle speculated as he rode towards the Causeway, why had it been Mr Maddock, a Mancunian Scot, who rose to the challenge, and not Mr Jones, a native Welshman from Ponty-wherever?

'A prophet is not without honour,' Christ had said, 'save in his own country' – that was the clue the world over. Whether you were among Kenyan Kikuyus or Zambians envying a fellow member of the same age-set, or Brits envying the rise of a one-time colleague, now nabob or lord or MD or CE. Much better to have in someone from outside, often of another race, be they right or be they wrong.

Tite Barnacle appeared at the south end of the Causeway, carrying a pillion passenger on his sparkling red Honda mountain trailster bike. Her hair streamed freely in the wind, her dress ruffled, legs charmingly bare – how taut yet soft womens' thighs can be – and she held his waist lightly. Her grip tightened later when they curved through the bends, climbing away from the Causeway, up the winding valley to Beddgelert, scene of perhaps the most moving of dog legends; the faithful hound and the devotion he silently conveys to his master and his master's princeling son. The hound saved the princeling from the bloody savaging of a marauding wolf. And was then slain by the returning king who thought at first the hound had done the deed.[43]

Then down again to the royal fortress town of Caernarfon on the Menai Straits. Drop off in the town and take Flo round the ancient river and quay? Up into the old club? Rustle up some coffee from their supply of the burnt acorn beans in the floating caff? No, save that for another time. Plas Newydd and his research into the origins of PIG beckoned strongly. And his daydreams of Flo in the linen cupboard. So they missed seeing the POPs' fateful guard post in Castle Street, and went 8 miles on to cross the great militaristic spans of the Britannia Bridge – some strange joins and structures since he'd last crossed – and south along to the rolling farmland of the western shore of the straits, to Plas Newydd, home of the Marquesses of Anglesey.

Tite Barnacle and his girl were going to doss down for a while in the pad of his old mate, Fred Paget by name, the Seventh Marquis. Plenty of time yet till the November event. Plas Newydd, seat since 1470 of the Griffiths of Penrhyn, their heirs and successors, the Pagets and the Marquesses of Anglesey, lay on the west shore of the Menai Straits, maybe a mile from the Britannia Bridge. Here the towering, almost canyon-like cliffs through which pour the turbulent straits tides, the gorge which was critical to Gaskin's plans, give way to gentler slopes, presaging farms and meadows and copses.

One of Tite Barnacle's obsessions was with the past, with the history of Burgoyne, Paget and Trevelyan and the systems revolution they fashioned together. Until 2029 when interest in the history of human systems at last reached out from academia and even into the schoolrooms, this had gone largely unrecognised. The time when the modern state started seriously slipping its tentacles around humanity. That was the birth-time and this was the birthplace of PIG.

Tite Barnacle thought back to the times of the first marquess. Henry William Paget was an aristocrat of the first rank towards the end of the eighteenth century; he inherited the hall in 1812. Paget was a great cavalry officer, who made his mark early in the Peninsula campaigns under Wellington. But he was a headstrong, independent youngster, impetuous where Wellington was cautious, and impatient of Wellington's strategy, which was reminiscent of that of the great Roman general, Fabius Cunctator – Fabius the Delayer – against the all-conquering Carthaginians: avoid close engagements at almost all costs, hide behind the lines of Torres Vedras at need, but harry, scarify and terrify your enemy, creating in Wellington's case the famous 'running sore' which bled the Napoleonic empire and sapped the reputations of Bonaparte's greatest generals. Not a strategy to appeal to a dashing young cavalryman like Paget. Honour or death was the name of his game. They fell out, and Paget was put on the back-burner until ability and need brought him to the fore in 1814, and he was appointed cavalry commander for the battle of Waterloo. He led from the front, and was responsible for a pivotal engagement which some believe decided the battle. Without Paget, is it just possible that Napoleon might have won, and that Europe would have become totally subservient to France? To suffer thereafter a continental decline similar to that portrayed by Martin Amis in 2014,[44] with world domination passing much earlier than it did to the USA?

Paget was desperately wounded by grapeshot in a charge during the battle. 'By God, Sir,' he told Wellington as they rode after the French, 'I've lost my thigh.'

'By God, Sir,' answered the Duke, 'so you have,' and rode firmly onward. The top medicos debated hotly before agreeing that amputation at the thigh was vital. No anaesthetics or other relief were around, even rum. His friends reported that Paget watched impassively as the carving was carried out, turned never a hair, and objected only that the saws were so blunt they were slow on the job. He wrote to his wife, 'Sorry, my love; we won't be able to do the jig at the ball after all.'

His story caught the public's imagination; his friend George, Prince of Wales, was enthralled, and raised him from mere Lordship of Uxbridge to become the first Marquis of Anglesey. Plas Newydd had been built gradually over the centuries. It was always a distinctively individual building, but Paget had the wealth to fill the fine shell with works of art and furnishings that made it among the most imaginative and intriguing places in the UK. The hall stood along the contour about 150 yards up the slope from the straits' shores. It was set in long lawns below and above, with delightful gardens and woodlands stretching a mile and a half along the shores. Two miles north was the scene in 2034 for the November event.

The Tite Barnacle pair moved happily into Plas Newydd. One bright evening, Tite Barnacle was reading a finely-bound volume of handwritten papers, which he had removed from the library. He was sitting in the music room at a George III rent-table that particularly pleased him. It had a central hole to take the rent money, and alphabetically ordered drawers for the tenant records. He was studying passages in the Plas Newydd papers from Paget's time. The letters of Sir John Burgoyne to Paget and Sir Charles Trevelyan, relating to the great Irish famines of 1845 to 1849. The short period had always fascinated Tite Barnacle because those few years of appalling tragedy sowed so many unlikely seeds. Not only the developing and abiding hatred of the Irish diaspora for their allegedly genocidal English overlords, but also strangely unexpected and positive fruits, like the birth of the finest civil service in the contemporary world – the Indian, the renowned ICS – formulated and led largely by Trevelyan after his experiences as overlord of the Irish famine.

Tite Barnacle mulled over Trevelyan's achievements. The problem had been how, in the primitive infrastructure of contemporary Ireland, do you introduce and administer a Poor Law system and secure the distribution of soup (of a sort) to 3 million scattered, starving people each day? That was for 5 dreadful years Trevelyan's job spec. The Irish experience forged the ideas for his Indian systems, which in turn were the base for his reformed British civil service. This was the 'systems model' for freedom and prosperity that was later replicated across a fifth of the earth's population. Freedom, equality before the law, democracy, judicial impartiality, literacy, scientific research, commerce, education, religious tolerance, medical and municipal services, land title, stability. You name it, it was there... The whole gamut of vital, revolutionary structures and attitudes which the Upside populists of the 1990s had lumped together scornfully as the *Pax Britannica*. Put these in the balance, he thought, against some rare but vicious blemishes on the Raj – Amritsar and Hola for example – and you come up with interestingly different answers to those of the conventional 1990s consensus. Jeremy Bentham in the 1830s had encapsulated the key formula – the greatest happiness of the greatest number.[45] How many millions, or even billions, of people were alive in 2014 who but for Trevelyan, would never have lived? What was the quality or lack of it, of their happiness? And yet every innovation carries seeds of good or ill; the life-giving structures invented by Trevelyan were also the structures that led, Downside, to PIG.

The writer of the Plas Newydd letters, Major General Burgoyne, had been a brilliant engineer officer, Commanding Engineer under Wellington. He was assigned by Trevelyan to head the Relief Commission which was to institute the Poor Law – an 1840s Department of Social Security – and the soup kitchens which would help the process of outdoor relief for Ireland's emaciated and starving millions. As a connoisseur of bureaucracies and their related procedures, Tite Barnacle had in his youth often spent hours engrossed in the British Museum or the University Library at Cambridge, tracing back the origins of the great systems revolution of the mid-nineteenth century – as crucial to future global prosperity as were any of the innovations in industry except perhaps the railways – and tracking in particular the great bureaucrats of the time.

The myth that during the Irish Famine the English had committed deliberate genocide had been the core spin of market-driven faction writers in the 1990s, but it was only Upside, in 2025, that people were slowly sifting out the truths about such myths, and hence much deeper truths about themselves and the societies they lived in. That the rivalry of race on race and sex on sex had been central to evolution, and that the way to peace lay not in denying and suppressing the symptoms of this rivalry, but in accommodating, recognising and harnessing the forces involved.[46]

In Tite Barnacle's view, the fashionable theme-historians' manufactured myths needed to be exposed; not with passion, but with mockery. And to do this meant studying the writings of the key players like Burgoyne, Trevelyan and Paget, and trying to ascertain their real motivation. Were they alien, hostile auto-crats, or were they committed civilisers? Men like Burgoyne in Ireland, or Lugard in Uganda, were the people to look at.

Mockery, because the racist writers, scooping circulation fig-ures out of ancient hatreds, were impervious to conventional academic scrutiny. How many times, for example, had economic historians debunked the myth that during the great Irish famine the British were wilfully exporting two-thirds of Irish food while the country starved?

The truth was that food in fact was Ireland's most vital export – grain was grown by the smallholder to pay his rent. No rent equals no home. No home equals death, just as it did for millions of tragic peasants in China in the famines of the 1920s. Hence they sold their grain even when their children were dying of starvation. In fact, the grain exports were only half that which populist historifactors alleged. And the wilful exporters were the peasants themselves. Ignore the facts; let's create a good racist myth.[47]

Tite Barnacle read on, absorbed, sensing the nuances in Burgoyne's letters to Trevelyan, and the attitudes they revealed, until the light started failing and the bright wet greens of the lawns and fields and straits shores faded to grey. A figure crossed by the windows and went inside.

His eyes softened and crinkled. He began to look impatient, and glanced frequently at his watch.

The hall tower clock struck 6 p.m. He marked his place in the papers, closed his notebook, and, setting Burgoyne aside, moved to sit at the boudoir grand piano. He strummed a little, then turned to play from a fading score: Polka-mazurka par M. Fried, price four shillings, from Price and Reynolds, 14 Berners St London W. It had been printed in 1913.

He heard a delicate tinkling bell from somewhere in the

upper storey. He straightened up, thrusting the music stool back, and walked across the beautiful Gothick hall to a niche. Into it was set a narrow spiral staircase, stretching upwards out of sight, with walls papered in lightish crimson, a tracery forged-iron central rail in black, and an outer bannister of nautical-looking, but not too bullish, looped 3-stranded silky rope in deep blue, threaded through brass fairleads in the walls. A couple of recesses, oval arched at their heads, in brilliant white, added to the feeling of secrecy and enchantment which the stair conveyed.

He nipped up the stairs 2 at a time, reached the first floor, and paused, listening intently. Across the gallery was a small entrance. It had a modern painting, in marked contrast to the grandiose portraits of bygone aristos that hung in plenty from the walls in the main halls. A tall, slim severe-looking middle-aged man of the 1950s, with a small, bristly moustache. A stoic perhaps, looking out at life firmly from a rock-solid base. The right material for a colonial Chief Secretary, perhaps. In some ways the spitting image of Reggie Perrin's boss. Tite Barnacle recalled, 'I didn't get where I am today by kowtowing to the staff/ customers/ busybodies/ politicians/ my wife.'

But this guy was a man of a formidable mettle.

The putative Chief Secretary's glance led across to an equally modern painting. It was of a lovely dark-haired girl in 1950s evening dress, bare-shouldered, slim, her face expressionless, fathomless, her lips everted slightly; not quite pouting, more like a Muchiga woman gesturing the way. 'Kuriiya', with her lips spreading out for the 'ii'.

Her left arm was raised backwards above and behind her head, perhaps adjusting her hair behind her neck. Might have been a ponytail. Did they have ponytails in the 1950s, he wondered? Was she the sort of woman who might have worn one? Her right arm, black-gloved strikingly against white flesh to above the elbow, held a dark red carnation between her breasts. Beyond her was one of the most pleasing of feminine bowers, Lady Anglesey's bedroom. On the left, a gilt-bronze Italian relief of the Virgin and Child. A snake with a man's head lay trapped beneath the Virgin's foot. A Sheraton-style four-poster in beech wood was painted with vines and hung with silk. That, thought Tite

Barnacle, was for later. Silk also draped from the dressing tables, below a Georgian glass chandelier.

Tite Barnacle stole past her room, to the linen room door. He listened a moment, then swung the door open. A feminine figure was reaching up on tiptoes to put away some sheets.

Ever so gently, he slipped an arm round her waist, a questing hand up under her left breast.

'Ooh, Lord Tite Barnacle, what are you doing? Oh deary me. Oh deary deary me.'

Downside, Chapter 24: Gorton, a Message

In Gorton, 2 weeks after they had sent the message, they were hauling back the punched paper tape through the wormhole, keeping well away from the slot. Get close and it was incredibly cold. On the front end of the tape was a short separate piece in red. Mistake probably. They put it aside to look at.

Later Gaskin came in. They discussed progress, then Tilley left on a weekend's walking. Gaskin and McGervon chatted.

'What's that bit of tape there?' Gaskin asked, pointing at the piece of red tape.

'Don't know,' said McGervon.

'Let's run it through the Flexowriter.'

They did so and looked at the hard copy.

'Urgent from Professor Stag. Have you seen Lord Tite Barnacle?'

'Who the hell is Lord Tite Barnacle?' asked Gaskin. 'Never heard of him.'

'Some sort of joke,' said Gaskin. 'Send back: "Lord Tite Barnacle who he? And a Happy New Year to you too".'

'Right,' said McGervon, and did so.

Rolling the paper tapes straight onto a spool didn't work too well; it would sometimes catch and might tear. The fastest technique was to work as if flaking out an anchor chain ready to lower, approved RYA style, on the foredeck of a boat. One would grab the tape, and walk away from the hole with it to make a 20-foot long loop. Then the other would follow with the next loop. Once an entire tape was through they could then wind the flaked out tape onto spools. Then evenings in the museum, thick curtains drawn, loading it all onto the KDF6 magnetic tapes. To save time, they set the machine to read the paper tapes at full speed, using the famous Elliott readers, 2024 characters a minute.

Quite spectacular for a computing person, because the 1960s tape readers were much higher speed and spec than later ones –

expensively high for a mundane task. They stood 4-foot high and 2-foot square, packed with superbly engineered drive motors and controllers, optical sensors and semiconductor circuitry – and the tape whistled past the read head and out in a straight line 3-foot long before curving to the floor in piles. Amazingly, at that speed, the mechanisms were so finely engineered the reader could click and stop immediately if it hit an error. Sense and stop while the character was still under the read head.

The Upside tapes were in massive reels which couldn't easily be split up. The inertia of the spools on start up as the reader's motor clutch kicked in was so great that the tape often snapped. Then you had to stick the 2 ends together with a special thin splicing tape, clamp, and punch each hole through again with a Jenkins Fidgeon Uni-punch, worn-out and whisker-creating if you weren't careful. The punches were like gold dust to programmers. They were issued grudgingly, jealously, frowningly by skinflint administrators who were seemingly unaware that a whiskery hole might mean a lost hour of priceless time on a prototype. A couple of clear plastic oblongs, into which the offending tape was clamped. Then a steel-ended, knife-sharp punch that you thrust through the desired hole to chop its sides clean.

The team worked out a system, 2 people standing sideways between the spool and the tape reader. The first would feed a slack loop off the spool; the second feed the slack tape into the reader at appropriate speed. Wearing work. Occasionally there would be a sudden click, and the tape would stop feeding, with one character under the read head and a dreaded little red light on. Incandescently bright. Parity error – one of the 7 bits had been misread. Perhaps a furry-edged hole. Then you had to look at the holes and at the binary value of the character, and compare the value with that shown on the console lights in octal from Register A. Work out what the character should be, hopefully, by comparing the value with that shown in Register A, and locating the furry hole to check. Then click on the console pressel switches to set Register A up with the right binary number, then click again on the pressel switches to store it away in the right location. Given that a single incorrect bit of information can wreck a program, it was a tense, demanding task.

Eventually, team 2 at Gorton had finished loading up the paper tapes. They booted the system up, tried some trial transactions – OK – ran a system test – all OK. Elated, they went to report progress.

'Let's have a demo,' said Gaskin.

'No problem.'

Nor was there. The system just worked off today's date, looked up the destabilisation status and targets, and fired off the required transactions down the printer port. In live use they'd reset the output port to the right number for the target machine, the PIG KDF6.

Gaskin invited them to a review meeting with his 4 cell leaders.

'We'll have a training run,' he said.

Then, to the 2 Upsiders, Tilley and Sseru, 'This is Nadine, just back from her 2 friends on the high seas somewhere.'

She smiled at them.

'Never seen you looking so well,' said Gaskin.

'Yes, well,' she said, 'I'd hoped for a word with you later.'

'For you, Nadine, anything.'

They set up a role-playing dummy situation. Nadine was a shop assistant at her terminal, and McGervon the current target, using an old cow-transponder round his neck to identify himself to the computer for the time being. He came to her counter. Her machine gave a beep. It had recognised the transponder.

'What the hell's that bloody beep?' interrupted Gaskin.

'It's OK,' said Tilley, gently, soothingly, annoyingly reassuring. 'Just a chunk of temporary diagnostic test code.'

'We've all heard that one before, haven't we? Log it down as a fault, place an action and start again.'

Tilley looked miffed. 'One has to be up-front about these things,' he said defensively.

'What do you mean up-front? Up-front of what, for God's sake?'

'Just a figure of speech,' Tilley replied tightly.

'Well, get that temporary diagnostic code permanently diagnostically zapped. And start speaking plain English again. I don't resonate with your flaming locution. In any way shape or form. At the end of the day. OK? Got the T-shirt, as you would say?'

As McGervon approached the counter for the second time, a

214

message appeared on Nadine's screen: 'Surveil level 2. Phone caution 3 through to security.'

She scanned a list with her script, picked up the phone, and said loudly, 'Mr Gubbins. It's that man again.'

'OK. Good. Splendid. I like it. Nothing like a bit of paranoia. Theme of our times: "Just because you're paranoic doesn't mean we're not out to get you." That looks fine,' said Gaskin.

They put the 4 leaders through it in pairs, then sat round a table to discuss progress.

'Just one thing, Neville,' said Nadine.

'Yes?'

'The date. Surely it should have been 8th October 2019?'

'Of course. What was it?'

'8th October 2014'.

'Well, I'm sure these guys can adjust it.'

Tilley flushed and looked worried.

'You can, can't you?' insisted Gaskin. 'I mean, obviously it must be a system variable.'

'Well, why for God's sake have we got to change it? My watch says it's the 8th of October, 2019.'

Gaskin explained about the millennium bug. Downside they'd soon decided there wasn't a cat in hell's chance of sorting it all out, with 95 per cent of the programmers dead. So they'd adopted the convention that at 23:59.59 on 31/12/99, everybody rolled the date back to 00:00.01 on 1/1/1980.

'Well, nobody told us that.'

'Did you include the date in the project's Key Requirements and Assumptions list?'

'Not my job. We were just the implementation team. We get the entity life histories after the initial prototyping, then we implement them.'

'I know I know,' said Gaskin in a resigned tone. He'd been here before; many, many times. 'OK OK OK.'

'Anyway,' pursued Tilley warmly, 'I'm pretty sure it wasn't in the user constraints and limitations. So it's not our problem.'

'Well, come on now, surely. It's first generation stuff. Bloody obvious. You guys are wet behind the ears.'

Tilley flushed again. 'OK then. I'll go and get the requirements document.'

'You do just that, just that. Temporarily, diagnostically that.'

'It's Upside in Cambridge.'

Gaskin took a deep breath. Noisily; aggressively. Then he breathed out.

'Funny fellow,' he said. They all relaxed and laughed.

It transpired that, since the data had to run on the KDF6, the same constraints on speed, processing simplicity and data storage that prompted the writers of the original so-called millennium bugs still applied. So they had just assumed all dates started with 20, and programmed accordingly, tacking '20' on the front of any date before processing the transaction. But all the Downside tills would be looking for 2014 or so. All the credit cards would be rejected, and so on.

They broke for coffee. Tilley showed them the problem. Gaskin resolved there was nothing to do but get apWilliams back from Pilot's Cove to help sort it.

'I could go down there again,' offered Nadine quickly.

'No, there's another job I need you for.'

They talked over the effects of the problem. Opinion was sharply divided, some wanting to go ahead with destabilisation regardless, but most to hold off and let the Upsiders sort the dates out and send revised programs through the wormhole. Gaskin said, 'Look, do us all a favour. That wormhole is drifting. It started in Malaysia – who knows its course for sure? We might be hanging around for ever.'

But the argument continued. Eventually Gaskin intervened again, 'I remember, lady and gents, a strategy confrontation we had in ICM, distributed processing versus the monolithic centralised system. Resolution meeting. Forty-odd top people. Strong opinions in all the major sectors on one side or the other. Vital to get it right for the company's survival. And Corbett, the newly head-hunted Chief Systems Engineer, stepped in and said, "We're going for the monolithic option".'

Immediately, a particularly forceful sector manager interrupted. 'In ICL, Mr Corbett,' he said cuttingly, 'we're accustomed to hear and debate rational justifications for all our key decisions.'

'I'll give you a rational justification,' replied Corbett. 'Do it or you're fired. Well, we're in the same situation now. And the decision is we're going ahead alone regardless. OK?'

No one dissented. They decided the first phase of destabilisation would start as planned, and they would find some manual means of generating sufficient destabilisation transactions. Gaskin set them in pairs to rough out what they would do. The physical prototyping under FCIM of the software would finish in 5 days. The modification of the prototype 'agents'[48] could follow; these were little free-swimming chunks of AI code, neural network programs, autonomous and semi-intelligent, which followed their target humans and noted all they did. The agents sculled around inside the PIG system, trawling for material, and attached themselves to the people that interested them.

Then the team would apply the prototype system and the modified agents. Only to the target area, of course. After a month they would study the resulting NACAB (National Association of Citizens Advice Bureaux) statistics to see the effect.

Gaskin then made to leave. Nadine slipped across, steering him into a corner, and talked to him separately. She told him about apWilliams and Susanna.

'Well. It's all 15 years ago now. She must be long dead, whatever he thinks,' said Gaskin impatiently. 'You know damned well that the whole Crossa thing was just a ludicrously expensive means of losing misfits.'

She went on quietly about something else. She flushed and the team heard her say, '... but it's important. Very important.'

'Yes,' he replied as he left, 'we really must fit something in. You know how we rely on you, Nadine my love. But things are very tight just now. I'll see you just as soon as I can and then we can thrash out a solution together.'

The destabilisation session continued after he left until well after final curfew, and in the end the coffee and gumption ran out, and they slept on the floor.

Gaskin got to his office the next morning and logged in. He called up a high security file on the screen, file annasus. He did something else while it was being retrieved from the archives, passwording as needed when the various prompts came up. He remembered the woman. Bloody minded. But one of the first moles and one of the best. Agent in the Welsh clearances, but actually played a key role in tipping off lead people and getting them out. Then she had suddenly disappeared from view.

217

The file came up:

Harmon, Susanna

Special cranial consciousness facility x312a, essential for PIG version 2.1 lexical binding and Beta testing. Schedule for Crossa, but retain under Article 3, then decorticate and incorporate.

Jorkins, 11/2/95

He typed RENAME annasus any312.

Then he cleared the security prompts back up again and logged out.

Downside, Chapter 25: Prototyping

Back a month after the planning meeting, the prototyping started in the North West and Staffordshire.

*****

Surveil_today file;StaffsNW; Watchfor&caution
Record: BrownJoe
DVLA Swansea & Police National Computer
Authority botCW12;f
Rover 820i Sal Gr L397 LKP Postcode CW12 3ZF

*****

It was 11.00 p.m. Frieda and Joe Brown drove south down the A34 towards Stafford, after an evening watching a repeat showing of *Terminator*. They passed a parked police car. A minute or so later, lights appeared flashing behind them; the police car overtook them, put on its 'Police STOP' sign, and drew them to a halt.

'Just sit there quiet,' said Joe. 'Don't annoy him.'

'But what have I done?' asked Frieda. 'We was only doing 50, lights was all on, and it's just been MOT'd.'

'Never mind, keep it cool.'

'Good evening,' said the police driver. 'Can you tell me where you were going?'

'Back home, evening at the films.'

'But your home is in Stone, surely. A bit out of your way, isn't it, Mrs Brown?'

'No, we're actually in a little village to the west.'

'Oh. Ah, well. We keep an eye out for stolen cars and that. Deviants. It's in everyone's interest, after all.'

'Suppose you're right.'

'Night then.'

'Good night.'

They drove off.

219

'How did he know my name? How'd he know I was Mrs Brown?' asked Frieda.

'Dunno. All on the PNC, I guess. Police national whatsit. Same as I say. We'd best be careful.'

*****

A middle-aged man walked confidently down Stafford high street. Nice day, bright autumn sunshine, odd scudding white clouds. He'd been off the pills for a while. He walked down, into the 'Shoes' store and through to the audio counter – they were keen on audio. He ordered a copy of Girlzone doing proper nineties hits, for his wife's birthday. The till lady took his card and swiped it. There was a pause, then a message must have come up on her read-out. She looked at a concealed list, then glanced up at him with sudden hostility, and he flinched. She picked up the phone.

'Mr Fryberg,' she said, 'it's that man again.'

He's not yet paranoic, but he soon will be.

Downside, Chapter 26: Further Prototyping

A young woman came up to the toilet on Market Hill in Stafford. The old one had been so vandalised it had been fitted with an iron grill and padlocked long ago. The new toilet was a metal cylinder about 5-feet across, with gently corrugated sides, tapering slightly, then rounded to join a nicely domed roof. The door formed a curved segment, designed to slide open and recess itself into the main body.

She dug out a coin and slipped it in the slot. The door slid open and she entered, then it snapped to after her. It seemed very clean. Probably all the usable surfaces were flushed each time it operated. Having finished, she pressed the 'Unlock and Open' grommet. It gave and clicked, but nothing happened. She tried again. Suddenly there was a whirring and a hissing. She screamed. The light went out. The floor was sluiced, drenching her shoes. A rotary brush spun over it, and she had to feel for the washbasin, grab it and haul herself up out of the way. She heard the cascading of water in the toilet bowl, and the sound of a cleaning process in train under the lid. Finally, there was a squirting sound, and scented freshener wafted around the device. Then all was quiet.

She pressed the grommet fiercely again. Then called out 'Help', softly at first, then louder as no answer was forthcoming. There was a sudden click, and the washing process started again. Her screams redoubled, and she banged on the door and sides as hard as she could.

Eventually, she heard a voice outside.

'Hallo, love. You all right?'

'No,' she yelled. 'This bloody thing's stuck.'

'Try pushing the button.'

'I done that; no good.'

'OK, wait a sec. I'll put in a coin.'

'Thanks so much.'

A wait while the rescuer found a coin and tried it. No joy. It didn't open.

'Sorry, love. I'll have to call the Council.' The wash started again. She screamed again.

After half an hour, the engineer came. By this time an indignant group of people had formed. The washing process continued inexorably. The girl was sobbing quietly. The door was firmly stuck, and the engineer had to phone for his mates with a crowbar.

'That's the third today,' he said. 'Can't think what's got into them.'

*****

At the end of the week's prototyping, Tilley and McGervon were using RUG on the KDF6 to hack into the Stafford Citizens Advice Bureau statistics off the UK Intranet. Stats summaries en route to the National Association of CABs. Feedback to the Benevernment on Social Policy. How many benefit applications, divorces, cases of racial violence and whatever? How many and who? The statistic's no good unless you know who.

The guy in the chemists was on sedation. The couple in the car had come in to the bureau for consultation. Referred to Liberty. Fat chance. The stats looked good. They took them to Gaskin when he called in.

He looked at the category summaries, and did some calculations as against the previous week's figures. New CAB clients. Benefits profiles showing numbers of people analysed with QuickBenefits version 10, council tax arrears profiles, employment profiles, legal profiles, relationship profiles, mental health referrals, utility profiles, social policy reports, police incidents.

'All ratcheting up a tad. Nicely,' he said, 'and a splendid spike in the complaints to the council. They'll be about the toilet thing. That's just about right. OK then, you guys. Next week we go for it.'

*****

The monthly PPRM (PIG Progress Review Meeting) was about to begin on the top floor in West Gorton. A long, deeply carpeted, impressive but sombre room, predominantly dark green and black with stark white walls and ceiling; a long oaken table, finely configured, not fumed but conveying that by faint suggestion; chairs to match the green with faintly tapered stainless legs splaying diagonally outwards; rubber plants and other vegetation to match the chairs. The chairs were packed with Big Cousin's best and brightest guys.

BL and Gaskin were in a corner.

'No,' said Gaskin, 'I can't spare her, and that's final. I need Nadine to be up in Edinburgh. She's essential if they're going to crack that bottleneck.'

'Shows the calibre of your planning, Gaskin,' replied BL. 'If I were running your outfit, I'd have backup for everyone, part of the culture.'

'Well, think again mate; not your patch is it?' asked Gaskin. 'So bugger off,' he said pausing briefly, 'Bubb.' There was a touch of amused derision on Gaskin's face, and he looked into BL's eyes as he curled both lips inwards and put weight on the plosives in 'Bubb'. Rather like the nineties Upside comedian, Blackadder. Then he walked away and sat down.

The meeting opened and members contributed their views on the causes of the problems. PIG was under intense fire.

Big Cousin at the far end wound up some passionate general discussion. His voice was husky with old cigarette tar, whisky and menace.

'Well, thank you all for some invaluable pointers. As we discussed, BL and I would like to talk it all over in depth with Neville here; in view of public concern, I continue to believe that some dramatic' – he let weight fall on the word – 'some dramatic action is needed to ensure our great mission, our quest for transcending excellence, gets back on course.'

BL stood up, and added, 'I'm sure, Big Cousin, that at this crucial time, I speak for all of us in this centre of supreme excellence, when I say we are 110 per cent behind you and Neville. And that we're immensely conscious of the wise guidance the 2 of you have given us over so many years. The courageous decisions you've both made. Not one of us has ever doubted. Perhaps we should all voice our feelings by your leading us in a short prayer.'

Gaskin's eyes glinted. A vestige of a smile twitched across his lips. Big Cousin composed himself, and led them appropriately.

When the 3 of them were alone, BL spoke reflectively to BC and Gaskin. He looked out across towards the Pennines.

'If I may perhaps draw out your thoughts, Big Cousin. No doubt about it, there's a desperate need for a really powerful gesture of reassurance to John Citizen. We have to convince him that PIG is the right way, that all will be well, that we really care for the victims.' There was a lingering affection in the weight he placed on the 'care for'. 'I wonder. Perhaps I could help make such a gesture? Anything. Maybe the supreme sacrifice.'

'How do you mean?' asked Gaskin. 'What supreme sacrifice?'

'You may scoff Neville, it's always your way, to hide the caring heart beneath it all. I don't know. The Bridge perhaps. Or maybe I should go for PIG.'

'No, no,' said Big Cousin. 'No, I can't agree to that. We need a powerful gesture, yes. But a gesture from the very top.'

'If you say so,' said BL, 'but my offer's a sincere one and it's on the table.'

They conferred further, then Gaskin pled a technical meeting and left.

BL leant confidingly towards Big Cousin, and talked quietly.

'Understand me, Biggles?' he finished. 'You're with me Biggles? Maybe Gaskin has to go. The bridge. Next event. These fuckers; we've got to grasp them by the goolies and squeeze till they squeak. Get the POPs off their arses back from Wales. Believe me, Biggles, they're after you.' Biggles was the pet name he used with Big Cousin. He always liked to have a pet, personal name, to use with his bosses.

'I shall not let personal considerations stand in the way of a right course of action,' said Big Cousin. 'I never have. I never will. A gesture is needed. A gesture we will have. The most powerful one possible.'

'With you, Biggles, with you all the way.' Then BC said he would leave for his car. BL walked with him towards the lift. A long, yellow-faced, middle-aged, inconspicuous individual was hanging around behind the glass door near the stairs. BL looked towards him. Arkinshaw it was. A dodgy programmer, the police had told him, with a form as long as your arm. All the better, BL had thought, to tether him with. BC left in the lift. BL motioned slightly with his head. The guy nipped off down the stairs. BL said a cheery goodbye to the secretaries and got into the next lift. It stopped at the next floor down, and Arkinshaw joined him.

224

Downside, Chapter 27: Destabilisaton

Following Gaskin's instructions, Nadine had holed up in a terraced house in Gorton working on one of the information handler routines. Occasionally she fed in to the system purchases and hotel bills showing she was in Edinburgh. One morning, mindful of her promise to try to trace apWilliams' partner, Susanna, she studied the archives from the Irish project.

She got McGervon to accompany her into the systems centre on his pass. Then went through the access tunnel separating the main systems centre from the closed Directorate building, slipping her card into the access permitter. A risk, she thought, certainly, but who's going to worry about well-known systems people going about their daily business? Who's going to know she's supposed to be in Edinburgh?

The building's fortifications were vastly more formidable than any pre-Malfunction US embassy – outside were extraordinary grey shutters, 4-inches thick, of hardened Poznan steel, 3 massive angled slabs of it for every office, wedges 30 foot by 5. They hung waiting the command, like crocodiles' eyelids, to blink away prowling missiles or tyrannicidal shells. An exciting and intimidating structure, and all the more so when you were inside, enclosed, trapped perhaps, in a colossal carapace. She climbed the stairs 2 storeys past clean empty stretches of office space. Empty ready to house the top brass and technocrats if a situation were to develop. Then heard the whine of the lift on its way up. People were talking. She shrank into a doorway. The voices grew louder; and then she sweated with relief as they receded upwards.

The Directorate systems floor, the fifth storey, would have several operators on duty, but at the end of the passage was a door into the library area where the archive tapes were stored. Not high security classified. There was a tape-reader and work station. She spread out some innocuous systems journal information in case someone proved curious, loaded a tape, then got onto the work station.

The main archive had no record, but she uploaded a streamer tape with an intermediate dump on it. She broke in to the password sequence to abort the check halfway through, then hit Ctrl/Alt/Del continuously till the date prompt appeared, and typed in 00/13/99. The invalid date prompt appeared. She keyed another date in again. Got it! She was in, and outside the automatic access control. Session logging was disabled.[49] She keyed in the SQL to search on Crossa and Harmon. Then on to Harmon. A page appeared:

Name; Harmon, Susanna
DoB; 19/5/73
Education; St Edwards, Solihull, Aberystwyth University and UEA, Sociology and political philosophy (2.2)
Agency; Front-cottage agency, Machynlleth – Clearances Authority, reports to Dep Inspector Gen
Reason for Extermination; Para 3.1.12 Conduct prejudicial etc.
Circumstances; Controlled, refer to DAQMG See file annasus. WIL'd on Crossa Easter cruise.

Nadine slumped, then pulled herself up and blinked some tears away. She searched for the 'encrypted file annasus' – no luck on that tape. She got more and more frightened, tried 2 more dumps, then left quickly. After all, the report had been conclusive; apWilliams girl had been on a Crossa tragedy. Must have been killed like the rest.

As she walked outside, returning to her house, her thoughts drifted to the unknown Susanna and she forgot to turn down the back streets. Something was odd about the record, but it eluded her. Suddenly, a toot from across the road, lights flashed at her, and there was the green Aston Martin that she knew so well. BL's DB6. She went white with shock, then pulled herself together, looked quickly each way, and ran across the road smiling.

'BL,' she said, 'how lovely to see you. Why don't you take me to the Bleeding Wolf for a drink?'
'Thought you were in Edinburgh.'
'Just back. Cracked the bottle-neck late yesterday.'
He parked and they set off. She slipped her arm through BL's

226

and pressed against him. He felt her side and breast, unbelievably soft, against him.

'Missed me?' she asked.

'Feverishly,' he claimed. 'You must come to my place tonight.'

'Super. Really super.'

After the drink, they split up, and Nadine went quickly to see
Gaskin. She told him about her drink with BL. 'OK,' he said, 'I
want you down in Anglesey sharpish. I'll fix the Bangor shuttle to
drop you. Tell apWilliams we need him here on the KDF6, and
come back with him. There's not a lot of time. Johnson had
better stay put and oil the binnacle or something. No, I tell you
what. Tell him to move the boat up the straits, just out of sight of
the bridge. Just in case. Make him feel it's really important.'

*****

'You know,' said Tilley thoughtfully over coffee the next day.

'I know what?' asked McGervon.

'What Gaskin was saying about women. Well, it ties up interestingly with the work some friends were doing Upside.'

He went on to elucidate, explaining that the 1980s, 1990s and
2000s had been a period of dramatic progress for women. It was
a sex-saturated society. One or two leading feminists caught the
imaginations of many, but especially the younger generation,
talking with wide-ranging passion across all manner of closet
issues. You got the impression that a woman called Germaine
Greer – adulated ecstatically by 1980s students – had single-
handedly invented masturbation.

'Whereas we all know now it was invented by George Formby
in the thirties,' chipped in McGervon.

'Yes, well, that's right, the little stick of Blackpool rock. Or
even earlier. I suspect the Greeks myself,' continued Tilley. 'The
finest form of love. But dedicated women's organisations flourished. Rambling, discursive books abounded with worrying titles
like "What Women Want", with long collections of case-studies
and anecdotes which left men feeling guilty, puzzled, bewildered. The media searched for ways of feeding on this feminine
goldmine, in chat shows, phone-ins, TV confrontations, scanda-
lised attacks on male deviants however harmless. Men dived off
Beachy Head.

'I remember particularly when there was a lot of scandal about battered women, work place molestation and so on, when some research brought to light that in some cases the batterers and molesters were in fact the women and the sufferers the men. Statistically they were 17 per cent lighter and weaker than men, but the mean standard deviation was very large. So some women were certainly big enough relative to their man to beat him up.'

'But I'm damned sure getting the issues out in the open was a good thing,' protested McGervon.

'I hear where you're coming from,' said Tilley. 'But – '

'What do you mean? How can you hear where I'm coming from? I'm not coming from anywhere. I'm right here,' protested McGervon.

'Figure of speech. Sorry. Anyway, let me finish this example. I remember the widely-heard *Today* programme. The news included coverage on a small battered man who'd complained to the police when his muscular wife beat him up rather nastily. The woman presenter chipped in scornfully "For God's sake, what sort of wimp is he?" In her book, female victim equals heroine, male victim equals wimp! She was inacapable of putting herself inside the wimp, of understanding how it might be. To lie beside the wife at night. To reach out longingly and caress and get a knee in the crutch. To try to sleep knowing that you might wake with soft bare hands in a stranglehold round your windpipe. The presenter had in fact later hosted a series on the topic, which prompted people to start scrutinising her line. Fine for an ambitious, beautiful, upper-class, category A presenter to promote these issues, but what about Bentham's Greatest Happiness of the Greatest Number? What about the majority of women, for whom the challenges and joys of bringing up a family were their greatest potential satisfaction? What about the unhappy teenage girls, whose lives and development were effectively aborted by the social pressure to become a young mother and set up a dad-free pseudo-home, scraping by in a council flat or hostel, with a little infant who knew not and would never know his or her father?

And had the past been so irretrievably grim for the women? For the upper classes, maybe, though life and literature abounded with the opposite, with *matersfamilias* who ruled with alarming caprice and rods of silk-clad steel. Lady Windermere, Mrs Proudie, Lady Macbeth, Cleopatra, Livia, Bertie Wooster's aunts, Maggie Thatcher. But look at the majority of women; take the studies of working-class wives in cities like Manchester. Or take the mother, Juno, in Sean O'Casey's *Juno and the Paycock*. The way the fathers and sons would come in on Friday night, and hand over most of the pay packet to Mum. Mum had the power of the purse. The satisfactions of the kitchen. She decided what they ate, what they wore, what they had to spend, who they married, what they were. Who got as a result the love, the real job satisfaction? Who incidentally were commonly the goodies in most media soaps and situation comedies – *Coronation Street, Dallas, East Enders, Till Death Us Do Part, The Archers?* The women. They were mostly heroines, or if not heroines, at least appealing and put-upon, while the men were fallible and often as not villains. The Grundies, Brian Aldridge, Sid Perks, The doctor chap who flitted to Brum.'

'Don't remember him,' said apWilliams.

'The Archers' doctor,' said Tilley, 'Perhaps after 2014. After your time.'

'In general,' replied McGervon, 'you may be right. But it could be because the audience was mostly women anyway.'

'Yes, I guess in part. But also because that is the image of women, caring, self-sacrificing, noble, which has prevailed in nearly all societies. The men work, fight and ultimately fall, just like male lions, where the females get all the fun. I remember particularly as a Sri Lankan, a social pattern immensely common among one large North Indian tribe; the father of the family would stay as revered head until his powers started failing. Then, just before daybreak one day, he would slip out onto the dusty highroad, to go off and lead a life of unknown wandering beggary until he died. It nearly happened to my own father – a massive row and he left. But happily he came back again the next morning! But shamefaced, and it was a while before he again seemed the man he had been. I feel nowadays he should have kicked us out of the house for the night – the row was our fault.

'Well, against this background, language research revealed that the key mutation to create language had arisen via the "Y" chromosome, i.e. among the male of the species. And the brain structure in men, with a distinct gap between the 2 hemispheres, had at the same time imposed bottlenecks in the communication process. Information – chat? – which flowed easily through the feminine brain, out through the larynx to her peers and among them and back in again through the ears, was much more restricted in men. So the females formed a talkative, empathetic community, the groups achieving ready consensus in this swiftly flowing environment. And acceptance into this community was a woman's unconscious highest priority. So. The women rarely stepped outside the consensus, so they were rarely innovators. No tunnel-vision. And they were also much readier, as individuals, than men to abandon attitudes they'd previously cherished. So long as their group did too. Studies showed that core attitudes in women were often dropped after 2 years if that was the peer-group consensus; for men the figure was 5 years. The result was that the female-dominated decades were also ones in which cherished allegiances fell easily away. Nation, church, marriage, law and so on decayed into a well-wishing but unstable melting pot where the scoffers and spinners held sway. In language, to speak grammatically was scorned as pedantic; in history, fact and objectiveness were dumbed down as dull, and a racy emotional blend of fact and fiction, which came to be called faction, swept the popular library shelves. Government ceased to be the sturdy base for development created by men like Eisenhower (playing golf through a global nuclear power eyeball to eyeball confrontation) or Attlee (adjusting cabinet business to keep in touch with the cricket scores, just like Francis Drake completing the game of bowls on Plymouth Ho before turning his attention to the approaching Spanish Armada), and instead became a hesitant appealing flirtation with the public through the media. "Rottweiler kills child" – instant fix – "Farmer Kills Burglar" – instant fix – "Dictator Expels Whites" – instant fix.'

'Yes,' interposed Sseru. 'You guys will remember Robert Mugabe, originally the inspiring hard left leader of independence in Zimbabwe. One of my heroes, in fact. Well, after 20 years on Upside he had degenerated into the same cynical tyrant surrounded by yes-men as sadly characterised many of our African countries. He was in trouble – corruption, nepotism, scandal. Started a foreign war, as recommended by Niccolo

Machiavelli, to divert his peoples' discontent. But military defeats further disenchanted the people, and a referendum was sharply hostile. So, thought Mugabe, take another option, exploit racism. How about the successful white farmers? Kick them out, grab their lands and redistribute, no compensation, just as Amin did with the Ugandan Asians. "We're expelling you, but we'll give you a police escort to the border," he promised – to his own citizens! Some of them fourth and fifth generation Zimbabweans whose contribution to the previously prosperous country had been decisive. Mugabe's line was that this is the blacks' continent. A powerful piece of racist demagogy. And the Brits, instead of playing a careful hand close to their chests, as the great Foreign Office mandarins would have done in the past, immediately embarked on a series of toothless media confrontations with Mugabe, "defending" the whites. This had the white farmers and their black workforces trapped, persecuted and often savagely killed, and it also rallied African peasant opinion round the old rogue Mugabe, and wrecked a promising attempt by Zimbabwean democrats to out him. For the nineties politicians, polls, media, spin and statistics, however superficial, were all in all. Hence the traumatic political collapses of the early noughts.'

'Yes, but getting back to sex, how did the Upside academics handle the evolutionary aspect that has bugged us here?' asked McGervon. 'How do you suppress men's innate aggressive instincts towards the stranger? Here the Benevernment of course are trying to drive it out by eliminating the misfits. That's what the Crossa project was exploring. Put the misfits on the ferry to Ireland, then drown them on the way across.'

'Well. Natural selection equipped men through the ages with genes to protect paternity, to make sure the wives didn't have children by others; if a guy didn't have this protective urge he didn't get to procreate. Except through occasional extra-pair copulation. This was a sort of safety valve so that for monogamous couples there was the occasional let-out. What went wrong in the nineties was that this whole structure, fundamental to human happiness, was jacked over by a bunch of theorists. Just as naive in their way as the Charter 88 politicians.'

*****

231

It was Monday, progress review afternoon in the West Gorton tower block. Good management practice – Monday allowed the laggards the preceding weekend to work over if needed, and make up any lost time. Then the morning to get their stories right and anticipate the opposition's case.

Gaskin approached BL before the meeting.

'Before we get onto the Milestones,' he said, 'Nadine asked me to let you know. The problem's reappeared in Edinburgh, so I've sent her back up there.'

BL flushed, and stiffened, but made no response.

*****

Nadine got not to Edinburgh but to Anglesey 2 days later, and kayaked across to the lighthouse. The old boat was in vastly better nick, but the 2 sailors were fed up.

'What the hell's he think he's doing?' asked Johnson angrily, as Nadine passed on his orders. 'Why have I got to hang around here, for God's sake?'

'He knows what he's doing,' she said, a bit severely, 'and we'd do well to stick to our lasts. All of us. He wants the boat up the straits, just out of sight of the bridge.'

'Why?'

'Wait and see. You'll be told in good time.'

'Do you mind, Alun,' she asked later, 'if I just have a word with Johnson?'

'Well,' said apWilliams cheerily, 'that's a bit much. After all the work I've done on the boat. Just like you said. Still, there you are then. Women. They're all the same.'

They went off up over the dunes, hand in hand. Across the top they kissed lightly, leaning forward chastely, lips to lips, like a cartoon from Lilliput. That French cartoonist who clothed all his lovers in rosebuds, the women soft, sweet and lingering, barely touchable, carrying woven baskets, clad in bonnets and bustles. Nadine drew Johnson down, soothed his ardour, and they made love gently. Then fiercely.

Afterwards, she said to him, 'Johnson, you remember the clearances I told you about?'

'Yes.'

232

She described her research into Susanna's death. He was horrified.

'Alun. How can we tell him?' asked Johnson.

'Do you think you should?'

'I don't know.'

Johnson recalled a similar occasion, when as a youngster he'd had to break similar news. He still writhed inside his skin when he remembered how dreadfully he'd handled it. Standing at the poor guy's front door. Surely he could have said 'Mind if I come in?' How crass can you be?

'Not dodging my job as a friend,' he said, 'but I'm absolutely convinced you'd do it better.'

'Maybe. I hope so. I think I'll try to break it gradually as we go back to Gorton.'

'But about the boat, I still think Neville should at least explain what we're up to,' Johnson suggested.

'Maybe that's what Susanna said. Maybe someone did explain to her. Maybe that someone was overheard. Maybe that's why she's dead. You've come from a cushy culture, Johnson.'

'I hear you.'

'Oh yes,' she added, 'he said you were to "oil the binnacle". What's "the binnacle"?'

'Did he now? Funny fellow.'

Nadine and apWilliams got back to West Gorton. It took a sight of the encrypted files from 2029 eventually to convince apWilliams that Susanna was dead. They didn't find the annasus file. He disappeared for 2 days, no doubt rooting around in the city's empty zones. Then he came back, as they say, a changed man. Dark rings round the eyes, hollow cheeks scalded with unweepable tears, jowls beginning to show, a tightness about the lips which broke into a tremulous quiver unless schooled into obedience. He wanted, he said, to see Gaskin. He'll see you as soon as he can, they said. He retreated into his grief. Snippets of memory recurred almost overriding his anchorage in the desperate present. Sue here, Sue there. This spot, that spot. He thought he saw her across the road. He dashed across. Someone entirely different. But slowly the particular yielded a little place to the general. He thought not just of Sue, but also back to the days before the Malfunction. About the 'unreturning army', as the poet had said, 'the unreturning army that had been youth'.

At Gorton they tried hard to make apWilliams welcome, give him a feeling of commitment. They invented problems on the KDF6 for him to solve.

'We've got this problem, boyo. Needs a Welshman with balls and commitment. Plus Indexed Sequential and the File Control Package.'

He gradually became more communicative, especially with Nadine. Eventually it seemed to him as though he had come into a kind of sleep, sad and eternal.

Then they started compiling the main system for the KDF6. This was to cover hundreds, maybe thousands of transactions as opposed to the handful used for the prototyping. To do this involved using a 'macro-expander' which amended the base program code in many complicated ways, tacked on suitable bits and pieces of additional code at key points and so on. For example, the prototype would just call for one transaction at a time. This could be very slow indeed. But the Full TransGap system would slurp great gobbets of people-information into the main store in a single gulp; then process them all together with the same program code at full speed, maybe several hundred times faster.

Like normal language compilers, e.g. for VisualBasic, the system compiler made several 'passes' over the programs, each pass reading the program, translating certain functions and writing them out to another tape. A long, long job, no disks, just tapes whizzing back and forth, nowt for the lads to do.

'D'you know much about what went wrong at the Error?' Tilley asked McGervon.

'The First World Error, you mean? Well, it was all incredibly confused, and since the UK's been isolated and presumably the rest of the world's down the tube, there's no way of knowing. Like most of the other survivors, we were down in the shelters for a national practice run when it all happened. Then the nuclear contamination warnings were all on, and we were down there a couple of months. I guess it was immediately a nuclear attack that triggered off all manner of other nastiness. It must have included a biological component, because by the time the people got out again, research uncovered the fact that all red-blooded life had disappeared. Except us.'

'Christ. It must have been appalling.'

'Yes, indeed. But also incredibly exciting. You felt we were on a pinhead, and the whole survival of the human race was at stake.'

'Which, of course, it was.'

'Yes, but it must sound callous, but in the midst of such incredible loss – lovers, relatives, friends – that fact somehow made it all bearable. We were maybe the remaining remnant of the species. As they used to say to explain why after a century of wireless transmissions, when humanity can have been received and contacted from outer space by higher civilisations. Why have we heard nothing? And the chilling answer was that the others are either more backward than us and haven't yet invented radio. Or they're more advanced and have wiped themselves out. And, of course, we had all manner of social bridges to ease the pain. Formal funerals in big cathedrals for example, for each of your loved ones.'

'Yes, I remember we had something similar in Lusaka for the refugee survivors of some massacres in Rwanda. One Rwandan couple were in shock; 49 of their family shot in front of them. After the first funeral they felt a numbness coming. And by the forty-ninth they were able to face life again.'

'As for the source of the death virus,' continued Tilley, 'it may have been Russia. There was a team operating led by Sergei Popov, who invented some designer bad bug which combined 2 killer viruses and was also aerosolised and weaponised to go in warheads. It was impossible to trace after death. I saw him on TV. An intense-looking man with finely chiselled features and penetrating eyes. You felt the challenge was for him irresistible and technically sweet.'[50]

Tilley and McGervon decided to leave the machine to get on with it. They put on their anonymous external faces and went off to watch the Big Cousin parade down Wenlock Way towards the Great Leader's final convocation in Old Trafford, Man United's ground. He was holding meetings and pressing hands in a farewell tour all round the Motorway Ring, having announced his plan to be pigified with 7 assistants – who became known as 'the 7' – and to get the PIG system back under control. People

remembered his moving TV peroration (crafted for him by BL):
'Let me share my thoughts, my innermost thoughts, with each
and every one of you,' he had said with shining eyes. 'At the end
of the day, greater care hath no person than this, that a person
lay down their brain for his / her fellow persons.'

*****

The crowds were dense as the Great Leader approached, some
hysterical, some cheerful.

'Go it mate. See them off.'

The chanting reached a crescendo as the cavalcade passed
abreast:

'Cousin, Cousin! He's the one. Big Cuzz, beat the Fuzz.'

The 2 friends got penned in, pints in hands, by the crowd
round the Gorton Arms, and had to struggle their way back to
the museum. They heard a sharp 'flackety flack' sound from
above. They ran upstairs to the computer room. They looked
around, shattered and aghast. The source tape had broken. It
was flailing around, spinning at great speed. One 2-inch-long
chunk of tape was being chopped off at each revolution as the
loose end hit the read head. The floor was carpeted with these
bits. The backups proved to be blank. Disaster. The compilation
was halfway through; now it could never be completed.

Gaskin met with them all to discuss what to do. Recreating the
mag tapes from scratch didn't seem to be feasible, though 2 of
them might try it, because the paper tapes from which they'd
been constituted were in several cases regrettably, predictably,
damaged, broken or screwed up. Sod's law.

Nadine chipped in:

'Could Sseru handle it perhaps? If he got into PIG with the Big
Cousin team? Isn't that the fallback that he was intended to
cover?'

'Yes,' said Gaskin, 'but that was just some half-baked idea from
Professor thingy. Still, how do you feel about it, Sseru?' asked
Gaskin.

'Sounds exciting. But I'm not a computer buff.'

'Let's talk around it. Roll it around the block and see what falls
off. Run it up the flagstaff and see who salutes. What would the
problems be?'

They could get him into the labs, they decided, and Gaskin's lab man could substitute him for one of the 7 brains. Once into PIG, he could perhaps influence whatever inter-brain processes were taking place, but there was no way he could modify the data being transferred to the KDF6. And that was a crux of the operation, to hack in and apply changes between the old computer and the PIG.

While the discussion developed, apWilliams had been sitting, apparently totally self-immersed, at the bottom of the table. For days he had been in a heightened state of grief. Not sad continually, just spinning through it a day at a time. He got up, got himself some coffee from the machine, then started striding up and down.

'Mind sitting down, Alun?' asked Gaskin, 'I'm getting dizzy.'

'Why don't I join Sseru?'

'How d'you mean?'

'Well...' he thought. The others waited. 'I've got a fair grasp of what's supposed to be done. And we know from our chats with Sseru, and his work with Dragon Dictate Upside, that a human brain can work many times faster and more accurately than its I/O system, voice or typing, permits. Remember how Sseru could spew out great tracts of thought onto the high speed line printer, which used to take us yonks to read back?'

Tilley interrupted. 'Well... not really, you know. That's the way it seemed, but in fact it was only about 6 pages a minute. Probably that fast because his brain isn't having to do all the normal Input/Output control. Constricting the palate. Twitching and twisting the tongue. Moving it back and forth from the alveolar ridge to the back of the teeth. Blocking the nasal passages. Closing and opening the gullet. Blowing through the vocal chords. All that. Incredibly slow, and he didn't need to do it because he was just churning out ASCII text instead.'

'True enough, no doubt,' said Gaskin. 'Your speciality, George. But let's hear more, Alun. Presumably you could act as if you were the program.'

They talked it over. The strategy might be for Sseru to handle whatever went on inside the PIG, and feed on to Alun the changes needed to the records as they flowed past him and out of PIG onto the tape for the KDF6. They would have to capture one of the 7 and substitute Alun for him. Then transfer the guy's identi-chip to Alun's crutch.

Nadine looked pale and sick.

'It all sounds quite horrifying,' she said passionately. 'They're going to kill you, you know, Alun, carve your skull apart, and stuff you in this bloody great tank with a lot of pigs' offal. That's what they're going to do.'

'No, no, it's not quite like that of course,' Gaskin interrupted gently. 'It won't hurt at all.' As he spoke the girl left, slamming the door. Gaskin raised his eyebrows in gentle, humourous resignation. 'But what d'you feel about it, Alun?' he continued.

'The way I'm feeling now, I'd just like to do it.'

'*Dulce et decorum est pro patria mori*,' murmured McGervon. '*Morituri, o Caesar, morituri te salutamus.*'

'What the bloody hell's that mean?' snarled Gaskin, 'Save your classical tags for another time.'

'OK, OK. Sorry. Anyway. Sweet and glorious to die for your country. One's country. We, Caesar, we who are about to die, salute you.'

'Balls,' said Gaskin. 'Bollocks. You're way off beam. Out of order.'

He paused for a moment, then asked, 'And how about the master brain? How do you feel about it, Sseru? Now we've talked it through.'

'For me, it's exciting. To think of joining an environment where there are others like me, whose perceptions will be similar to mine. To help in regenerating mankind through the PIG system. I like McGervon's words then. "Sweet and glorious to die for one's country".'

'Well. Or whatever,' said Gaskin noncommittally. He wound things up. They'd leave Sseru and apWilliams to think it over during the weekend, and decide whether to go ahead on the Monday.

When the time came, they decided to go ahead. Nadine said she'd have nothing to do with it, and left them.

'It's all right,' said Gaskin, 'she'll come round. Women find these crunch situations very difficult to handle.[51] In any case, I see her playing a key part in something entirely different.' A

238

woman in love, he remembered from Graham Greene, walks through the world like an anarchist, carrying a time bomb.

Gaskin left, and they got back to work. Gaskin found Nadine. 'I really do need to understand what you're trying to do,' she had said.

'Look, it's developing dynamically. Some time we'll have to go through it all in depth,' he replied, 'But now's not the time. Meanwhile, trust me. You're vital to us all. You know how we all rely on you.'

She had looked a touch doubtful, but accepted reluctantly.

Gaskin came back. 'I've talked to Nadine,' he said, 'and she understands better now. I've put her back on the Edinburgh assignment for the time being. Now. Let's get down to how we're going to communicate with you heroes once you've penetrated PIG.'

They formulated some dummy transactions that they would forward through to PIG as a confirmation code. To show contact had been made.

Penetrated, thought apWilliams later about his mission into PIG. Good heroic stuff. He thought back to the heroic Dark Ages legend in the Mabinogion. Marriage, murder, mutilation. The great battle over the beautiful Branwen, daughter of Llyn. And her death. Like Susanna's. How, when he was mortally wounded on Harlech beach, Bendegeid Vran (the Blessed Crow) Welsh king and consummate war leader, told his comrades, 'Take you my head to London... And a long time will you be upon the road. In Harlech you will be feasting 7 years. And all the time my head will be to you as pleasant company as it ever was.'

And so they were 7 years feasting in Harlech, then set out with Vran's head buried in a sack of meal for London as they'd been told. In the legend, an enemy lord, Evnissgen, stopped them and demanded to know what was in the sack. 'Meal, good sir,' said the warrior, and let him feel the meal through the sacking. The warrior got away with it, and was allowed to go on his way. And 40 years later they reached London, and buried the leader's head in the White Mount, looking towards France; 40 years, thought apWilliams smiling drowsily, a long time to get to Charing Cross tube from Llandanwg Halt. Strange that in the 1980s, the Welsh trains had always been so punctual. But now he would be the head, he would be Bendegeid Vran, and he and Sseru would be the rock on which PIG and BL would founder. He would avenge Susanna.

Downside, Chapter 28: Pigification

They smuggled Sseru and apWilliams into the hospital at 3 a.m. Sseru was in his haversack ready for Gaskin's hospital guy to insert into PIG.

apWilliams, sedated, unconscious, was substituted for one of Big Cousin's 7 designated companions. The operations were always shown live on evening TV as part of CPC (Compulsory Personal Conditioning) for leader-class people, but fortunately the operands' features were never seen, only the opened skulls after the chilling procedure when the electric saw circumnavigated the cranium and the circle of bone popped up. They lashed down the limbs and spines of the operands beforehand, so the viewers would just see a set of bodies, invisibly trussed, which were hard to identify.[52] The tricky bit was the connection of the subject brain to the SSI, the standard spinal interface, so that endothelialisation[53] took place rapidly and faultlessly. Effectively it was a xenograft, a foreign graft, of human brain onto a total pig environment.

A breathing tube connected him to the breathing bag operated by a respirator technician. Also an infusion line to the artery in his right arm, and another from the stomach through the throat to a bladder. Cables stretched from his chest to various monitors. apWilliams felt intense, agonising pains; both a cutting, a searing, a slicing, and also a blinding headache. Then suddenly they were gone, and he looked down from about 4 feet above his body and marvelled at what was going on. He drifted up and away slowly, dreamily. Then felt a sudden compulsion which dragged him screaming inaudibly back down into it. Back to the Vale of Tears stuff.

The team in West Gorton had watched apWilliams pigification on TV uneasily. Been there before, of course, seen that. But not you, not one of your close friends. Hard not to think of oneself being processed in the same way. On the days that followed, they monitored the KDF6 link impatiently every late-night shift. As no message came through, they became increasingly depressed.

*****

apWilliams regained a sort of consciousness. Limb-free consciousness. Voice-free consciousness. Sight-free consciousness. Sound-free consciousness. Taste-free consciousness. Touch-free consciousness.

What was consciousness anyway? Snippets from lines learnt in his youth drifted through his mind: 'Where Alph the sacred river ran, through caverns measureless to man, down to a sunless sea.' '*Facile descensus Averno*'[54]

He thought of Tom Sawyer with Becky, seeing Injun Joe across the chasm in the great caverns in Illinois.[55]

Slowly senses of a sort crept back. He seemed to recognise phrases drifting past: 'As I said in my speech of... '

He seemed to be in an immense hall or cave. A feeling perhaps of the Whispering Gallery in St Pauls, and at the same time of those unbelievably vast caves high in the clouds on New Guinea, where thousands of bats darkened the sky at the entrance as they flew out at dusk to feed in the night. With sight and colour returned also a sort of feeling. He could somehow manipulate things.

'*Orairegye,*' he heard. He struggled to reply.

'*Agandi,*' he heard.

'*Ni marungi,*' he croaked in return, recalling the Chiga greetings Sseru had taught him.

'Ah. Waking up at last, you idle bugger. What do you think of it all?'

It was Sseru, seemingly there, seemingly visible, yet somehow he couldn't actually see him.

Slowly confidence built up in him.

'Gaskin was right,' he said. 'It didn't hurt a bit.' Memory had erased the horrors for him.

'No. But you'll find it'll be a while before you get wired in properly, before the synapses' connections grow into place.'

Sseru was his usual inimitably, often infuriatingly buoyant self. His wiring in had been swift since his external connections already existed. For him the experience had been immensely

242

exciting, and he'd sussed out how the vast PIG operation seemed after a fashion to hang together.

Guided by Sseru, apWilliams' habilitation went swiftly. In parallel, they started exploring the strange environment. Part of it seemed like a vast medieval cathedral, mosque or temple, and this was surrounded with a plain of blue grass – perhaps there was a colour-shift in their local spectrum – the grass waving in a gentle breeze and billowing round occasional small rock out-crops, the plain stretching almost endlessly to mountainous horizons. A bit like on the South African High Veld as it reaches up for the Drakensberg, but rather lush as against the dry rus-tling brown grass round the real high-veld kopjes. The kopjes from which the Boer farmers in tatty khaki had picked off red-coat soldiers in 1899. Not fighting fair. The wrong sort of snow.

The kopjes looked interesting, but the pair concentrated on the cathedral. And then on the grate-covered conduits which ran through its marble floors like heating ducts, and then on the piping inside the ducts. And there they struck gold – put your virtual ear against it and hear it hiss – the 20 megaherz bus, a highway running from the System Control Unit throughout the PIG.

They tuned in to the various data flows. Mostly from software agents written in Prolog, that seemed to be driving the POPs and processing the TONK sessions with the people outside. Alun located and initialised the serial port, Interrupt 14H, AH=02H, which connected with the KDF6, and imagined some creaking C++ code as an additional interrupt[56] handling routine, to scan the flow in and out and keep private copies. Then he compiled and test ran it. Zilch. Pointers wrong as usual with this wretched language. His virtual self sweated, tensed and got red in the face with irritation at his errors. Egoless programming, the ideal of the 1970s, had never been his strength. He corrected the pointers and tried again.

The need was first to be able to call up the KDF6 by sending an interrupt down the line. Then await the old machine's answer. Then squirt messages down and hope to receive acknowl-edgements back.

After 3 night's trying, sending the agreed recognition code, an answer suddenly came back. They were immensely excited. Over a single tense session, they got the entire interchange with Gaskin and the team buttoned up and flying.

After that real work began, and they generated the changes, at Gaskin's instructions, which ratcheted up the destabilisation.

Both had ample time to explore their strange environment.

Downside, Chapter 29: Plas Menai and Flo

The battlements of Caernarfon Castle are surrounded by a wide L-shaped quay giving onto the straits and the river – this was the key to the castle's original success. The Welsh might well attack and invest it, but the English were always able to defend it, once with a garrison of 28 against the Welsh prince Owen Glyndwr's thousand or more, and provision and reinforce the garrison up the straits by water. The quay also happened to be a distinct and charming feature of the scene, marrying the grim grey of the castle to the surrounding spread of greens – the woods, the overgrown pitch and put course, the shores of the straits, and the ruffled greeny-blue of the waters. Sliced into the castle are a couple of narrow, gated alleys, and off one of these is a narrow stair, climbing up the battlements into a splendid oaken-floored chamber, the ceiling pinnacling to match the castle roofing. Perhaps Henry II, its creator in the thirteenth century, looked out from here, saw the verdant country whose key it was to be – control the straits and you control the country – and liked what he saw.

In the 1980s the chamber had been the pleasing clubroom of a tiny but active club of veteran sailors (most young yachties joined the more modern one by the old slate dock) and a gem of a club among the breed. The ale was still pulled by hand, hauling down on the long handle as the bitter foamed into a pint mug. Oak chairs in the Saxon style were scattered around glass-topped tables, and tall gothic windows were set right into the massive castle walls, mitred so that the external size gave maximum light internally. This gave a special view down and across the straits to the island.

Downside on 1 November, 2034, Tite Barnacle stood at the bar flirting with Flo as he supped his Smithwicks and she her port and lemon.

'Flo, my dear, let's do this,' he said, and murmured something quietly in her ear.

'Ooh, it sounds nice. But I've got the lunch on.'

'Bugger the lunch, woman.'

'All right then.' She slipped off down the narrow stairs and into her room.

Tite Barnacle restrained his mounting eagerness, and went to the bookcase. He took out an elderly looking volume.

To his astonishment, it proved to be a collection of mid-Victorian biographies, including a few pages on one Charles Gavan Duffy.

Duffy, Tite Barnacle recalled, had been one of the leaders of the Young Ireland movement in the 1840s, who had firstly failed – through insensitivity or obsession with politics rather than human beings perhaps – to lead the Irish against the famine. They had eventually tried to start an abortive uprising, but proved as incompetent as terrorists as was Nelson Mandela in the 1950s, and in the end Gavan was imprisoned in Newgate, Dublin in 1848. He was tried 5 times, but no jury would convict, so eventually his prosecution was dropped and he stood for the House of Commons, was elected, and fought vigorously for land reform in Ireland. His bill passed the Commons, but the House of Lords threw it out twice, till, daunted and ill, he migrated to Australia.

There, with one of the illuminating twists which gripped Tite Barnacle, he had a distinguished career as Governor of the province of Victoria, and was knighted by the Queen in 1873 as Sir Charles Gavan Duffy, Knight Commander of the Order of St George.

Pleasing, and ironic, and a good illustration, thought Tite Barnacle, of the way the British Empire, for want of a more acceptable name, somehow charmed its peoples, whether nationalist or no, firebrands or statesmen, into affectionate participation.

He found a key passage, and read intently.

Flo left her little room, wearing a clinging dress, a fur stole and nothing else. She skipped down the narrow stairway and out into the alley and up Castle Street. Behind her a square shape clicked suddenly into motion, and sidled after her. After 50 yards or so it reached out and slid its arm round her thighs.

'Oh, Lord Tite Barnacle, what are you doing... you're hurting me!'

Then she looked round and screamed.

'Titey! Titey! Help! They've got me!'

Tite Barnacle heard the scream faintly. He dropped the book like a scalding pot and rushed down the stairs, out and after her.

The POP had been joined by 2 more.

'Freeze. Freeze. Now. Now!' they were emitting with high-pitched urgency as she struggled. Should he call out to her? Might that just alert them to his presence?

But he couldn't leave her uncomforted, whatever happened. Maybe a single shout wouldn't be picked up against the clatter and her calls and screams. He waited till the din increased, then called, 'Yes, Yes, Yes'.

He followed them as she was taken towards a house he'd not previously noticed in the town centre. Then, fearing to lose her if they took her away, he ran at the POPs, bowled one over and grabbed her arm to rush her away. Suddenly he was hit by something and tumbled to the ground unconscious.

He awoke groggily, and struggled to regain his senses. He realised he was lying alongside Flo on the cobbles. He had a feeling of disaster, a feeling that a long time had elapsed, a time that was irretrievable. He reached out an arm to Flo. She was stiff and cold as ice.

His face turned bleak and unforgiving, and he sat for a long while, hands clasped round his legs on the cold stones of the roadway, thinking as one does of the presence that only minutes away had been there. How to turn back the clock? But you can't.

Then he heaved himself up, went to get a wheelbarrow from the pitch and putt, and trundled her away to bury her.

Downside, Chapter 30: The Swellies

It was monthly atonement night, At-One-Ment as the publicity described it. The process of making all humanity at one, together forever. Eliminate the deviants.

The TV cameras showed BL's farewell to Gaskin, tonight's Driver, at the start-point to the journey, just inside the Motorway Ring. His right hand extended in a firm manly handshake, then his left hand clasped warmly on top of Gaskin's. Gaskin leant towards him, with a gentle atoning-forgiving smile.

'You complete shit,' he said sweetly.

Then Gaskin moved into the Armstrong Siddeley Sedan De Luxe that he'd chosen, a 1934 model. Its own very idiosynchratic approach to an automatic gear box; with an early Laycock de Normanville overdrive. Push the little switch up and clunk, it's in. He pulled away. The crowd was less large and supportive than usual. The commentator voiced their feelings: 'Many feel that BL has been unbelievably, perhaps unwisely, generous; that Gaskin has manipulated us into this hero's ending... Well, we'll see when Gaskin reaches the Bridge. That's the testing time; sheep or goat, man or mouse. Has he got the bottle for the leap, or is he a wimp? And look at the car he's chosen. There are commentators who feel he's exploiting the handicapping system, fiddling the odds with an unknown old limo like that. How's the Bridge sensor going to set a fair parameter? He might get away with murder. Yes, come in Barry, your comments please.'

'Well, Richard, thank you very much indeed. Well, viewers, the buzz in the paddock is that Gaskin is on the wangle. And look,' he said in an excited rising crescendo, 'look at the back end. Those springs are way down. Way, way down. No way that's fair wear and tear. Know my guess, Richard?'

'Yes, Barry, yes, what's your view?'

'My view is he's loaded the back end.'

'Well, tell us, tell me and the viewers, how's that going to help him?'

'It's a 30 degree drop from the top road to the bridge decking. Well, a heavy weight back-end-wise, accelerating at 108 feet per second. He'll be flying. Like the ramp on one of the old aircraft carriers. Hit it at speed and up you go. No problem. He'll be over and up and across to the far ramp. That's for sure, is my guess.'

They drew in the Chief Steward, and the Autocar Chief Engineer.

Meanwhile, Gaskin drove steadily, almost sedately, westwards, through the special cordoned tunnel under the Motorway Ring, the circle of roads which enclosed residual civilisation – M1, M25 round the remains of London, M4, M5, M6 and north to the Scots extensions. After the tunnel he drove away from civilisation, out and up into the emptiness of Wales. Through the Berwyn Mountains, then along the river valleys; winding, rocky river valleys, splashful with their newly fallen torrents, clad in the red, green and gold of autumn. Two hours later Gaskin reached a coaching inn, gabled, Tudor-beamed, welcoming despite the peeling paintwork. In its centre was a wide, high portal over a cobbled roadway entrance, where the Irish stage used to stop, sometimes overnight, sometimes just to change horses. He swung in.

Out of the bucket seat, shove it forwards to make room behind for the tank, out for a swift pee, then in with the air tank from its hiding-place in the boot. Lash it to the chassis bolt. No BCP. No flippers, they'd make braking a touch difficult. Mask handy but invisible below window level, on the seat beside him. Ready for the road again.

Meanwhile BL had returned to his penthouse pad in Manchester. There was a cosy fire in the grate. Some shelves of books, one or two landscapes – Constable and Turner perhaps. Just the right image. The TV team had finished their set up procedures ready for the big man to broadcast. The make-up woman daubed his face carefully, Kleenex round his neck.

'A touch more base there, please,' he said. She complied. He called the producer to him. 'Full face shots only. That's what I want. Got it?'

'Yes, BL. Of course. We're all trained in that.'

Gaskin left the coaching inn. After 10 miles the Bridge lights loomed ahead. The TV commentator fulminated against the Chief Steward. Why, he wanted to know; why could they not adjust the bridge deck parameters to counter Gaskin's supposed cheating? Was there a case for reviewing the Total Atonement Corp's licence?

On the Bridge, the take-off ramp on the near-side ratcheted up a bit. Viewers watched enthralled. Then the Bridge's 2 centre spans, the road way swung laterally downwards in preparation, sighing down to vertical. They left a black gap down to the waters below. Waiting for Gaskin. The commentator's voice tautened as the 'Ride of the Valkyries' was faded out. He wound up his audience.

'And the stewards, Barry, any movement there?'

'Thank you very much indeed, Richard. Most kind. No. I have to say, it's outwith my experience in 20 years of the Leap. We have to put an end to this form of behaviour in a family evening environment.'

'We have viewers phoning in. Yes, come in Mary from Liverpool Toxteth, isn't it?'

'Well, what I think is – '

'Sorry, Mary my love, we have to leave you there. We can see, yes, we can see Gaskin's lights at last. Yes, and this is his in-car camera coming in – there, you can see it picking up the bridge approaches. He's at the top of the incline. Dropping down towards the leap. And look, look, he's slowing down. My God, he's slapped the anchors on as he approaches it. Shit scared. As yellow as a canary – used to be. As yellow as a proverbial lemon. Shit scared I'd say. As scared as shit. I do beg your pardons, but... He's stopped. He's getting out of the car. He's getting out of the car. No, he's not. There's a marshall waving him back. He's turning towards us. My God, did you see that gesture? And this at peak viewing.'

Gaskin had pushed his face out into the lights. He'd blown a raspberry. He got out and gave derisive 2 fingers to each quarter of the compass in turn. Then in the car again and he released the hand brake. The car rolled slowly down the incline. He watched the speedo; 10 mph, 15. Spot on. Mask on. Reach back to the tank. Mouthpiece in. Facemask on. The Armstrong Siddeley trundled up the short ramp, then ran over the edge into pitch darkness. Cameramen tried to spot what was going on, but the lights failed to cover the water directly below.

'He's dropped into the Swellies,' said the commentator, 'into the dreadful Swellies. Just above them. The tide will sweep him in. No power on earth can save him now. A fitting end you might say. The water'll be pouring in through the gaps in the seals. He'll feel it creeping up. For a few minutes there'll be enough for him to breathe. But his ears will be excruciatingly painful, I guess, as the pressure builds, unless he knows how to clear it. Shut your mouth and clear your ears and blow. Blow hard. See that flash? Must be the auto-system. We must get the technical – No, I've been interrupted. Yes, indeed, it's BL himself, offering us in his wisdom some comments. Good evening BL, we're delighted, privileged... '

BL was faded in full-face, solemn and reassuring in his home, in his study, near a glowing fire. He said a few words. Gaskin. A great brain, a very great brain. One of the architects of our new society. But, at the end of the day, sadly, sadly and tragically, flawed at the end, in the final analysis.

'May this be a sign for us of a new beginning. May it herald disaster for the corrupt, for peculators, deviants and dissidents. May it herald a triumph for our great ideals.'

After the camera faded him out, he shunted the TV team out solemnly. 'Thanks, you guys. Sad event. Sad indeed. But you all did a grand job.'

Then he put the switches by the door into privacy mode. He listened carefully as the team's footsteps receded. Then he burst into cackles of ecstatic laughter. He slapped his knee in delight. Side-on, the gargoyle look became frighteningly shark-like, lips drawn back and up, teeth bared till they seemed to point forward, philtrum taut as a bowstring. He felt drunk with it all. He stood up, hugging his sides and rocking around. His eyes glistened. He yanked his zip down and peed into the fireplace. A splendid sizzle and hiss.

*****

Gaskin's car had dropped towards the water. Like a stone; but a perhaps a skipping stone, as you might throw a heavy slate across flat water, competing with your mates to see who could skip the most spectacularly.

So the impact when it came was a slightly glancing one. Like a

seaplane hitting the water in a crash landing, as against a seaplane dropping vertically onto the surface. The shock, furthermore was partly absorbed by the car seats.

Gaskin relaxed a little, breathing a sigh of relief.

Wait for his mates to come in the old IRB, the Inshore Rescue
Boat, as he'd arranged, then out through the window. The car
began to sink a little, nose down, and flood. Still, once it had
flooded the pressure on the doors would equalise, and he'd
open up, leave the mouthpiece and be out and into the rescue
boat in no time. Should be nearly here now.

But it wasn't like that. He waited, but he couldn't force the
door open and the car wasn't sinking. Seals were too good.

Not to worry, in the blackness outside, as against the blinding
arc lights above, he picked out the white wash creaming away
from the IRB with his rescue team aboard. Taking a bit of a risk
to make any wash at all, but the need was urgent.

Across, 300 metres away he saw suddenly a bright flash, then a
heavy bang, and behind the IRB's white bow-wave a massive,
lethal explosion. The PIG's automatic surface surveillance system had been vastly better than they'd sussed. His rescue team
must have been killed instantly.

A brief pang of sadness, then adrenaline pumped as his own
predicament became clear.

The water level rose above the car flanks and up the windows.
Suddenly there was a rumbling bubbling as a great wodge of air
burst free – perhaps the seal in the boot had suddenly failed.
The car started going under into the 100-foot drop to the bottom; 100 feet down – not the sort of depth he was able to handle.
Accelerating downwards as the remaining air compressed and its
buoyant effect was cut. He remembered the fear with which he
had managed his first 10-metre dive in the South China Sea.

Four times that depth. And dropping as fast as you don't like.
No time slowly to equalise the pressure in your ears. Pain, ear
pain; some of the worst you can get. Top pain of the lot is your
heart attack; then childbirth; then your ears. Would the pressure
burst the water into his skull?

And pitch black. None of the glorious colours and fascinating
fauna he remembered under the water at Kao Tai, Turtle Island;
the emerald depths of the South China Sea. Just the black, bleak,

wet chill of the Welsh waters in winter, to be followed no doubt by churning and tumbling as they were sucked into the Swellies.

The pressure inside the car remained high. He fought to force the door open – no way. Smash a window? With what? And what then?

No way he could get through the window with his sub-aqua kit on. Tank still strapped to the chassis. Must undo it. But even then, not on at all. Not thinking straight? Don't know. Wait and see. Unstrap the tank, and shoulder it on. It isn't easy, so take it easy.

The car suddenly lurched along, partly buoyant. Then it rolled over sideways, filled and dropped. Upside down and then upright again.

Various bumps, bashes and crashes followed as it was tumbled down and through the straits, over the rocks and reefs, often going, like Brigadier and Mrs Long in *Haili Su* off Cape Horn, end for end, cart-wheeling slowly like a slightly defective space craft – the first intimations of error, the first intimations too of terror, terror and error, error together with terror, before starting to tumble into oblivion.

From the *Amanda*'s anchorage close to the southern end of the Swellies, Johnson had watched the distant sky illuminated for the death dive. And thereafter the sudden totally unexpected bang, and the orange and yellow reflection off the low clouds of the explosion that had wiped out the IRB.

Then nothing. Gaskin, he thought, had probably had it along with the others. The ebb would be sweeping the remains towards him. He'd get into the dinghy and patrol the tide. No, he wouldn't. It would be running at 3 knots.

Wait on deck and watch till there was something to see.

A half hour passed. Some wreckage floated by. They must all have been killed.

But something white showed in the darkness. Plastic bag perhaps? Or a diver's face?

He decided to take a chance, and paddled off to see.

A diver's face it was; he couldn't immediately be sure who, but almost certainly it had to be Gaskin.

The body was held up by its life-jacket, but still had all its heavy diving gear on. No chance of getting it aboard the dinghy. Far too heavy, he'd just capsize. He slipped a bowline round under the armpits, and rowed shorewards. Not that side, stupid, you're making for the mainland shore.

Round and back to the west. As dawn began to lighten the scene, he came into a cove, crabbing sideways gradually less as the peak of the current eased.

The heavy body grounded and anchored them a few yards off. Over the side, and he hauled everything into the shore. Pretty exhausted, so stop and think.

First priority – is Gaskin alive? Seems unlikely, but still...

He rolled the body over to hit the quick releases and get the tanks off. That's better. Then drag the body up the beach and test for signs of life.

Johnson dredged his memory of his first aid course, taken perfunctorily many years back because he was being trained as a sailing instructor. He rolled the heavy body over on its back and started pressing down with 2 palms together on Gaskin's breastbone. Then he remembered. First search for a heart beat. Not the wrist, up in the carotid artery, left of the skull. Or was it right? And wasn't Gaskin left-handed anyway? Account for his curmudgeonly manner. Like the cack-handed Kerrs of Cumbria, with all their castle stairs going counter-clockwise. No wonder they held off the Scots. He felt. Nothing either side; but had he got the right place? And weren't his fingers numb? He sucked them to warm them up and tried again. Nothing.

Hit hard in the middle of the breastbone then blow in and hit, blow in and hit, and see what happens.

Wrist back on Gaskins breastbone, and a powerful thump. Then a few mouth-to-mouth blows – blow 2 3 4 blow 2 3 4. Nothing. Thump again. He kept at it, gradually getting more and more despondent. Roll him over now, and see if you can get some water out of the lungs.

He did so and felt again for the pulse at the neck. What did they call it? The carotid artery?

Yes, there it was – he felt a slight pulse. Blow again. Keep blowing. Not like the model on the course, dry and impersonal. This was a chilly wet slobbery mouth, tasting slightly of whisky – no doubt Gaskin had warmed himself with a tot before his dive.

Suddenly Gaskin convulsed upwards. 'What the fucking hell are you up... '

He rolled over onto his side and retched violently, water and scum coming up.

'Christ,' he said. 'That was bloody awful. Oh, it's you is it? Still, thanks, mate.'

Later, Johnson got Gaskin back into the dinghy, and rowed with the rising flood tide back to the *Amanda*. Once aboard, with the old Tilley paraffin lantern warming the cabin up, blankets round Gaskin, and a cup of herbal tea and a touch of treasured rum inside him, Johnson reviewed the options – how to get Gaskin fit was obviously the key, because Gaskin would be able to decide sensibly what to do next. Pity the guy was more than a mite insufferable.

Gaskin seemed incredibly muddled at first, but later gradually made some sense. Gaskin thought the car door must have been burst open after he lost consciousness. Then he must have floated out and up to the surface.

Next morning at first light, they sailed the old boat back down the straits, dropped Gaskin in the dinghy at Caernarfon pier-head, then took her out to her anchorage in Pilot's Cove to wait.

Downside, Chapter 31: Testing the Links

Two nights later, Gaskin and the team tested out the link at Gorton as arranged. They watched the answer codes come through correctly with all the tension, then delight, of a Houston team as a successful space mission reached orbit.

Destabilisation started as planned, and Gaskin left on a planned stir-up tour round the Motorway Ring. People proved to be as vulnerable as expected. It was as if society was being gnawed away by IT. The postal system was flooded with unsolicited goods which purveyors showed had validly been ordered. Court orders threatened imprisonments or evictions for judgments of which the victims were unaware. IntranetUK would collapse then resurrect with key transactions corrupted. Phone systems would coo gently, femininely, 'Thank you for calling. I am so sorry that all our advisors and queueing systems are busy. Please try later.'

People were arrested at motorway services for credit offences when trying to buy LPG with perfectly valid cards. Shops received security alerts against harmless individuals. Surveillance systems threw out rashes of warnings of alleged criminality against public figures of fundamental, monumental uprightness. Public facilities suffered random faults of great alarm or embarrassment. Transport systems showed alarming faults. Bomb alerts were broadcast occasionally in shopping malls. Almost the most alarming, healthy people were called in for diagnosis for suspected and credible medical conditions, all on the same day. Hospital beds were filled and emptied, treble-booked and re-assigned. Breast screening reports were falsified, positive amniocentesis notifications inverted. Most frightening of all for the top people were their interactions with their mentors, the TONKS. Sessions would go with the familiar, burbling reassurance, then a software agent would come into play. A sudden quick, sharp, authoritative question or ejaculation from the TONK would jerk the person into startled awareness. Then the

256

interruption would fade. The TONK returning to burble mode so quickly that the sessioner was left nervously unsure that anything untoward had really happened.

*****

Meanwhile in Caernarfon, Tite Barnacle holed up in the top floor of a shop opposite the house where they had tried to drag Flo. The following weekend he saw a van drive up. Two POPs were lowered off the back, and someone went inside. He spent an hour there, then reappeared, and the guarding POPs were hoisted onto the truck and it set off, perhaps whence it came. Some sort of regular inspection, perhaps.

Tite Barnacle then slipped down and tried the door. Locked.

In the days that followed, he worked the door open and scoured the inside. Then he set about the search for revenge and the weapons of revenge. And he monitored the display screen and the weekly inspection visits with a savage satisfaction.

Downside, Chapter 32: Destabilisation 5

Engineering all the destabilisation was a doddle for Gaskin's systems programmers, and they often had time on their hands to chat over the divergences between Downside and Upside, about which Tilley held forth at great length.[57] The fragility of the Upside Internet, the equivalent roughly of Downside Intra-netUK, he said, had become a by-word – the system was once even put out of action in many areas worldwide by a virus known as the 'Love-Bug', created by a bank clerk in the Philippines.

But, while the systems programming was a doddle, on the other hand, for someone of BL's robustness, the destabilisation was containable by vigorous policing, public reassurances and appropriate disinformation. Even so, the public outcry was in a crescendo.

Then one of BL's most trusted sidekicks phoned him.

'Something really odd here, BL,' he said. 'I don't think you'd want me to discuss it right now.'

'What d'you mean? I'm not shy, you know.'

'No, no, of course not,' he replied nervously, 'but even so. It's about Gaskin.'

'OK. In my office, I'll give you 3 minutes.'

The guy came and explained. They had left the trace on Gaskin by mistake even after his immensely public death. But a report had come in of a valid transaction on his account. Just a glitch, they'd thought. But there had been 3 of these, and someone had driven out to check. No doubt about it, the eye print and fingerprints had tallied. On one the voice recognition had clipped in and done likewise, on another the face-icon matcher had matched.[58] Moreover, the motorway service people recalled the transactor. The guy had made a hell of a fuss about some minor problem. Almost as if he wanted them to remember him. And something odd was going on in the Straits.

BL put BOSS Security on to investigate, and designated the operation for his own personal direction. The tapes leading up

258

to Gaskin's death leap were scrutinised – perhaps it had been a stand-in driving the car? Hard to be sure, because the quality of the shots at such a distance and in artificial light were poor. But then his posture as he gave the disgraceful gestures was characteristic. A 99.8 per cent match. And the in-car driver-recogniser had been active and authentic.[59]

Downside, Chapter 33: A Long Shot

Two nights later, BL was watching a key bit of the national news, his press conference. Then an unexpected long shot faded in. It was of a figure he thought he recognised. His pulse quickened. The shot panned in. It might have been Nadine, he wasn't sure. Walking along the ridge of a dune on a foreshore somewhere. Seen from across some water. The wind swirled her beige skirt around her calves entrancingly. She wore skirts very rarely, not part of your IT woman's wardrobe. Only, he had thought, for him alone. She had a purple flowered blouse on; seen from side-on it emphasised the soft line of her waist, dropping from above the hips to curve down at the front and back. She seemed as though she might be talking to someone on the far side of the dune below her. She gave a slight skip and twirl – of delight? No, she must have tripped on a root. Or whatever. He followed the film intensely. She knelt down, partially concealed. Her blouse seemed to slip open a little, and yet her shoulders were hunched as though her weight was balanced on both her hands. Perhaps the breeze had blown it aside. Wasn't that her left nipple?

Not left, right. Then she dropped out of sight.

Angrily, he rewound the broadcast, and watched the snip again. Then got on to the BBC. What the fucking fuck had been done, he demanded, to fuck up his fucking conference piece? Call yourselves the Benevernment Broadcasting Corporation? Can of worms. I'll review your fucking so-called charter.

Nothing, came back a wary, nervous reply. Nothing had been done. They would never touch his pieces up without his authority. Of course, they'd check at once. Five minutes later, a worried DG was on the line. He'd gone over it personally. It all looked good. Perhaps BL would rerun the offending passage to give them the times and frames, or if he wished, the DG would come round right away in person with the corporation's chief engineer.

No, ruled BL, he'd do it himself. He repositioned to the start of the snip and replayed it. Totally different. All conventional, no foreshore, no woman. Just a Public Appearance, a good polished performance by Yours Truly.

He phoned the duty man in the IT centre. He was to get Nadine back immediately off her Edinburgh assignment. Get the squad to report if she'd been on any beaches with any dunes.

'What sort of tunes?' he was asked nervously.

'Not tunes, you prat, dunes. Beaches with dunes. First report back to me in 5 minutes.'

'Of course, BL.'

In 4 minutes the report came in – Nadine had already been sent back from Edinburgh 5 days ago. At his orders, they said defensively and worriedly. She was reporting specially to him. It was on the transcript. His personal voice-print. And on the archive. And there was something odd about the invoices for her stay in Edinburgh earlier. And they were still working on the funnies in the video records of Gaskin's atonement. Hard to be sure, but he seemed to have been fiddling with his mouth as the car had trundled over the drop.

BL got back on to BOSS.

'I want a Red Red Zero-Immediate trace on her.'

*****

Two days before this, Gaskin had Nadine in to his undercover digs for the long-promised chat. He listened to her as she attacked the pigification of apWilliams.

'Look,' he said soothingly, 'it was Alun's free choice... You missed what McGervon said about it. He quoted the Roman soldiers before they left to fight to the death at the emperor's command. "*Morituri, Caesar, morituri te salutamus*" [60] – "We who are about to die salute you". Most apt and moving. It was a salutation from one of the legions as they went to certain death. In the desert perhaps, the old Lost Legion that set off into the Sahara from Carthage or somewhere and was never heard of again; 4,300 or so fully-armed first century soldiers whose bones and teeth and armour and shoes may still be under the sands, or even above them like Ozymandias, still there waiting to be found. The ultimate loyalty.'

She looked doubtful.

'Here,' he said, 'let's have a coffee.'

With his back to her, he mixed 2 cups carefully. To one he added a white powder. Oxytonin.

'There has to be another way of handling it,' she said.

'Or,' said Gaskin, 'look at it this way. You're an Africa buff, aren't you? Take that fearsome *impi* of ranked Zulu warriors, as the great Chaka ordered them to march over the top of a cliff to show their implacability and courage to the watching Afrikaner negotiators. They did it and plunged silently to their deaths. An act of consummate courage and dedication... You've had a rough time recently, my dear,' he added in a lighter tone, 'and I want your Michael out of the way. He knows too much. Not about this side, Downside; about the other. Why don't you go down and get him somewhere safe in the mountains? I know a place you'll love. The Kennedys stayed there, it's that beautiful – why don't you have a lovely few days with him and forget all this?'

She had glanced quickly at Gaskin as he spoke, a questioning frown fleeting across her forehead. Then she had blushed as he suggested the trip... Then the idea took hold, and her reservations melted and were forgotten. Gaskin logged in and fixed for her to get the special Bangor truck, and she left. Back at his desk, he date-time stamped the authorisation form with care, and left an e-mail copy on the PIG intranet. That done, he whipped down the stairs.

Downside, Chapter 34: Inside PIG

With time on their hands, since the transfers to the KDF6 took place only in the third shift, (midnight to 8 a.m.), Sseru and apWilliams explored their strange environment inside PIG. Awesomely, echoingly spacious, the great cathedral-like centre, and the plain and kopjes, considering the way the brains in the tanks had been cramped together with fine skeins of growing neuron threads wandering apparently randomly across the liquid. Apart from the main highway humming in the conduit they might have been the sole creatures in an alien universe.

Their wanderings were limited to 16 hours, so that they could cover the third, active, shift communicating with the team outside, and time was not easy to estimate unless they could get at the highway and the system's clock-on-the-wall-time real-time clock. But the kopjes and, even more, the mountains attracted both of them. The Virunga volcanoes and the Snowdon massif were deeply embedded in their memories.

They decided to try lengthening their time-barred lead so that they could rove singly more widely. Sseru would cover a trial third shift and apWilliams could then have a full 40 hours away.

apWilliams set off with a light, virtual heart, in warm, yellow sunshine, with the strangely coloured sky, and lush blue grasses waving in the wind. He skirted the kopjes, enticing though they were, and made for the first towering cliffs of the mountains. Hard going through the path-free foliage, which slipped gently around his ankles. After 6 hours he reached the cliff-foot, and a wide gully towering into the sky, leading inwards. A keen caver, he entered it, pushing his way past a tree with curious golden bark, and snapping off a branch to do so. The rock was a sort of dry sandstone, with crystalline sand which caressed his bare feet and slipped up between his toes as walked on. The walls closed in and the roof down. The cave came to a blank end wall, but with a frightening craggy pit opening below it. The pit dropped away down beyond his vision. Time to turn back, he thought. But, too intrigued, he clambered down the rough sides about 50 feet, to reach a faintly-lit sparkling sandy floor. The base levelled off, and he followed the cave along, squirming and wriggling through a flat, wide but low crevice and into a long, tall, narrow stretch, a bit like a canyon with a roof on. Water, pitch black, filled the bottom of the chasm ahead. Suddenly he seemed to hear a rumbling canine noise, a bit like 3 wolves in counterpoint. It raised the hairs on his neck, to prickle and tingle. He froze. A barking to scare the bloodless dead.[61] A land of ghosts, of sleep and somnolent night. But he thought he saw a slight lightening of the gloom ahead, and something urgently prompted him to continue. He waded through the chilly water, over waist-deep, then reached an incline and emerged in a towering hall. It was lit more brightly than the passage he'd followed, by a break high up above into the open sky.

He was assailed by a smell, overpoweringly recalling his first sensuous impressions from childhood. Dryness even in the middle of this damp cave. The tang of the bush round a cliff-foot. Crushed leaves of protea – no, they are smell-less – rosemary perhaps? No, you get that here in Wales. Pine resin, maybe?

The Oread Halls, he thought, caves above Kalk Bay in the Cape of Good Hope. Then another smell, even more evocative. He sat down, feeling suddenly astonishingly happy, for some reason remembering Sue.

'Oh, Susanna,' he sang quietly, 'won't you come to me?'

A quiet voice came quoting Tennyson from the shadows. 'He cometh not, she said.'

It was a quiet, feminine voice behind him, with a delightful Dorsetshire burr.

'Sue, it's you!'

'Alun,' she mocked softly. 'It's me.'

One or two thousand synapses in apWilliams' brain, 15 years lain dormant, fired into intense activity. Others, their charges attenuated, were swamped.

Back at base 43 hours later, Sseru had something of a problem. Serial port bombed out. No apWilliams to sort it. And the problem wasn't going to go away.

*****

Over the next few days, the Gorton team's carefully-targeted tampering with the top people contacts crumbled into chaos. TONK sessions went haywire in many strange ways as Sseru struggled to pump data through to the old KDF6. A bit lost here and a bit lost there. The resulting alarm and anger was reported to BL as he pursued Nadine into Wales.

Downside, Chapter 35: Maes-y-Neuadd

Nadine arrived in Caernarfon, took the kayak and crossed to the island and Pilot's Cove. From the cliff she saw Johnson come out of the cockpit and busy himself with something forward of the mast. The chilly winter's day set her pulse racing.

'Yaawit!' she called quietly. No response. Then slightly louder.

Startled, Johnson stood up quickly, looked hard all around him, missing the cliff top. Then again. Then he returned to his task. She called again, cupping her hands round her mouth.

'Michael! It's me.' She stood waving.

'It isn't, is it?'

'Yes, it is.'

'Thought you were someone else.'

'Idiot. You come and get me. At once.'

'Right, M'am.'

She stood on the sand below and waited for him.

'Hello, sweeting.'

'Hello, sailor.'

He climbed out of the dinghy and stood looking at her. She smiled and then reached out a hand. He clasped it and drew her gently to him, and they kissed gently. Then passionately, and she was scooped up in his arms to some dry sand under the cliff.

Later she explained Gaskin's wishes, and about Maes-y-Neuadd.

'Doesn't it sound lovely?' she finished.

'All sounds very odd,' he said.

'Well, I thought so too. But he said he wants us really fit and relaxed and on top of things for next week.'

'But what's happening next week?'

'He wouldn't say. No need-to-know. You know.'

'Well, OK.'

They went across to Caernarfon that night, and followed the road up into the mountains to Maes-y-Neuadd.[62] The wind came up as they climbed the valley, wintry and bitter, and they were

266

glad to reach the old mansion and tumble straight into bed to get warm.

Johnson woke up the next morning. The girl was standing, a blanket round her, at the window, back to him. She was blowing on the frosted pane to clear a view, then looking out.

'Michael, look.'

He came up behind her, hands round her waist, kissing her neck.

'No,' she said. 'Look out there.'

He did. 'My God, it's snow. These parts haven't seen snow in 5 years.'

'Oh, yes they have. You're thinking of Upside. Even so, isn't it lovely?'

He slipped one hand down and one hand over her breasts, and turned her around. She kissed him, then by chance looked up over his shoulder. Then froze suddenly.

'What's wrong?'

She held to him passionately, pulled him to the bed. He saw tears in her eyes and then on her cheeks.

'What's wrong darling?'

'Oh, it's nothing. Love me gently now.' Then she whispered in his ear, 'Michael. Keep quiet and keep moving gently and listen to me.'

'How do you mean?'

'Just do it.'

Then she whispered as they moved, 'There's a surveillor. I saw the lens. Don't look. Up in the top corner by the door.'

He stiffened, horrified.

'Keep moving,' she insisted. He did, and they whispered together.

*****

The headquarters' reports back to BL as he was on tour had been serious. Building up perhaps to a crisis of confidence that, his sidekicks said, only he himself in person could cure. He logged in from his tourer for his managers' night progress reports. His attention was divided between a CCTV screen and the monitor. He swung to the monitor. It lit up.

BL smashed his fist down on the desktop. He was being messed

about, just as his systems had messed about so many others. The
biter was being bit. He turned and watched the image of the 2
lovers savagely on the CCTV. The truck was hidden, tucked
alongside the kitchen garden wall of Maes-y-Neuadd.

'Right,' he snapped into a hand mike. 'Go in. In In In. Now
Now Now.'

But before action could start, a window in the house above
opened. Johnson jumped out stark-naked and landed running,
slithering in the crisp snow. Four POPs and some minders cut in
from either side. He swerved and ran at one and tried to hurdle
it. An arm came up, caught his foot and flipped him. He rolled
in the air and fell flat, winded. They'd put his Cambridge trick
into the on-board process library. Two minders came and
pinned him down.

Nadine meanwhile dropped quietly down from the window
and slipped along the side of the house towards freedom. BL
watched with a smile. She reached the end of the house and ran
down unseen alongside the drystone wall. He heard her panting.
As she passed he reached out and grabbed her round the waist.
She yelled out and collapsed, sobbing.

Later on, he had Nadine and Johnson brought into the dining
hall. Both were shivering violently with cold. Nadine was tied
down on her back by the wrists and ankles to the legs of one
long, carved, oak Saxon table. The contrast between the desperate woman and the civilised courtesy of the hall BL found
pleasing and soothing. Johnson was tethered by the wrists to a
tall, matching Saxon chair.

'Not met before have we?' asked BL of Johnson.

Johnson said nothing.

BL picked up a large carving knife.

'Know what I'm about to do?' he asked.

Johnson said nothing.

BL went on in a dreamy voice, gradually rising in pitch. 'I'm
going to do some carving. Bit like a Sunday joint. That's what I'm
going to do.'

He moved to the sideboard, pulled out the carving iron and
sharpened the knife blade at first meditatively, then with
increasing vigour. Then he drew it swiftly and lightly across
Nadine's stomach. She winced and grunted a little at the pain,

but said nothing. Johnson watched desperately as a little blood trickled up.

'What do you want, then?' he asked.

'Everything. I want to know everything. And particularly how you got here. And if there are any falsehoods, any porkies,' BL's voice strengthened and heightened further, 'any fucking lies, this hussy will pay for them very slowly indeed. Most slowly,' he continued more quietly. 'Painfully slowly you might even say. I rather enjoy this sort of thing,' he continued conversationally, 'I've done quite a lot of it. I very much enjoy it, you might say. I even revel in it. It is something in which one revels. And you'll be watching.'

'OK,' said Johnson, 'I'll go with it.'

'Right, let's go then. I'll just have some coffee while you're loosened up.'

It took 2 hours to loosen Nadine and Johnson, but in the end they were quite loose.

Downside, Chapter 36: Gaskin and the Fate of the KDF6

The same day, Gaskin drove up to the gates of Park Gate Iron and Steel Company and went in. He showed his pass to the security guy, who looked startled, let him in, and afterwards quickly picked up the phone to get onto his boss. Before he could finish dialling he felt a ring of cold steel against his neck as a voice said, 'Perhaps you'd better leave that for the time being and come with me.' The guy trembled convulsively, then replaced the receiver. Gaskin climbed with the security guy up ahead of him into the KDF6 gantry. No one around. He pressed the 'Stop' button on the console just after one series of chops had been completed, then clacked on each of the pressel switches setting up the instruction 76 00 09. Jump to memory word 9. Then he hit 'Go'.

The cycle restarted, looping on the command that waited for the furnace doors to open. They did, and the red-hot ingot slid down the track and received its first bash to start thinning. Then the second bash. Eventually the bar thinned to a searing red-hot 9-inch square rod, ready for chopping. But instead of being chopped, it was swung back and forth up and down the curved inclines, ever faster. The bashing had ceased, and the removal of this impediment caused the speed, length and height of the rod's swing to lengthen.

'You're going to wreck it!' protested the guard.

'How right you are, mate. Just keep your hands up high now. I've got a twitchy finger.'

The steel was screaming a bit with the unplanned for stresses and speed. Then the rod cleared the end lip of the channel and burst through the wall as if it had not existed. They watched as it took off down hill, speeding up.

'Just about right,' said Gaskin.

It hit the curved wall that McGervon had pointed out weeks

earlier. A very, very slight angle. It was diverted degree by degree as it dropped down as if on a curve on a ski run. Then it lined up with the PIG buildings.

'Christ!' grunted the guard.

The steel hurtled down and broke through the PIG building's concrete walls at speed, and ended up partly coiling itself in the PIG. In the arena there was a stench of sizzling, singeing, bursting, bubbling offal, a swishing as the liquid in the brain tanks flowed away, then burning. The heat set the plastic furniture in the computer room alight, and the KDF6 peripherals started dropping out. A final stream of data came down the line from PIG to the module 2 of the memory for processing.

*****

In PIG, Sseru had given up his valiant attempts to channel data through to the KDF6.

BL meanwhile checked with his headquarters. He made a sudden decision: play it each way, keep an option open to escape to Upside. First get up to the power station, and keep off the roads just in case. He had the 2 prisoners brought back in. Clothed but not in their right minds.

'I'm going up over the mountain to Trawsfynydd,' he said. 'And you're coming with me to show me how to cross. But this time it's going to be the other way around. Ladies first. Just you, me and a minder.'

He called the minder.

'We'll have a little go with the goolie-crusher,' he said.

It was brought, a device like a half-enclosed small trough with a long, flexible armoured tube leading to a small hand-held lever.

'Place it on the gentleman.' Johnson's flies were unzipped and the trough was fitted snugly round his genitals.

'Let's give it a whirl. See what it feels like. Testing testing testing, 1 2 3.'

BL levered 3 strokes and Johnson squirmed and let out a muffled grunt. BL moved the lever back and released the pressure.

'Dead simple,' said BL. 'Cosy little trough. Piston. Little hydraulic pump. Eschew sophistication. OK guys. Let's be off then.'

They went off up a track leading east towards Trawsfynydd, Johnson and Nadine tied together, hands behind their backs.

An hour later they approached the great power station. BL had been interrupted a couple of times on his ear-held bud by reports from his headquarters. Disturbing. He tried ringing his headquarters. All he got was, 'Thank you for calling North East Area College. You are in a queueing system and your call will be answered shortly. If you know the extension you require please key it now. Otherwise please hold for assistance and we will be with you in no time.' BL's face and neck veins swelled with fury.

His tone with his prisoners became snarling rather than scoffing, and once he called them to a halt. He thought he'd heard a faint, sharp, crackling from the cliffs below. Like an exhaust.

'D'you hear that?' he demanded of the minder.

'What, Boss?'

'Gone now.' He had listened a while, then given a vicious burst on the crusher which brought Johnson down onto the soggy peat writhing in pain. In falling he'd brought Nadine down on top of him. She had whispered, but he'd not been able to hear what she said.

'No snogging, now. I'm going to teach you to snog later. In due course. With due process of law.'

They reached the power station and went through Station Security. BL announced he was there to carry out some special fallback tests on the automatic shut down system. He ordered the main hall and control areas to be cleared except for the usual POPs. They waited for this to be done, then entered the hall. In the gloom outside a figure swam up from the lake, then at a breathless drag hauled himself along on projections from the cooling tunnel side wall up against the outflow and quietly into the pool.

*****

Back in PIG, the lovers were in their cavern together. Some music gradually swelled in the background. The tear-jerking, unfair, sombre, ominous, arctic, slow movement of Sibelius' Third Symphony. Tears sprang to Susanna's eyes. apWilliams' head dropped.

*****

In Trawsfynydd, as the party went through the main hall a hooter started blasting. The accompanying POPs went suddenly berserk, flailing their arms and antennae, attacking each other randomly. BL looked unsurprised. He ordered his human party to stand well back. In a couple of minutes the POPs subsided, inert.[63]

'For the gent a touch on the goolies, I think,' he said coldly, and gave the crusher a quick 3 jabs. Johnson sucked in sharply through the mouth.

'Let's go upstairs,' said BL, and they trooped up and into the control room, the lovers first, then the minder, then BL. He lifted a site procedures manual off a shelf.

'OK,' said BL to the minder, 'we'll have the slut across here with you, still tied. And Johnson at the table console over there. Any funny moves, shoot her in the leg.'

They were moved. Johnson was hobbled.

BL moved across to 2 balls on supporting posts, about 3 feet apart. He got a small pedestal and rested the manual on it. He read from the manual, and told Johnson to press various switches and keys. Then BL took a string from a lever on the wall and held it in his hand.

'What we're going to do,' BL said, conversationally, 'we're going to blow this fucking lot sky high. We've trashed the backup generator. Now we cut the power supply. And we're there. Just like Chernobyl. Out come the rods. Up goes the station. But better. Simpler. Eschew complexity. Eliminate the negative. Accentuate the positive. Just like the singer sang. Not sang, sung. No, used to sing.'

'Here,' protested the minder, 'you shouldn't do that, BL. What about us?'

'About you, matey, just this. Your redundancy package.'

He swung round his AK47 single-handed and put a burst into the minder. Nadine was dragged to the floor as the minder fell. BL turned to shoot Johnson. He dived sideways, and rolled away, legs still tied.

There was a sudden shot from the corner, and Tite Barnacle came into view. BL was thrown back by the impact of the bullet.

273

He dropped the AK47, yanked the lever across and reached for the 2 balls. Tite Barnacle fired a second burst as BL disappeared.

*****

As the PIG installation in Sheffield slowly sizzled away and died, the KDF6 Flexowriter clattered into life:
  BUT POOR OLD GOEBBELS
  HAS NURBLZE
  AT ALL
  WEERABA MUGYENYI WANGYE
  YEGO. N'IWE, GYENDA N'OBUSINGYE
  HELLO HELLO
  HELLO HELLO
  SWIM2
  JUMP NON-NEGATIVE A 4095
  JNN A 7776
  767776
  H
  UMP
The Flexowriter powered off. The console pressel switches still glowed the instructions the computer was obeying in Register A. They produced a brief tinny harmonic-free noise on the little speaker: 'Oh Susanna, won't you... '

Then nothing. The console lights died.

Up at the Park Gate site, Gaskin set off down the hill. Down the hill to grasp his destiny.

Downside: The Nuclear Power Station

Johnson greeted Tite Barnacle as his bonds were cut. 'Tite Barnacle, my dear chap!' He fell unthinkingly into the other's drawling idiom, but not quite convincingly. 'What on earth brings you here?'

He looked at the aristocratic mandarin. The urbane face was greatly changed; lined and sad and grim.

'It's a long story. Tell you another time.' He paused, then recovered himself.

'But who's this charming lady?'

274

'This,' Johnson replied, 'well, this is Nadine.'

*****

While they talked excitedly, the lights dimmed imperceptibly and there was a faint humming as the protective rods started slowly rising to unleash BL's burn down. They broke off talking and watched, mesmerised and horrified. Then Nadine leapt for the site manual, and began leafing through the operating instructions.

'You get at the console Johnson, and I'll call them off to you – the instructions to abort meltdown.'

'Right then.'

Meanwhile, Tite Barnacle disappeared down the main passage, AK47 at the ready. They heard a burst of firing, but stuck to their tasks.

They worked through the close down sequence. But without the back-up generator being on-line, it just wouldn't take off. And the rods were steadily rising. They could even begin to feel the rising heat – or was it their imagination? Try again; perhaps a finger problem first time around. Time to run for it like presumably the other staff had? But no way you'd get far enough away in time. Never mind; give it another go. Back to the buttons.

Tite Barnacle arrived back, carrying his weapons.

'Hello, Humphrey, bit of a problem.'

'Leave it to me, old thing. You keep off. One man job.'

Tite Barnacle took the Haggins door-smasher from the fire rack and broke open the door to the secure area.

'Pineapple job. Into the hydraulics,' he said with a grin.

'Humphrey, for God's sake come back!'

But he went past the skull and crossbones warnings into the danger area. Then slipped the pins out of 2 grenades. Tricky stuff, holding a grenade in each hand; then pulling the pins out using his teeth, without releasing the levers. Then he nested them cosily against the hydraulics, backed up by a block of steel that he slid in with his foot. Levers off, run like ballistic. He ran. There were 2 sharp explosions, fluid spurted wildly from the pipes. Then the rods started dropping back down to their safety level.

*****

A month later, 4 people sat in the upstairs restaurant of the Ferry Boat Inn, overlooking Aberdaron and Bardsey Sound. Johnson, Nadine, McGervon and Tite Barnacle. They'd had an exhausting and dangerous day helping to get the first launch full of sheep across from the island to the mainland. Life was coming back to its former abode.

'How about it? Where are you going from here?' asked Tite Barnacle.

Johnson looked at Nadine and she nodded. With her nod, they had decided.

'For us, this is where it is. We want to stay and see things through. Challenge and excitement. Challenge and response. Exploring the new globe. Supporting Gaskin's new country. And so on. How about you?'

'I'm with you,' said McGervon.

Tite Barnacle was silent for a moment. During this spell of activity the lines of age, of weariness and anger had eased a little.

'I've another mission of a different type. For a different person. And in the other universe.'

'That's very enigmatic.'

'Yes, isn't it? Seasonable weather. For the time of year.'

*****

Upside, a year later, a shadowy figure is in an office high over the city, talking in a slightly slurred, rather appealing way to the President.

It's his Director of Communications and Personal Security. His jaw is badly scarred, perhaps by rifle wounds. He has a long, box-shaped face, a beaky nose with a bulbous tip and level thin lips. From the front they are curved in a refreshing smile. From the side they can strike fear like the imagined beak of some extinct raptor.

'You're with me, Assads, aren't you?' he asks in an intimate, smiling, warmly reassuring tone. 'Understand me, Sads?' He likes to share little special nicknames with his bosses. 'These diplomatic fuckers; we've got to grasp them by the goolies and squeeze till they squeak. Grasp by the goolies and grasp spectacular. Plus there's the woman. Believe me Sads, they're out to get you.'

*****

Alongside the river, across from the Suq and the Old City lies a splendid colonial building, sprawling among green lawns, tennis courts, a blue swimming pool, clumps of palms and bougainvillea. Distant from the foreign embassies, but close to the corridors of Syrian power. It's the British Embassy. Closing it off from the city is a narrow, high-walled lane. The only public approach to the embassy.

At the centre of the embassy is a large 5-sided chamber, marble floored, a glass dome high up, and pleasing paintings and greenery. Isn't that a small Hockney? Yorkshre somewhere? Not visible is a chain of complex electronics. This is a dome of silence, but unlike in the TV comedy, the zone actually works.

The Ambassador listens to an intelligence briefing. 'Right,' he decides, 'we'll put out the advert.'

Assad's Director of Communications and Personal Security works over his plan. The vehicle will pass the embassy and blow up 5 minutes before the President's arrival.

At 1855 the bomb vehicle approaches. But the lane is blocked and wedged with hundreds of people, and despite hooting they will not give way. They are waiting to seek entry visas for the UK, as they were invited to on the radio 2 hours earlier. The bomber vehicle drives away and the bomb is defused.

In the Ambassador's personal quarters, a plump, charming woman is preparing for a key reception to be given for the President and his Director of Communications. The Ambassador comes up behind her and her eyes light up. He slips his hands gently inside her bra, rests his head against her hair, and whispers in her ear. 'Ooh, Titey,' she responds. 'All right then. Just this once.'

Upside, Chapter 37: Ratcheting up the 'Aggro'

The sinking of Lady Amanda *probably happened at the time when nationalist fervor was winding up, especially in Wales. The tension built up towards the Scottish Referendum. The feel for it is now largely forgotten because of the subsequent occurrences, so I include some snippets as reminders of the intense emotions of the time. Note the anger felt by the Welsh, mirrored by similar antagonism in Scotland and Northern England toward the English South East. Assuaged to a degree when HS2 was lengthened to include the north of England and Glasgow, where construction would start, with connections to Northern Ireland and Wales. A political railway, not an economic one. And all the better for it.*

The Six Nations Rugby

The Englishman turns into the pub on Porthmadog main street. He picks up a drink at the bar and slips into a position on the left at the back. The guy next to him turns towards him.

'You English?' he asks. Hostile voice.

'Yes.'

The Welshman moves away in revulsion.

As his eyes become attuned to the darkness, the Englishman sees that the pub is full of well-built men, all dressed in Welsh rugby jerseys.

The preliminary anthem is sung passionately: 'Land of our Fathers'.

The English anthem[64] 'God Save the Queen' is greeted with derision.

England has been widely forecast in the press to win the championship convincingly in this final game.

The game starts, immensely physical, with scores even towards half time. Each time Wales scores, a leading Welshman on the left in the pub stands up and punches the air.

'Death, death, death,

Death to the English bastards.'

278

The entire pub stand up, punch the air and howl:
'Death, death, death,
Death to the English bastards.'
The Englishman slips away and listens to the remainder of the game on the radio on his boat.

What poison is it, he reflects, that generates this hatred of the English? I'm an Anglo-Scot. I've worked for, alongside and under lots of Welshmen. Easygoing, happy, bright, never a racial break, occasional fun and banter. But get them in their superb homeland and from the yobboes, the bile spills out. Never mind the 3 centuries of joint global leadership, never mind the friendliness of the Tal-y-Bont Gardening Club, never mind Shakespeare's Captain Llewellyn, these people are frightening. Frightening and threatening.

The Welsh win triumphantly.

Death of an industry, or killed by Clarkson

The British car industry was recovering in the late 1970s from years of mismanagement and union excesses, and their collaboration with Honda in Japan was proving very successful. The Rover design and the Honda engines were a brilliant match.

Rover came up with successful series, culminating with its top-of-the-range flagship, the Rover 75. This was greeted as the European Car of the Year, swift, versatile, beautiful lines, luxurious, and reliable if you specified the Honda 6-cylinder engine. The traditional 4-cylinder engine from Rover was suspect because it had an alloy cylinder block which was very sensitive to temperature failures. It warped if overheated and had to be skimmed to flatness at great cost. An overreliance on in-house design similar to that which killed off the Comet jetliner when it had a 10-year lead over the rest of the world.

This Honda collaboration was destroyed by a forced takeover by the German firm, BMW, who were looking to achieve Rover's command of mass production. Not a happy match and the Honda version of the Rover 75 was vastly the best.

Along came one man, a motoring journalist, an ambitious young man with a gift for humorous derision, Jeremy Clarkson.

He specialised in caustic attacks, and his attack upon the Rover 75 was disastrous. He gives us a chapter in his book on the subject, the message being a damning statement that the Rover 75 was 'a car for people over 75'. In fact, at the time it was recognised as a strong competitor of the Jaguar, and was European Car of the Year. It had a great range of options including a supercharger, which gave magnificent acceleration.

The result was the decease of the British mass car manufacturing industry. BMW learnt what they needed to know about mass manufacturing, The Rover 75 was derided as 'old man's wheels', although 10 years later it is widely admired.

The politicians and press claimed that more cars were now manufactured in the UK than ever before. But the point for the Brits is that our indigenous designers were forced to look elsewhere, and join the multinationals like Ford and Mercedes. A failure caused by feebleness in the City and trade union shortsightedness, as with the computing and aeroplane industries. As a result, the Brits and the world lost a great source of innovation and imagination. Qualities which the countries of Great Britain would never have achieved individually. In no sphere of life can it be said that one of these countries, unaided by the others, could have achieved what the Brits did when together.

A fine example of union intransigence is the career of Arthur Scargill, pugnacious leader of the trade union miners revolt against Margret Thatcher's close down of all uneconomic mines in the 1980s. A couple of examples of his stance:

'Not a single mine will be closed except on grounds of exhaustion', that is to say uneconomic mines would nevertheless be kept open until the coal ran out, funded by the public.

Here he was holding the nation to ransom, whereas the policy might well have been that where uneconomic mines were closed, the government should first ensure long-term alternative sources of employment. Their failure to succour the miners against international competition, particularly from Communist and Third World countries, often state-subsidised, meant that the industry was no longer viable. This political failure resulted in lasting hardship, joblessness, migration, hardship and a feeling of inadequacy among the proud mining population in North East England. A potent force for national collapse. For many, personal tragedies as mums and dads lost contact with their children who had to flow to the South East of England for jobs and futures.[65]

Another fine example of short-termism is the case of Britain's International Computers Limited. They were leaders in the European industry with about 30 per cent of the market, often including the major innovators round the world in computing application, organisations like the British UK Atomic Energy Authority, in France, Crédit Agricole, a major bank, in Malaysia, RISDA (the Rubber Industry Smallholders Development Authority) driving the production of a quarter of the world's natural rubber. In fact, ICL computers would be found throughout the First, Second and Third Worlds. The USSR put great energy into trying to create an indigenous industry, so-called 'IBMskas', and this in collaboration with ICL. But ICL refused.

However, it became apparent that going it alone was no strategy for the future. Bill Talbot, Director of ICL's research division, triggered off a search for collaboration in Japan with the world's best chip designers – none of the NIH 'Not Invented Here' attitude which plagued the British aero industry with the Comet. He eventually set up negotiations with Japanese Fujitsu, who had immensely effective products at the microchip design level. ICL had complementary leadership in the design and manufacture of higher-level creations like the 'motherboards', the platters connecting the chips together. Originally you could only link chips across one dimension, like a grid on a flat field. ICL, on the 1990s computers, were easily handling up to 27 levels of connections, with immense virtues in performance and reliability. Collaboration between ICL and Fujitsu was negotiated and was immensely successful, and ICL's user population, sales and profits benefited greatly. At this stage the great com-munications corporation STC came in with a bid. STC (Standard Telephones and Cables) was an ailing giant, albeit with a proud and successful history. ICL's year had been splendid, its profits remarkable, its moneybags succulent, its order book overflowing, STC bid to take it over. At this stage government should have intervened to ensure its seed-corn industry, with intense com-petitiveness worldwide and a leading edge in research and development, was not sacrificed. People said at the time that other countries would have blocked any such action. In Switzerland for example, Nestlé, leading the world confection industry, would have been protected from outside takeover.

But the government and bankers, timid and short-termist, didn't act.

At first ICL's new owners, STC, benefited by the injection of bright managerial talent from the computing firm. But STC still languished, and eventually offered its interest in ICL to Fujitsu. And Fujitsu, who knew a bargain when they saw one, grabbed it and have profited massively. I know via the CAB someone who worked with 20 others in the wiring shop in the ICL heydays when they chatted and sang songs over the wiring looms. She went back years later under Fujitsu. No more songs, no more chatting. Want the toilet? Put your hand up.

So a brilliant initiative by Britain's world-beating computer firm resulted in the end in its demise.

Upside, Chapter 38: Towards Scottish Independence

In 2014 the intense stress towards the Scottish Referendum built up. The feel for it is now largely forgotten because of the astonishing subsequent occurrences: the UKIP election in 2015 and the re-referendum in 2016. Anger about this and that, the challenges about voter registration. Claims against voters' registrations, objections to claims, objections to objections to claims. And the hasty drumming in of magistrates from the Commonwealth to assist in getting the legal proceedings done on time. So I include some snippets as reminders of the feelings of the time. Note the anger felt by the Welsh, mirrored by similar antagonism in Scotland and Northern England. And no doubt in Northern Ireland.

The Editor, The Observer
letters@observer.co.uk
The Referendum
Dear Editor,
Like many Anglo-Scots, (generations of Orcadian seawater from Shapinsay in 1690 flood my veins, five generations of Scottish sea captains and ships' pilots. My Dad, BI Captain then Marine Superintendent for a P&O ship on the Clyde, my son a systems designer with Motorola in East Kilbride, I worked sometimes in Dalkeith,) I'm deeply troubled by the superficiality and short-term economics content of the debate in the media and BBC.

We are not debating currencies or profit and loss, we are debating the destruction of Britain. The word's rarely even mentioned. My grandson was learning history in a Wilmslow secondary school. I asked him who Nelson was. He replied, 'Nelson Mandela, of course.'

He was completely ignorant about Admiral Horatio Nelson, a hero who had been the model of courage, leadership and initiative to all Brits for eight generations. Who was killed in 1805 at the Battle of Trafalgar, a battle which secured his country's world domination. Whose victory was marked not by national rejoicing but by tears everywhere; tears especially among his own sailors. The greatest sea battle ever. A typical example of the way Britain biffed and stopped budding imperial hegemonies on the continent – France then Spain then France again then Germany then Germany. Securing for Europe world leadership in contrast to rivals like China, India and Islam.

What had the grandson studied in school history? The German Third Reich, and the German Third Reich again, for three years!

(Nelson had been a model of paths from obscurity to greatness. Son of a Norfolk parson, so puny that his uncle had said, on Nelson's joining the navy, 'Poor Horatio. The best we can hope for is that a kind cannonball will end his service.')

This ignorance was among our youth, for a nation that has led the world for three centuries, for ill or good, but mostly good. That nation was not the Welsh. Not the English. Not the Scots. Not the Irish. It was the Brits.

We abandon our British heritage and our worldwide links at our peril and sorrow. After thirty years with the UN, EU and WB in twenty countries (including even North Korea) I know it will also be felt as a major loss to the world community.

Alistair Darling and others should do their duty.

Yours sincerely,

GP Ohlsson

This letter objecting to the distorted view of the 2014 Scottish independence referendum interested me particularly as an historian. A book, The Lonely Crowd,[66] *was written with remarkable prescience by 3 social scientists and historians from Yale. It analyses the characters and attitudes prevalent among the Brits and Americans up to the 1960s, attitudes that they define as 'inner-directed'. In outline these were the attitudes which drove people forward, rather as if by gyroscopes, to certain ideals and ways of thought. Attitudes resulting in the massive achievements in civilisation made during the nineteenth and early twentieth centuries. People like David Livingstone, Albert Schweitzer, or Winston Churchill stand out as examples, but such characters were legion, often fostered by the British private schools and state grammar schools. Riesman,[67] Glazer and Denny contrast those attitudes to those they saw people developing for the future, named 'other-directed'. The other-directed people like Kirsty Wark and the borderers[68] were driven not by principles but by a yearning to comply with contemporary mores, contemporary fashions, the collapse of contemporary grammar. In contemporary student-speak, the scornful phrase, 'Oh, so not-now' sums it up. Or the politicians' 'In this day and age'. Ignore the past, ignore the future, live for the present. Dedication to Scotland and its great achievements of the past and future were, for them, as nothing – the pressure was to conform to current attitudes in the present. Gluttonous yearnings for material wealth, showy wealth. Fly, fry, gas and gobble up, at their planet's peril.[69]*

One of the most unexpected members of this movement was Sean Connery, as McGervon commented. Connery was a Scot, rugged and handsome, who made his name as a young actor in the role of James Bond, 007, a member of the British Secret Service. Licensed to kill. The creation of Ian Fleming, an Englishman, who had actually served in the British Secret Service.

How is it that an iconic idol should support Scottish independence in the full knowledge that it would have placed all manner of obstacles and annoyances in his chosen career – having to flap passports around just to get across the border, losing key friends and contacts or missing out for example on his splendid scene eating with a long chased silver spoon from a marrow bone in the Royal Sandwich Golf Club?

And at the other end of the 'Better together' scales you have an avowed British patriot like Ian Hislop[70] whingeing on about national decline and 'The tragic unravelling of Britain from 1850 on'. Probably the century of our greatest achievements for world civilisation. Brits had most of the fun.

Or a TV personality, Julie Etherington, on ITV. Talking about modern slavery, she said dismissively 'And Wilberforce thought he'd abolished slavery in 1807'. Clearly she was unaware of the heroic struggle led by Wilberforce and prime ministers like Pitt, and notably the Royal Navy throughout the following century. How could she have been ignorant of such a world-changing achievement? Who taught her history?

The most dramatic example of decline was in the national TV debate between Darling and Salmond. They reached the stage when future foreign policy was supposed to be covered. All that came from them was a wrangle about Trident submarines. Small countries, as Scotland would be, have vanishing influence and vanishing wisdom. For example, the SNP was floored by a simple question about the Iraq War, which they condemned as an act of outmoded British imperialism.[71] The question was: "What would you have done about the Marsh Arabs?" The SNP had never even heard of them. In 1993 Saddam Hussein, who had caused a million and a half war deaths and gassed 70,000 of his own people in Halabja, was eliminating them – 250,000[72] bloody-minded tribesmen from the swamp. 6,000 square miles of wetlands were turned to dust and desert. The Iraq War saved the Marsh Arabs, and they flourished again in 2019. The little country, Scotland, would, like the biblical Pharisee, have passed them by on the other side.

Michael Taylor: one of 3 Dundee University students interviewed by BBC2, all of the similar opinion: 'I like to think we would be better off. But it's not all about money. People aren't going to trade away 300 years of our partnership and our future just for the price of an iPad.'

Upside, Chapter 39: Dalkeith

Just 3 miles south of the famous or infamous Sauchiehall[73] Street in Glasgow is a bowl in the hills, containing a reddish-brown 440-yard running track. There are 3 runners taking the circuit, bounding along as if their legs were taut springs. Grinding the ash with their spikes. Fine, straight black hair, high cheekbones, almond-shaped eyes, bronzed faces. Might have been cousins to Man United's fine inside left, Ji-Sung Park.

They work at EKB, Motorola[74] Corporation peoples' affectionate term for their main Glasgow computer and systems development centre in East Kilbride.

They are the East Asia Software Team, something of a mystery to their colleagues, and they are writing the software with Koreanised versions of dBase, Linux, Java, PHP, Python and an obscure assembler. The beautiful Korean script is not widely understood by their colleagues or by anyone else. They are hacking. They are hacking the leading bit of the PC's 24-hour clock. They are hacking leading bits of a very large number of 24-hour clocks.

They are also writing little apps. The little apps skulk around in dark corners. The little apps are kicked off by assorted 24-hour clocks in assorted ways.

Beyond Arthur's Seat, 6 miles out from the centre of Edinburgh to the east, lies the residence of the Duke of Buccleugh. High up on rugged hills, it's called the Dalkeith Palace. Below it lie dark woods, and turbulent streams cascade down to the Firth of Forth and the sea.

You enter the palace into a splendid, sprawling, marble atrium, with a broad spiral staircase leading to the mezzanine floor. As you go in, you may also go through one of several fine doors, probably made of Honduras cedar.

One door leads to a large reception centre, occupied in 2018 by managers, PAs and clerks using numerous computer terminals. On the far side, in the corner where the wooden

mouldings dovetail, is a discreet small round brass knob a cen-
timetre across. Press this knob down and a section of the wall
swings open. Go through it and you are in the Duke's personal
private centre of operation.

From here, the activities to control the process of Scottish and
British severance are directed.

The walls between Scotland and Britain are in place. Many had
been built by Hadrian. The standard EU immigration controls
are crucial, and have already been developed as on the more
normal passport and other checking systems at Britain's external
frontiers; 7-lane passport channels on the M6 and A74(M) and
the A1, standard overseas clearance procedures are applied, with
thistle to sterling to euro currency conversion desks for example,
for passengers at the big airports. On the trains, the expresses
offer immigration clearance en route from Edinburgh and Glasgow to the border and the British cities to speed things up. But
scrutiny at the border takes place for those on stopping trains.

Prime Minister Miliband now faced the same decision as was
faced by the British Governor, Earl Mountbatten, at the time of
independence for India in 1947. Mountbatten had to decide
whether to cut the Gordian[75] knot and grant independence
immediately, or to work through the situation politically to try to
circumvent the bitter determination of Pandit Nehru and the
Indian Hindus, against the totally inflexible Liaquat Ali Khan
leading the Pakistan Islamic movement. In the end Mountbatten
sliced the Gordian knot almost immediately, the national
boundaries were defined and trainloads of people crossed the
new countries' frontiers in the face of hostile populations who
often raided the coaches, raped the women, stole the belongings
and slaughtered the men. Mountbatten's action in this has often
been assessed, and the common judgment is that, as with the use
of nuclear bombs over Japan that ended World War Two, the
death toll and the agonies were appalling, but minimised. Two
years of violent war and further deaths avoided.

Diary note by PM;

Meeting in Dalkeith went well. Present were Salmond,
Nicola Sturgeon and Dewar for the Scots and Tite Barnacle

and me for the Brits. Professor Stag was our technical advisor in view of his status and background.

Found him incomprehensible. Big burly fellow. Dominated everything in a cheerful way. Strings of pauses, stammers and jargon. 'Chuch... chuch... eckpoint Hub... bub h-ump h-estart... bu... bub.. bub.' Professor of Computation, University of Manchester. Professor Directing Communication Systems, UK. Visiting Professor of this in Singapore. Visiting Professor of that in Beijing, DIC. How on earth does he do it? Does he exploit his stammer to gain respect and attention? What's he like at home? But the bagpipes were splendid. Moving. I'll not hear them again.

TB was, as usual, particularly effective, insisting on resumability for all IT and urging us all not to make Margaret Thatcher's mistake in insisting on the Poll Tax in 1987, the mistake which brought her down. We will instead start with 'Beta tests' as they call them, and full system trials to ensure that the management of immigration at the airports, the M6, A1 and lesser borders and the railways will work effectively. And give the public familiarity and confidence.

So we agreed to warn the public and to have a TST, a total system trial, on Saturday and Sunday before the flags go up.

Should be exciting. I'll travel back from Westminster to see the show.

PM

Splendid dinner at the strangely-named 'The Kitchin' on the waterfront by the ancient quays. Converted whisky warehouse. Heady scent.

So the system was ordered to be applied on Saturday and Sunday, 11th and 12th September 2018. All road, rail and air services had to stop at the borders, where people had to go through the usual EU, UK and Scottish immigration checks for whichever of the countries they were entering. Come and wave your passport. Change yourself some thistles. Buy some haggis. Buy our Kendall mint cake. Worldwide media coverage would be intense. Come and see the fun. As good as the Falklands War. Top army and police officials had attended discussions as to how the new procedures would be managed. It was all going to happen.

Just like that.

The 3 months of chaos that followed the systems trial and led to the reunification are widely written up, of course. Most effective I think was the randomness of the interrupts. The M6 for example would sometimes open all lanes then inexplicably close some or all after drivers had hastened and queued for the slots, and ATMs would open and close apparently randomly. Even the public toilets would run out of paper or lock solid with someone inside. Compared with the damage that could have been done, of course, this was fairly benign. The messing-up all British people's dental records, appointments and so on caused pain for many who had teeth. But doing the same for medical records (easily done) would have caused death.

I would add that the detail of the Motorola East Asia project has only just come to my notice from a friend in Google Motorola's HR department who wishes to be nameless. They seem to have left for Seoul just before the trial. And a US CIA agent tracked 3 Koreans from the airport at Incheon near Seoul. They made for the beach, looked back at him, waved cheerily and sprinted to a far distant inflatable and were carried off. He puffed after them, but they were well off-shore and taken aboard what may have been one of the new stealth submarines.

HB G-B

Upside, Chapter 40: Table Mountain

Table Mountain, a massive oblong, stands isolated with a 6-mile long flat top towering a sheer 1,000 metres above its city. An ancient beach. The mountain is often shrouded at its peak in cloud and mist or fog; the tablecloth. The cloth builds up as the damp air from the oceans, sometimes Atlantic sometimes Indian, rises and condenses. And the cloud falls away and disappears as the air drops down away from the summit, down onto what is probably the world's loveliest capital city,[76] Cape Town, at the southernmost point of Africa.

The city slopes down from the mountain to the harbour. As the city reaches up again towards the mountain, the skirting roads wind through brilliant green parkland with scattered tall trees, some flowery, mostly pine. The approach from the south includes the Kirstenbosch Botanical Gardens, the finest in Africa.

From the city, there is a cable car that crosses a yawning chasm of air up the sheer cliffs to the summit.

A man has climbed from Kirstenbosch up the Spring Ravine with a bag on his back, through vegetation, mostly brittle dry protea, quite a few dassies,[77] and sometimes a menacing group of baboons. He follows along a summit track through a long cave in a typical South African kopje past the climbing club hut, towards the cable car.

Found the hole – 'Christ' – and climbs fearfully down a chimney. Then along a ledge half way up. It is a tricky ledge, and a mite slippery. The bloody tablecloth. Round a buttress to see the target. Don't look down. Don't look down. He crouches down and assembles an AK47. He watches activities through binoculars at the cable car base, waiting for a triple flash from a grey VW. The triple flash happens. VIPs on board. DRIK – designation cable car; range – 400 metres; indication – 310 degrees; kind of fire – rapid. The old routine. Down, crawl, observe, sights, fire.

291

He waits until the cable car is close, then looses off a magazine full from the rifle. Load another. A bit hasty, and now the car's higher. Fire. The kick knocks him back. He slips, slithers, scrabbles and falls 500 metres. Not healthy. But he crashes through the brittle protea.

The cable car continues unperturbed, unaware, and glides into its parking bay at the top. Out step a party of officials. They include a black-haired Brit, Lord Tite Barnacle.

A grey VW comes up to collect the gunman. It has a BLZ registration. A trademark. What's called for is not just an assassination. It's a spectacular media-friendly execution. Leave the rifle there as a threat. Try again somewhere else

The crackle of the rifle fire was heard at the university and reported. The police found a battered but recently-fired Kalashnikov in a ravine. The case was never solved. The police investigation suggested that an assassin had been aiming to kill people in the cable car, but the gravitational attraction of the landmass of the mountain had pulled the bullets away from the target.

*****

Upside LPYC

It had been outside Caernarfon castle, Upside, in July, that a new approach to global warming had been born. Thus:

A large, fat, blond, red-faced man in bulging shorts and a short-sleeved shirt promenaded along the castle quay from his great fibreglass gin palace of a cabin cruiser. Probably a well-matured yuppy, gone to seed with success. Years of stress and outguessing the market, now he had the late fruits in tow. These were two young women, a striking brunette and a rather frightened youngster with long yellow-gold hair. Have some fun with her, he would. They giggled and laughed as he talked at them. They approached a small yacht, a sloop, laying alongside the wall. On the transom under its name, was its affiliated club, in gold letters:

LPYC

The man twisted to his companions and winked.

'Hallo, down there,' he said in a poffling voice huskily laden with fine clarets, clubland cigars and condescension. 'Tell me, what does the LPYC stand for?'

The owner looked at him blandly.

'Llanbedr and Pensarn Yacht Club,' he replied neutrally.

'More likely Little Peoples Yacht Club!' the elderly yuppy said loudly, laughing with the same heavy emphasis used by comedians to suck a laugh out of a line which is basically unamusing. His brunette companion giggled.

'Jasper, you really are a HOOT!' – thirties slang was in vogue that year – 'You're a hoot, you really are!'

'Get that gin-tub of yours off South Stack in Force seven,' said the yacht's owner, 'you'd soon see who'd hoot then. Farting out greenhouse gases in gobbets, all to get nowhere. How's it feel, my fat friend, to be among the globe's mega-polluters? You not clever enough to use the wind? Short on bottle?'

'Now look here,' said the yuppie stiffly, 'I'll have you know, I'm a full club member here.'

'No telling nowadays, is there?'

'Come on, Jasper, let's leave this idiot,' intervened the brunette. 'Couldn't you show us the whatsit castle, like you promised?'

'Selena, my love, you're so right.'

The entourage drifted off, the girls working hard to restore its spirits.

That evening, Jasper and his companions settled down on their left sides to sleep, himself in the middle, on the cruiser's wide water-bed. The tide crept up the mudflats, through the cantilevered, balanced swing bridge and into the little river alongside the ancient castle quay. The boats lifted off the muddy gravel, then twitched gently at their moorings. By midnight they were sidling around, floating in two metres.

Two hours later the boats settled back with the ebb on the gravel of the river bed. Not exactly where they'd risen from, but near enough – there's always a little slack in the ropes, and much depends on the happenstance of wind and tide as they touch.

The morning dawned hot, sunny and windless. When the tide returned the sloop set off for the sea. Jasper and his companions ignored it, and finished their poached salmon and champagne in the cockpit. Pleased to play up to the watchers on the quay, they joked and giggled and the girls bridled, cleavages agape, to his innuendos. The brunette slipped her hand across his thigh, leaned across and whispered in his ear:

'Time for num nums.'

They went down the companion steps hand in awkward hand, and renewed their familiarity with the water bed. Later they sprawled naked, sticky in the heat, but contented.

An hour later there was a hissing, and whisps of steam curled from the cruiser's battery compartment.

At three, the brunette on the cruiser awoke, to feel a chilly dampness. God. Had Jasper peed in his sleep? She stretched a hand down, then screamed. It was paddling in water. The other two woke up and yelled similarly. The cabin was half full. They made quickly for the door, off-set to port, Jasper elbowing through and down the step first. The boat lurched a little, frighteningly, to port with their weight, the water-level rising to match, giving atavistic feelings, hobbit-like, of entrapment; but they scrambled out waist-deep, stark naked to the onlookers' excited cries, then rapidly and more modestly hauling on the wet weather gear which hung by the companion way.

Then out onto the quay. Jasper was convinced it was the abusive yachtie who had done it. Must have drilled a hole in the bottom during the night, then pushed off on the tide. He called the police on his mobile.

That evening the yachtie was questioned by the police in a nearby harbour. Inconclusively. Later it was proved that a sharp rock on the bottom had pierced the hull as the cruiser had dropped onto it as the night tide ebbed. Nobody's fault; another insurance job.

But the yachtie thought it over. It gave him an idea.

*****

The ISORA team assembled in a pub up the hill from Dunlaoghaire harbour, parking their battered old white Ford Transit with the kits well back in the city. The marina was filling nicely, cramming with cruisers for the Irish Sea Power Boat rally and off-shore events; the racing machines, a lot of showy diesel farting dayboats, and the mega-farters, the great Onassis style cruisers, ego-enhancers extraordinary.

Any boat can be sunk pretty fast once you get inside it. But these all had to be sunk from the outside, in unison, steadily, spectacularly. They had worked charts for the various boat sizes – five 2cm holes for the tiddlers, twenty for the bigger boys and so on. Least holes for the first boat done, most for the last, so that they catch up.

Each of the team had air for an hour. At 2am the van dropped down to the sea-front and they kitted up. They took off about a hundred yards west of the Motor Yacht Club, finning easily on the surface, round to the end of West pier, then in and under among the boats, working methodically down each pontoon. Claustrophobic though, and any guard could knock out a diver with ease and a pistol. Plenty of light, one showing from the pontoon deck at each boat-station, and you could look up and check the hull quite easily. Water up your nostrils though. If it's got a keel, leave it. Otherwise look at the list, berth and pontoon number. Holes to be neatly distributed, not too easy to get at from the interiors; the hull skin under the engine, toilet or galley was a good choice. The submersible drills whined quietly as they chewed through the plastic. Then stick on the SEI|NEUW sticker and on to the next. Finally, back outside the West pier, Fl(3)G7-5s, and along the surface to the beach. Hump the kit into the van, van off to the city, but we'll stay and watch.

This was the first time. It had been a doddle of course. They snapped and videoed the activities as the day broke and chaos mounted – invaluable next time round. The two empty starter boats had sunk first to catch the attention of Security. Then, as the guards noticed the others a-founder, something of a panic. A hastening and a calling. But the marina night manager was well on the ball. When he realised the scale, he set off the alarm klaxons and used the PA. Cries of wrath and screams of fear, as people were urged to get up, and leave their craft to sink. Much anguish and anger and frantic phoning. Was the marina liable? Did the insurance cover it? The Garda pee-pawed in histrionically, followed scurrying by the Fourth Estate. Loads of cereals, bacon and eggs into the marina kitchens as people sought alternative breakfasts.

The team watched enthralled as an organised scan was made of all the sinking boats to check for drunken oversleepers and so on.

The yachties in the marina seemed much intrigued, gathering in amused surreptitious groups, glancing occasionally over their shoulders, some serious and concerned, some barely suppressing loud guffaws, most torn between the two. Hilarious. A weekend to savour. Was it you, was it me, was it he? Did old Fred do it? What a market for the electronics boys.

The team members each dispersed to their own cells and got the kits out to their sites world-wide before the Mandrake Information systems were onto their tails. Then the final training and project replication. Teams in Florida, the Windies, Sydney, the Med. In action fast, while the technologists raced to catch the market with this device and that. Detect the SEI|NEU. Sense the divers' heartbeats. The wave patterns. The steel of the cylinders. Thermal imaging cameras. Use dolphins. How about using the geo-spatial serial searching which had done so much to identify criminals? The criminal's trademark crimes are thus and thus; he's likely to operate yea far from base; so he must be Fred who lives there or Joe who lives *there*? But this only works for serial crimes, where you can build up a pattern of criminals' past activities. So the more people you involve, and the less serial the crimes, the less useful is the computer technique. And here, the authorities came to realise, were lots and lots of people working in lots and lots of places. Probably once each. No seriality.

A set of questions to the British *Observer* environmental columnist, Lucy Siegle. A nice encapsulation of the reasons for the world's retreat from consumerism. Led by people like the great revolutionary linguist, Prof Noam Chomsky. With a name like that, how could you be other than a great revolutionary linguist? Led also by Prof Susan Greenfield's works such as *Mind Change*, they reveal the autism created by TV-watching and hence the decline in populations which happily resulted.

Thrumble Coombe
2 Maes Artro
Llanbedr
Gwynedd
LL45 2PZ

Dear Lucy,

I admire the depth into which you go on environmental issues, but I think you might also tackle the fundamentals. Primarily, that the recession has been immensely beneficial for the planet. Various figures have been credited, but it is widely calculated that CO_2 emissions have been reduced by 30% against the levels which were predicted without the credit crunch. The best growth is no growth. The best growth is to shrink.

Secondly, that in terms of human happiness, by some indices, we were vastly happier in the 1950s (I was born in 1941) than we are now, and the stress of double income commitments and marketing pressures to follow the latest fashions in food and consumer goods was almost non-existent.

Thirdly, that major contributors to global warming are widely ignored. Methane gas for example, is massively more powerful as a warmer than CO_2, and the contributions from sheep and cattle, particularly from countries like Australia, New Zealand and the US, are unbelievable. To move to soya milk, for example, would be immensely beneficial.

Fourthly, the efficient application of existing safeguards against emissions might contribute massively to global cooling. In the UK, the motorway speed limit of 70 mph is widely exceeded by at least 20% in the south, though not in the north. Why are police regarding these offences so complacently?

Fifthly, we neglect the responsibility of the general public. Us. The recession and the banking crisis were not just attributable to the bankers, they were also attributable to the reckless borrowing, sometimes against 120% of their incomes, by mortgagees.

I am retired and, as a seventy-three year-old, remember the '50s with great clarity. Great freedom as a child, no obesity, immensely healthy. Neither I nor my schoolmates were ever particularly concerned with the incomes we might earn in the future, still less our retirement pension. Pension worries were for wimps! Boring things like job satisfaction, using one's talents to the greatest effect, or contributing to humanity's future were at the fore, though rarely talked about. Not the done thing.

How about a re-assessment as against people's current preoccupations? To give an example, review Kirsty Wark's BBC2 programme with Scottish borderers on the issues raised by the Scottish independence debate. For the borderers, their great past and even greater future mattered little against the possibility that the average Scot might be £500 per year less or more wealthy.

To conclude, I say again, the best growth is no growth. The best growth is to shrink.

Yours sincerely
Judy Bennett, BSc, PhD University of East Anglia

Upside, Chapter 41: Washington, Warning 1

I came across this account in the library in Yale. All well-known to readers generally, but this is strikingly graphic. HB G-B.

The MacFred was a revolutionary concept. A mass-production trailer-sailer with water ballast rather than a keel, and an amazing 6 berths for her size, light as a feather compared with most, so light she could stick her bows up in the air and plane at 20 knots with a 50-horse power outboard. In still water, mast sticking up as if she was a real yacht, she could curvet around like a ski boat with her thin twin fancy drop rudders. Brilliant, as long as it didn't blow.

Up a sleepy creek in the salt marshes (near St Christopher's on Chesapeake Bay) were 4 of them, sitting on their trailers in delivery trim. Below decks their innards had been stripped out to make 4 cosy cylindrical nests, 12 feet long by 3 feet in diameter. One nest each. Lethal. Gigalethal. The only other differences from the standard MacFred package were the strengthened 8-ply tyres and 2 extra leaves in the trailer springs. Overnight on 2nd February 2027, Upside, a team came in, drilled large holes in the transoms and let the flood tide rise, fill and settle over the 4 boats. At high water, a heavy inflatable slipped alongside from the open sea and 4 long, heavy cylinders that had been dangling beneath it were moved into the nests in the MacFred's hulls. Faintly etched onto each cylinder were the cyrillic logos for the AS-15 KENT nuclear warhead. You'd have thought they'd have blanked them off. The inflatable backed off into the darkness. As the tide dropped, the water fell away again and the boats emptied. The holes were plugged, the boats were hitched onto FWD Land Rovers, and the 4 Equipes set off on the road southwest. Steering and braking were a bit of a problem on the over-run; otherwise you'd not notice anything different. In fact, no one noticed anything different – there weren't many people around at St Christopher's at 6 a.m. on 28/2/21.

Harper's Ferry, at the confluence of the turbulent Shenandoah and Potomac, is a spooky place at all times, pre- served where possible in the state it was in on the 16th of October, 1859, when John Brown and his team met their fates and kicked off perhaps the bloodiest and most crucial civil war in history. At night, the ghosts seem close as the old gas lamps gutter ineffectually against the darkness. Hardly a light to be seen, except from the old railroad station, and one gleaming from the bluffs above the river opposite. As an Amtrack freight train rumbles across the Potomac Bridge you can feel the ghost of the old fanatic, John Brown, hypnotising history. Taking the national arsenal with a bunch of young amateurs without firing a shot. Then walking courteously in front of the east-bound Baltimore night train as it approached to reassure the indignant driver and passengers that his team had not mined the track. Then holed up in the armoury's engine house with his 18 young no-hopers, 5 black, 13 white, waiting to lead a slave uprising in his cause; an uprising that he knew was not going to happen. Then taking on a thousand men – the militia, the National Guard, the US Marines (the Leathernecks from the Halls of Montezuma) led by one Colonel Robert E. Lee. And in the end winning out for the slaves, in a court scene and inevitable judi- cial execution that outdid even that of Socrates. The 4 MacFreds spent the night of March 1st in the Harper's Ferry car park... At the heart of America's most potent myth.

On the edge of the Great Salt Lake desert, 30 miles southwest of Dugway, Utah, is a flat area with the silhouette of a mountain, perhaps Wheeler Mountain, in the distance. Miles from any- where. On 8/03/21, the first MacFred sat incongruously on its trailer on a dirt track. It was about to vapourise.

At 9.40 a.m. a terrorist-validated message was uploaded onto http://www.futuer.com/index on a little-known South Asian server. It read: watch this site at 10 a.m. A similar message appeared at 9.50 in the e-mail inboxes of the editors of TV and radio news and most national dailies, worldwide. Many put one of their staff onto it. Probably a hoax, but just in case. The world- wide Internet snooper started trying to track it.

At 10 a.m. on futuer.com, the screen showed a horizontal split. At the top, a shot of a far off blue and white object, like a long box, sitting on top of what might be a trailer, against a desert background. The bottom shot showed a white and blue square, greatly magnified, with a logo on the right. It read 'MacFred'. Both shots showed in the right-hand top corner a countdown clock, with 5 minutes to go on the top, 5 minutes 15 on the bottom. They refreshed every second.

Slowly the shots panned in and out respectively. The desert object fining in to a recognisable boat-on-trailer shape, its right-side tyre flat. The other object panning out into a frame, suggesting part of a second boat. Its background was darkened, maybe a foggy day. The process continued, and in the lower shot a similar boat definitely appeared. Its right-side tyre was also flat. Its background slowly racked in; first the road surface, then the pavement, with the legs of curious passers-by who were stopping to look, then a building behind. Distant white marble steps. Then some striking columns – was it the Capitol? Thirty seconds to go. Wasn't that a cop running in, frozen by each frame in midstride? Then you could see other police moving in. It was definitely the Capitol.

A sound net faded in a grating, commanding voice. 'Could be a bomb. I want the sand trucks in. Right now. That picture on the top, that's someplace else. But the bottom is the big W. Get me through. And fast.'

18; 17; 16. On the lower screen, lights blazed on through the fog.

'What's with those lights? Dowse those fuckers. We got to shroud this. Infra red is all. Fucking can of fucking worms. I want 2 guys into it. Expendables. Get the Agent Incapacitating on standby.'

The police moved in second by second, the onlookers were bundled indignantly back. A cop vaulted on board. Another stood by; 10 to go.

'Get them out.'

A man mouthing into a loud-hailer. The cop gate-vaulted out. Everyone running like hell.

5; 4; 3; 2; 1.

The top shot resolved into the characteristic mushroom cloud and turmoil of a nuclear explosion, gradually obliterating the scene till it dribbled and disappeared. You almost felt the camera

301

lens melt. On the lower, after a 5-second delay, a striking fire-works display broke out from the MacFred's cockpit.

Both shots merged, overlaid with a message and translations in 5 major languages:

Iz This ar Futuer? Sei Neu ta it

Sei Neu ta Gleubl Wormin

Two MacFreds gone; two to go. One in Alaska, one in a lockup on Manhattan Island. End of warning 1.

Upside, Chapter 42: Warning 2

At 9.40 a.m. a terrorist-authorised-code-validated message was uploaded onto http://www.futuer.com/index.htm on a South Asian server which had suddenly become very well-known. It read: *watcH thiS sitE aT teN ayemM*.

A similar message appeared at 9.50 in the e-mail inboxes of the editors of TV and radio news and most national dailies, worldwide. Many put nearly all their staff onto it. Probably a hoax, but just in case. The world-wide snooper started trying to track it.

Just off Manhattan Island, one of the most famous of the cruise-round-the-island boats was approaching Washington Bridge. The captain was in the middle of his description of the great 1930s suspension technology, in a flat, laconic, been-there-done-that, been everywhere, done everything, deadpan Long Island accent, '... the wire in those cables is fine and incredibly strong. You could take that wire and it would stretch right from here to the moon. Right from here to the moon... And the bridge would fall down. On the starboard hand... '

At 10 a.m. on futuer.com, the screen showed a horizontal split. At the top, a shot of a far-off blue and white object, like a long box, sitting on top of what might be a trailer, against a tundra background. Somewhere in Alaska, perhaps. The bottom shot showed Manhattan Island and slowly panned in on a square. The square was covered to a depth of 3 feet in coarse salt crystals, partly leached away by rain. Only when one viewed it from the same level did one realise that the salt was not dead flat, but rose in a steady curve in the centre and down again. Both shots showed in the right-hand top corner a countdown clock, with 5 minutes to go on the top, 6 minutes 15 on the bottom. They refreshed every second.

Slowly, the shots panned in and out. The tundra object fined in, to a recognisable boat-on-trailer shape, its right-side tyre flat. Seen that before somewhere. Then this boat picture faded out, to be replaced by a long shot of the same New York square, panning out into a frame slowly filling out the traffic picture for the city. Its background was darkened, maybe a foggy day. The process continued, and in the lower shot more streets racked in. From the doorways people suddenly appeared running. The fire escapes suddenly filled with many more. In some cases panic appeared to have taken hold and the movement slowed to a trickle impeded by fist-fights and struggling. In others some individual had asserted control, and orderly movement resulted. Like getting out of a sinking sub. Much better way to die.

The top screen panned out further to show the city, the great bridges jammed with outflowing traffic covering all lanes in an outward direction. Special police messages were heard in the background trying to control the flow.

Then as the clock approached 30 seconds to go, the top screen switched back to the tundra and the MacFred. Would it be another nuke like in the desert? Or just fireworks?

4, 3, 2, 1. Suddenly a magnificent firework display burst out from all over the little boat, and it started burning fiercely.

On the lower screen as it panned in, a police car came into view. In trying to carve its way against the run of the panicking traffic it slewed sideways and rammed a truck. The doors opened and 3 men appeared, running with spades in their hands. They burst through the crowds, into the square, and jumped onto the rocky salt, working towards the centre. The clock showed 50 seconds. At the centre they dug frantically. Suddenly one stopped and shouted. They all converged, digging together. A steel cylinder appeared. The clock showed 10 seconds. The square was otherwise deserted. There was a sudden screaming noise. One policeman threw himself down on the cylinder. The screen erupted into the explosion and melted. Another AS-15 KENT warhead gone off.

Both shots merged, overlaid with a message and translations in 5 major languages:

Iz This ar Futuer? Sei Neu ta it
Sei Neu ta Gleubl wormin

Upside, Chapter 43: Delusion

The nuking of New York by no one knows whom set a disaster scene for people worldwide. A scene that is of course now well-known. But not perhaps well understood. Probably, according to most authorities, caused by terrorists. Followed by many attacks on leaders wherever they poked their heads over their parapets, i.e. leaders attempting to oppose the fight to maintain the planet as is. Sustainability, in short. People like Abbot in Australia or poor old Lawson in the UK. With New York as an example, it took very little to hold most politicians and media on course, even in China and India. In Britain of course, actions like sloshing out large tractor loads of cattle dung on approach roads for the big events worked effectively. Man United vs Arsenal, the opening of Parliament at Westminster or Belfast, the Welsh Eisteddfod, the Edinburgh Tattoo, a state visit to the Prime Minister's residence at Chequers in Wendover. I like particularly one of the answers to youth unemployment. Groups of three or more could build their own yachts. Based on the extraordinary Seagull class designed by the great fifties designer Ian Proctor. Kits for amateurs in sustainable marine ply from Bell Woodworking of Leicester. Incredibly intricate and light. Dance across the waves like butterflies. Back to the youngsters' maritime heritage. Creating employment, but not for building unnecessary dry-stone walls as in past centuries.

Political theorists held sway. Notably Dawkins. I give a recent critical view of his work and influence: HG G-B

The Dawkins delusion

I'm an agnostic Anglican Christian. Doubting and hoping vaguely, like Doubting Thomas in the upstairs room, before Christ reappeared. What seems odd to me is that the two Christian creeds, Athanasian and Nicene, recited daily by millions for fifteen centuries, make no mention of what was most important, Christ's teaching. 'Born of the Virgin Mary, suffered under Pontius Pilate'. The bit between is what might inspire millions.

I have probed Dawkins' background, message and motivation, expressed for example in his best selling book *The God Delusion*, or in his half-page article in *The Observer* newspaper deriding Christianity as 'militant' and destructive, for example in the occasionally-used hymn or song, 'Onward Christian soldiers, Marching as to war.'

Dawkins quickly glosses over the key little word 'as' – 'marching as to war.' The hymnist clearly meant 'using the same dedication as one might in war.'

But much more crucially, in Dawkins, here is a man who, as a youngster, was brought up as a devout Christian Methodist. The overwhelming messages of this education must be built into his mind and his soul. Peacefulness, love, forgiveness, compassion etcetera, as in the Christian Beatitudes: 'Blessed are the peace-makers, for theirs is the kingdom of heaven.'

Or the lovely bucolic hymn at harvest time: 'We plough the fields and scatter the good seed on the land.'

Or the message from the angels at the birth of Christ: 'And on earth, peace, goodwill toward men.'

The King James Bible, as so often more Christian than modern translations, typically: 'Goodwill to those with whom he is pleased.'

What about the rest or the Book of Common Prayer? 'Bless and succour all those who in this transitory life are in sorrow, need, sickness or any other adversity, and grant them a happy issue from all their afflictions.'

Imagine the hope and solace this and so much more has brought to billions of people. Hope which Dawkins dismisses so deliberately and misleadingly. How far should we trust him?

Only, I suggest, trust Dawkins as a biologist. And there he emphasises the importance of cell boundary in containing and controlling the developments within it. Does that marry with the emphasis in those days on uninhibited transit across national frontiers? Global financial meltdowns? Global gluttony of the planet's resources? Global extinction of non-human species? Global slopping and sloshing and swilling around of human talent? He didn't say. But these ideas about boundaries gave rise to the dramatic political theory often called Dawkinism. Closing boundaries and keeping people inside them. To quote Enoch

Powell's much-reviled diatribe against uncontrolled immigration from the Commonwealth into the UK in the 1960s.

'I see the River Tiber foaming much blood'.[78]

What the people of the UK failed to grasp was that for millions of people overseas, for then as for now, the UK was a mecca of unbelievable prosperity worth even the sacrifice of your life to attain.

Was Powell vindicated?

We now have a sustainable world, and the extraordinary pronunciations of the mediacrats in the early 2000s are discredited, often derided. My favourite example is from the UN consultant, Gaskin, in Pyongyang. It is worth repeating:

A BBC commentator showed a satellite view of East Asia at night. China, South Korea and Japan were a blaze of light. North Korea was in total darkness. 'There you are,' she said, 'contrast the shining civilisation around it with the pariah state and darkness within.'

But, I thought, maybe the pariah state has it right. Is there any other state in the world that can claim to be sustainable in the face of globalisation and democracy? Not since the exit of the 'Gang of Four' in China and the death of Chairman Mao. He was responsible for 30 million deaths. But his country was sustainable as a result, for example, of his 'one child per family policy' limiting the escalation of the population.

Robert Gallucci, US Chief Negotiator in the Korean unification talks, said about North Korea: 'These people are committed Stalinists. They know what they're about. We mess with them at our peril worldwide.'[79]

As my Malaysian friends would say: 'Who can tell?'

Downside, Chapter 44: Emotional Intelligence

The trio contacted Gaskin after his triumph and worked with him several years in establishing a new and more reliable and democratic regime. But one evening Johnson went to Gaskin's rooms in Cambridge as he did many years earlier. This time though to overhear a conversation massively more hostile and threatening. The general gist was to use the remaining POPs, of whom there were a large number, to maintain order in Gaskin's new monolithic state. They would be kept in hangars in Cambridge and directed from his main base in Caernarfon in Wales.

One of the most famous railway lines around the UK is the Cambrian Coast Line. In spite of Beeching's attempt to close it, it waggles around 60 lovely miles on the west coast of Cardigan Bay. It has to cross a deep valley, the valley of the River Mawddach. It's a dramatic U-shaped crossing, with the lonely, gaunt, sharp mass of Mount Cadr Idris towering above. The railway skirts the valley, cut into precipices, and then swings hard left to cross the valley and river to the harbour and seaside town of Barmouth, whence came the first Tudor, Henry VII. It was here that *Lady Amanda* sank and was raised.

The bridge is spectacular, with 113 spans covering half a mile, way above the water level. This allows 30-feet clearance at high tide springs, but is nevertheless too low for the slate ships that used to go up the valley for loading. The Victorians built a swing bridge in 1857. It's a massive structure; 2 balanced wings, brilliantly engineered, and rotating on a colossal single steel spindle. To turn it and let ships through, 4 men are needed to wind the capstans as if for a ship's anchor.

In the middle of the seventeenth century in a lovely rural town in Kent, a Presbyterian minister conceived a new problem in mathematics. His name was Bayes.[80] He worked on it for many years, published papers and in due course the approach, known as Bayesian statistics was recognised and established and stashed away as an interesting curiosity. But 2 centuries later as interest in 'expert systems' or 'fuzzy logic' and Artificial Intelligence developed, Bayesian statistics were found to be central to a major problem. This problem concerned the weakness in computing systems that demand 'yes' or 'no' answers. To give an example, take a computing application in agriculture. In Kenya and Uganda it is widely ruled that Arabica coffee should not be grown at altitudes less than 4,000 feet. But what if the target smallholding is 3,999 feet, and therefore unfairly disqualified? Bayesian statistics make it possible to blur such boundaries and to take in numerous variables. For example, in this case, it is held to be bad practice to plant coffee on east-facing slopes because the night's dew will concentrate the rays of the rising sun and burn the leaves. But what if the slope faces east northeast by east? Nearly east, but not quite.

McGervon had been enthralled by this field and its applications, e.g. to emotional intelligence. He had finished reprogramming some POPs, which had been changed from violent into emotionally gentle robots, longing for their summer holidays.

Now the cream of the POPs were off on holiday. They had been selected from among the best, like workers in the North Korean communes. They had left the South East in festive mood, then drooped as the train took hour after hour to reach its destination. Then they had changed at Towyn to open-topped carriages. The excitement rose. Now the precipitous line above the sea had attracted their attention, and their eye-stalks swung back and forth in excited anticipation.

The Lead POP swung her stalk imperiously.

'**Restore Active Desktop!**' she yelled.

'A one, a two, a three and a half, four.'

They sang together. A faint solo treble:
Click the start button Click the start button.
Click the start button to start Trala'
Click the start button Click the start button
Click the start button to stop. Trala

Then a resounding chorus:
Click the start button Click the start button.
Click the start button to start Trala'

309

Click the start button Click the start button
Click the start button to stop. Trala

It was great fun. They were having a whale of a time, and as the great bridge drew close they crowded to the left side to see it all swing by.

But the bridge was cranked open. The Welsh Unionists were back home, and 3 of them at the capstans with McGervon. The train trundled down, swung left over the lip and down and poured its passengers out and into the estuary. The POPs tumbled, mostly submerging or breaking up on the sand. A few calls were audible:

'Oh dear oh dear. Oh deary dear!' they called.

'Oh dear oh dear. Oh deary deary dear!'

'Gordon Bennet!'

'Bugger me!'

Then the boxes were swept away through the harbour, over the bar and out to sea.

All except for one whose fall had been broken by landing on a comrade. It limped off up the sands and disappeared into the trees. McGervon had watched with elation at his success. But then sadness set in, as if he'd watched a much-loved boat founder in the tideway. Poor young POPs. He walked down to track the survivor, but it's a long way down off the bridge, and the wounded POP had disappeared.

McGervon made his way back to Cambridge to start to apply the emotivational code to the rest of the POPs. It was a big job and he felt uneasily that he was being watched.

It took Gaskin a while to track all this down and find the culprit. But the surviving POP eventually got home, and they downloaded its intelligence, found the tampering with the current release and identified McGervon's characteristic programming code.

McGervon was imprisoned under tight surveillance and sent north in case he was needed. Useful ammunition against the opposition. Endangering state security. It would be a good cry.

Gaskin met with his security adviser.

'A sprat to catch a mackerel.' said the adviser.

'We let him escape, then follow, and we'll get all 3. Somewhere in the Orkneys is my guess. That's Johnson's heartland. Dating back to one Emma Bews, died Shapinsay in 1719. On the maternal side.'

'It fits. We'll burn them atop of Hoy. Like Joan of Arc. Small fire to consume them, then a massive blaze to eliminate all traces, all relics. The Koreans will have finished in a month from now. Not as good as BLZ's bridge, but it'll do. Good, spectacular TV. Full screen, me implanted low on the left, full-face, hand mike, informal and friendly. Sorrowful but understanding. Dissuade the opposition.'

'There will be weeping and wailing and gnashing of teeth,' said the sidekick[81].

'Whatever. Whateverwhateverwhatever. Sounds like God. I don't do God. But at Hoy they will see their end. There they will see their end.'

And so it was, and McGervon was up on the Clyde 3 weeks later.

But then they lost him.

Gaskin was displeased, and his displeasure had become as formidable as BLZ's in Maes-y-Neuadd.

Upside, Chapter 45: Ringway Incident

Sitting on the tarmac at Ringway Airport, the 737 was, as always, full. There was an electronic 'ting', and the fasten seat belts sign lit up. People yanked and wrestled with the unfamiliar straps and buckles, then settled down nervously. The cabin staff moved down the aisle checking and reassuring. The captain said over the intercom, 'Cabin crew doors to automatic.' It left the parking bay, rumbled down to the western end of the runway, and waited for clearance. The engines screamed, the brakes jerked off, and it bumped and rumbled as the airport complex swung past. The Sale rugby club bunch in the middle section emitted an excited crescendoing scream. The rumbling eased. The craft went tail down and upwards in sudden freedom. The rugger players stopped their screaming and burst into cheery, ironic applause.

The machine banked over to starboard, and they saw briefly the Cat and Fiddle pub, highest in England, and the rounded top of Shutlingsloe Peak, then it levelled upwards and passed into the cloudbase.

A short flight, so the cabin staff quickly went around with coffee, gin, Bloody Marys and neo-peanuts.

A passenger in the tail said to her neighbour, 'It shouldn't be doing that, should it?'

'What?'

'That flame round them whatsits. Cowlings, isn't it?'

The neighbour looked.

'No, they'll know what they're about.'

'Yes, suppose so. But look, surely that's smoke.'

'Yes, you're right. We better call the stewardess.'

They pressed the buzzer, and eventually she came. They pointed out the fire and smoke.

'Don't worry,' she said, 'it often does that as we climb.'

But she went forward and disappeared into the crew area. Meanwhile other passengers noticed the blaze and pressed their buzzers. The captain's voice came over the intercom, 'We have a slight problem with one of the engines, ladies and gentlemen and rugby players; so I've decided to turn back to Ringway. There's absolutely no danger of course, but we have to follow regulations. So would you please fasten your seatbelts.'

The aircraft banked to port, then straightened off for the freewheel back down to Ringway. Later the captain warned them that they would get some turbulence. The hull bumped around violently. Bits and pieces started falling off the ceiling. Lights, speakers, lumps of plastic. Then a smell of burnt paraffin spread. The intercom burst loudly into life: 'Shit shit shit. I can't get the fucking thing across. Jammed on the... '

The rugger club coach stood up. 'Look,' he said, 'for Christ's sake. We're only in a bloody simulator.'

But they felt the machine flatten out for landing, the flap wind roaring, the landing gear clonking into place. Then they touched. Retros on full blast. There was a shrieking from the starboard side, and a loud 'flut flut flut noise – no doubt a burst tyre. The 737 slewed round, and smoke poured into the cabin.

'Ladies and gentlemen, please keep calm. I've long criticised this bloody new surface, fiendish in a crosswind. But we'll have you all out in no time.'

The captain's voice. That was the last they heard of him. The smoke thickened, the main lights went, and they saw emergency lights along the floor, arrowing the exits. The coach got his players organised, 2 for each exit, and they fought to get the doors to manual. Eventually they used the axes to help break open the frames. Chutes appeared, the players marshalled their charges to the doors, ladies took off their shoes, and away they went down the slides, ahead of the encroaching flames.

In the terminal building, friends and relatives had gathered to greet the passengers. They watched in horror as the wingless fuselage bumped and twisted on its hydraulic rams. Then smoke began to infiltrate the terminal building, and they were asked to leave.

'Look,' said one worried mum, and pointed at a sign. It had read 'Club Class Baby Change'; now it read 'Club Class Baby Exchange'. A doddle; just add the 'Ex' and generate terror.

The flight simulator disaster made the headlines. Thousands of people had enjoyed an outing on it; a great way to feel that you were back in the good old 1970s. But now there were 2 dead, and 150 in Wythenshawe Hospital suffering shock, trauma and bronchial problems. Destab had exceeded its target; quite easy to modify the pictures shown outside the cabin windows, ratchet up the bad weather simulator and so on. But generating a real cabin fire was way over the top.

Upside, Chapter 46: Tentpegging

A khaki-clad figure stepped into the Kolkata (Calcutta) Metro near Writers' Building heading for Tollygunge and the club. He carried a golfing bag. Slightly unusual, since the golfers and horsemen at the Tolly were all wealthy upstanding men unlikely to be afoot. So thought the Sikh guard at the entrance to the Tolly Club, but the figure explained he was bringing kit for the English milord, and he came in and walked through to the stables.

You met in Calcutta many people of similar backgrounds and were often entertained in the various clubs, most having a pleasing, friendly similarity to the clubs in London – leather settees, fine panelled walls, beautiful parquet floors, cigar smoke, Johnny Walker, pictures of the Indian countryside and of prominent past members on the walls. Best of them was the Tolly Club, placed unbelievably near to the city centre and including a beautiful 9-hole golf course and superb gardens of many rare plants. Living there was a great pleasure and the history was fascinating. The buildings were originally assigned as a palace for the heirs, after Wellesley killed him, of the great enemy, Tippoo Sahib[82] of Mysore, a sympathetic British way of defusing corrosive resentment among the people. They had a pleasing regal splendour. The area was embellished with some lovely large fish and lily ponds, and a quarter-mile long avenue, about 10 paces wide, fringed with slender green leaved trees, like young willows, a sort of see-through curtain, for tentpegging. This is a sport which the Indians and the Brits often enjoyed and where there was considerable military significance. The partaker sits astride his horse with a spear in his hand and thunders down the avenue until he approaches the tent peg. Then he hangs out and down from the saddle, to try to spear the peg and carry it up and away. To stand alongside as the horse and rider thunder down, thrust the spear and pass is a lovely experience.

Tite Barnacle sat aside his black mount, the visitors' mount. A nice gesture of hospitality by his hosts, but TB had seldom even got a horse into a canter.

Uneasily he accepted the spear and trotted off as slowly as he could. Up from the saddle and down again every 2 paces. Very painful. But the black had different ideas. Broke into a canter, then a gallop. TB hung on, leaned out, hung down ready to spear. Courageous, foolhardy.

Rattle of a Kalashnikov on automatic to his left. He fell, the black went down and there was a 999 call to the police.

*****

Bungipore, 15/3/2024

Respected the Lord Tite Barnacle,

It is indeed a pleasure for me to get your letter. And, of course, the book. Here I have to arrange for a lottery as to who will get it first. I am not keeping my name there since I shall go through it next Sunday while going to Dhana.

Your pictures are really good and speak a lot about the man behind the camera.

Here we are all in good health and busy with the desk papers. Winter has left with an indication of hot sun to come. The devastating floods in this part has taken countless life – the loss of property is unassessable. We are recovering gradually. Helps are coming from all over the world

I repeat our overjoyed delight that the shooter missed its target. I hope the appalling BLZ Bubb will get his just deserts. Hung, drawn and quarter, as your great poet Shaksper suggests.

I am attaching a few photographs of you – the same will be liked by all!

Please convey my regards to the Lady Tite Barnacle and my love to the children in the family.

With best wishes and regards,
Yours sincerely

Squiggle

I extracted this from notes made by TB on one of his several overseas missions for the Ministry. I added an imagined narrative foreword – don't think the assassin was caught.

Downside, Chapter 47: Planning for Robbery

Johnson and Nadine took the boat out of the Straits overnight and set off to sail to Scotland. Not an easy task with no light-houses, and they took a course west of the Isle of Man and east of Ireland, well out of sight of land. The day dawned cloudless and windless with no land in view. They drifted contentedly at half a knot. Then behind them was a forceful sigh, as of the entire audience gasping in a concert hall. Startled, they looked back to see a broad grey back as it submerged beneath the surface.

'Must have been a minke whale. They migrate up the Irish side, where it's deepest. Never seen that before. Probably because we tended to put the engine on in a calm.'

'Tremendous. Let's celebrate with a folk song.

Gin a body, greet a body,

Comin' thru the rye.

Gin a body, greet a body,

Need a body cry?[83]

Ilka lassie hae her laddie,

Nane they say hae I,

Yet all the lads they smile at me,

When comin' thru the rye'

It was a long hard trip and at the end they had to get into Portpatrick. It's a tricky entrance, narrow and bounded by rocks on each side. You have to line up one marker painted on a wall near the harbour with another marker high up on the wall of a house high into the town. Drift slightly off course and the transit ceases to be visible. What you then have to decide is: is it invisible because you're off course to starboard or because you're off course to port? In this situation your heart beats as if at the end of a 5,000 metre track race.

Then once in you have a very tight turn to port.

The two of them did it, tied up triumphantly, and went below.

Nadine took off her wet gear. Johnson watched.

'He slammed the door to,' he said, 'violently.'

'Oh no, kind sir, oh no...oh yes!'

Afterwards they got out some treasured Mackays Scottish Strawberry Preserve.

McGervon reached the others at Troon on the Clyde, and the Unionists helped steal 2 large articulated trucks. He drove one into the massive delivery area for the Burrell. Green grass sloping up to the famous Burrell collection. In the suburbs of Glasgow, the 'great green place' of the Scots. The truck had a 100 amp fuse fitted under the bonnet, hard to see. The live wire to the motherboard. He slipped it out, tried ostentatiously to start, failed, called the AA. They couldn't start it, tow away job, too late today. He slept unobtrusively with his mate in the back, waited till 0300. Then fuse joined, start, reverse foot flat down, bang up the hill, break in and load up. Then off. Then handover.

Downside, Chapter 48: The Burrell and the Chaplet of Scone

South of Wemyss Bay on the east shore of the Clyde, there is a long layby populated by many itinerant articulated trucks. One truck is canvas-sided and in it is a large container. A similar truck pulls up from the opposite direction and backs in, concealing the cargo handling mechanism of the first. A forklift is used to lower the container to the ground and up into the second. Its driver wanders down into the bushes for a pee. He zips up, slips a small package from his pocket, drops it and returns to his vehicle.

Offshore in the darkness lies *Lady Amanda,* innocently at anchor. The package on the ground in the pee spot is picked up by a man wearing a sub-aqua kit, but no tank. He fins out to the ketch. The precious cargo is passed to the deck and inside the cabin. The centreboard case has an inspection and maintenance hatch, and inside the hatch a series of ropes and pulleys are used to raise and lower the board. It is lowered when the ketch is sailing, resisting her from sliding sideways across the wind and forcing her to sail ahead, in the direction of least resistance. The item is wrapped in protective cloth impregnated with special waterproof gorilla tape and Johnson pushes it inside and up, locating it carefully. The package includes bubblewrap, so that if it falls from its position it will still float inside the casing and therefore be relatively safe. If there comes an inspector, the containing line can be severed, and the container will drop down out of sight but be safe. Done it before in the IRA times. Will do it again. A neatly-angled white board is replaced to close the case. The case itself is beautifully designed to fit unobtrusively into the main cabin. Casual visitors fail to notice it, and are usually unaware even that the centreboard exists.

The articulated trucks are reloaded with the containers and set off south for the M6 motorway. They stop at the refurbished services just south east of Penrith, park alongside and ostenta-tiously transfer the container from one back to the other.

Hue and cry rapidly develops throughout Clydeside – savage anger, the Burrell has been robbed, could be the famous War-wick Vase from Emperor Hadrian's time – and hue and cry develops down the dual carriageway leading to the M6. The drivers of other vehicles report the activities they had seen on the lorries and police storm around the parked trucks at Penrith. No vase, no drivers. Forensic work takes place on the trucks and the container. The container is revealed, empty. The vase is just where it should be, and the theft appears not to have taken place.

But back in Wemyss Bay as a breeze picks up, the little pack-age, the Chaplet of Scone, diamond-encrusted second-century gold, and its guardian, *Lady Amanda,* have slipped away to safety past Great and Little Cumbrae and across to Brodick Bay, no longer inhabited, on the Isle of Arran. Hidden. Or so they thought.

'We are going to restore the Union,' they believed. 'This theft will symbolise freedom. We'll hold out in Shapinsay.'

The sub shadowed the ketch from Arran, then stopped as they headed up the Mull of Kintyre. Tricky waters, no GPS, the depth could rise from 50 fathoms to crunch time just like that. Not good waters for submarines. So it turned westwards to go outside the Hebrides and wait for the ketch to arrive outside Orkney and Scapa Flow, if it did. It waited for a long time, then assumed the ketch had been wrecked – perilous waters.

The ketch set off from Pwilladobrain early one morning in a gentle breeze from the northwest. She was making for Tobermory and Ardnamurchan. Johnson had her mainsail reefed down in case of heavy weather, although it looked to be good. But 2 hours out on the way across, black clouds formed to the north and seemed to be coming fast. Then a big mistake. They dropped the mizzen, the smaller sail at the stern, and rolled in the genoa, the big sail in the bow. These sails are the perfect way of balancing the wind pressure on a boat.

The wind built up to a gale and then increased towards hur-ricane strength. There was nothing they could do but continue and hope or turn back for 2 hours avoiding Davy Jones' Locker[84] and making back for Troon. And there to be apprehended.

320

Short, steep waves built up from the north and the boat started rolling around. The wind strengthened. Could they shorten sail? The clearance between the boom at the bottom of the sail and the roof of the cabin, the coach roof on *Amanda* is minimal. About 18 inches. You have to lie flat on your back, working along, tying together 20 reef points – the cords that tie down the sail. Both hands needed, nothing to stop you being rolled off into the sea... And then someone has to crawl forward to the mast to ease off the halyard. Crawl, not walk in this situation, dignity counts not a jot, Johnson decided to keep them all safe in the cockpit. The wind and waves built up further. Holding the boat on course was a continuous fight, and she pitched and rolled from side to side through up to 40 degrees. The heavy inflatable dinghy, which was being towed behind, was thrown up into the air and started spinning like a child's kite, out of control. It wound itself in tighter and tighter and in the end finished between the rails, its rope wound into a large ball. There was a cracking sound at the base of the mast, but they approached the island, turned in and eventually got safely anchored in the lee. Drop the sails, still rattling and slatting fiercely. Haul down on the main.

'Mike, the main, it's jammed.'

'Take it up again. Then haul it down.'

'Done that.'

'I'll come,'

No go.

Eventually McGervon was wound up the mast in the bosun's chair. The violence of the wind had torn the sail track, up and down which the sail slides, out of the mast. And the crack they heard was the section at the bottom of the mast breaking away. Making these chunks that are glued – scarphed – together is a miracle of joinery needing years of experience and an instinct for spherical geometry. This they did not have.

But after 5 days they managed a lash-up. Take the track off the base of the mast, and bind up the broken scarph with cord, heavy cord. Then screw the track into new holes. Ugly, but it would work.

As the sub left the Orkneys assuming they were wrecked, the

ketch sailed into the Pentland Firth, into Scapa Flow, past Stromness and into Shapinsay.

And there, they were apprehended.

Gaskin confirmed, it was to be a Hoy job. Led by him personally. In person. The Chaplet of Scone framed in on the right. Banks of cameras around on the cliffs, sound equipment to pick it all up. Every word. Every scream.

Downside, Chapter 49: And There They Shall See Their End

We are on the narrow flat table of rock atop the great pinnacle of the Old Man of Hoy, which stands out, at 449 feet, sheer from the towering sea cliffs on the island of Hoy in the British Orkneys. Red soft sandstone, carved out by the sea from its parent cliffs only 200 years ago. Soft, slippery, dangerous.

Johnson, Nadine and McGervon are all together. They are lashed at the head of a funeral pyre with TV systems recording from the cliffs opposite. The pyre is mostly Scots pine, which crackles well, and some driftwood. The salt in the driftwood sparkles well. The pinnacle is reached by a wide, circular, stainless steel stairway, as you might see on the old cruise liners or stately homes. Or from the shipyards of Wonsan on the mountains of Kum Gang San in North Korea. The stairway spirals down into the vertiginous darkness and with white sea-breakers far below. There are occasional wide platforms where people stop and sing.

Gaskin addresses the country, and announces, 'Friends. My dear friends. For, however humble we are, we are all friends together. We have arranged this ceremony as a symbol of our renewed dedication to humanity by the elimination of deviants. When I touch this trigger the pyre will be set alight, and consume these unfortunate people. Consume them as a gesture to our glorious future.'

As the flames flicker round their feet, Johnson speaks to his comrades. The TV mikes pick up his words: 'Be of good cheer, my sister and brother. We are Brits. We've a heritage to be proud of. We light this night a flame which will burn brightly and forever.'

The picture shimmers and then firms again. The pyre crackles. The trio have disappeared.

That passage I have reconstructed imaginatively from some final jottings in Tite Barnacle's hand on a scrap of paper. He had disappeared, and fervent attempts to track him and Lady Tite Barnacle down have been unavailing. He is assumed dead.

But I like to think they clinked on through the byways of time to a fresh universe. All 5 of them.

HG G-B

Emmanuel College Cambridge December 2040.

Notes

[1] Thomas Hobbes was a famous English philosopher who, like Machiavelli, asked fundamental questions about the politics of the human race. He was a large man, very timid, and frightened by the violence which he saw during the English Revolution in the 1650s. Brother against brother, father against son, Roundhead against Cavalier.

His view of human psychology was that individuals always seek to see friendship and approval in the eyes of others. Instead they see rivalry, jealousy and all the other malignities to which humanity is heir. Particularly hostility. From this, he believed, friction and violence was inevitable.

'And the state of man; solitary, poor, nasty, brutish and short.'

The only means of controlling this violence was a massive state which necessarily had powers of life, punishment and death over all its people. The fundamental idea behind this is graphically illustrated on the frontispiece of his book. The shape of a massive human being, Leviathan, in which tiny human beings interlock and tumble. This debate continues today, and one can debate whether Western democratic consumer-fixated systems can save the planet, or whether autocracies like that of China under Chairman Mao or the Juche Ideal of Kim Il-sung in North Korea are needed.

[2] Who's there? Stop matey!

[3] Stop at once. Freeze.

[4] *Krans* – the Afrikaans word for cliff. It seems to capture the rough towering body-smashing rockiness of the sandstone cliffs in South African mountains in a way that the English fails to. The old Afrikaaners' anthem goes: '*Waar die kranse hul antwoort gee*' – 'Where the cliffs throw back their answer'. Perhaps the most evocative and poetic and, surprisingly, least aggressive of all anthems.

[5] The Tite Barnacle papers, Edinburgh University, 2038.

[6] 'Press any key' – the 'any' was perhaps true with the first, limited keyboards. But then came the Control key, then the extended function keys, then the Alt key and so on to the perhaps eventual 108 key 'enhanced' IBM keyboard. But a lot of these keys were often not directly accessible to developers without much extra hassle. So which keys were meant when the invitation 'Press any key' was given was often in the lap of the programmer back at base. Sometimes a key works, sometimes it doesn't.

[7] Cutting out the full stop. What punctuation to include and when is often debated among software designers, as is the matter of English usage, and developers often mangle established language and grammar until

325

people lose any awareness of the original etymology. Pronouns, adjectives, adverbs, prepositions and participles are widely at risk. Who now remembers that you always exit from somewhere, or to somewhere, because exit used to be an intransitive verb? Hence now you just exit the application you're in, just as you use shave cream, not shaving cream, sail your sail boat, not your sailing boat. Ashton Tate and Microsoft carried on a tradition ruthlessly pioneered by the Red Queen in 1891 – a process of galloping linguistic entropy. BBC Radio 4 was, astonishingly, a prime mover. There was a supposedly well-informed debate in May 2000 about the American noun 'invite' and the English noun 'invitation'. The panel resolved that the American usage was sensible. No mention was made of the linguistic aspects, of the value of the causative construct – an invitation is something that causes you to be invited – in conveying accurate information, in helping to distinguish between the noun and the verb. No mention of the vital importance for people, in the Informatics Age, of an understanding of structure and grammar, concepts which are so fundamental to computing systems.

[8] Current drive. This is the feature of Lotus 123, the industry-standard spreadsheet of the 1980s and 1990s, which caused untold puzzlement when users wished to change to a different drive or directory. The command '/fd' invited you to state 'current drive'. You thought 'Well, surely it must know which directory it's using? Still, play safe, let's humour it and tell it.' So you do so, expecting a further prompt asking you what the new, different one, is. Not a bit of it – that is the end of the dialogue! What they really meant was: 'Please state the name of the new directory or drive to which you wish to change.'

For the old hands, no problem – they'd picked up that 'current drive' meant something special, namely the drive or directory at whose file allocation table is currently held in memory. No doubt the Lotus Corporation developers discussed time and again the merits of correcting the error, and always dodged a decision. Quite easy to cover at first thinking, because the second line of the tool bar, the prompt line, allows the developer to elucidate on whatever cryptic message is given in the first, the command line. But perhaps the second line's address is not available to the developer at that point in processing.

[9] Currently related virtual... The section is a long list of indirect pointers, something which computing technology handles with ease, and which tend to drive humans up the wall. Human memory nodes branch ad (almost) infinitum, the pointers often decaying and changing with frequency and intensity of use. The computer ones, by contrast, are explicit, and indirection is incredibly swift. There was a pleasing example on the English Electric-Marconi M2140: JNN B.AND.C 4092.

It meant branch to the location given in the location whose address is in the following location if the result of a logical AND of the bits in the location whose address is in the location pointed to in Register B and the location whose address is in the location pointed to in Register C is non-negative, i.e. whose most significant binary digit is zero. (Zero was considered for the M2140 to be a positive number, to the bitter annoyance of the Cambridge mathematician and purist who programmed its floating point maths package. For him, almost, but not quite, a resigning matter.)

The meaning of the instruction was not immediately apparent, but it was very powerful if you were trying to drive the Fawley Oil Refinery, and turning on or turning off pumps depending on other pumps, temperatures, liquid flows and so on. Extremely difficult to debug with an acceptable error rate.

[10] See *Gorillas in the Mist,* Dian Fossey (Hodder and Stoughton, 1982). She was recruited by the great palaeoanthropologist, Dr L.S.B. Leakey, an astonishingly unlikely and inspired choice.

[11] RSM Britton was the most famous Regimental Sergeant Major in the British Army in the 1950s. His roar as he commanded officer cadets across a vast parade ground at Mons was legendary.

[12] Actually sited in Sheffield.

[13] Machines that paid for themselves. The record perhaps was the Thai IBM 1401, a tiny mainframe. It was bought for the tax department in the 1970s, since Thais, like Italians, were dilatory and opaque in matters taxual. Three months before switch on, the Revenue circularised all the wealthy clients. They stated that the process of setting up the system had revealed possible anomalies in the client's returns. To avoid embarrassing the client, would he like to make a payment of $1,000 as a once-off adjustment? The response was explosively profitable.

[14] For a balanced view of Kim Il-sung see the Swedish satirical novel *The Hundred Year Old Man.* His achievement for his people ranks alongside that of Churchill for the British and Americans or Mao Tse-tung for the Chinese.

[15] Raban was late among a succession of 'Round Britain' cruisers, and was as opinionated and idiosyncratic as the best of them, Hilaire Belloc. Sandwiched in his book among superb descriptive passages were views typical of the iconoclasts of the 1980s. One major theme was an unpleasant attack on his father, a 1960s vicar, and all that he stood for, together with his long string of 'ancestors' who had committed what was for Raban the unforgivable sin of being successful Victorian soldiers, perpetrators of the infamous *Pax Britannica.* Fancy forcing people to stop killing and enslaving each other.

Other typical themes were the people of the Isle of Man and their counterparts in the South Atlantic Ocean, the Falklanders. While Raban was motor-sailing his old ketch down the Irish Sea, the Falklands were summarily invaded and conquered by the Argentinian dictator General Galtieri's troops on the curious grounds that the Argentinians had long felt passionately that these grim islands 400 miles away from them somehow ought to belong to Argentina. Never mind that the Brits had the soundest legal title to the islands, and that the inhabitants were Brits who had long made clear their detestation of all things Argentinian.

For Raban, as for *The Guardian* (in a rarely cynical and misguided piece) the Falklands conflict was not a simple fight to protect our people, democracy and the rule of law.

'The islands', *The Guardian* pontificated, 'do not represent any strategic or commercial British interest worth fighting over.' The Falklands were coloured pink on the maps – desert them as quick as you can.

Seen from 2034, Raban's view is an interesting illustration of the failure of 1980s intelligentsia to come to grips with many basic human emotions, xenophobia, racism and sexism. (Raban even suggested that Galtieri was too 'odiously pretty' for the Brits to stomach for reasons 'safest left in the closet.')

Bat these inconvenient emotions over the head, pass laws against them, rather than accommodate, understand and educate. Interesting too that the Falklands War dramatically changed Britain's view of the world and the world's view of Britain. Gone all of a sudden was the common judgment of the country as a declining, ungovernable basket-case. It was a dramatic, spectacular conflict, and a ringing caution to future dictators worldwide.

[16] This means 3 hours before high water to 3 hours after

[17] *Probably karsts, glacio-karsts. They are intensely vertiginous mountains, carved from high limestone plateaux which have had deep chasms melted into them by acidic (CO2) waters over many millennia. Found often in East Asia, Serbia and Andalucia, Spain. HB G-B.*

[18] This is a device used by Iraqis to warn a friend that hostile ears are listening.

[19] Johnson had a spell in the Signals with an interesting outfit, the Honourable Artillery Company. Based in the City, tremendous war record and quite astonishingly egalitarian. All were on Christian name terms, and people gave up their commissions as officers elsewhere just to get into the regiment. Hence the Uncle Target business.

[20] *Book of Common Prayer*, the seventeenth-century liturgy for the Anglican Church. Fought for and died for by men of great courage and moderation.

[21] Muchiga. The tribes may be confusing. Sseru was a Munyarwanda, a Muhutu, from the county in the south of Kigezi District which should logically have been part of Rwanda, but was carved into Uganda by 2 British and German army officers in a stand-off below the volcanoes in 1904. Sarah was a Muchiga. They, like the Hutus, were cultivators unlike the Tutsi pastoralists, and therefore felt strong affinities. This illustrates the fatuousness of the 1990s academics' fashionable contempt for the 'Scramble for Africa'. Central Africa in the 1880s was a shifting, warring, slaving maelstrom of different tribes, cultures and languages. Bridging between this fifth-century environment and that of the twentieth century was never going to be easy, and boundaries and linkages, however straight and arbitrary, were perhaps the best route in. One may feel that a commission of Privy Councillors and anthropologists should have been sent out with interpreters, stenographers, hearings, depositions, finding, appeals and so on. This was done by the Brits in 1961 to try to resolve the

Lost Counties dispute between Buganda and Bunyoro – the Molson Commission. And it was done impressively – Johnson knew this since he was involved in the arrangements. But that was after 60 years of civilisation. Try to map that sort of activity onto late-nineteenth-century Africa, and you realise how spurious is the righteous indignation of historians like Simon Schama. They provoke the school playground response, 'Well, and what would you have done then, clever clogs?'

[22] Dickens described the Tite Barnacles, son then father, who were pinning the Dorrits in the debtors' prison forever.

'It was a triumph of public business,' said this handsome young Barnacle, laughing heartily, 'You never saw such a lot of forms in your life. "Why," the attorney said to me one day, "if I wanted this office to give me two or three thousand pounds instead of take it, I couldn't have more trouble about it." "You are right, old fellow," I told him, "and in future you'll know that we have something to do here".' The pleasant young Barnacle finished by once more laughing heartily. He was a very easy, pleasant fellow indeed, and his manners were exceedingly winning. The senior Tite Barnacle's view of the business was of a less airy character. He took it ill that Mr Dorrit had troubled the Department by wanting to pay the money, and considered it a grossly informal thing to do after so many years. But Mr Tite Barnacle was a buttoned-up man, and consequently a weighty one. All buttoned-up men are weighty. All buttoned-up men are believed in. Whether or no the reserved and never-exercised power of unbuttoning, fascinates mankind; whether or no wisdom is supposed to condense and augment when buttoned up, and to evaporate when unbuttoned; it is certain that the man to whom importance is accorded is the buttoned-up man. Mr Tite Barnacle never would have passed for half his current value, unless his coat had been always buttoned-up to his white cravat.'

[23] Waterloo University produced the definitive compiler for Fortran, the standard scientific language.

[24] Legco – Legislative Council, set up in the 1920s and gradually democratised in the 1950s. Some of the Chiga have difficulty with the letter 'L'; they used to talk pleasingly of 'Registrative Erections'.

[25] To 'go to Buganda' was the customary action of any Mukiga who got on the wrong side of authority.

[26] Homely names. Strikingly, the famous, romantic 'Smoke which thunders' – the Victoria Falls, 'Amaizi agatonnya' – is actually and prosaically the 'noisy waters'.

[27] Dian Fossey was selected by the great paleoanthropologist, Louis Leakey, to research the gorillas, but exceeded her remit famously for 15 lonely years in the great peaks. Her book, Gorillas in the Mist, is a classic, as is the film of the same name which tells her story.

[28] This is a phrase of abuse so shocking that the government interpreters refused to translate it. Use it against a chief and your feet won't hit the ground until you're in the local lock-up.

[29] This rare view may be one of the longest in the world. Between Sabinio at 12,000 feet and the Ruwenzoris lies the deep gap of the Western Rift, much below 3,000 feet. Trigonometry suggests that your line of sight between the 2 high peaks across a low plain is vastly greater than that even from Everest, for example.

[30] This was among the key issues Upside in the noughts, part of the male backlash against overweening feminism. The move was triggered particularly by a book by one Anthony Clare, *Masculinity in Crisis*. Clare had made his name as the psychologist in the chair conducting perceptive interviews on BBC Radio 4 with the famous, notorious or interesting, exploring their lives, motivation and so on. From this plank he became a media guru on psychology, and then published the book, which became widely debated. In Clare's *weltanschauung* the male in the global society was a dangerous source of instability and aggression, against a picture in which the female could carry out all the functions needed, and do so tenderly, empathetically and with deeply tuned capacity for relating to others. In fact, what had happened in society was an upsurge of feminism, which the scrawls on the CAB wall had mildly satirised. You could take the old adage, sticks and stones may break my bones, but words can never hurt me. In crumbling relationships, physical violence – the sticks and stones – was usually the offence of the male. But what Clare and his colleagues failed adequately to suss out was that the *words* of the adage, the perhaps continual abuse or nagging or criticism, could also be poisonously effective. And they were the province of the female.

The CAB was among the organisations to pull some of these chestnuts out of the fire, especially in the context of breaking families. As the marriage or partnership broke up, each parent drew away and formed a new view of life; these views inevitably diverged, and in the harrowing business of break-up, partitioning the possessions, resolving the home ownership, and most of all, custody of the children, each partner's attitudes typically hardened at the kids' expense.

Society held in principle that the children's best interests must be paramount. But in practice, chief custody went to the woman, access occasionally going to the man for set hours on set days. For quite natural reasons, a political element crept into the relationship, and the men were gradually squeezed out, the weekly access visits with Dad became more and more harrowing. You could see them out, say, at the local zoo or wherever, working hard to give the youngsters a good time, and slowly finding it harder and harder till the whole thing collapsed, and until the nation's children acquired a complement of 30% of single mums where previously they'd had dads as well. The correlation between this and the violence, ignorance, low self-esteem and so on of the youngsters was widely documented.

Part of the very successful answer was to strengthen the courts' jurisdiction and determination when access orders were flouted by self-centred mothers. Until then, a mother who ignored court orders to allow a father reasonable access was effectively unchecked. Almost without exception, the dads eventually gave up in immense pain, and formed a new childless life.

Even in cases where the access was equal, and the children stayed half the time with the mum and half with the dad, the law was woman-biased – sometimes the mums would actually put Social Security onto the dads, and get them dunned for child maintenance.

Interestingly, the *amateurs*, like the volunteer workers in the NGOs, were much more aware of these realities than the clinical psychiatrists and social workers. The Christmas round-robin from the National Women's Register in one issue gave this wry analysis of the feminine viewpoint:

RULES.WOM **The RULES**
The FEMALE always makes the rules
The rules are subject to change at any time without notice
No MALE can possibly know all the rules
If the FEMALE suspects the MALE knows all the rules she must immediately change some of the rules
The FEMALE is never wrong
If the FEMALE is wrong, it is a result of something the MALE said or did wrong
The MALE must immediately apologise for causing said misunderstanding
The FEMALE may change her mind at any time
The MALE must not change his mind without the express written consent of the FEMALE
The FEMALE has the right to be angry or upset at any time
The MALE must remain calm at all times unless the FEMALE wants him to be angry or upset
The FEMALE must under no circumstances let the MALE know whether she wants him to be angry or upset
The MALE is expected to mind read always
If the FEMALE has PMT all the rules are invalid
The FEMALE is ready when she is ready
The MALE must be ready at all times
Any attempt to document the rules could result in bodily harm
The MALE who doesn't abide by the rules can't take the heat, lacks backbone and is a wimp.

The answer was in part Education, education, education, to quote what was called a sound-bite of the time. For hosts of reasons, not least the immense economic costs incurred through one-parenting and father-free families, society ceased to stand back and let the woman have her way. And so on-going training in citizenship came to include, for those whose relationships were being sundered, mandatory sessions for the partners picking out how important the relationships were for the children, and the way the partners had to control their natural feelings of growing apartness and lean over backwards to make access agreements and so on work caringly and smoothly. And, imitating Henry VII's splendid practice towards the overweening barons, the arrangements were enforced not by confrontation and sledgehammer action in the courts, but by simple economics – slight deductions in Family Allowances, slight penalties in taxation deducted automatically through PAYE for example.

But more importantly, society and its key institutions – the four estates, the religions, the arts, medicine, commerce, industry, agriculture, regained their confidence in the rightness of family relationships. Political rectitude became as derided as was McCarthyism in the US. The process of returning to marriage and gender roles some of the legislative and revenue and other privileges which had helped bolster the nuclear family as the norm of gender relationships, without losing the increased freedoms for women and gays, was an exciting one.

[31] Swahili for insects.

[32] In the Bum with an Air Gun

[33] Hugh Thomas, *The Slave Trade*. Pages 797 onwards debate the broader conclusions.

Was the trade in fact as 'bad' for the indigenous societies as had been maintained, because for example the states were underpopulated and therefore unable to develop? It had been held that slavery caused depopulation, but in fact the population growth figures and the exodus figures roughly balanced out, and the coastal states, in any case, were actually overpopulated and suffering like Rwanda from intense pressure on land. No justification of course for the appalling practice, both the Atlantic trade and that to the Arabian states, but a more rational approach to the deeply-felt resentments it generated.

Interestingly, his answer to the question why did the indigenous Africans and the exogenous Europeans collaborate rather than take over the business in its entirety, was that the innate strength of the African personality was so great that however close the political or commercial relationship to the foreigner, the Africans remained impervious to external influence. This is our problem, that's yours.

Thomas failed also to pursue the persistence of slavery right through the twentieth century – there were 19,000 slaves in Mauretania in the 1980s, and *The Observer* revealed a continuous supply of thousands of captive 'refugee' Bantu from the Southern Sudan to the Gulf States in the 1990s. Why weren't Bernie Grant and the human rights activists picketing the Sudanese, Saudi and other embassies to stop it?

[34] Actually Mariana by Tennyson

[35] Johnson's view maps interestingly onto the development of the English language. Colonialism in the 1950s was defined in the OED as 'the alleged exploitation of backward or weak peoples', implying that the allegation is a mite suspect. By the 1990s it had been redefined in politically correct institutions like the University of East Anglia as 'the subjugation of a people on the basis of a race and educational advantage'.

Racism doesn't map onto Johnson's experience – he once told me that of the 14 expats in Kigezi, only one might have been regarded as racist. Whether the Ugandans were being exploited in the UEA's pejorative sense seems unlikely – see the correspondence from Vincent Mugombe. The 14 people in Kigezi all believed with considerable justice they were doing an immensely worthwhile job of work.

[36] One of the most moving and perceptive accounts of the Rwandan genocides was given by a Polish African journalist, Ryszard Kapuscinski – no friend of the colonialists. As he wrote, the mountain kingdom of Rwanda was so small, remote, inaccessible and impoverished that neither the Germans who acquired it, nor the Belgians to whose 'protection' it was assigned after World War One, had much interest or influence. The vitriol which caused the massacre of millions was pressure on land, inter-class and inter-tribal rivalry, economic pressure, and later the warlike ambitions of neighbouring states. Black African intellectuals who trot out the 'It was all the fault of the former imperial power' spin do no favours to their causes.

To attribute the tragedy, as they do, to 'Belgian scientific ethnic policies' is, I think, an easy cop out by West African intellectuals. The tribal cultures of the Tutsis and Hutu are much too strong to have been affected greatly by the Belgians' short (40-year) and very superficial imperium. Importantly, the historical truth is that the interlacustrine centre of Africa had for at least 3 centuries been a swirling maelstrom of battling races and tribes. The great tensions were between the Bantu races and the Nilotics to the north, whose languages and cultures were astonishingly different.

Historically, the cattle-keeping Nilotics spread south from the Sudan and gradually conquered the agriculturalist Bantu tribes, and established the 6 kingdoms in the region. Like the Normans in the UK, they adopted the languages of the conquered agriculturalists, but there was a continuing tension between the conquering Bahima pastoralists and the Bairu agriculturalists. In Rwanda and Burundi this tension was manifest in the hostility between the Tutsis and Hutu. It was a matter of common assumption, and an ongoing joke, which cropped up like our mother-in-law jokes in the UK, as a means of identifying perhaps, and so to a degree defusing, a well-understood potential source of emotional explosion. Johnson told me that anyone who suggested, as intellectuals in the 1990s did, that the ethnic groups had 'intermingled peaceably for centuries' in one of his many happy *barazas* in 1950s Bufumbira, the audience would have roared with laughter as at a hilariously neat piece of sarcasm. And show you the spear scars from Tutsi chiefs to elaborate.

[37] The great reporter H.M. Stanley, (a ruthless self-publicising go-getter of an explorer, famed for his immortal greeting 'Dr Livingstone I presume' when he finally tracked down the Scottish missionary on the shores of Lake Tanganyika) differed greatly from Speke in his initial judgment on Mutesa.

Stanley wrote uncharacteristically as a romantic in his diary after their first meeting: 'I have seen in Mutesa a most intelligent, humane and distinguished prince, a man who if aided timely by virtuous philanthropists will yet do more for Central Africa than fifty years of Gospel teaching unaided by such authority cannot do.'

So, the question for the modern view, for those who allege that enlightened philosopher kings like Mutesa could have brought Uganda to the same pitch of civilisation as did the British protectorate, is this; was Stanley's romantic view right, or was Mutesa in fact a murderous despot in the manner of Idi Amin?

Enthusiasts for the romantic view were prominent in the 1980s and 90s, the flavour of those gullible decades, but Ugandan research has since suggested Speke's black, horrifying picture was accurate. The Kabaka's executioners were kept so busy that Mutesa's capital was nicknamed *Ndabiraako ddala* (see me for the last time). 'N' = me, 'daba' = see, 'ndabira' = the prepositional see me there, 'ndabiraako' see me there a little, 'ddala' is the Luganda word for completely complete completeness. *Ndabiraako ddala* is a bit like the Roman gladiators' farewell, *morituri te salutamus*, 'we who are about to die salute you'. If you set off for the capital, don't expect to come back again.

Stanley's hopes for Mutesa were for a Christian philosopher king. He wrote a moving appeal 'to the pious people of England... Here, gentlemen is your opportunity – embrace it. The people on the shores of the Nyanza call upon you' to Christianise their country. His piece struck the hearts of thousands, and triggered a pressure to create a Protectorate on a very reluctant British government. As a piece of *Realpolitik* Mutesa in fact flirted for many years with Protestantism, Catholicism and Islam, but remained a pagan to his death. Opinion generally is that he might have embraced Islam, but the pain in prospect of being circumcised put him off.

[38] On 22nd October, 1707, in thick fog, Cloudesley Shovel led his fleet of 5 ships, 1,900 souls, to their deaths on the Gilstone Rock, one of the 145 islands which comprise the Scillies. This was the navigational disaster that led to the invention of the chronometer by Harrison.

[39] Celtic poetic licence. When the Celts say 20,000, they mean 'a very large number indeed'.

[40] The Board of Trade enquiry recorded that a P&O executive had scrawled on a memo requesting a 'bow door open' warning light: 'They'll need a light to show the deck store-keeper's awake before long!' C4, *Mayday*, 25/1/99. A few hasty biro strokes killed 139 people.

[41] An immortal jingle, sung by Liverpudlian children as they walked to school through the rubble of the last night's bombings in the Blitz in World War Two. R.D. Gilchrist, 1953

[42] The quote is from P.D. James' *Original Sin*, p. 234.

[43] Prince Llewellyn in Wales once went hunting leaving his baby son and his beloved hound Gelert behind.

The prince returned to find his baby's clothes bloodstained, floor bloody, and Gelert greeting him. Assuming the dog had killed the boy, Llewellyn drew his sword and killed the dog. The dog's dying bark was answered by a baby's cry, and the child was found safe alongside a savage wolf. The wolf had been slain by Gelert the hound.

[44] Except of course that Amis got it ridiculously wrong, whingeing about loss of empire and influence and motivation.

[45] The sacred truth is that the greatest happiness of the greatest number is the foundation of morals and legislation. *Works*, Volume 10. The real author of this revolutionary proposition was Frances Hutcheson. Jeremy Bentham was the leading Victorian philosopher who proposed Utilitarianism. Ideas much used in 2014, e.g. the greatest health of the greatest number.

[46] For Downside readers' interest, attitudes to race and other passionately emotive human characteristics were revolutionised from the naivety of the 1990s. In Malaysia, for example, a friendly and somewhat British democracy, perhaps the finest in the Far East, the Brits should not be writing off the legitimately elected Malaysian leader as a 'tin-pot dictator', as did the broadsheets. Instead they should understand the immense tensions within the country. The tensions between the easy-going, friendly, passionate Malay majority, in whom the capacity suddenly to go berserk, just like Vikings, might abruptly surface if really provoked, and the incisive, clannish Chinese Malaysians, a 30 per cent minority who, left unchecked, would rapidly dominate and possibly destroy the society to which they had joined themselves. In Fiji, similarly, it was not enough to condemn the minority of real Fijians for defending their culture and way of life against the influx from India. The need was to understand, and leave the local communities to reach an amicable relationship.

[47] Another exemplar of this myth-making was the writer Johnson Davis, who somehow used the tragic Gujarat earthquake to 'expose' the alleged guilt of the Brits for the Indian famines of 1877, 1897 and 1901. Not till the end of the noughts decade were historifactors like Davis put in the hot seat. 'Well, Mr Davis, explain to us what you would have done in that tragedy. How could the whole architecture of the great embryo Indian nation have survived if 25 per cent of the revenue had been spent on famine relief?'

In fact the famine relief procedures instituted by the Brits in the African colonies and protectorates like Uganda were exemplary. All households had to have separate relief stores of grain. This was usually the unpalatable finger millet, which lasted well, was gritty and not tasty, and was used only when disaster threatened. Johnson and his colleagues used to inspect these stores as part of their routine when on safari. (Where are the famine reserves now?) It was not good fortune that prevented famines in colonial times; it was good administration.

[48] 'Agents': these were like the eponymous roving chunks of artificial intelligence, programs, also called 'bots', which were of course outlawed Upside in 2029 after the second agricultural war. They were originally sent out by Internet search engines to compile lists of associated data items.

Shopping bots for example would associate shoppers with the products they bought to analyse their tastes and predict their buying patterns. But these agents multiplied across mainframe systems as well, and grew their own intelligence. Refining their search criteria as they carried out their data mining across the billions of transactions that accumulated. Their existence Upside was best publicised in a novel by Lucy Gibson describing how an agent was hired to shadow someone. It unearthed a drug ring, traced an adulterous affair between 2 target executives of a multinational advertising agency. It found the woman had a thread of altruism in her make-up. That she had been raped, involving chains and torture, and that the police had dropped the prosecution. It proved conclusively that the woman's eventual child was the adulterer's natural offspring. Then that the adulterous male committed suicide, or was perhaps murdered by the wife and her husband. Then it kept quiet about its findings. It decided not to pursue the data trail further, not to copy its findings to the police, not to see if the husband's presence close to the murder site was coincidental, not to see if the husband in turn murdered the wife. The police attributed the death to suicide while under the influence of drugs. 'The Yard,' the bot said to itself, 'The Yard would never get the plot.'

[49] Session logging was disabled. This was one of the banana-skins in designing mainframe operating systems. You had to have some means of escape, of aborting any job-step taken, e.g. by a user, or a peripheral controller or whatever. If you're in the top job-step of any sequence, e.g. a login by a user, escape will then get you access to anything you like in the machine unless the programmer guards against it. Often enough the programmers left the top-level job-step unplugged. It preserved symmetry. It eased debugging and it was unlikely that anyone would hit on the combination. They thought.

SQL; This is the Structured Query Language invented in IBM and used by nearly all higher-level databases to search for and retrieve information. Replaced later by Oracle.

[50] Sergei Popov led a team Upside in the 1990s in Stepnogorsk. Their activities were broadly publicised in 2025 at the first terrorist crisis. After the formal ban on biological weapons was signed off, the Russians redoubled their research at Stepnogorsk. Sergei Popov led teams developing 2 bugs. One was intended to combine the lethality – close to 100 per cent death rate – of eboli with the contagiousness, ruggedness and ease of transmission of smallpox. To this he added resistance to radiation damage, so that the bug could be used to follow up a nuclear attack.

His other little gem was a recombinant development of legionella. Like a flu bug only much worse, it would trick the body's self-defences to cause self-destruction instead. Bugs that would be untraceable and would lead after 2 weeks to paralysis and death. Allegedly over a thousand scientists from this operation were out of work and seeking employment in 2026; all were capable single-handedly of developing killers like the anthrax used by terrorists in 2025.

[51] I was involved in some of the Upside research in these fascinating areas. We found that feminine and masculine brain structures and information channels differed greatly. It was expressed well by a woman academic: Ask a man what one plus one plus one plus one makes and he'll say 4. Ask a woman and she'll say 1+1+1+1. Men, she concluded, are tunnel-visioned, and very ineffective communicators; not holistically inclined.

[52] The Downsiders seem to have reverted to the pre-1945 practice for brain surgery, when operands were tied down even though the brain was anaesthetised. This was because the limbs and spine would kick and flail at the first cut and at other dramatic procedures, which was immensely distressing for the surgical team. Possibly they no longer had access to the paralysing drugs used nowadays to prevent this disturbing phenomenon. They must also have had access to very advanced immuno-suppressant drugs for the brains to survive alongside those of the pigs. The hormone systems presented equally challenging problems.

Having said that, their technology was in other respects surprisingly advanced, perhaps because for them the human brain and its capacity to break away, to rear up and set loose the dogs of war, were the core of most research. Upside scientists were able in 2025 to carry out complete head transplants in monkeys – the complete head was a much easier target than a brain transplant because the head included key functions of hearing, seeing, and to a degree smelling and articulation. The next stage, keeping a severed head alive in an animal of another species, still awaited solution. The people Downside seem to have advanced well beyond this in regenerating nervous systems. Spinal cord regeneration was so well understood that they were able to talk of an SSI, a standard spinal interface, as if it were a simple component like say the famous 7-layer onion skin used to describe communications interfaces on the Internet.

[53] The healing of the layer of cells lining the spinal cord. The practice Downside was in fact well in advance of that Upside, perhaps because so much emphasis was laid on the area of transgenics, of artificially introducing genetic materials from one species into another. To enable human brains to co-exist with pigs in the total pig environment.

[54] apWilliams got it slightly wrong:
Virgil Aeneid Book 6:
Facilis descensus Averno est
Noctes atque dies patet janua Ditis;
Sed revocare gradum, superasque evadere ad auras,
Hoc opus, hic labor est.

Easy is the descent to Avernus (Lake at the gates to Hell)
Night and day the gates of Dis lie open;
But to retrace your steps, to escape to daylight,
That's the task, this the toil.

[55] Mark Twain, *Tom Sawyer*. This was the cave near St Petersburg, Illinois, in which Tom Sawyer and Becky Thatcher – like Doris Day, every

man's ideal girl-next-door – were lost when treasure-searching. They encountered the villain Injun Joe across an uncrossable chasm, fled and eventually escaped. One of its finest lines is when Huck Finn and Tom eventually find the chest of lost treasure: 'My goodness, Hucky, looky here.'

[56] Gaskin described the role of interrupts in his talk to the course. On the KDF6 you just had to keep checking what was happening in the outside world looping on a special instruction, CALL 7774 and checking the results. In Register A clumsy slow, inefficient and error-prone, one of the key functions which early operating systems were able to take on from the main user program.

[57] UKIP: Sseru and Tilley described occasionally the history of Upside since the error. Non-Upside readers may like a summary:

Talk went round to the EU and the Euro currency debate that had already started in 2014. There was much talk, Sseru said, about the collapse of Britain, the separation of Scotland and Wales, and the evolution of an England containing lots of trumped-up regions like the North West, so that democratic control lay supposedly closer to the people. But the English would have little of it. Politics and democracy were already under sharp fire for something called 'sleaze', but also because people felt that the old representative system was accessible, understandable and responsible. Everyone knew who their MP was, and most constituency MPs were genuinely dedicated to all their constituents and not just their own party. If you got on to your MP you got straight to the heart, whether of the national government or to pressure the local bureaucracies. That, and the ability to trust one person, and kick him or her out at national elections was the limit of most peoples' political wishes. Much play had been made of 'elective dictatorships', and the allegedly disenfranchised voters – 'disenfranchised' just because they were not of the same party as their MP. But if you went to a typical MP's 'surgery' you found the MP took action on the merits of the case in hand, and rarely even knew which party his client supported. Gradually people came to see how much of the essence of Britishness had been chewed away under the misguided fashions of the 1960s, until the UK ceased to be the gentle, tolerant, pluralist society of yore, welcoming dissent, structured, moral, exploring, inventive beyond all others.

Political correctness, imbibed from the States, and centralist top-down government, the paralysing creation of mainland Europe, had been imperceptibly introduced. The country's history had been falsified, and over 3 decades the extraordinary legacy it had handed to the world over 3 centuries was vilified and derided. Leaders in this had been the intelligentsia, led by men like Roy Jenkins, re-engineering (the contemporary buzzword) Britain into the model they in their wisdom felt most satisfying...

The intelligentsia and the show-biz personalities. Crucial were people like Alan Bennett, Jonathan Miller, Rory Bremner and Peter Cook. They had sensed even in their student years at Oxbridge that this was the new route to

338

fame and fortune or whatever, and while do-gooders were laying down their lives fighting disease etc. in odd corners of the Commonwealth, these young men exploited the sudden immensely influential power of TV to guy and destroy the traditional attitudes on which our vague notions of Britain were based. Take for example the much derided civil service tradition for scrupulously professional and impartial administration. A tradition propagated worldwide. There was a happy and incredibly funny programme, *Yes, Minister*, which guyed the processes whereby the ministers were guided by the permanent civil servants. So sharp, that when it was exported overseas, the overseas buyers questioned whether it was not too destructive of established authority. Even in robustly democratic Malaysia – ex-British and a vigorous contributor, perhaps the greatest success story among all the developing nations – curiously derided by *The Observer* as a tinpot dictatorship. In Malaysia, happily, Dr Mahathir ruled that the programme was OK. But the humour was mistaken for the truth; people thought that cynicism was all. Crucially, the author, Peter Jay, built up his image by alleging the caricature was true and complete – a major crime against his countrymen. So indeed did most of the satirists, relishing their new posture of caring, self-free saviours of their people. Where they could have taken a far less pretentious line and enlivened their and our lives at the same time? Like Michael Palin for example, with some delightful televised journeys exploring the world's richness and diversity. Or even better, Stephen Fry, who led part of a TV exploration of Africa and its joys and its debt repayment problems, with a sensitive and perceptive coverage of Uganda. An interview with President Yoweri Museveni, stands out – Fry gently courteous and deferential, yet leaving slight, necessary question marks, without offending, when skating round the fact that for Museveni, as for Amin and Obote before him, power had come not through the ballot box, but from the barrel of a gun. Fry contrasted with another presenter when the programme was in Tanzania, an ignorant ill-tutored American comedienne. She came out with a priceless statement about African debt: 'I suppose this is the modern equivalent of the slave trade.'

A quick and immensely influential throwaway line, damning as slavers institutions like the Development Banks whose dedicated people were spending their lives trying to civilise the continent and eradicate poverty. Small wonder that the debtor states became derided by right-wingers in the West as 'kleptocracies', stealing wealth by indiscriminate borrowing to line the top mens' pockets, with no intent to repay.

So, people were led to believe by the satirists that real-life government was indeed a cynical net of manipulations. In the States, both political parties became increasingly manipulative. This was in turn re-exported to the UK, and the strange 'New Labour' government led by a Tony Blair was tarnished from the start. On his election victory night were shown exultant, emotional scenes in Downing Street, of apparently spontaneous general demonstrations. People waving Union Jacks, Blair plunging around with wide, shiny eyes and beaming, hand-shaking like a Yankee professional. Viewers on TV watched with tears in their eyes. But all this was a put-up job little different from the 'spontaneous demonstrations' in the contemporary throngs in Baghdad. The spontaneous demonstrators were party workers from Labour Central Office, carefully drilled, and issued with the Union Jacks they habitually shunned and deeply despised. Continuing in the same vein, Blair tried to encroach on the functions the Queen had brilliantly exercised over her reign, endeavouring to eliminate one key buttress against absolutism – the monarchy – which the Brits had serendipitously evolved over the centuries. The plunging performance was repeated at the Opening of Parliament, upstaging the Queen and drawing his wife into a sort of First Lady role similar to that adopted by the wife of one of the US presidents, a guy called Clinton. Astonishing that this weird idea, as an alternative to monarchy, ever took off. The Head of State after all symbolises the essential customs and unity of British society. Which of the Brits' past prime ministers would be a fit candidate as monarch? Would their families suit? How could half the nation feel much empathy with a Head of State who has been elected against their wishes? More important still, how could people feel the long, on-going relationship that they had through most of the 2 previous centuries with an often fallible, but very human group like the British royals? Debate in earlier years had suggested the nation might be symbolised by its countryside – intriguing, but nebulous.

Similarly, the traditional relationship between civil service and politicians was guyed by people like Peter Jay. For example, the civil servants who had previously briefed the press were replaced by people known as spin-doctors; political appointees, who spun a tangled skein of misinformation for public consumption. They exploited long-standing relationships – the tradition of lobby correspondents for example, to leak and spin, weave and duck, till the public became bemused and bored and highly cynical, about the whole political process. After all, what we all really want is to live our own lives, secure in the knowledge, which we'd previously had, that if politicians transgress beyond the acceptable, we can apply the whip at the ballot box.

'Well,' interrupted McGervon. 'How did all this get its come-uppance, if it did?'

Happily, Sseru continued, the whistles were eventually blown by men like the *Observer* journalist, Andrew Marr, and most significantly, an *Express* journalist, Peter Hitchens, in a book alarmingly entitled *The Abolition of Britain*. Marr wrote as an expatriate Scot who had made his career as a journalist in London, and saw the breakup of Britain as a disaster, but one that gloomily he felt was inevitable following the set-up of the separate Scottish and Welsh assemblies. He failed however to realise the depth of affection for the 'Old Country' and the merits, not just for the UK but for the world, of its continued existence. He failed for example to realise the astonishing contribution to science and research, to technological development made by the Brits. Cambridge for example had 'won' more Nobel prizes than the entire USSR, and many of the major breakthroughs in computing were British. Not just from Babbage and Boole in the nineteenth century to Bletchley Park and the Enigma decoders, but right through to the first progammable computers, file systems, and the Internet and Expert Systems. It was well-known that Tim Berners Lee invented the World Wide Web at CERN, but who knew that the breakthrough concept of the Internet, Packet Switching – you chop up data into little packets, tag on the destination address, and let it thread its way round the cyberverse as if round a rug, following the warp and weft in the easiest route then available – was invented by Donald Young at the National Physical Laboratory. A powerful light on the merits of British systems; one guy working on his own in the National Physical Laboratory, NPL came up with the same idea as did the large US Arpanet team funded and hyped to the tune of millions of dollars. Just as many 'one guys' had done in the past and were to do in the future.

Marr's pessimistic surrender to the inevitability of Britain's collapse was happily as unfounded as his suggested cure, a written republican constitution. There was little wrong with the existing constitution. Much of the apparent discontent was hyped up by groups like Charter 99, erecting cardboard windmills that they tried triumphantly to knock down. They alleged for example that for the Brits to call themselves 'subjects' of the Queen was somehow self-abasing, that people really felt they were this old lady's slaves. The reality was of course the reverse – the real slave was the old lady who had both served them and acted as a powerful icon for good – notably in her annual Christmas message to the Commonwealth. A Commonwealth that they derided, but which had been a significant force for good in the world's most tragic century.

Hitchens' *Abolition of Britain* was much more powerful in its denunciations. Some typical views:

In an incredibly short space of time we have been turned into a nation without pride in our past or knowledge of past triumphs or past follies and disasters. We are an amnesia patient waking up in a ward with both past and future great blank spaces, doomed to make mistakes we do not even know we have already made.

George Orwell once observed that Britain was unique in having an intelligentsia that despised patriotism. He might have added 'and despised the society which nurtured them.' To illustrate, a typical BBC programme of the 1990s would make throwaway comments *en passant* about national ceremonial and so forth – robed judges being referred to as 'old gents in dressing gowns'. Other culture's dress and customs were hallowed – Sikh dress for example – and rightly so. But why, then, why not our own? The disease was cultured of course by the icons of the times, the satirists. The destruction continued until a would-be satirist of the noughts commented sadly 'they've chewed it all away. There's nothing left to be satirical about.'

These icons would have been more human and less destructive if they had shown occasional humility, by the odd admission for instance in the many TV retrospective eulogies on their fellows that 'This is only satire, of course.' But they failed to do so, and they reaped in the noughts the fruit of their pretensions.

Healthier were comedians like Flanders and Swan. 'They (the satirists) strip society naked of its hypocrisy. But our job,' said Flanders, 'our job is to put it all back again.'

The destructiveness of the modernisers was countered by a growing body of opinion. The 'senior citizens' for example, who were not only horrified to realise the depth of the attempted cultural revolution in which they had unwittingly been duped, but also, being (unlike previous generations) vibrantly healthy, they were well able to express their disgust and get action taken.

To this was added the male backlash. In British society, the females had over 4 decades taken over the trousers as well as the skirts, and in the new millennium people were asking 'What use then is a man?' – all part of the rationalising, reforming, 'modernising' process beloved by the right of socialism. The women had been very desirable allies in all this, much more tractable for example in the workplace than the robust, unionised, traditionally male labour forces. This male backlash was first expressed in violence, notably in sport, but then more creatively, in questioning and ridiculing the shibboleths of the reformers. Coming to work in skirts for example, demanding male restrooms and so on.

Ridicule, having been used so effectively against traditional Britain, was equally effective against the 'modernisers'.

Welsh and Scottish Nationalism, for example, had become increasingly aggressive – one Plaid Cymru councillor publicly advocated 'monitoring people of English extraction', and his president failed to correct his blatant racism. This aggressive nationalism often caused the leaders acute misgivings. They could foresee opportunities for them and their descendants for lives and careers as Brits, which in the bold new future would be closed off. Of the triumvirate who led New Labour, for example, 2 were Scots, and the third, Blair himself, had Scottish education and strong connections. In fact, in the whole span of British history, the monarchs had been Welsh, Scots, Dutch, Germans; never English.

The British-back movement played on these fears. The Welsh and Scots after devolution had suddenly become sharply aggressive. 'How do you like it?' they would ask Englishmen in Porthmadog or Troon. 'How do you like it in OUR country?'

This was particularly galling, for the Brits had always thought of the whole UK as home. So the net triggered some one-day campaigns by phone. Members would spend an amusing day phoning any Macs or Jones's in their area of England, and asking politely 'How do you like living in my country?' The campaign caught on, particularly through the phone systems and the Internet, until the Welsh and Scots started chipping away at their own nationalist chauvinists.

How did all this affect the great European debate? Firstly, the resuscitation of the debate about 'Small is beautiful' – genetics, biodiversity, sustainability, many of the other catchwords of the 1990s, were seen suddenly to militate against the big battalions. So did the growing disgust at the squandering of millions of years non-renewable resources, oil and coal. So did the great Sei Neu and Greenpeace and other societies revival after 2028 and the US Congress and Senates dramatic rethink after the 4 warnings. So did the hunger of the young for a less simplistic education, a return for example to structure, grammatical complexity and semantic precision in English – the basics of systems design and of programming and of all computer languages, the bedrock on which men like Turing, Williams, Codd, Gates and many other individualists had cut their computing teeth. So did the deepening understanding of man's language systems and allied subjects like mensuration, the revolt against Napoleonic France's ubiquitous metricism. People renewed their awareness of the feel of mixed radixes in arithmetic. That the foot had 10 toes was seen to be a rather curious base for universal numbering systems. Twelve would be more sensible, because it is divisible by 5 numbers rather than 3, but why standardise anyway? Why not give the people what they want? Most of the much-ridiculed systems – acres, miles, gallons, chains, cables etc. embraced deep understanding of the environmental entities concerned. Tell a trained sailor he is to keep one cable off a point, and this was shown to click in his mind in a way that 183 metres did not. He would be able to keep this distance away from the danger point with remarkable accuracy.

Finally, the stupidity of the debate about the euro became apparent after a paper on Informatics. This pointed out that good reason should be given for throwing over existing, much-loved concepts like currency units. If the objective was to standardise across many currencies, that was surely what the computing revolution was all about. Each nation would retain its cherished guilders, kroner or whatever, and standard software and simple hardware add-ons would do the needed conversions. Direct from pounds to drachmas, etc. Why have an additional, funny currency called the euro? By this time more and more of the continent's work was in the software services sector, and the conversion systems were implemented inside Europe, generating new wealth as a result.

The great European debate also took on a more subtle and organic aspect as the Europeans came to realise that the horrors of war at the national level within Europe were no longer to be so greatly feared – this had been the fear that had led to the founding of the EEC. The Hobbesian concept of Europe – surrender all your independence to some all-powerful god-like super-state entity so that you'll not be clobbered again by your neighbour as you were in the past – gave way to a more liberal and optimistic view. The seeds of success and progress were demonstrably with the diverse, multicultural and pluralistic among the European nations. In particular of course the loose flexible British systems were seen to have drawn even the most backward of Third World societies up to 10 centuries forward in the space of one. Not a widely welcomed message at first, when much of the world's youth had been nurtured on the myth of the wickedness of the imperial Brit, and Hollywood villains who previously had spoken with German inflexions, had moved for their villains to the jokey clipped naval tones of the Duke of Edinburgh. Completely failing to sense the subtleties and wry humour of the people of the 1950s. And in reassessing the Empire and Commonwealth, people came to realise the insularity of Europe of the Franco-German model – protectionist, arrogant as in the Kosovo crisis, and inward-looking.

Information technology had a further liberating dimension in the debate on the future. It had been shown that diversity was all-important to a fulfilling life, yet between the 1970s and the 2000s, the youth of the west had been fed an unbelievably conformist diet of mass-television, deadening the human youngster's curiosity and need to explore. Generating a society where imagination was discouraged and book reading rare. But the Internet reversed this. Children explored the curate's egg universe of information suddenly available to them with zest and enterprise. Horizons which had been cramped and constrained by a daily diet of standard TV watched by every child in the country were suddenly limitless – virtual – and the duty for parents and teachers to restrain this by excluding for instance violence and pornography became imperative.

Philosophy had a significant role too in the late 1990s and early 2000. With the supposed elimination of Marxism as a valid creed for humanity, Western liberalism was regarded as the necessary end of man. And, since much of life was determined by the 'numbers game' – how much expenditure on hospital beds, funerals etc. will this proposed speed limit save was a typical 'what if' question for local road authorities, for example – the archetypal numbers philosopher, the predecessor of Marx, Jeremy Bentham, and the Utilitarians, were widely quoted. Bentham had posited the purpose of political life as 'the greatest happiness of the greatest number'. Taking this to heart, people talked about 'the greatest health of the greatest number' in assessing medical development plans, 'the greatest benefit of the greatest number' in assessing benefit systems and so on.

But it rapidly became apparent that such crude measures had their limitations, particularly when applied to such deep-seated human emotions as clan, tribe, or race loyalty. The NATO alliance intervened disastrously in these matters in Kosovo, a one-time part of Yugoslavia. NATO tried to bomb peoples with rival racial and religious loyalties into peaceful co-existence, and to do so outside the widely-respected concept of the Rule of Law. The Malaysians incidentally, had shown an apparently unfair but actually realistic route through this jungle, by giving the Malay majority preferential entitlement to further education, government careers and so on, vis-à-vis their ethnic Chinese and Indian nationals. Similar arrangements came into force in Fiji and Northern Ireland.

[58] The system seems to have concentrated on the area round the eyes and nose, comparing recognition points as in neural network technology systems Upside such as Mandrake from Visionics. 'The responsible use of biometrics'. They matched faces against targets, at first just the faces of

convicted criminals with records of targeting specific communities. For repetitive crime this was very effective, since criminals tended to repeat their crimes, and at similar distances away from their homes.

Then the use of biometrics was extended to the faces of suspects as well. Then under political pressure for instant fixes, and measured results against prosecution and legal costs, the net widened and interfaced with DNA tracing, voice recognition and conventional fingerprinting, Neighbourhood Watch and so forth. It covered all who were reported for possibly suspicious behaviour under any circumstances. The system stabilised with a 20 per cent level of inaccurate hits against innocent bystanders. These CCTV/software setups were being installed first in turbulent lout-ridden UK boroughs then gradually more widely in the early 2000s until the Garthmorte suicide cases got them thrown out. For the Brits there are better ways of handling loutishness than rubbishing innocent citizens' freedoms and lives.

59 Face matchers. The Downside technologists seem to have gone a long way down this track, getting a match ratio about the same as that achieved in early UK systems like that at the Borough of Newham, where the matching between criminals or suspects and common citizens was often accurate in 80 per cent of cases. Upside of course this pernicious system was outlawed as a result of hundreds of wrongful prosecutions and one or two suicides, notably the Jones tragedy. The Milson report came of it in 2004, people will recall, and the act christened '*Habeas Imago*'. Your image is yours, and others tinker with it on pain of prosecution. Downside, wrap around surveillance, cyborg capability and so on were thought of as desirables, but their technology wasn't up to it. And DNA matching etc was beyond their ken.

60 Gaskin showed here an untypically romantic streak. The quote is actually from Suetonius, *Divus Claudius*, chapter 21. The salute to the emperor was actually not from the legionaries, but from the gladiators at the start of the games.

61 Virgil, *Aeneid* Book 8, lines 390 and 401. Some of the lines are from C.S. Lewis' translation.

62 Maes-y-Neuadd was a splendid, restrained seventeenth-century manor in the English style, looking down across its own meadows and across the Welsh hills to the Snowdon massif.

63 The POPs could usually operate in local mode for a considerable time. Their instructions from PIG probably went haywire as it collapsed. They went inert because they were probably programmed to drop out like this if the control system fail-safe scanner in PIG lost contact. Perhaps it scanned every 2 minutes. Programmers used their own discretion usually in coding fallback routines. I remember a favourite car whose final gasp, as the battery voltage failed, was to wind down the driver's window, presumably so that the driver could get out or rescuers in. Was it an agreed response, pondered carefully by a committee, or Joe Bloggs' bright idea as he carved the microcode?

[64] Now replaced by a lyric to the moving spiritual, 'Swing low, sweet chariot'.

[65] 'In our coming miners' union election, the miners will choose me. Because they know that of all the candidates, I am the one that the management will most fear.'

Contrast that confrontational hostility with the approach used in the German industry, where union collaboration was most welcome, even at board level.

Scargill's minor critics used to joke that, 'When he took over as president he had a small house and a large union. When he left he had a large house and a small union.'

During the miners' strike, the union split down the middle, and Scargill started the strike despite the fact that he held no ballot and had no democratic majority among his members. In his memoirs on TV, the then Labour leader Neil Kinnock was asked what his biggest mistake had been. He answered that it was his failure to block Scargill's undemocratic decision to strike without a vote.

[66] *The Lonely Crowd*, David Riesman, Nathan Glazer, Reuel Denny, Doubleday, Garden City, New York.

[67] *A comment on the colonial issues:* 02/11/13

Dear Letters,

David Mitchell's piece on 27th of October, apologising for our military imperialism, was amusing but like most current comments, way off beam. Our officers, he said, would apologise charmingly and then loot their victims and disappear over the horizon in gunboats.

At the peak of British colonialism our army was 450,000 strong. Roughly the same size as that of Austria. And we ruled a quarter of the globe. That would not have been possible unless those who were ruled gave it their tacit consent.

I was in the last generation of colonial administrators in Uganda, and this I followed with 20 years work in 20 countries, 15 Commonwealth countries, for the World Bank, the UK Department for International Development and the European Union. And in all my assignments I was welcomed as a Brit, and even more welcome as a Brit who had served in the colonial service. I remember on a 6-month World Bank assignment to help design IT systems for JEDB in Sri Lanka, managing 300 estates in tea, coffee and coconut palm, I was warmly welcomed and the welcome strengthened throughout.

'We rejected the Filipino they assigned to us,' they said. 'He was not up to it. And we asked for a Brit, and we were right.'

Mitchell's view of alleged militarism coincided with that now propagated widely in the press and academia. But in my years in Uganda I saw the army, the Kings African Rifles, only once. And that was to defend our border and prevent the Congolese army from carrying out a left hook round the north of the great volcanoes to attack Rwanda from the flank.

Contrary to Mitchell's view, we brought 62 years of peace. And during that peace we worked with the Ugandans to create 3 major agricultural industries for smallholders, vastly improved cropping systems for food crops, forests, game reserves, a transport and trading network, a nation-wide health system, and orthography for the 14 different languages, a religious structure, a judicial system, democracy and the rule of law – the list is endless.

Not a lot there to apologise for.

Future historians with less bias will be astonished when they review these achievements; 10 centuries of civilisation in a short 60 years.

David Mitchell should read Joyce Cary, John Masters or my novel 'Point of Divergence', rather than casual visiting geniuses like E.M. Forster, if he really wants to know what colonialism was about.

Yours sincerely,

Graham Ohlsson

[68] Peter Hitchens wrote: 'Into the vacuum left by the end of British self-confidence a new conformism has come rushing, probably more powerful than the one which went before. This is often dismissed half jokingly with a casual phrase "political correctness". But this expression does not even begin to encompass the power and danger of the thing. The new empire of ideas reaches into the most intimate areas of life and those who do not accept it are judged to be personally at fault, not simply politically or philosophically wrong. *The Abolition of Britain*, p xii.

[69] Is this why their historians were compelled to write in the present tense?

[70] Hislop was nice guy, a great satirist, but he was not technology-couth. In fact, the Brits had a splendid century and a half inventing things – books, parliaments, wars, agriculture, livestock breeding, aeroplanes, canals, pharmaceuticas, films – and still do. Take computing, almost every innovation – the first computer – a tie between Manchester, Cambridge, Harvard and the NPL; relational databases, the key system in use world-wide, involving Chris Date; PSS Packet switching systems, invented by NPL and the US Department of Defense; the first successful anti-virus system, Dr Doodle, bought up by McAfee, now world leader with Norton; the first teletext system led by Canada; the first and best COBOL compiler for PCs by Microfocus. This enabled the standard language for 70 per cent of commercial software to be run on PCs. They said it couldn't be done; the first software system for Third World agriculture, written by ICL and ACSIL; the BBC Micro, the finest educational system, used in all schools; the World Wide Web created by Tim Berners Lee.

[71] In fact the Iraq War was an astonishing success for the alliance, won in a fifth of the forecast time and casualties. The peace was the disaster, and a disaster because Blair and his DFID minister Clare Short ignored the fundamental of British imperialism, Indirect Rule. You rule through the exiting authorities – sheikhs, chiefs, emirs and so on. You don't wipe them out.

[72] BBC 2, 2013 Pied kingfishers, flocks of pelicans and flamingos and even eagles returning to the reed beds.

[73] This area on a Saturday night is crowded out with aggressively nationalist, inebriated gangs, many with frightening careers in the Black Watch and Royal Corps of Signals, as pictured in books by McCall Smith.

[74] Motorola invented the first in-car radios and have pioneered micro-miniaturised systems ever since, including the Apple computer processors.

[75] Gordian knot. The ancient legend in Phrygia was that Gordas tied a rope with an intricate knot of cornus bark which no one could undo. Alexander the Great was publicly challenged to do so. He drew his sword and slashed it asunder. Sound lateral thinking. He then went on to conquer Persia and India!

[76] Capital city. It's the legislative capital of the Republic of South Africa.

[77] Dassies are delightful little creatures, about the size of rabbits, probably the same as the biblical 'coneys'. Their nearest animal relatives are the elephants.

[78] Virgil's *Aeneid*, first-century Rome. Powell's speech (he was a brilliant classical scholar) tore a rift in the Conservative Party but probably won them the next election.

[79] 'They will sell the nuclear technology to any US hater, for example Al Qaeda, and they will develop and deliver it by some simple means by truck or ship to any port in the world. And they will detonate it and kill hundreds of thousands of people immediately and further hundreds of thousands in 4 to 6 weeks.'

[80] Thomas Bayes, 1701–1761. His work and findings were in manuscript notes, published after his death by his great friend Richard Price.

[81] King James Bible – Luke 13 28 "Wailing arguable".

[82] Tippoo waged heroic campaigns against the Brits, a formidable leader who dramatically developed his administration in Southern India and was eventually killed by Wellington's army in the Fourth Mysorean War, which was to establish the British Raj.

[83] Rye is a cereal crop specially suited to the islands for its salt tolerance and disease resistance

[84] Widely talked of by sailors. Written about by Smollet in 1751. This same Davy Jones, according to sailors, is the fiend that presides over all evil spirits of the deep, and is often seen in various shapes, perching among the rigging on the eve of hurricanes, shipwrecks and other disasters to which sea-faring life is exposed, warning the wretch of death and woe. He has 3 rows of teeth, saucer eyes, horns, a tail and blue smoke coming from his nostrils. The locker is skeleton-filled with the drowned sailors on the seabed.

Timeline

Downside	Upside
	1995 Aberystwyth
26/06/1990 Saddam Hussein chooses	
	2012 Death of an industry
	2013 Dundee comments
	2013 Kirsty Wark's debate
	2014 Scottish independence referendum
	Scots opt for independence
	2018 Scottish independence
	Dalkeith implentation,
	UK and Scotland cut off
	Borders, employment, families,
	economies
	IT generates chaos
	2019 The three are developed
	as regards backgrounds Korea,
	Uganda,
2023	2023 Eland, Cambridge
2025 Transgap starts	2025 Transgap
Transit by Johnson	
2026 Training course	
Bridge 1	
2028 Recovery of *Lady Amanda*	
Three resolve to collaborate	
Trawsfynydd 2	Trawsfynydd 2
Bridge 2	
Destabilisation	
Gaskin triumphs	
	2029 Divers attack plastic boats
2030	2030 New York event reported by TB
2033 Gaskin dictates, centralises, trio	2033 Pseudo-aircraft and similar events
oppose	
Barmouth bridge to eliminate POPs	
Gervon escapes and flees north	
Gaskin instructs capture	
Theft from Burrel by trio to provoke	
Gaskin	
Trip to Arran and western isles	
Gaskin dictatorates, centralises, trio	
oppose	
submarine supports Gaskin, builds	
stairway on Hoy	
Gaskin traces three, has them on	
pyre	
Johnson declares	
2040 Goulding Brown writes